COLD SKIES

COLD SKIES

A DreadfulWater Mystery

THOMAS KING

HarperCollins*Publishers*Ltd

Published by HarperCollins Publishers Ltd

First edition

HarperCollins books may be purchased for educational, business,
or sales promotional use through our Special Markets Department.

HarperCollins Publishers Ltd
Bay Adelaide Centre, East Tower
22 Adelaide Street West, 41st Floor
Toronto, Ontario, Canada
M5H 4E3

www.harpercollins.ca

Library and Archives Canada Cataloguing in Publication
information is available upon request.

ISBN 978-1-44345-706-4 (HARDCOVER)
ISBN 978-1-44345-514-5 (TRADE PAPERBACK)

Printed and bound in the United States

LSC/H 9 8 7 6 5 4 3 2 1

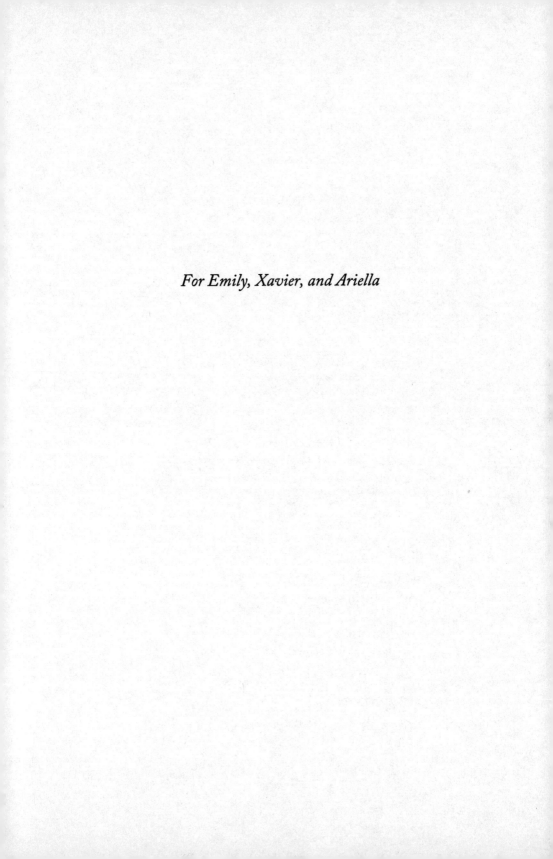

For Emily, Xavier, and Ariella

ONE

ob Tatum wheeled his suitcase from the baggage area to the car rental desk and tried to work the stiffness out of his back and legs. The flight from Seattle to Great Falls had been on time, but the commuter from Great Falls to Chinook had developed a mechanical problem and had sat on the tarmac for almost five hours.

Always a crowd-pleaser.

He had wound up next to a bony blonde with a collection of shopping bags, which she arranged around her seat like party pillows. Tatum had tried to ignore her. He rolled up against the window, his neck bent at an awkward angle, while the woman opened packages, removed cellophane, and pulled tape off designer boxes. In the confines of the small plane, it sounded as though she were ripping tin off a roof.

And the sandwich.

The flight attendant had called it a "Ham and Cheese on a French Roll." Tatum had never been to France, and he was reasonably sure that the roll hadn't either. A little lettuce would have been nice. Maybe a slice of tomato. There wasn't even any mustard or ketchup to set an edge and brighten the taste. The sandwich had been the size of a small log, and each time he tried to take a bite, a glop of thick white goo had squeezed its way out the sides of the bun.

It wasn't mayonnaise. He was sure of that.

THE YOUNG MAN at the car rental desk had a gold badge that said, "Orem."

"I have a reservation. Tatum."

"Mr. Tatum," said Orem, looking at the computer. "Seattle."

"I reserved a compact."

Orem glanced at the computer. "It's your lucky day, Mr. Tatum. We'd like to upgrade you. How does that sound?"

Rental upgrades, along with airline food, delayed flights, and irritating passengers, were just another of the many minor annoyances of travel. In his years of moving around the country, Tatum had only gotten a compact car once. Every other time he had been "upgraded," which was the expression the car rental companies used to make you feel as though you had won something, as though getting a larger, clumsier gas guzzler was first prize in a lottery.

"I reserved a compact."

"Unfortunately, we're out of compacts at this moment, but there won't be any additional charges for the Suburban."

Tatum set his bags down, closed his eyes. "Do you have anything else?"

"It's very comfortable. And it has a sunroof."

"Something smaller?"

Orem looked slightly hurt, as though Tatum had just told him that they couldn't be friends anymore. "Well, there's a Jeep Cherokee. It's sort of a compact."

REGIONAL AIRPORTS HAD the advantage of having everything within walking distance and the disadvantage of not having a shuttle to take you and your bags from the terminal to the parking lot when you were worn out and grumpy.

The night air was cool. Tatum dragged his bags toward the cars and wondered, once again, if life would have been different if he had finished university. His major for the first three years had been sociology, but then Kathleen had come along, complete with a job in her father's company. At the time, the job had looked good. Kathleen had looked good too.

The rental cars were lined up like horses at a hitching post with not a compact among them. The black Suburban was more elephant than horse. If he had his way, he'd drive a sports car, something agile and quick. But sports cars didn't seat a wife, three kids, and a six-figure mortgage all that well. Maybe when he retired and the kids left home, he'd get a used Jaguar or better yet a Corvette, an older model with red and white tuck-and-roll upholstery.

There were two Jeeps parked next to each other. He checked the key tag. It simply said, "Jeep." No licence plate number. No indication which horse was his. It was hard to tell colour in the dark, but one of the Jeeps looked as though it might be green. He'd try that one first. The colour of spring. The colour of new beginnings.

The door wasn't locked, and, as Tatum pulled it open, he tried to remember if today was Tuesday or Wednesday.

The man slumped across the front seat didn't look as though he was going to tell Tatum any time soon.

Tatum stood by the open door and looked up at the heavens. That's what he liked best about the West. There were still places where the world seemed enormous and full of promise.

"Excuse me."

Tatum had a momentary urge to shake the man awake, but the smell stopped him. It wasn't your usual rental car mix of air freshener and Armor All. It was more a taste, bitter, like copper, with an unpleasant undercurrent that brought the airline sandwich back into focus.

"You okay?"

There had been a CPR seminar that Tatum had had to attend as part of the company's workplace-safety program. He tried to remember the three steps of CPR. The first had been to call out to check for responsiveness. He had done that. Twice. The second step, if he remembered correctly, was to tilt the head back and check for breathing. If the victim wasn't breathing, you were supposed to pinch the nose and blow into the mouth. Step three involved some form of chest compression.

He had never seen a dead body, and he wasn't sure he was looking at one now, but whatever the man's problem, Tatum didn't think CPR was going to help. Or more to the point, given the disagreeable odours that had rolled out of the Jeep, step one was as far as he was willing to go.

Tatum closed the door softly, just in case the man was asleep and easily startled. Then he looked up at the bright stars in the cold sky one last time and trudged back to the terminal.

TWO

Thumps DreadfulWater crouched under the folds of the dark cloth and examined the upside down and backward image of the river and the mountains on the ground glass of the field camera. The air was crisp. The land was quiet. The only sound was the mosquitoes as they hovered about trying to get at him, and Thumps was reminded once again what he disliked about spring.

Bugs.

Not all bugs. Mosquitoes and blackflies to be exact. They came at you in clouds, the blackflies first with the mosquitoes hard on their heels. The flies lived and bred near moving water, which was where some of the best images were, while the mosquitoes would go anywhere for a warm meal.

Thumps came out from under the cloth, slapped at several of the bloodsuckers that were stuck to his neck like darts, and shooed away a flock of gnats that had settled in front of the lens. He set the aperture and the speed, cocked the shutter, removed the dark slide, tripped the shutter, and slid the slide back into place.

The sad truth about photography was that even the best lens was a poor substitute for a good set of eyes. Under the bowl of the sky, looking in all directions at once, you felt small and lonely and calm. The finest photograph in the world couldn't match standing on a bluff overlooking a river valley with the light streaming through the clouds, and it couldn't capture the feel of the wind or the smell of the sage.

What a landscape photograph captured was romance, an emotion to hang on your wall so you could remember an imagined moment and forget that the wind had been sharp and that the smell of sage had been cut with diesel fumes from the trucks as they lumbered along the interstate.

Normally, photography had an invigorating effect on him, but today the trip out to the river and the hike up to high ground had been exhausting. And for no good reason. Sure, the camera and the backpack and the tripod were heavy, but it was more than that. Claire would have told him it was depression, but that was because women liked depression, did not see it as the weakness or loss of control that men did.

So, he wasn't depressed. Didn't feel depressed. As a matter of fact, life had been unfolding rather nicely lately. Claire was affectionate once again, and he had just finished arranging his kitchen, a task that always made him feel good. There was nothing like imposing a little order on spices, cereal boxes, and cans to make a person believe he was in charge of his world.

The fatigue, however, was annoying. It was as if someone had opened a vein and drained him dry. The sudden urge to pee was a different matter. Both had come out of nowhere. He had made the mistake of sharing these anomalies with Archimedes Kousoulas, who owned the Aegean bookstore in Chinook.

"When was your last physical?" Archie had asked.

"I don't need a physical."

Archie's glasses were too large for his head and made him look like a Greek barn owl. He was the kind of friend everyone needed. Whether they wanted one or not.

"All men over fifty need to get a physical every two years."

"I'm not fifty."

"You look fifty."

Archie had pulled several medical books from the shelves, looked up Thumps's symptoms, and cobbled together a diagnosis.

"You're not pregnant," Archie had told him, "so it's either cancer, a bad thyroid, or diabetes."

"Archie . . ."

"Course, there's no reason it couldn't be all three."

THE LIGHT ABOVE the river had brightened, raising the contrast beyond the levels film could manage. Thumps checked to see if there were any clouds on the way to soften the glare and smooth things out, but the sky was high and fierce.

A year ago, Thumps had gone to Toronto for a week-long photographic conference that included exhibitions, workshops, and seminars. One afternoon, he had wandered the city and stopped at a camera store near the corner of Queen and Church, where most of the sales staff was under thirty. There was only one guy who looked to be Thumps's age.

"I'm John," said the man. "You look like a film guy."

"Four-five field camera," said Thumps. "Goerz Dagor lens."

"Good gear," said John. "And you're wondering if it's time to switch to digital."

Thumps shrugged. "Is it as good as film?"

"Nope," said John. "It's just different. What's your pack weigh?"

"About forty pounds."

"With the tripod?"

"Fifty pounds."

"That's the difference," said John. "You looking to trade in the four-five?"

"Probably not."

"Good," said John, "because it's not worth shit."

Thumps looked at the rows of digital Nikons and Canons and Fujis on the shelves behind the counter. They did look compact. And light.

"The big companies have stopped making most of their films and papers. Even the chemistry is being phased out. Another five years or so and it could all be gone. You remember electric typewriters? Most of the kids in this store have never seen one."

"I do my own chemistry."

"Sure," said John. "I did the same thing. Used to love to sit in the dark and mix up nasty shit in graduated beakers like some mad scientist. Course the fumes pretty much ruined my liver."

John gave Thumps a quote on a Nikon body with three lenses, a canvas camera bag, and a lightweight tripod with a quick-release head. "You know the one thing that hasn't changed about photography?"

"What's that?"

"The cost."

OKAY. NO MORE photography today. As Thumps hogged the backpack onto his shoulder, he felt his stomach nudge him in the ribs. Time for breakfast. His favourite meal. In Chinook, breakfast was limited to two choices. At least so far as Thumps was concerned. Either you made it yourself or you ate at Al's. Thumps could certainly construct a fine breakfast, but one of the pleasures of modern life was to have someone else make it for you. Especially if that someone was Alvera Couteau, or Al as everyone in town knew her.

Normally, quaint local hangouts with a reputation for good food and fair prices, in interesting but out-of-the-way places such as Chinook, turned into hot spots during the summer months, forcing locals to stand in line behind tangles of tourists bristling with backpacks and guidebooks. But even though Chinook had its fair share of visitors, few of them ever made their way to Al's.

First of all, the café was difficult to find. It was sandwiched in between the Fjord Bakery and Sam's Laundromat, with no sign marking the place other than the turtle shell Preston Wagamese had superglued next to the front door, with the word "Food" painted on it.

Tourists did occasionally find the place, but they didn't stay. Not that the café looked threatening in any way. It was, in fact, unremarkable. Little more than a long, narrow aisle with plywood booths huddled against one wall and a run of scruffy chrome and red Naugahyde stools wedged tightly against a lime-green Formica counter.

To be sure, the place was dark. The only light came in through the window next to the grill. And it was damp. With the sweet smells of grease, burnt toast, strong coffee, and sweat forming currents and eddies that ran through the café like tides. Thumps imagined that the main sensation people had, when walking in off the street for the first time, was that of being shoved under water.

The regulars all sat at the counter as close to the grill and the coffee pot as they could get. Al's wasn't going to be featured in one of those restaurant-beautiful magazines any time soon, but the food was five-star.

Al was one of the few people in the world who knew how to scramble eggs. Most places polluted perfectly good eggs with milk or water and cooked the unholy mixture in a non-stick pan. The secret to scrambled eggs was to whip the eggs gently with a fork and pour them *au naturel* into a hot cast-iron skillet seasoned with butter, and just as they began to firm up, toss in a chunk of cold butter. This slowed down the cooking process and allowed the eggs to come together in a smooth and delicate dish.

By the time Thumps got to Al's, the place was empty. He found his favourite stool, seventh from the end, and settled in.

"You missed everyone." Al strolled the length of the counter. "You want coffee?"

"Absolutely," said Thumps.

"You out taking pictures again?"

"I'm a photographer. That's what I do."

"Used to be a cop," said Al. "You used to do that, too."

"Yeah, but I'm not a cop anymore."

"You look a little tired."

"Photography's hard work."

"Maybe you should try some B12," said Al. "Supposed to kick-start your energy levels."

"My energy levels are fine," said Thumps. "I just need to be fed."

"Your little buddy thinks it's cancer."

You could get breakfast out at Shadow Ranch. The ambience was nicer, the portions were larger, and no one there cared whether you lived or died. But the food wasn't as good.

"Archie's full of shit."

"That's not news." Al waved the coffee pot at Thumps. "You get that new stove yet?"

"Not yet."

"Must be expensive as hell."

Actually, it was more expensive than that. When Thumps bought the bungalow on Water Street, the house had come with an electric stove. It was adequate enough, but Thumps wasn't fond of the time the elements took to heat up, or the way they created hot spots in his sauces, or the springy, tinfoil feel he got whenever he set a pot on a burner.

Four burners. How could anyone cook effectively on four burners? If you put a large pan on the front burner, it took up space on the back and side burners as well.

Six burners. That was the only way to cook. And gas. But not one of those sealed systems where the heat roared out of narrow ports like an acetylene torch.

Open flame. That was the trick. Where the heat gently rolled over the bottom of the pan, warming everything evenly.

"This about that stove in the window of Chinook Appliances?" Al snorted. "No way Danielle is going to put that on sale."

"Almost the end of the model year."

"You should give one of those induction thingies a look-see."

Induction cooktops were all the rage. Thumps had looked at them and decided that he would rather cook in front of a microwave with the door off.

"That electro-magnetic stuff is supposed to be quicker than hot grease."

"Not so sure it's good for your health."

"That's what they said about microwaves." Al tossed a clean towel on her shoulder. "You going to the conference?"

"Conference?"

"The big water conference at Buffalo Mountain," said Al. "Archie hasn't signed you up yet?"

Thumps had already heard Archie's name enough for one morning. "You know what I eat, don't you?"

"Sure."

"You think I could have that?"

"Archie said I should cut back on your potatoes," said Al. "Just in case it's diabetes."

"Potatoes are vegetables," said Thumps, slumping forward on his elbows. "Vegetables are good for me."

"Actually, they're starch." Sheriff Duke Hockney stood in the doorway. The light behind Hockney wanted to get into the café, but it wasn't brave enough to try to push past the man. "Christ, DreadfulWater, you look like hell."

"He always looks like hell," said Al. "Coffee, sheriff?"

Thumps was in no mood for a double team. "I'd look better if someone would feed me."

"So, get married." Hockney hitched his pants and slid onto a stool.

Al shook her head. "Pretty high price to pay for a meal."

"Tell me about it," said the sheriff.

Hockney had been sheriff of Chinook since before Thumps had arrived in town, and Thumps was sure that Duke would be sheriff long after he left. Duke's wife, Macy, thought her husband looked like John Wayne, but that was because of the way he walked, his feet set wide apart as he pitched from side to side. Mostly he looked like a bag of boulders in short sleeves.

"You remember that convention Macy and I go to every year?"

"Law enforcement? In Toronto?"

"That's the one."

Thumps knew that Toronto wasn't Duke's idea of a good time. It was Macy who liked the city. And with Chinook paying Duke's expenses, it allowed her to squeeze a holiday out of a man who thought a vacation was sitting by himself in his backyard with a beer.

"Sure."

"They moved the venue to Las Vegas." Hockney put the cup to his lips. "Woman's not happy."

"She doesn't like Vegas?"

"Thinks it's tacky."

"It is tacky." Al refilled both cups. "So instead, Macy's found Duke an anti-terrorism summit in Costa Rica. Fancy resort right on the beach."

Thumps shrugged. "Costa Rica could be fun."

Hockney dragged the sugar bowl over, leaving a furrow in the Formica. "Anybody ever tell you that you're an asshole?"

"Tropical forests, ocean, fun in the sun," said Thumps. "What's not to like?"

"You know how much Macy's ticket is going to cost me?" said Duke. "You ever hear of leptospirosis?"

"It's a tropical disease," said Al. "Nasty piece of work."

"And there's Chagas," said Duke, warming to the discussion. "You get it from blood-sucking bugs that bite you on the face when you're sleeping and then take a crap in the wound. That sounds like a good time to you?"

"Then don't go."

"Have to go." Duke held his hands out, palms up. "No living with her if I don't."

"Okay," said Thumps, "then go."

"He can't go," said Al. "He's got no one to play acting sheriff while he's away."

Suddenly, Thumps was awake.

"So, I figure that if I have to go to Costa Rica and pretend that I'm an expert on terrorism, the least you can do is stay here and pretend you're a sheriff."

"Sheriff?"

"Acting sheriff." Hockney reached into his pocket, fished out a badge, and slid it across the counter. "You used to be a cop. Even heard a few rumours that you were a pretty good one."

"I don't want to be acting sheriff."

"Yeah," said the sheriff, "and I don't want to go to Costa Rica."

"Not happening."

"You're just out of practice."

"Not out of practice," said Thumps. "Not interested."

Duke reached across and helped himself to a piece of Thumps's toast. "And as luck would have it, something has come up that will help put you right back in the game."

THREE

By the time Duke pulled into the Chinook airport, Thumps had used up most of the good reasons he could think of as to why he couldn't play sheriff.

"You got four other deputies."

"Not enough experience," said Hockney.

"What about Lance Packard?" Thumps kept his voice calm and reasoned. "Lance could do it."

"You know the big law-enforcement conference in Toronto that Macy always drags me to?"

"The one that got moved to Las Vegas?"

"Vegas and Costa Rica are at the same time," said the sheriff. "Packard's going to Vegas."

Thumps could feel the first stirrings of desperation. "What about Andy?"

Andy Hooper had been Hockney's deputy for more years

than Thumps liked to remember. Andy was one of those
delightful combinations of bigotry and ignorance, an arrogant
man who had no mind to speak of and spoke it.

"Hooper quit," said Duke. "Remember?"

"Sure," said Thumps, "but he might help you out if you
asked."

"He sells used cars for Norm Chivington."

"And I take photographs."

Hockney parked the cruiser in front of the terminal. "Would
you buy a car from Andy?"

"That's not the point."

"But you don't mind if he's sheriff?" Hockney shook his
head. "How about we just deputize you now? Give you a chance
to ease into the position."

THE YOUNG MAN behind the counter was dressed in black
slacks, a white shirt, tie, and red blazer. His gold name tag
said, "Orem." Thumps wondered if Andy Hooper had to wear a
blazer when he was selling cars. And whether he had a name tag.

"I'm Sheriff Hockney." Duke took out his badge with practised efficiency.

Orem went to the computer. "State or county?"

"What?"

"For the government discount," said Orem. "Do you need
GPS?"

"Don't need a car." Hockney opened his notebook and stared at it for a moment. "A Bob Tatum called my office about a dead body he found in one of your vehicles."

"Oh, that," said Orem. "That was a mistake. The guy was just drunk."

"Tatum?"

"No, the guy in the car."

"Big difference between drunk and dead."

"Head office wasn't too happy," said Orem. "I can tell you that."

Hockney leaned on the counter, his palms flat, his elbows bent. "Why don't we start at the beginning."

"Sure," said Orem. "Mr. Tatum was supposed to arrive on the 6:10 from Great Falls, but it was delayed. Almost five hours. You believe that? He wanted a compact, but we didn't have any, so we upgraded him to a full-size car. It's company policy."

"So there wasn't a dead body?"

"It was late at night," said Orem. "We had two Jeeps left on the lot. A blue one and a green one. Mr. Tatum thought the green Jeep was his."

"And the body was in the green Jeep."

"Wasn't a body," said Orem with a wistful look that suggested he had been disappointed. "Mr. Lester was just . . . under the weather."

Thumps wanted to jump in and say "Dead drunk," but Orem was already doing a fine job of annoying the sheriff all by himself.

"Lester?"

Orem played with the computer for a moment. "James Lester. From Sacramento."

"Any idea how this James Lester wound up drunk in one of your vehicles?"

"He rented it." Orem looked at Duke and then at Thumps. "Not when he was drunk, of course. Two days ago. When he arrived."

Hockney turned to Thumps. "Why don't you give it a try?"

Thumps had been thinking about his new stove and how much easier it would be to do a vinegar reduction over an open flame.

"Was Lester returning the vehicle?"

"Don't think so." Orem checked the computer again. "He had another four days left on the rental."

"So, maybe he was picking someone up."

"You mean like . . . a woman?"

"Sure," said Thumps. "Like a woman."

"Maybe that's why he was drunk," said Orem, gathering speed. "Maybe she didn't show. Maybe she sent him an email or a text message to say that it was all over."

Thumps glanced at Hockney. The sheriff still had his gun in his holster.

"Maybe when Lester realized that he had lost the love of his life, he decided to drown his sorrows in a bottle."

Hockney grunted. "Drown his sorrows?"

"Okay," said Thumps quickly, "so you went out to the car and woke him."

"Oh, I didn't do that," said Orem. "I didn't even see Mr. Lester. We're not allowed to leave the desk. Normally there are two of us, but at night, when it gets slow, Mr. Chivington doesn't like to pay for the extra personnel."

Suddenly, Duke was back into the conversation. "Chivington?"

"Our CEO."

"CEO? Norm Chivington?" Duke's eyes were alive. "This is Norm Chivington's rental agency?"

"It is," said Orem. "So when Mr. Tatum told me about the problem, I called Mr. Chivington, and he came out and took care of everything."

"I'll bet he did," said Hockney. "I'll just bet he did."

Thumps looked around the airport lobby. There was a large poster that showed a happy couple on a beach. The ocean was impossibly blue, the sand impossibly white, the man and the woman impossibly fit. It was a scene that existed only in Photoshop.

"It's not Mr. Tatum's fault," said Orem. "Anyone could have made the same mistake."

Duke nodded. "What do you think, DreadfulWater? You think you would have made that mistake?"

"Sure. Drunk and dead are almost the same thing." Thumps gestured to the security camera on the wall behind Orem. "Maybe we could see the security footage."

"Unfortunately," said Orem, "that doesn't work."

"Of course it doesn't." Hockney shook his head. "Are there security cameras in the rental lot?"

"No," said Orem, "but there is a guy who checks the lot at night. Sometimes people park and forget to pay the fee."

"And this guy keeps track of the cars?"

"Randy, I think," said Orem. "Or Sandy."

"Andy?" asked Thumps.

"Right," said Orem. "Andy. He works for Chivington. Not here. At the dealership."

WHEN THEY GOT back to the sheriff's office, Thumps made a hard beeline to the bathroom. It was the sudden onset that bothered him the most. One minute he was fine, and the next he had to bear down to keep matters from getting out of hand. Maybe Archie was right. Maybe he should get a physical.

"You can even sit in my chair." Duke poured himself a cup of coffee.

Thumps didn't know how much coffee Hockney stuffed into the old percolator or how long the sheriff boiled the grounds. Just seeing what came out the other end was enough.

"And you can drink my coffee."

Thumps had watched Duke drink eighty-weight coffee for years, and he had never once seen the man flinch. "You ever get a physical?"

"Physical what?"

"Medical physical."

Duke set the coffee cup down on the edge of the desk. The desk didn't flinch either. "You worried about what Archie told you?"

"Why don't you ask Archie to be sheriff?"

"Why don't we get you oriented in the new job?"

"I don't need an orientation," said Thumps. "I need a new stove."

"You play sheriff while I'm gone, and I'll buy you your new stove." Hockney held out a meaty hand.

"You'll buy me my stove?"

"Sure," said the sheriff. "How much can it cost?"

Thumps smiled, wrote the figure on a Post-it pad, and slid it across the desk.

The sheriff stared at the number in disbelief. "You're joking."

"Nope," said Thumps. "Take it or leave it."

Hockney was staring at the figure when the phone rang. "Sheriff's office."

Whoever was on the other end did all the talking, and by the time Hockney hung up the phone, all the fun was gone from his face.

Duke pushed the Post-it back to Thumps. "You remember your concern about being out of shape for law enforcement?"

Thumps closed his eyes. "More practice?"

Duke stood and straightened his belt. "And you know what they say about practice."

FOUR

The Wagon Wheel motel had been built sometime in the 1950s. The original sign, a large wagon wheel with neon spokes, which flashed on and off to simulate motion, continued to roll along. The split rail fence at the front of the property was still standing, but it had been repaired with baling wire so many times that it was now more rust than wood. There was a portable display panel parked at the edge of the driveway that promised free cable television and high-speed internet along with whirlpool tubs and free coffee.

When Hockney pulled into the motel parking lot, Eleanor Lake was standing outside the office with her hands on her hips. Thumps's mother had struck the same pose whenever her son had done something to displease her.

"Eleanor doesn't look happy."

"Eleanor's never happy," said Duke. "Woman's vinegar and gristle."

Beth Mooney's station wagon was parked in front of one of the units. Thumps could think of only two reasons that she would be here.

"Beth is here." Thumps waited to see if Hockney was going to confirm the suspicion.

"I can see that."

Beth Mooney was a family doctor, but she also doubled as the county coroner. Beth made the occasional house call for patients too sick to come to see her, but, for the most part, if Beth and the sheriff were at the same place at the same time, it generally meant that there was a dead body nearby.

"Just what the hell are we paying you for?" Eleanor stood about five foot two, with cropped steel-grey hair and the temperament of a straight razor.

"Morning, Eleanor," said the sheriff, tipping his hat the way John Wayne might have done.

"Morning, Eleanor," said Thumps, but without the tip.

"Why'd you bring the photographer?" Eleanor bore down on her hips. "Sure as hell don't need any postcards."

"Maybe you better tell me what happened."

"Told you over the phone," said Eleanor. "Went to make up the room, and there he was. Suicide. Pure and simple."

"Actually, you didn't call me." Hockney tried to keep the annoyance out of his voice. "You called Beth."

"Course I called her. Don't need the law for a suicide. She's the one takes bodies away, isn't she?"

"When I tell her to," said Duke.

"How about you tell her to do just that," said Eleanor. "And toot sweet. Can't make money off an empty room."

Thumps left Duke to argue the protocols of effective law enforcement with Eleanor and ambled down the row of motel rooms. Beth was standing in the middle of Number 10. A tall, gaunt man was slumped in a chair in front of the television. He was dressed in a light grey suit. Cream shirt. Blue tie. In his early fifties. Not that his age mattered a great deal. He wasn't going to get any older.

"Hi, Beth."

"Sheriff with you?"

"He's chatting with Eleanor."

"That could involve stitches." Beth moved to the far side of the room and took several photos of the body. "Good thing I'm a doctor."

"You want me to do that?"

"You asking as the photographer or as the acting sheriff?" Beth walked back to the body and took a photo of a gun lying on the floor next to the chair. "'Cause you're in the middle of my crime scene."

Ever since Beth and Ora Mae had broken up, Beth had been somewhat irritable, and it didn't appear that time, which is supposed to heal all wounds, had worked its magic just yet.

Thumps gave Beth a quick smile. "Eleanor figures it's a suicide."

"Archie tells me you're dying of cancer."

"Since when do you listen to Archie?"

"When was the last time you had a physical?"

"Don't need a physical."

"Let me rephrase," said Beth. "Have you ever had a physical?"

Thumps circled the bed. "That looks like a head wound."

"What else do you see?"

"Dead guy. Medical gurney. Good-looking county coroner with a camera."

"Body dies," said Beth, "the muscles relax and . . . ?"

Thumps didn't like the picture that flashed on the screen in his head. "Bladder and bowels," he said quickly.

"Bladder and bowels." Beth took several close-ups of the side of the man's head. "Archie wants me to give you a physical."

"His pants are stained," said Thumps. "But the chair cushion looks clean."

"You feel like shit and you don't come to see me?" Beth picked up the revolver and placed it in an evidence bag. "But you tell Archie."

"I didn't tell Archie anything." Thumps considered going back outside to watch Eleanor tear strips off Hockney. "Looks like you've been working out. Is that a new hairstyle?"

"We talking about Ora Mae?" Beth crouched down by the chair. "Because if we are, that's old news."

"I'm just being . . ."

"Sensitive?"

"Observant."

"And that particular piece of old news," said Beth, "is dead news."

Thumps was trying to think of something else he shouldn't observe when he felt Hockney's large shadow at his back.

"You two solve the case yet?"

"It's a suicide," said Thumps. "Just like Eleanor said."

"Not even Andy is that stupid."

"Yes, he is."

Hockney walked over to the chair. "Don't see that much anymore."

"A dead body?"

"A vibrating bed." Duke looked almost nostalgic. "You put a quarter in and the thing shakes you to sleep."

"Formica and chrome table and chairs," said Thumps. "Shag carpet."

"1950s," said Duke. "What's not to like?"

Beth stood and stretched her legs. "Let me know when you two are done with the home-furnishing segment."

"Can I move him a bit?"

"Be my guest." Beth stepped back from the body. "You know what suspicious deaths and natural deaths have in common?"

Thumps knew the answer to that one. "They're both dead?"

Hockney patted Thumps on the shoulder. "See, you still got all the right moves."

Beth pulled off her gloves and opened her notebook. "The bodies normally don't get up and move around after they die."

Duke bent over the body for a closer look. "You got a time of death?"

"Don't you want to know how he died?"

"I know he didn't die in that chair." It wasn't a question, and Hockney didn't expect an answer.

Beth held up an evidence bag. Inside was a wallet. "James Lester."

"Lester?" Thumps turned to Duke, but he could see that this was not a surprise.

Duke flipped open his book. "James Lester. California licence. Sacramento address."

"The same James Lester who was passed out drunk at the airport?"

"So it would appear." Hockney shook the bag. "You two find any car keys?"

"No car keys."

"Remarkable." Duke turned to Thumps. "Don't you find that remarkable?"

"Happens all the time," said Thumps.

Duke put on a glove and fished the pistol out of the bag. "Smith & Wesson, internal hammer, .22 magnum."

"Kind of cute," said Beth. "For a gun."

"Holds seven rounds." Hockney cracked the cylinder. "Three rounds fired."

Thumps wondered if the stove he wanted came with a removable grill or if he would have to buy it separate. Next time he stopped by Chinook Appliances, he would ask Danielle about that.

The sheriff dropped the gun into the evidence bag and handed it back to Beth. "So, DreadfulWater, what do you think?"

"I'm a photographer."

"I do so love wasting my time watching grown men work." Beth resealed the bag and turned to Thumps. "Two o'clock today," she said. "My office."

"I don't need a physical."

"Don't be late."

ELEANOR DIDN'T CHEER up, even after Duke and Thumps loaded Lester's body into the back of Beth's station wagon. "Can I clean the room now? The day ain't getting any younger."

"Room's a crime scene, Eleanor."

"How the hell do you arrest someone for shooting themselves?"

"Don't suppose you heard a gunshot."

"What the hell kind of place do you think I run?"

Hockney hitched his pants. "I'm going to get some tape and seal the room. Then I'm going to send a couple of my deputies over here, and they're going to process the place."

"You mean make a bigger mess," said Eleanor.

"And when we're all done, you can have the room back."

"You got two hours," said Eleanor. "After that, I start vacuuming."

The sheriff shook his head. "Eleanor, my deputies find you in that room with your vacuum and you'll wind up in my motel. We clear on that?"

Eleanor stormed back to the office, kicking up sparks as she went. Duke leaned against a post and leisurely scratched his back.

"You know that woman used to be a nurse."

"Maybe she'd like to be acting sheriff."

"Let's take a walk," said Duke. "Enjoy the spring air."

The sheriff walked to one end of the parking lot and then he walked to the other.

"How's your math?"

"One bullet in Lester," said Thumps. "Two bullets missing."

"Maybe he tried to kill himself," said Hockney, "but missed the first two times."

"We looking for a green Jeep?"

"We are." Hockney took off his hat and rubbed his head. "You see one?"

"Nope."

"How's that Volvo of yours doing?"

"It's doing fine."

"Maybe you should forget about that stove and start thinking about another car."

"I don't need another car."

Duke opened the door of his cruiser and slid behind the wheel. "And seeing as you're in the market for a new ride, I know just the place."

FIVE

Chivington Motors was a sprawling acreage of used cars and trucks on the western edge of Chinook. Norm Chivington liked to boast that his business was the largest used car lot in the state. Not that the claim mattered to anyone except Chivington.

"You ever buy a car from Norm?"

"Nope."

"I did," said Hockney. "This is going to be fun."

"This about that Buick you got for Macy?"

"It is."

"The one with the cracked engine block?"

Hockney hummed a few bars of something bright and bouncy. "You got any ideas as to how our Mr. Lester wound up dead in his motel room?"

Tatum had arrived after eleven. Maybe he had a checked bag,

34

maybe he didn't. Ten minutes at the car rental desk, another ten to stroll to the parking lot. Half hour maximum. He discovered Lester in the green Jeep that Lester had rented and reported the problem to Orem. Orem called Norm Chivington, who came to the airport, roused Lester from his drunken stupor, and drove him back to the motel.

"Lester was dead before Tatum's flight landed."

"Yes, he was," said Duke.

So what Chivington would have found was a dead body. Even if rigor hadn't set in, there would be no mistaking a dead guy for a drunk.

"And Norm didn't call you."

"No," said Duke, "he didn't."

"You got it solved yet?"

"Nope. But I'm pleased as peaches that Norm is involved."

FROM A DISTANCE, the car lot looked impressive. Thumps had to give Norm full marks for curb appeal. Chivington Motors was a glass-and-aluminum prefab showroom and sales cen-tre set on a slight rise overlooking a regimented field of cars and trucks, their windshields decorated with exhortations, low-mileage stickers, and clearance prices. Off to one side, Norm had set up a long, white tent to protect the more expen-sive vehicles from the sun and from the hailstorms that could hit the prairies any time of the year.

Thumps had almost forgotten about Andy Hooper, but as the sheriff pulled into a parking space in front of the sales centre, there Hooper was, grinning as though he had just spotted his two best friends in the world.

"Sheriff!"

"Hello, Andy."

Andy Hooper was one of those tall, lean, young men you see in catalogues, posing in underwear and swimsuits. He had been a football star in high school. He had been prom king. He had been voted most likely to succeed.

"And Thumps." Andy grabbed Thumps's hand and gave it a good pumping. "How the hell you been?"

Hockney tried to approximate a smile. "Your CEO around?"

"What?"

The only thing missing from Andy's arsenal was a brain. Which, in some ways, was just as well. So far as Thumps could tell, Andy hadn't yet figured out that high school was probably as good as it was going to get.

"Norm?" said the sheriff.

"Hell, Duke," said Andy, holding on to his grin, "anything Norm can sell you, I can sell you. Keep it in the family. If you know what I mean."

"Afraid this is official business."

The smile remained fixed on Andy's face, but it had lost much of its sparkle. "Norm do something wrong?"

"Suppose I'll have to talk to him first."

"Got some primo units," said Andy. "No charge for looking."

"You know," said Hockney, "now that you mention it, Thumps here has been talking about getting another car."

Andy brightened again. "Nothing like a new car to put zip in your life."

"So, while I'm talking to Norm," said the sheriff, "maybe you can show him around."

"You bet."

"You might want to start with a Jeep," said Hockney. "Thumps has always struck me as a Jeep guy."

The late model cars were under the big tent, every one of them polished and sparkling. Thumps thought about his Volvo and tried to remember the last time he had cleaned the vehicle.

"A lot of people buy private," said Andy. "Craigslist, AutoTrader, classifieds. But that's always a mistake. I had a guy come in who had sold his car for cash to some stranger. Guess what happened?"

Thumps ran a hand along the hood of a late model Ford Mustang. He could feel the soft wax of the finish.

"The clown who bought the car didn't bother to transfer title or take out insurance. A few days later, he hit a delivery van and totalled the car. Guess whose insurance had to pay for the damage?"

There were four Jeeps under the tent and not a green one in the bunch.

"A woman I know bought a used car off the bulletin board at a supermarket. Turned out to have been stolen." Andy stopped and shook his head sadly. "You got to do these things right. Work with a professional."

"These are all the Jeeps?"

"Low mileage, fully loaded," said Andy. "Which one you want to take for a test drive?"

"I was thinking green."

"Green?"

Thumps held his face in check. "Yeah," he said, "green's a traditional Native colour."

"No shit." Andy wrapped his arm around Thumps's shoulder and hurried him back toward the showroom. "Then today is your lucky day."

THE GREEN JEEP was sitting in one of the mechanic bays, all shiny and wet.

"This little beauty is a steal," said Andy. "Hey, you're Cherokee, right?"

Thumps nodded.

"Jeep Grand Cherokee." Andy tried a wink that was more twitch. "That's got to be an omen."

"Somebody washed it."

"No charge for that." Andy tried to open the door.

"Locked?"

"Let me get the key." Andy hustled off toward the show-room. "Don't go anywhere."

Thumps walked around the Jeep and tried the rest of the doors. Of course, this might not be the green Jeep that Lester had rented. This might be a green Jeep fresh off a three-year lease, looking for a good home. Thumps tried to imagine himself behind the wheel. It was a Cherokee after all, and maybe Andy was right. Maybe it was an omen. Four-wheel drive would be handy in the winter, and the Volvo wasn't getting any younger.

Then again, neither was he.

"So what do you think?" Andy was back on the run with a large ring of keys. "You name the price, and I'll work with you."

"What's the mileage?"

"I'm on your side." Andy began trying out the keys. "If I don't make the sale, I don't get the commission."

Thumps was mildly fascinated watching Andy work his way through the keys, and he didn't hear Hockney until the sheriff was standing at his side.

"Hey, sheriff," said Andy. "Can you picture Thumps behind the wheel of a great car like this?"

Hockney had two cups of coffee. He handed one to Thumps. "Norm's got one of those fancy one-cup brewing machines in the showroom. You ought to see the different kinds of coffee the damn thing will make. I got you a Pumpkin Spice Latte."

"You're kidding."

"Got you a bottle of water too. Just in case."

"I'll take the water."

"Customers are crazy about that machine," said Andy, as he began to run through the keys a second time.

Hockney set his cup on a tall metal tool box. "Looks like you're having a little trouble."

"Not to worry," said Andy, picking up speed, "key's right here."

But it wasn't. Thumps and Hockney stood by the side of the Jeep and watched Andy work his way through the keys a third time.

"You know what," said Andy, "I'll bet Norm has the keys."

Hockney nodded. "And Norm seems to have disappeared."

"Must have gone to lunch," said Andy. "He probably took the keys with him."

"Now that's awkward," said Hockney. "Can't sell a car without the key."

"He brought it in early this morning," said Andy. "Must have forgotten to leave the keys on the board."

Hockney turned to Thumps. "Just how keen are you on this particular vehicle?"

"Very," said Thumps.

"Hey," said Andy, "I'll bet you got a slim jim in your car. Am I right?"

Hockney smiled. "So long as Norm won't mind."

"Hell, no," said Andy. "Norm's motto is 'Anything for a sale.'"

It took the sheriff less than thirty seconds to open the Jeep.

The rental agreement with Lester's name on it was in the glove box.

"Can make you a great deal." Andy rocked back and forth on his heels. "I'm in a crazy dealing mood today."

THUMPS GOT THE crime-scene kit from the cruiser while the sheriff called his office to arrange for a tow truck to take the Jeep to the police impound lot.

"You smell that?" Hockney wrinkled his nose. "You normally use ammonia to clean the cars?"

Andy had lost his good spirits. "How the hell should I know?" he said. "I sell the cars. I don't clean them."

"Ammonia destroys blood evidence," said the sheriff. "You'd know that, wouldn't you?"

"Blood? What blood?"

Hockney stuck a crime-scene seal on each door and handed his former deputy a business card. "Tow truck's on its way. Norm's not answering his cell, so when you see him, tell him to call me."

"Not my job," said Andy. "Tell him yourself."

Hockney turned to Thumps. "Then I guess we'll have to take old Andy here down to the office and get a signed statement from him."

Andy shoved his hands into his pockets. "Okay, I'll tell him."

"Don't want to put you out."

"I said I'll tell him."

"And while we're being all co-operative," said Duke, taking out his notebook, "what time did you get to the airport last night?"

"Airport?"

"You were there checking on Norm's rental cars."

"Sure, it's part of the job."

"Eight o'clock," said the sheriff, "nine o'clock, quarter to ten?"

"What the hell difference does it make?"

"Now think hard," said Hockney.

"Nine, nine-thirty. Something like that."

"And was this particular green Jeep at the airport at that time?"

"Wasn't there." Andy tapped the side of his head. "If it had been there, I would have noticed it."

Duke gave Andy a quick smile. "On behalf of the city of Chinook," he said, "I want to thank you for your assistance."

"Norm's not going to like this," said Andy, "you taking his car and all."

"Yeah," said the sheriff, "I know."

As THEY WALKED back to the patrol car, Thumps noticed that the sheriff had acquired a noticeable spring to his step.

"You forgot your Pumpkin Spice Latte."

Duke shook his head. "No, I didn't."

"You know," said Thumps, trying to sound concerned. "You may have to arrest Norm."

"God," said Hockney, "some days I just love this job."

SIX

Hockney dropped Thumps off in front of the Aegean. "I'm betting that one of Andy's old uniforms will fit you."

Thumps shook his head.

"Don't be like that," said Duke. "Think about Macy. She's not going to be pleased that you won't play acting sheriff for a lousy week."

"Macy's your wife," said Thumps. "She's your problem."

"Woman takes her vacations seriously," said the sheriff. "You know what I mean?"

"I'm not the man you want."

"That's true," said Duke, "but you're the man I've got."

THE AEGEAN WAS Chinook's only authentic bookstore. It was located in the old Carnegie library, which Archie Kousoulas had rescued from the jaws of a Denver developer who wanted to tear the building down and put up condominiums.

The idea of heritage armageddon had sent Archie into a frenzy, and he rushed to city council with a counter-proposal. He'd buy the building for a nominal price, apply for federal funds to fix it up, and turn the Italian Renaissance structure with its columns, semicircular arches, and hemispherical dome into a high-end bookstore and community centre, thereby adding to the cultural life of the town and, at the same time, preserving a piece of the city's history.

As THUMPS WALKED into the old library, he tried to decide whether he would simply remind Archie, in a gentle and generous way, that personal information—such as health—should remain a private matter.

Or whether he would forgo the niceties and just wring the little Greek's neck.

The lights in the store seemed unusually dim, as though the place had fallen on hard times and Kousoulas had been forced to cut back on the utilities.

"Thumps!" Archie was standing at a small display table next to a large poster. "Do you have any idea how worried I've been?"

"Have you been telling everyone that I'm sick?"

"You are sick," said Archie. "We just don't know what it is."

"I'm not sick."

"So what did Beth say?" Archie folded his arms and waited. "Did she take blood? Is it serious?"

Thumps rubbed his eyes. "For one thing," he said, "Beth doesn't jump to conclusions. For another, I don't need a blood test."

"You're kidding," said Archie. "You haven't seen her yet?"

THE DENVER DEVELOPER got the council's blessing. Most people would have given up at that point.

Not Archie.

He spent the next several months haunting city hall, annoying the mayor and council, badgering the planning department, and excoriating the heritage committee. He wrote the governor. He phoned every representative and senator in a four-state area. He called the National Register of Historic Places in Washington, D.C., and wrote letters to the editors of all the major newspapers in North America.

When that didn't work, he got a portable sound system, chained himself to one of the fluted columns, and read sections from Norman Tyler's *Historic Preservation: An Introduction to Its History, Principles, and Practice*, Robert E. Stipe's *A Richer Heritage: Historic Preservation in the Twenty-First Century*, and Jane Jacobs's *The Death and Life of Great American Cities*, until finally, the city had him arrested for trespass and being a public nuisance.

* * *

THUMPS TOOK a deep breath. "Archie, we need to get something straight. I'm not sick."

"It's the first stage of dealing with mortality."

"What?"

"Denial." Archie stared at Thumps's jacket. "What the hell is that?"

"Where?"

"There," said Archie. "In your pocket."

"What?"

"Bottled water?" Archie slapped the side of his head. "Are you crazy? Indians are supposed to be environmentalists."

THE ARREST DID IT. The video of Archie being hauled away as he shouted quotations from Thoreau and Marx, his fist raised defiantly in the air, made the national news, and in a media minute, Archie and the library went viral.

The major networks descended on the town like hawks on a rabbit, and the publicity forced the council to reconsider the matter. Over the next year, the air in Chinook was filled with angry words and fur, as a travelling circus of injunctions, lawsuits, and legal clowns tumbled their way through the courts. In the end, the developer folded his tents and slipped away. Three months later, Archie bought the building and set about restoring the old library and turning it into a bookstore.

* * *

"THE FIRST THING you need to do," said Archie, "is sign the petition."

Around a large table in the centre of the Aegean were a series of posters, all of them exactly the same: a photograph of a man in a business suit standing in the middle of a desert with his back to the camera. "Bottled Water," the caption read, "And You Were Worried About Oil."

Archie had enlarged articles from various newspapers on aquifers and watersheds, had mounted them on boards, and arranged them on wood stands. Two smaller tables were stacked with books on the history of water conservation and water management.

Archie pushed his glasses up on his nose. "Do you know the greatest threat our planet faces?"

"Something to do with water?"

"The commodification of fresh water," said Archie. "And here you are drinking it."

"I didn't drink it." Thumps pulled the bottle from his pocket. "See, it's still sealed."

Archie grabbed a form off the table. "Here, give me fifteen dollars and fill this out."

"Fifteen dollars?"

"The Chinook Water Watchers," said Archie. "When you join, you get a stainless steel water bottle."

What you couldn't fault Archie for were his enthusiasms. The man was a civic dynamo. If there was a worthy cause, you could count on Archie's support. If there was an important event, he'd be there. The only thing he hadn't done was run for public office.

Thumps glanced at his watch. He was supposed to be at Beth's at two. "I don't do a lot of joining."

"You don't do much of anything, but that's because you're sick." Archie rolled an old, grey metal office chair out from behind his desk. "Sit down so you don't fall down," he said. "Now, what do you know about aquifers and watersheds?"

ARCHIE HAD STARTED his book business on the second floor of his house. Back then the Aegean had been mostly mail-order and it had been reasonably successful. But the old library gave Archie just what he had always wanted.

A grand storefront.

Over the course of two years, he painstakingly restored the building. He sandblasted the granite facade, replaced the weeping tile so the basement didn't leak in the spring, patched the plaster walls, and painted the interior. He talked various people into donating their old couches and chairs and placed them among the stacks so there would be places to sit and read.

Thumps remembered the day the old Carnegie library reopened as the new and improved Aegean. It was the civic event of the year, and everyone showed up.

Even the mayor.

Archie rented a tuxedo and gave all his guests a copy of a best-selling novel by a Canadian writer no one had heard of, a book that Archie had purchased as remainder stock. On that day, the store had been hung with banners and flags, with Greek music playing in the background.

FOR THE NEXT twenty minutes, Archie took Thumps through a crash course on water conservation, and in spite of his desire to lean back in the chair and go to sleep, he found most of the information interesting.

"There's no reason for bottled water. The corporations have suckered us into believing that it's better than municipal tap water, but it's not. Between the toxins that the bottles give off and the lack of controls in the bottling process, municipal tap water is better and a hell of a lot fresher. And that's before we get to the environmental disaster that plastic bottles create. You still awake?"

"Tap water is better and fresher."

"That's right," said Archie. "Did you know that a gallon of bottled water costs more than a gallon of gasoline?"

"It's right there on the poster."

"Knowing something isn't the same as knowing something," said Archie. "And you're going to need a ticket."

"Ticket?"

"For the conference." Archie rushed to his desk. "The tribe is hosting the event at Buffalo Mountain Resort. Twenty dollars if you buy one now, twenty-five if you wait and buy it at the door."

Thumps could feel the fatigue rolling back in like a tide. "What's with the lights? You forget to pay your electrical bill?"

Archie rolled his eyes. "National Dark Skies Week."

Thumps tried to think of something to say.

"National Dark Skies Week," said Archie again. "We're all supposed to turn out our lights or at least reduce the amount of light we create. Don't you have a television?"

"And we're doing this because?"

"Light pollution," said Archie. "You need to read a newspaper every now and then."

Thumps tried a smile. "So we need to save the water and reduce the light."

"No one likes a smartass." Archie held up a flyer. "Here."

It took a moment for the photograph on the flyer to register. It was James Lester, smiling and full of life.

"Archie . . ."

"James Lester," said Archie, stabbing the brochure with his finger. "He's giving the keynote."

"Archie . . ."

"You know about the monitoring wells on the Bear Hump?"

The Bear Hump. Now there was a name Thumps hadn't heard in a while.

"Lester's company, Orion Technologies, has a lease out there. Company's developed a revolutionary method for measuring and mapping aquifers. Been running tests for the past year. Going to present their findings at the conference."

"Don't imagine the tribe's too happy about that."

"You talking about the old treaty dispute?"

"I heard the case is back in court."

Archie shook his head. "That's been going on for the last hundred years."

"One hundred and seventy-nine years."

"And I'm sympathetic," said Archie. "But Lester's keynote is going to change the face of water. Where else are you going to get that for forty dollars?"

Thumps held up a hand. "I thought you said the tickets were twenty dollars."

"Sure, sure," said Archie, his face suddenly aglow with enthusiasm. "But this is a moment in history. You're going to want to bring a friend."

Thumps looked back at the poster. "So, this technology . . ."

"Resource Analysis Mapping," said Archie. "RAM for short. There was an article on it in *Scientific American*."

"So, this technology is . . . valuable?"

"Valuable?" Archie glanced around the bookstore. Then he leaned in and lowered his voice. "Just between the two of us, there are people who would kill for it."

SEVEN

Thumps waited until he had turned the corner and was out of sight of the Aegean before he took the bottle of water out of his pocket, cracked the cap, and poured the contents into his new stainless steel container. It was a pretty thing with its silver body, matte black top, and bright blue carabiner, and Thumps made a mental note to use it whenever possible.

Especially when he was around Archie.

He should have said something, of course. Archie was going to find out about James Lester soon enough, and when he did, the little Greek wasn't going to be all that happy with Thumps and his failure to mention that the star of the water conference was dead. Not that it was his business to keep Archie up to date on police investigations.

* * *

THE INSIDE OF Chinook Pharmacy was bright and warm. National Dark Skies Week evidently hadn't made its way to the drugstore yet. Thumps picked up a small basket and strolled to the back. Chintak Rawat was standing behind the counter, immaculate in his starched white pharmacy jacket.

"Ah, Mr. DreadfulWater," said Rawat.

Rawat had arrived about six years ago, straight from Toronto, and had bought the drugstore from Harry Lomax when Harry retired and moved to the Oregon coast. At first, folks in Chinook had been cool to Rawat, and rather than support a local business, they drove to the big-box stores in Great Falls and Helena to get their drugs.

But then the price of gas had gone up and economics proved to be more powerful than prejudice.

"Mr. Archie tells me that you are not feeling well."

Thumps wasn't going to strangle Archie. He was going to borrow Duke's service revolver and shoot the little Greek.

"He is quite concerned about your health," said Rawat. "He tells me that you have never had a physical. May I inquire as to who your family doctor might be?"

"I don't really have a family doctor."

"Most disturbing. Everyone should have a family doctor. How else will you get the health care you need if you do not have a family doctor?"

"I wanted to ask you about vitamins."

"Ah," said Rawat. "Vitamins. The North American answer to good health."

"Something for low energy."

"I sell a great many vitamins," said Rawat. "I tell all my customers that most vitamins are not worth the buying, that the human body can get the necessary nutrients and minerals from a balanced diet."

"I hear that B12 is good for that."

"Yes," said Rawat. "Adults normally require around 2.3 micrograms a day. Beef liver and clams are excellent sources of B12, as are fish, meat, eggs, and milk, but it would be presumptuous of me to suggest a wellness protocol for you. That is the purview of your family doctor. The family doctor examines, considers, and, if necessary, prescribes, and I, as your pharmacist, then fill that prescription. As you can see, this is a very good system, though from time to time, there can be problems."

"Problems?"

"Oh yes," said Rawat. "There are unfortunate examples of unscrupulous doctors who will prescribe certain drugs to certain individuals who then sell them on the street. And there are drug companies who from time to time bring a drug to market before it has been fully tested because the potential profits are too great to resist."

"So, you don't have any recommendations?"

"But these instances are rare, and I will say no more about it."

* * *

THUMPS WANDERED the pharmacy looking at shampoos and the new shaving gels in neon colours. He considered sneaking a bottle of B12 when Rawat wasn't looking and moving quickly to the checkout line. Just in case a vitamin fix was all that was needed and he could forgo any further medical intervention.

Beth.

Thumps checked his watch. Beth had said two, and when Beth Mooney said two, she meant two. Not quarter past.

THE OLD LAND TITLES building was a two-storey, red brick affair with arched windows, checkerboard banding, and granite sills. Constructed in 1893, it had been home to land transactions, mining claims, and grazing leases as well as lawsuits, fist fights, and more serious disagreements. In 1902, a water-rights dispute led to a gunfight between groups of ranchers and farmers, who blazed away at each other for several minutes until both sides ran out of ammunition.

One of the ranchers shot another rancher by mistake, and a farmer broke an arm when he slipped and fell off the stone steps. Several windows in the building were shot out, and you could still see where the gunfire had chipped out pieces of the brick banding.

By 1910, the city fathers decided that the building was too

small to manage the demand, and a new Land Titles building was built next to city hall so that business and politics could be conducted in the same bed. The old Land Titles building was sold to a Mrs. Archibald Gibbons, a businesswoman from New Jersey who refurbished it as a boarding house, where young women of adventurous natures might spend their evenings entertaining adventurous gentlemen of all ages. In 1917, a more conservatively minded council changed the city by-laws and made such adventures illegal, and Mrs. Gibbons sold the building and moved back to New Jersey.

By the time Beth and Cora Mae bought the building, it had been a billiard parlour, a restaurant, a lawyer's office, and a short-lived men's club. The building had not weathered the years or the changes in usage all that well. The brick exterior had gone black, the window frames had rotted out, and the lath-and-plaster walls had begun to crack and crumble. Thumps had no idea how much work and money the two women had put into the place, but they had slowly restored the building until it was as crisp and spiffy as the day it was built.

Thumps hoped that the front door would be open. It wasn't. Which meant only one thing. Reluctantly, he pressed the intercom button.

"Yes?"

"It's me, Thumps."

"Basement," said Beth.

The second floor of the old Land Titles building had been

converted to living quarters. The first floor was Beth's medical practice. The basement housed the morgue. Thumps had nothing against basements. He had a darkroom in his basement. Beth had dead bodies in hers.

Along with an array of disturbing smells.

The basement was cold, dank, and gloomy. Thumps was relieved to find Beth sitting behind her desk rather than standing next to the stainless steel table, sorting through a corpse.

"When'd you get glasses?"

"Shit." Beth snatched the glasses off her head and shoved them in the drawer.

"They look great."

"I look like a librarian."

"Nothing wrong with librarians."

"What the hell do you want anyway?"

"This was your idea."

Beth frowned. "Right," she said. "The physical."

The white metal cabinet under the window was the only piece of furniture in the basement that looked as though it might have once been alive. Beth opened a drawer and took out a small plastic bottle.

"I need a urine sample."

"You want me to pee in the bottle?"

"That's the general idea."

"Here?"

"In the bathroom," said Beth. "Mid-stream."

It was a bit unnerving walking into the tiny bathroom with an empty bottle, knowing that Beth could hear him through the thin walls, and it was more than a little embarrassing walking out with a full bottle in hand.

"Just put it over there," said Beth.

"Is that it?"

On the table, Beth had laid out several test tubes, a piece of rubber tubing, and a sealed package, the contents of which Thumps was sure he wasn't going to like.

"Let's start with the blood work."

Thumps took a deep breath. "Couldn't we start with the questions?"

"Questions?"

"You know," said Thumps. "Do you drink? Do you smoke? What's your favourite colour?"

Beth was smiling. Thumps wasn't sure she was happy, but she was smiling. "Take off your shirt and sit on the slab."

Beth smiling or not, Thumps wasn't going anywhere near the autopsy table. "Aren't doctors supposed to be sympathetic?" Thumps could feel sweat forming on different parts of his body, and he could hear a distinct ringing in his ears.

Beth leaned over the desk and pressed the intercom button. "Yes?"

"Hockney," said the voice.

"Basement," said Beth.

Okay, so the ringing hadn't been in his ears, but the sweat

was real enough. Thumps had been happy to be rid of the sheriff earlier, but as he heard Duke stomp his way down the metal stairs, he felt positively euphoric. As though he had been found by search and rescue.

"Thumps?" said the sheriff.

"He's here for a physical," said Beth.

"Can I watch?"

Okay, maybe not search and rescue. Maybe just another psychopath.

"Put him on the autopsy table," said Beth, "and hold him down."

"My pleasure," said Duke.

"Costa Rica," said Thumps, as quickly as his dry mouth would let him.

"Which arm will it be?" Beth held up the needle so the metal gleamed in the light. "Left or right?"

Thumps was sure that, sometime in the near future, science would find a way to do blood chemistry without the barbarities of plunging a nasty steel tube into your arm and sucking out vast quantities of blood.

Hockney waited patiently while Beth listened to Thumps's heart, checked his reflexes, looked down his throat, probed his body with her fingers and asked him unnecessary questions about his bodily functions.

"You know," said Hockney, "this is fun."

"When was the last time you had a physical, sheriff?"

"Macy asks me the same question."

"And?"

"She gets the same answer."

Beth taped a piece of cotton over the wound. Thumps had been shot once, and as he sat in the chair, he tried to decide whether catching a bullet was as terrifying as getting a physical in a morgue.

"I hear our Thumps is going to play sheriff while you're away."

"He needs the money," said the sheriff.

"No, I don't."

"He wants to buy a stove that costs more than my car."

"No, it doesn't."

"Your car's free," said Beth. "City pays for it."

"The other car," said Duke.

"The Buick with the cracked block?" said Thumps, trying to even the conversation.

Duke paused and considered Thumps. "You really make a living taking pictures of trees and clouds?"

"I take pictures of rocks and rivers, too."

"How much you charge for a small photograph?"

"I'll give you one for free," said Thumps, "if you promise to leave me alone."

Beth snorted. "When you two are all done bonding, you might want to have a word with the recently departed James Lester."

"You know who killed him?" said Duke.

"I don't do who," said Beth.

Thumps's arm continued to ache. "Maybe someone gave him a physical."

"Okay," said the sheriff, "murder or suicide?"

"At this point," said Beth, "you can take your pick."

"Not much of an answer."

"Gunshot wound to the side of the head." Beth handed the sheriff a plastic container. "This was in his brain."

The sheriff held the crumpled lump of lead up to the light. "Any other wounds?"

"Nope."

"Don't suppose there's any chance of matching this bullet to the gun we found at the motel."

"Does this look like *CSI: Las Vegas*?" Beth walked to the far side of the table. "Angle of the wound doesn't discount suicide. Powder burns and stippling. There's a lot that feels like suicide."

"But?" Thumps moved his fingers one at a time to make sure they all worked.

"Not enough blood," said Beth. "Head wound like that should have more blood."

Hockney hitched his pants. "You saying he was dead before he was shot?"

"Only reason to explain the absence of blood is if Lester's heart had stopped working before he was shot."

"So, it's not suicide."

"Didn't say that." Beth shook a finger at the sheriff. "All I'm saying is the gunshot didn't kill him."

"So how did he die?"

"That's a better question."

"And you don't know."

"I don't know yet," said Beth.

"We're just charging right along, aren't we?" Hockney took off his Stetson and ran a handkerchief around the sweatband. "Lester dies of causes unknown. Maybe it's murder. Maybe it's suicide. Maybe it's natural causes. And after he's dead, someone shoots him and moves the body."

Thumps eased himself to a standing position. "Maybe the body was moved before it was shot."

"Possible," said the sheriff, "but not particularly helpful."

"How about you boys go play somewhere else." Beth picked up a small electric saw. "When I have more to tell you, I'll call."

Duke settled his hat back on his head. "Maybe you should give Beth a hand with the rest of the autopsy. You know, reacquaint yourself with the essentials of law enforcement."

"Now there's a great idea," said Beth. "And just what am I supposed to do with him when he passes out?"

"Sheriffs aren't allowed to pass out," said Hockney. "Even acting ones."

THUMPS TOOK THE STAIRS slowly, one at a time. His arm felt almost normal now, but he kept it close to his side. The street was quiet. The afternoon sun was bright, but the spring air was still wearing a chill. As he headed home, Thumps half-expected to hear Duke come charging up behind him with one of Andy's old uniforms tucked under his arm and a new inventory of reasons as to why he should play sheriff.

But the only sound in the world was the west wind sliding off the east side of the mountains on its way to warm up the land.

EIGHT

The house next door had been vacant for over a year. Thumps had watched potential buyers march in, and he had watched them march out. The realtor, a friendly guy named Ray or Clay, had stopped by to see if Thumps was interested in buying the property as an investment.

"Real estate in Chinook is hot right now," Ray or Clay had said.

Thumps asked the obvious question. If the market was hot, why hadn't the house sold.

"Vision," the agent had told him. "In real estate, it's all about vision."

Thumps remembered Ora Mae telling him that real estate was all about location.

"Why don't you take a look," the man had said. "I think you'll fall in love with the place."

So Thumps had looked. There was nothing wrong with the house. It was, in many ways, Thumps's house. With a tired paint job, a sloping floor, mismatched kitchen appliances, and a musty smell in the bathroom that made Thumps think of porta-potties in state parks.

"The owner's motivated."

Actually, the owner wasn't motivated. The owner was dead. The house was part of an estate sale, but Thumps supposed that Ray or Clay wasn't keen on sharing that information with prospective buyers, in case someone made the obvious but erroneous connection between the smell in the bathroom and Karl Vogler's death.

Karl had a daughter. Debbie. Thumps had met her when she came up from Los Angeles to bury her father. She cleaned the house, sold what she could, tossed everything else into a dumpster, put the house up for sale, and flew back to Los Angeles. Thumps suspected that the two of them had not been close, but he also knew the unpredictable nature of grief.

No one knew that Karl had died. Not immediately. It was Rose Twinings, Thumps's neighbour four doors down, who noticed that Karl hadn't been out for his daily walk.

"I suppose you know the story of the man who lived here," said the real estate agent.

"I live next door."

"He died in the hospital," said Ray or Clay. "The rest is just urban legend."

That August, Thumps had stood at his front window and watched Beth take Karl's body out of the house. It was not a pretty sight.

"Karl died in the house, in his recliner."

"It's misinformation like that," said the agent, "that hurts the economy."

As THUMPS CAME up the sidewalk, he noticed three things. One, Freeway was pasted to the front window, as though she had seen a carton of kitty treats strolling down the street. Two, the real estate sign at the Vogler place had a sold sticker on it. And three, there was a tall, thin man standing on the porch with a pile of dirty laundry at his feet.

The man smiled and waved, and Thumps waved back.

"You must be Mr. Awfulwater."

"DreadfulWater," said Thumps. "You buy the house?"

The man stepped off the porch. As he did, the pile of laundry stood up and followed him across the lawn.

"I'm Virgil Kane," said the man. "You know, like the Robbie Robertson song? Only with a *K*."

"Thumps."

"Most people just call me Dixie."

"Dixie?"

"Virgil Kane?" said the man. "'The Night They Drove Old Dixie Down'? Get it?"

"Clever."

"And this is Pops."

Thumps was pretty sure that Pops was a dog.

"He's a Komondor," said Dixie. "Real friendly, but he tends to fart a bit."

"Great."

"That your cat?"

Freeway was racing back and forth on the sill with her mouth open and her paws beating at the glass.

"Maybe Pops and your cat can be friends."

"Freeway?"

"I used to have a cat," said Dixie. "She and Pops got along real well."

Thumps tried to imagine Freeway and Pops frolicking through the neighbourhood together.

"I do computer programming and web design. And I'm into organic gardening. How about you?"

"Photography."

"Hey," said Dixie, "maybe we can do some business. I'm always looking for images for websites."

Thumps started to say something about photographs and computers when he was suddenly dropped into a septic tank.

"Sorry," said Dixie. "That's Pops. The move has been hard on him."

Thumps had to blink several times to clear his vision. He tried to remember if he had any gum.

"I better get back to unpacking," said Dixie. "Maybe when the dust clears we can sit down and have some coffee."

"Sure." Thumps glanced at Pops and wondered how any animal could produce such a stench and still be alive. "That'd be great."

"You like chickens?"

"Chickens?"

"Yeah," said Dixie. "I was thinking about building a coop in the backyard."

THUMPS STOOD ON his front porch and waited for the wind to blow the smell of Pops's digestive tract out of his clothes. Freeway was waiting for him when he came through the door. She twisted herself around his leg for a moment and then ran snarling out of the kitchen.

"It's not that bad."

The cat's bowl was empty. Freeway had been eating more than usual lately but was not gaining any weight. Maybe she was exercising when Thumps wasn't looking. It didn't seem possible. The only physical activities Freeway engaged in were yawning and stretching.

Thumps picked up the bag of cat food and gave it a shake. Freeway made a brief appearance at the doorway. She looked at Thumps and then she looked at the empty bowl.

"You want to play sheriff for a week?"

Thumps liked Duke. And he didn't mind doing crime-scene photographs when no one else was available. He had even helped the sheriff with the occasional investigation. But after Eureka and the aftermath of the Obsidian Murders, Thumps had put his badge and his gun away, and that's where they were going to stay. Duke would find someone else to look after the office when he and Macy went off to Costa Rica.

Or the sheriff could stay home.

Thumps settled in a chair. Freeway slipped around the doorway and climbed on the bag of food, but Thumps was too tired to care.

"Open it yourself," he told the cat. "Use your thumbs."

THE OBSIDIAN MURDERS. All these years and the case could still come out of nowhere and overwhelm him. The Northern California coast. The summer had started off the way summers on the coast always started. Foggy days that turned sunny around noon and then ran back to fog. By the end of August, ten people had been murdered, their bodies laid out in a strange, ritualistic fashion along the beaches between Fields Landing and McKinleyville, a small piece of black obsidian left in their mouths. Five women, four men.

And a child.

There had been no pattern to the killings, nothing to link the victims except their deaths. Anna Tripp and her daughter,

Callie, had been the last. A mother and her young daughter. Thumps had just come back from a forensics conference when their bodies were found on a stretch of beach below Trinidad Head.

He and Anna hadn't married. They hadn't even lived in the same house. Anna's choice. But they had been lovers, and during their time together, Thumps had, in small but significant ways, become Callie's father.

That summer the killings had started suddenly. Then they stopped just as quickly. And the police were left holding nothing but sand and fog. Three months after he buried his family, Thumps resigned from the force, packed his truck, and headed north and east for no better reason than that's the way the roads ran.

Just outside Chinook, the Volvo had thrown a fuel pump, and Thumps wound up stuck in the town. Frost was already in the air and, as he waited for a replacement to be shipped from Salt Lake, an early blizzard had come down from Canada. The roads were closed for the better part of a week, and by the time they had been cleared, he realized that he had no place to go.

So he stayed. Everybody died somewhere, and, for Thumps, Chinook had looked to be as good a place as any.

"YOU WANT A TREAT?"

Freeway had an extensive vocabulary, but there was only

a handful of words that could capture her attention. "Treat" was at the top of the list. Thumps forced himself off the chair. He took down the box of Kitty Num-Nums and shook out a handful of brown pellets that smelled like dead fish. Freeway slid off the bag and inhaled the treats whole.

"Don't be throwing up on the rug."

BUT HE DIDN'T DIE. One morning he woke up and the pain wasn't as bad as it had been. Day by day, in small increments, he made his way to where he could go to bed at night and wake up in the morning without feeling as though he had somehow killed Anna and Callie himself. He was not to blame. He understood that. But peace was fleeting and thin, and in the darkness that forms around sorrow, his own voice reminded him that neither had he caught their killer.

Death was a funny business. Whenever he saw a dead animal along the side of the road, he wondered if it had had a lover, children, a family, and yet, even if he knew the answer, he also knew that, in the end, he wouldn't stop.

Wouldn't even slow down.

THE PHONE SAVED HIM from slipping under water.

"Thumps?"

"Hey, Claire."

"Just thought I'd call to see how you're doing."

Women, Thumps decided years ago, had a need to know what people around them were doing every minute of the day. It wasn't curiosity exactly, and it wasn't control. It was more as though they were keeping track of the world so that if anyone hit them with a pop quiz, they'd have the right answer.

"Does Beth have the results yet?"

Archie had been working overtime.

"I just had the blood test today."

"Blood test?" Claire sounded confused. "What blood test?"

Thumps groaned silently. "The autopsy results, right?"

"The tribe is co-hosting the water conference. James Lester was to be our keynote speaker. We were supposed to get together today for lunch." Claire paused. "Why did you have a blood test?"

"Why would you call me about the autopsy results?"

"Roxanne said you were acting sheriff."

So, it was Hockney who was working overtime. "I'm not acting sheriff. Duke is just kidding."

"Didn't sound like he was kidding."

"He's going to Costa Rica. He *wants* me to be acting sheriff."

"Okay," said Claire, not missing a beat. "Then tell me about your blood test."

Freeway had made her way to the top of the scratching post, so she could watch as Thumps tried to explain that he wasn't sick, that he had just got the blood test as part of a normal physical, that, yes, he was a little tired, but that it was nothing to worry about.

"So you're tired."

"A little."

"And you're nauseous."

"Sometimes."

Thumps couldn't tell if the tone in Claire's voice was concern over his health or annoyance that he hadn't mentioned his health problems before now.

"All right," said Claire, her voice softening. "Call me when you have the blood test results. I don't want to hear about them from someone else."

Okay, so it was concern *and* annoyance. Thumps dragged himself to the sofa and lay down. Perhaps he should take lessons from Freeway and just ignore everyone and live life on his own terms. Now if he could just find someone who would feed him.

THUMPS HADN'T REMEMBERED falling asleep, but here he was waking up.

"Hey, uncle."

He could feel Freeway curled up in a warm ball behind his knees.

"You alive?"

There were only so many people Thumps could imagine

standing over him when he awoke from a nap. Cooley Small Elk was not one of them.

"The door was open. I thought maybe you had died."

"Cooley?" Thumps tried to sit up, but the cat wasn't interested in moving or being moved.

"Old people do that sometimes. Lie down and don't get up." Cooley grabbed a chair from the kitchen and sat down with a thud. "You want something to eat?"

Thumps looked at his watch. He'd been asleep almost two hours yet the feeling of fatigue was still there.

"Sleeping always makes me hungry."

"No, I'm fine."

"Okay," said Cooley, and he stood up and ambled to the refrigerator.

Most people who saw Cooley for the first time made the mistake of thinking that the man was fat and slow. It was an easy mistake to make, and depending on your circumstances, the error could be minor and embarrassing or major and fatal. There was little fat on Cooley's frame. He was simply huge. And fast. Thumps had seen him move, when moving was important.

"You got any ham or chicken?"

What Thumps appreciated most about the man was his innate intelligence and his gentle nature. Cooley seldom had a harsh word for anyone, and you had to work hard to get him angry. Thumps liked the man, but he always had the uneasy feeling that he was standing next to an impending avalanche.

"You want this juice?"

"Help yourself."

Cooley wandered back to the chair with a sandwich on a plate. From what Thumps could see, Cooley had shoved all of the leftovers in the refrigerator between two pieces of bread. Just beneath the romaine was what would have been his dinner.

"You're out of tomatoes," said Cooley. "Butter's almost gone, too."

Cooley wasn't as slow getting to the subject as Moses Blood, but he liked to take his time, especially if he was eating. Truth be told, Thumps wasn't all that keen on getting off the sofa.

"I need to go shopping."

"You should try the new sourdough bread that Milton is bringing in from Great Falls."

Cooley hadn't come all the way to town just to tell Thumps about Chinook's newest selection in bread.

"You plan on stopping by Moses's place anytime soon?"

"Moses?"

"He's expecting you." Cooley disposed of most of the sandwich in two bites. "Maybe I should drive you out there."

"Drive me?"

"You don't look so good."

"You don't need to drive me to Moses's place."

"That's true," said Cooley, "but it's a nice day and on the way, you can tell me all about the dead guy at the motel, and I'll tell you about Claire's new boyfriend."

"Boyfriend?"

"I don't think you have anything to worry about, but women see the world differently than men." Cooley gave the refrigerator an affectionate pat on his way to the door. "Oh," he said, "just so you know, you need more cheese."

NINE

The inside of Cooley's pickup was warm, and Thumps was having trouble keeping his eyes open.

"Stick said I should mention the boyfriend to you."

Stanley Merchant, or Stick, as he was known to everyone except his mother, was Claire's only child. The last time Thumps looked, Stick was twenty-two or twenty-three and still living at home because, to paraphrase the bank robber Willie Sutton, that was where the food was.

"He said he didn't want you to hear it from a stranger," said Cooley. "Blackfeet guy from Missoula. A lawyer. Roxanne says he's pretty good-looking. Got a bunch of muscles that show."

"Claire's a grown woman."

"Absolutely," said Cooley. "Don't figure she's all that impressed by muscles."

Thumps let his hand stray to his side. Part of his waist was leaning against the top of his belt.

"Now a lawyer might be a different matter." Cooley leaned on the wheel. "And he has a nice car. BMW or a Lexus."

"Why does Moses want to see me?"

"Don't you want to know about the lawyer's car?"

"Claire will tell me if she wants me to know." Thumps tried to keep his voice casual and uninterested. "What about Moses?"

"He needs your help."

Thumps couldn't imagine Moses Blood needing anybody's help. "You know what kind of help he needs?"

"Sure," said Cooley. "That's why he sent me to get you."

As THEY LEFT the highway and drove onto the reservation, Thumps realized that he hadn't been to Moses's place in several months. That was bad manners at the very least, with no room for an apology.

"What happened to the trailers?"

The last time he had come out, Moses had had an assortment of some fifty trailers spread out on the fifty acres of bottomland.

"They're migratory." Cooley held the wheel steady and let the truck find its own way down through the ruts. "They come and go."

"Migratory? Trailers?"

"That's what Moses says."

MOSES BLOOD WAS waiting for them under a large cottonwood. He was dressed in jeans, a blue work shirt, a white straw cowboy hat. Normally, he wore a pair of red runners, but today, for some reason, he was barefoot. The red runners had always struck Thumps as curious, but Moses told him that cowboy boots hurt his feet and that red was the colour of dawn.

"Hope you're hungry," said Cooley as he swung the truck around and stopped. "Moses cooked up a batch of his chili and cornbread."

Thumps had never had Moses's chili, but he had heard about it. Depending on whom you talked to, it was either wonderfully delicious or murderously hot. Duke Hockney had had the chili on several occasions and said it was "frisky."

"Ho," said Moses, "real nice day."

"Hi, Moses."

"Cooley," said Moses, "bring your uncle a chair. He's moving kinda slow."

That was how Thumps felt all right. Slow.

Cooley set up a folding chair next to the plywood table. "That chili ready?"

"You bet," said Moses. "It's always good to see young boys eat."

Thumps didn't feel all that young, but the smell of the chili and the cornbread reminded him that he hadn't eaten since breakfast. Cooley was already filling his own bowl. Evidently, the sandwich he'd made out of all the food in Thumps's refrigerator had only annoyed his appetite.

The chili was hot. It wasn't frisky. It was hot. Not so hot that you couldn't eat it, but hot enough to bring tears to your eyes and make your nose run. Even with the cornbread as a buffer, the chili was a lightning strike in dry grass.

"Chili's good."

"I got the recipe from a Mexican Indian who came to visit me." Moses leaned forward and lowered his voice. "He said it was a secret and not to tell anyone else."

"The recipe?"

"No," said Moses, "the ketchup."

The food was bringing him back, bite by bite. Thumps wasn't as tired now.

"Maybe you boys want to take off your shoes."

Cooley slid off one of his boots, taking the sock with it. "There was an anthropologist who came by and told Moses that Indians were in tune with nature. Said that Indians could feel the rhythms of the earth."

Moses stretched his legs and wiggled his toes into the short prairie grass. "What about it, grandson, you feel the rhythms?"

"Nope," said Cooley, "what about you?"

"Nope," said Moses, "but it always feels good to get out of those runners."

"Cooley said you might need my help."

"Yes, that's true," said Moses. "I might need your help twice."

"Sure."

"See," said Moses. "I knew your uncle wouldn't let us down."

"What do you need?"

Moses looked at the sky. Off to the west, the clouds were beginning to bend into an arch. A hard wind would be up by evening.

"A walk," said Moses. "First, we should probably go for a walk."

"A walk."

"See what all the commotion is about." Moses wiped his hands on a towel. "But the rumours are not good."

THUMPS FOLLOWED the two men along the river bottom. With any luck, the walking would be flat and the distance short.

Cooley gestured at the coulees on the far side of the river. "Last year, a company out of California got Indian Affairs to give them a ten-year lease on the Bear Hump."

Thumps had a flash of Archie standing in front of the water poster. "Orion Technologies?"

"That's right," said Cooley. "Orion is supposed to have a way to map aquifers."

"Whites like to measure things," said Moses. "They measure how cold it is, and how hot it gets."

Cooley held up his wrist. "They measure time."

"Yes, that's true." Moses chuckled and moistened his lips. "They even measure women's breasts. Have you ever measured a woman's breasts?"

"No," said Thumps, "can't say I have."

"Good to know the Cherokee are a civilized people," said Moses.

"But you've looked at them," said Cooley.

"Looking is okay," said Moses. "Just so long as you look in a respectful manner."

"Orion has their monitoring wells all over the Bear Hump," said Cooley. "There's one just on top of the coulee."

"Whites like to count things too," said Moses. "If they're not measuring, they're counting." Moses raised his face to the sky. "If I was a White man, I'd be counting those birds."

Thumps hadn't noticed the buzzards before, but there they were, floating above the land on the thermals.

"They arrived this morning," said Moses.

Buzzards weren't an unusual sight. You could always find one or two patrolling the skies. But now there were at least a dozen birds hanging above the land, turning in slow circles.

"Come on," said Moses. "We better go over and see what's got them upset."

"Upset?"

"Sure," said Moses. "Those ones are smart. Those ones are cautious. They don't like surprises. That's why they circle around and take their time looking. They see a dead deer or a dead cow, they say, 'Okay, we recognize that,' and then they swoop down and have a good feed. But if they don't like what they see, they stay away."

Thumps shaded his eyes. "Where exactly is this test well?"

"Across the river," said Cooley. "Right below those birds."

THE RIVER WAS low enough to ford at the sandbar. From there, Moses led them up a deer trail that wound its way along the side of the coulee. He didn't move fast, but he was steady, and Thumps had to scramble to keep up. Cooley kept jogging ahead and then coming back like a large puppy out for a run.

"You want to stop to rest?"

"No," said Thumps, "I'm fine."

"Breathing pretty hard."

"Feel good."

"The trick," shouted Cooley, kicking up dust as he bounded up the slope, "is to be in tune with nature."

"Yes," said Moses. "That's the trick, all right."

AT THE TOP of the coulee, Moses stopped and turned his face to the wind. "You smell that?"

The smell was faint, and it wasn't so much a smell as it was a vague stench.

"Not a deer," said Cooley. "And it's not a cow."

Moses wiped his hands on his jeans. "More bad news."

The monitoring well sat in the middle of the prairie. It wasn't much to look at, just a pipe and a wellhead boxed in by a cyclone fence with a padlocked gate. Someone had hung a large No Trespassing sign on the wire.

The woman lay in the prairie grass looking up into the sky, as though she were keeping track of the birds overhead. She had been shot once in the chest and once in the head.

"Margo Knight." Cooley squatted beside the body.

"You know her?"

"She came to council last year when the wells went in," said Cooley.

"I remember," said Moses, "because her name rhymes with *Fargo*."

"That was one scary movie," said Cooley. "Especially when they put that guy in the chipper."

"The other man did most of the talking," said Moses.

Thumps found the pamphlet Archie had given him. "This the guy?"

Cooley nodded. "That's him. We told him that he shouldn't be drilling holes on Bear Hump, that it was tribal land."

"They were nice," said Moses. "But they didn't listen so well."

"I'm going to have to call the sheriff. Tell him what's happened." Thumps looked back the way they had come. "Is there any easier way to get here?"

"Sure," said Cooley. "The highway is just over there."

"You mean we didn't have to walk?"

"There's nothing like a good walk," said Cooley.

"As acting sheriff," said Moses, "you could deputize me and Cooley."

"The acting sheriff thing is just a rumour," said Thumps.

"I always wanted to be a deputy," said Moses.

"And you can use my cellphone," said Cooley. "For official business."

The cellphone signal was weak but serviceable. As Thumps waited for Hockney to answer, he wondered if Moses was right about the buzzards. Maybe the birds were smart. Maybe they had taken a good, hard look at the corpse and had decided to give it a wide berth. All in all, Thumps couldn't fault their decision to stay in the sky.

If he had wings, that's exactly where he would be.

TEN

Cooley used his cellphone to take pictures of the dead woman and the ground around the monitoring station. Then he took a couple of shots of the three of them standing on the prairies with the dying sun stretching their shadows out across the land.

Thumps walked to the edge of the coulee and looked down on the river.

"We still on the reservation?"

"Yes and no," said Cooley. "Everything on that side of the river is reservation. Everything on this side is reservation land as well, but not everyone agrees."

"So this is Bear Hump?"

Cooley turned his face toward the mountains. "When we negotiated the Treaty of 1836, the Hump was part of the reservation."

"But the Whites changed the treaty when we weren't looking." Moses shook his head. "You got to watch them. If they're not measuring stuff, they're busy changing things."

"We've been trying to get the land back," said Cooley, "but treaty cases move slowly."

"Sometimes," said Moses, "they stop and stand still."

Cooley held his phone up and took a picture of the rolling hills and the dark forests in the distance. "My dad and I used to go hunting in the lodgepole pines. Good fishing streams up there."

The mountains were a deep purple now, and the light was fading quickly. Thumps zipped his jacket and turned up the collar.

"How long you figure before the sheriff gets here?" Cooley shoved his hands in his pockets. "'Cause I'm thinking I should take Moses home."

"*Say Yes to the Dress* is on at nine," said Moses. "Tonight the bride has to choose between a Stella York mermaid trumpet with cap sleeves and an Edgardo Bonilla ball gown with an illusion neckline."

"We've seen this one before," said Cooley. "So we won't be disappointed with the choice the bride makes."

"I can stay with the body." Thumps checked his watch. "Catch a ride back with Duke."

"You got a cellphone?"

"Nope."

"Too bad," said Cooley. "If you had a cellphone, you could call Stick while you were waiting."

Stick had never been happy with Thumps in Claire's life, and he sure as hell wasn't going to sit around and let some muscle-bound lawyer from Missoula come along in a fancy car and drive off with his mother.

"I think he's hoping you'll chase the guy away."

"Yeah," said Thumps, "I'm sure he is."

"Roxanne knows all about the guy," said Cooley. "In case you're curious."

Thumps had to admit he was curious. Claire didn't start relationships easily. He had had to work hard just to get her attention. And keeping her attention had been just as difficult.

"Not sure I want to do that."

"Don't blame you," said Cooley. "She's my auntie, so I've got blood to protect me."

Roxanne Heavy Runner was a thick, handsome woman who had been the band secretary through at least six different chiefs. People who didn't know her might think she was mean. In truth, she was just stern and somewhat inflexible. So far as Thumps could tell, there were few shades of grey in Roxanne's world. If there were any at all.

"If Claire wants me to know, she'll tell me."

"That's the attitude," said Cooley. "Make her come to you."

Thumps was fairly sure that's not what he had meant.

"Just like the sheriff," said Cooley.

"The sheriff?"

Cooley pointed his lips in the direction of the highway. "Make him come to you."

THUMPS WATCHED COOLEY and Moses drop down the side of the coulee and work their way back to the river. In some ways, it might have been better if he had gone with them. The sheriff was not going to be happy with another dead body, and Hockney was known to shoot messengers.

Claire hadn't mentioned the new boyfriend when she called earlier in the day, though there was no reason why she should. The two of them had never been exclusive. Thumps tried to think how he would describe his relationship with Claire. It was romantic, most of the time. And it was sexual, some of the time. By and large it was a series of starts and stops, warm with moments of high passion, but never hot enough to start a fire. A couple of years back, there had been some talk of living together, but then Claire was elected chief and that was that.

Comfortable? Is that how he would describe their relationship?

Thumps was trying to picture a muscular Blackfeet lawyer from Missoula in a German sports car when the sheriff's cruiser popped out of the prairies, kicking up a rooster tail of dust as it bounced along the uneven ground. It skidded to a stop by the cyclone fence, but the cloud the sheriff had been dragging along behind him kept coming, and Thumps only had enough time to turn his back as the whirlwind rushed by him and went sailing away into the evening sky.

Duke stayed behind the wheel, safe and snug, and waited for the storm to clear before he opened the door.

"Hear Claire has a new boyfriend."

Thumps brushed the dirt out of his hair. "We didn't touch the body. Left all the fun stuff for you."

"We?"

"Cooley took pictures."

"Wonderful." Hockney walked around the body. "Do we have any idea who she is?"

"Margo Knight." Thumps handed Duke the brochure. "She worked with Lester. They were in town for the water conference."

"You check her purse?"

"Nope."

Duke squatted down next to the body. "Shot twice."

Thumps stuck his hands in his back pockets. "Looks like we found our missing bullets."

Duke hooked Knight's purse with his little finger and stood up. "Your powers of deduction are amazing."

Thumps supposed that the sheriff had called Beth. It wouldn't do to leave a dead body on the prairies overnight.

"You catch up with Chivington yet?"

"Funny thing happened to Norm." Hockney's eyes narrowed into slits. "Seems he had to go out of town."

"Out of town?"

"On business."

The evening breezes were cool. The buzzards were still overhead, but there were fewer of them now. Thumps wondered where they slept at night, wondered if they slept on the wing. Moses would know that. So would Cooley. He should probably know it, too.

"Number 11." Duke held up a motel key. "Right next door to Lester's room."

Thumps rolled the sleeve of the woman's jacket between his thumb and forefinger. "Jacket's expensive."

"Do tell."

"So is the dress," said Thumps. "Purse is a Prada. Two thousand dollars, easy."

"You're kidding."

"It's all wrong."

"You can say that again," said Hockney. "Who the hell pays two thousand dollars for a purse."

Margo Knight was probably in her mid-forties, about the same age that Anna had been when she and Callie had been murdered on that lonely beach in Northern California.

"No," said Thumps. "What she's wearing. She wasn't dressed to come out here. She was on her way to dinner or a party."

Hockney sorted through the rest of the contents of the purse. "Wallet's here. Money. Lipstick. Condoms."

Thumps nodded. "Not a robbery and no signs of sexual assault."

"Along with a cellphone." Duke turned the phone over in his hand. It was a BlackBerry. Square, dark, expensive. The kind of cellphone serious business people carried to show that they were serious business people. "Notice anything about it?"

"It's a cellphone," said Thumps. "Every time you need it, the battery's dead."

"Same make and model as Lester's," said Hockney.

"If you say so."

Duke dropped the phone into an evidence bag. "You got a cellphone?"

"Nope."

"As acting sheriff," said Duke, "you'll be required to carry one."

"Then I can't be acting sheriff."

The sheriff got to his feet and dusted his pants. "Lucky for you, I've got an old Nokia you can borrow."

Over the sheriff's shoulder, Thumps could see a set of lights heading in their direction. "You call Beth?"

"Of course I called Beth," said Duke. "She has a cellphone."

"Then there you go," said Thumps.

"What?"

"She can be acting sheriff."

ELEVEN

It was late when Hockney dropped him off in front of his house. Next door, through a side window, Thumps could see the glimmer of a television.

"The place finally sold?"

"It did," said Thumps.

"Won't be easy, you know," said the sheriff.

"What?"

"Breaking in a new neighbour."

"He seems fine."

"That's the way things always start out," said Duke. "You ever see *Disturbia*?"

"He's a computer programmer."

The sheriff leaned forward on the steering wheel. "Now, what in hell's name is that?"

The light from the television flickered across the porch. In the shadows near the front door, something massive heaved itself up and then collapsed back into a heap.

"That's a dog," said Thumps.

"That's a dog?"

"A Komondor," said Thumps. "He's not as alarming as he looks."

"Komondor's a big lizard," said the sheriff. "Nature channel. Macy and I watched one of those suckers bring down a goat."

"You're thinking of a Komodo dragon."

"You ever see *Cujo*?"

FREEWAY WAS SITTING on the table in the kitchen, pretending to be an Egyptian figurine. Thumps and the cat had had several long conversations about where cats were allowed and where they were not.

Thumps had bought Freeway a fabric basket with a soft cream liner that had bird illustrations on the sides. He had positioned it in a corner under the kitchen table so she would have a comfortable hidey-hole.

"Haven't we talked about the kitchen table?"

Freeway had sniffed at the basket, and she had sniffed at the birds, and then she never went near the basket again.

"Cats aren't allowed on the table."

Freeway slowly leaned to one side, fell over on her back, and stretched out so Thumps could scratch her stomach.

"Really?"

Thumps glanced at the clock. Was it too late to call Claire? And what excuse would he make for calling at this hour? What if she wasn't home? What if she was?

Just wanted to make sure you were okay.

Your son said something about a new boyfriend. How's that going?

Freeway jumped off the table, but instead of slinking to her bowl and complaining that she didn't have enough food to survive the night, the cat went to the front window. At first she sat and stared out at the night, and then she began to meow and pace back and forth on the sill.

Thumps was about to tell her to pipe down when something large and dark leaped up against the glass.

"Jesus!"

It was a short, shaggy man with a long, pink tongue.

Freeway stopped pacing and considered the prowler. She cocked her head and put a paw out. The intruder did the same thing.

Pops.

Thumps imagined that he could even smell the dog.

"Great."

Freeway should have been hissing, her back arched, her tail fluffed out to resemble a baseball bat, but instead, the cat began to purr and rub her face against the window. The dog, for his part, began licking the glass with great slobbering strokes and waving a paw at Thumps to ask if he could come in and introduce himself.

That wasn't going to happen. The last thing Thumps wanted to do was to encourage Pops to spend his copious free time farting on the front porch.

Still, Freeway seemed curious, even friendly, and she didn't have any friends. If this dog was stupid enough to believe that he and a cranky cat could have a future, who was he to discourage a relationship when he couldn't even manage one himself.

"That's Pops," he told the cat. "Pops, this is Freeway."

There was a full moon out. He and Claire had spent one such evening not too long ago at her place, sitting in lawn chairs, watching the moonlight twinkle off the Ironstone River. That was then. This was a different moon, and he was tired. He should be asleep rather than playing chaperone to consenting adults.

"Don't stay up too late," he said to Freeway as he left the kitchen. "Don't make a lot of noise, and turn off the lights when you go to bed."

WHEN THUMPS HAD BEEN a cop in Northern California, he had lived his life on a schedule that had him up in the morning and out of the house before dawn. As a self-employed fine-art photographer, he could, if he felt like it, sleep in, lie in bed at all hours, wrapped up in a soft quilt with pillows braced against his side, while he drifted in and out of dreams.

Not that Thumps had dreams. Dreams, he imagined, were pleasurable fantasies bubbling with heroic escapades and erotic interludes. What found him in the night were the splinters of memory that tore through whatever peace sleep might provide. Nothing tangible. Nothing in focus. Just a vague assembly of assaults, desolations, and sorrows that rushed out of the shadows and swallowed him whole.

THE PHONE RINGING at six-thirty the next morning reminded Thumps of his standing resolution to have the damn thing disconnected. He buried his face in the pillow and let the call go to the answering machine. After ten rings, he realized that he had forgotten to turn the machine on. Again.

Thumps hit the talk button. "Mr. DreadfulWater is out of town and unavailable."

"Stop fooling around."

"Leave a message at the sound of the beep."

"Why didn't you tell me Lester was murdered?"

Thumps pressed the off button on the phone and pulled the quilt over his head. With any luck he could sink back into oblivion for another couple of hours.

Almost immediately the phone went off like a grenade. Thumps let it ring, hoping that Archie would give up.

"We got disconnected."

"No, we didn't," said Thumps. "I hung up on you."

"That's the cancer talking," said Archie.

"I don't have cancer."

"Diabetes then. Have you heard from Beth?"

"That's none of your business."

"I know who killed Lester."

The last thing Thumps remembered with any clarity was helping the sheriff and Beth load Margo Knight into the back of Mooney's station wagon. He didn't think anything else had happened while he was asleep. But maybe it had. And then again, maybe Archie was just making it up as he went along.

"Then call Hockney." Thumps tried to sit up. "He's the sheriff."

"Duke won't talk to me."

"Then bother Beth."

"She won't talk to me either."

"That makes it unanimous." Thumps hit the off button and rolled back into the quilt. He didn't expect that Archie was going to go away, and he wasn't disappointed. This time he answered on the first ring. "Archie, I'm trying to sleep."

"You're kidding. You're still in bed?"

"It's only six-thirty."

"It's nine-thirty."

Thumps squinted at the travel alarm on the nightstand. A moment ago, the first number on the clock had been a six. Somehow it had turned into a nine.

"I need your help," said Archie. "The water conference needs your help."

"I'm sure it will be a great conference."

"Great? Our keynote was murdered. How great can that be?"

"That's not what I meant."

"And now I can't find Dr. Knight."

Thumps struggled to the edge of the bed. His slippers were somewhere in the room. His shirt was over the chair. His pants were hanging on the hook behind the door. Where had he put his socks?

"Did you mention Knight to Duke?"

Archie snorted. "He wanted to know if Knight and Lester were close."

"And?"

"You too?" said Archie. "Not everything is about sex, you know."

"Archie . . ."

"Get dressed. The Aegean in an hour."

"Archie . . ."

But this time, it was Archie who hung up on him. Okay, so it was later than he had thought. Time to be up and moving. He felt his face. He had another day before he'd need to shave. The shirt he had worn yesterday still smelled fresh.

Yes, he could have told Archie that Knight's body had been found out at one of Orion's test sites, but sharing information about an ongoing police investigation wasn't his job. If the sheriff wanted to tell Archie, he would tell Archie. If Lester and Knight were sexually engaged, well, it wasn't his concern.

As he brushed his teeth, Thumps debated whether to make his own breakfast or to stop at Al's and start the day off right.

Not that the day hadn't already started without him. And he had eaten at Al's yesterday. Of course, there was no reason why he shouldn't treat himself well. He had read somewhere that one of the keys to good mental health, and by extension, physical health, was something called "tempered self-indulgence."

Thumps suspected that he had seen the phrase in an article in *Reader's Digest*, a magazine known more for its sappy anecdotes and right-wing grousing than for its accuracy. Still, he liked the general concept and was willing, for the moment, to suspend his disbelief.

The house was remarkably quiet, and it wasn't until he had dressed and was standing in the kitchen that he realized what was missing.

"Freeway?"

By now, the cat should have been dragging him out of bed. He had installed a cat flap in the door that led to the yard, but Freeway was not a fresh-air enthusiast. She preferred the luxuries of a toilet with water in the bowl, a soft sofa to scratch, a dish full of food, and a carpet on which to puke. She would go outside from time to time, though Thumps suspected that these forays were just to remind herself that inside was the better choice.

"Freeway?"

The cat's bowl was full. There was no vomit on the rug. No kitty corpse floating in the john. Thumps went to the kitchen and looked out the window. No Freeway. For just a moment, Thumps wondered if the cat had run away with Pops.

"Hey, diddle diddle, the cat and the fiddle . . ." There was a dog in there somewhere, but as Thumps checked the rhyme in his head, he remembered that it was the dish that had run away with the spoon. The dog in the poem had laughed, though Thumps couldn't remember why.

Thumps opened the refrigerator. It was more gesture than anything else. He had already settled on Al's, had decided he should give "tempered self-indulgence" a try and not be so dismissive of a new concept.

THE DAY WAS crisp and cheery as only spring days can be. As he stepped outside, Thumps noticed two things. First, Freeway was on his new neighbour's porch, lounging in a white wicker chair. Pops was sitting next to the chair beating his tail against the deck. Every so often, Freeway would casually wave a paw in the dog's direction, and, each time she did, Pops would quiver with what was evidently delight and beat his tail harder against the boards.

Thumps wasn't really sure he wanted to know.

"Hell of a nice morning."

Thumps turned to find a black Cadillac Escalade parked at the curb and two men standing next to the car. One was a Hispanic man in his early forties, shorter than Thumps but more powerfully built and in better shape, with black stubble for hair. The other man was taller and older. He was wearing a tan suit that had been made for him. And a cream summer Stetson. Thumps had no idea who he was, but the tall man looked as though he had just stepped off the front page of a fashion magazine.

"You must be Mr. DreadfulWater," said the older man in the Stetson.

Whoever he was, the man had a first-rate orthodontist as well.

"I'm Boomper Austin." The man ambled up the walk and thrust out his hand as though he were trying to punch a hole in plate steel.

Thumps tried to remember if he had ever met a Boomper.

"It's a family name," said Austin, reading his mind. "Historical artifact that we pass around every generation or so. And this is my associate, Mr. Cisco Cruz."

"Cisco," said Thumps. "As in *The Cisco Kid*?"

Cruz was dressed in jeans, a black T-shirt, and a black windbreaker that was two sizes too large. He wore a silver pendant on a leather thong around his neck and a thick, ugly watch on his wrist that looked as though it had been made out of old truck tires.

"Mr. Austin is in town for the water conference."

Austin took off his hat. "And I'll bet you're wondering what in the hell this idiot is doing standing on your property. Am I right?"

Thumps hadn't had much sleep and he hadn't had breakfast and the last thing he wanted to do was exchange pleasantries with a Boomper. "Bank owns the place," he said. "I just look after it for them."

"You see, Mr. Cruz, a sense of humour. It's one of the marks of a civilized man." Boomper turned back to Thumps. "You know V. Tony Hauser? Works out of Toronto?"

Thumps had never met Hauser, but at a show in San Francisco, he had seen a number of his photographs that had been shot on a Folmer & Schwing 12 x 20 banquet view camera.

"Large format," said Thumps. "Platinum and palladium prints. Does a lot of portraiture."

"Mr. Hauser did one of me," said Austin. "A Polaroid of all things. Amazing what you can find in a portrait that you hadn't noticed before."

Thumps tried to place the accent. Visually, the man was West Texas—white hair, blue eyes, tanned skin—but there was East Coast privilege lurking in his vowels.

"I have a set of his Algonquin Park images. I imagine you sell your photographs."

"I do," said Thumps.

"Then I'll take half a dozen. You pick them."

Thumps didn't know if the man was naturally charming or if he had worked at charisma until he had mastered it.

"Think of it as my way of paying you for your time."

"I'm on my way to breakfast."

Boomper nodded. "And I'm not one to keep a man from his feed."

Cruz took a card out of his pocket and handed it to Thumps.

"Austin Resource Capital," said Boomper. "That's me. R. B. Austin. The *R* is for Randall, in case you were curious." Austin took a postcard out of his pocket. "You probably recognize this."

Thumps nodded. "Ansel Adams. *Tetons and Snake River*. 1942."

"I have two original photographs of that scene that Adams himself printed. If you're agreeable, one of them is yours."

Thumps looked at the card for a long moment. He had always admired that photograph. Not that he was a great fan of Adams, but *Tetons and Snake River* was one of those images where, in that moment, all the elements had come together, and Adams had captured them. Thumps had seen any number of photographs made by other photographers of the same spot, but none had ever moved him the way Adams's effort had.

"I'm real fond of Adams," said Austin. "I don't just give these away."

"What is it you want?"

"You know the name Richard Throssel?"

"Throssel was a Native photographer," said Thumps. "Early nineteenth century. A contemporary of Edward Curtis. Cree."

"Adopted by the Crow," said Austin. "I have several original photographs and I can get others. You can take your pick."

Cruz shifted his feet. "Sir, you have a meeting in less than an hour."

"Cisco is reminding me that I don't have time to talk photographs," said Boomper. "But we're not talking photographs, are we, Mr. DreadfulWater? We're horse trading."

Cruz nodded. "Yes, sir."

"And I'm hoping Mr. DreadfulWater here likes the look of my horses."

Not many people knew about Richard Throssel. Austin might be a rich blowhard, but he knew photography. Thumps wondered what else he knew.

"I don't need an answer right away." Austin pulled the brim of his hat down and angled it to one side. "I'm having a little party up at Shadow Ranch tonight. Why don't you stop by? Bring a friend if you're so inclined. Cisco here will make sure you're on the guest list."

The sun caught the ring on Boomper's finger.

"Beautiful, isn't it?" He turned the ring back into the light and the deep red stone flashed with fire. "Just had it made. One of the perks of being filthy rich."

"Ruby?"

"Lot of people would think that," said Boomper. "Course it could be almandine garnet or imperial topaz or maybe a piece of cuprite."

"But it's not."

"Red beryl," said Boomper, his voice betraying his pleasure. "Stuff was discovered in 1958 by one Lamar Hodges while he was prospecting for uranium. The Ruby-Violet mine in the

Wah Wah Mountains of mid-western Utah is about the only place in the world where you can get gem-grade stones."

"Sounds rare."

"Extremely," said Boomper. "About ten thousand per carat. Red diamonds are ten times that price, but most red diamonds are small, less than half a carat, though in 2007 Sotheby's did sell a 2.26 carat red diamond for 2.7 million."

Cruz cleared his throat.

"But I do rattle on." Boomper rolled his shoulders. "Gemstones are a hobby of mine."

"Should I call ahead to say we'll be late?" said Cruz.

Boomper waved him off. "Mr. DreadfulWater is a patient soul, but I believe we have worn him out."

"Nope," said Thumps. "If I ever need a red beryl ring, I'll know just where to go."

Cruz opened the door and Boomper slid in.

"You think about my offer," Austin said. "No reason we can't do business."

Cruz walked around to the driver's side. The bulge in his jacket was noticeable.

"Big gun." Thumps pointed with his lips. "Shoulder sling. Combat boots. There a war somewhere?"

On the side of Cruz's neck, near his jaw, was a nasty-looking scar, as though the skin had been burned or ripped apart.

Cruz's face was impassive. "What are you, *vato*, a fashion consultant?"

"So you're the bodyguard?"

Cruz let his arms hang loosely at his side. "I'm whatever Mr. Austin needs me to be," he said. "Today I'm the driver."

"And tomorrow?"

THUMPS WATCHED THE Cadillac disappear down the street. Boomper Austin was a man who was disturbingly sure of himself. That kind of confidence might come from talent and skill, but in Thumps's experience, it more often came from money and the power that money could buy.

Boomper hadn't said what he wanted from Thumps, but the man hadn't come all the way to Chinook to pass out expensive photographs. And he hadn't come to town simply to attend a regional conference on water.

Freeway and Pops were no longer on the porch. They had disappeared. Maybe the cat was showing the dog around the neighbourhood, or maybe, as with people, the relationship hadn't survived the initial rush. Maybe the dog had quickly tired of the cat's surly nature, or perhaps Freeway had jumped into a BMW and run off with a Blackfeet lawyer from Missoula.

TWELVE

It was after eleven when Thumps got to the café. Wutty Youngbeaver and Jimmy Monroe were hunkered down on the far stools. Al was standing by the grill, singing to herself about a Holiday Inn full of surgeons.

"You just missed your little buddy," she sang out. "Flew in here like a crow with its tail on fire. Said to tell you to forget about the Aegean. You're to meet him at the Tucker."

"Not going to happen."

"Room 424."

"Archie has a room at the Tucker?"

"Has a girlfriend as well," said Al. "Brunette. Pretty, if you like hard thighs and pointy faces."

"What I'd like is breakfast."

Al tapped her watch. "Just turned the grill up for lunch. How about I grill you a nice piece of chicken with sliced cucumbers."

Thumps closed his eyes and slumped forward onto the counter. The fatigue was back. Out of nowhere.

Al slid a cup of coffee next to his head. "All right," she said, "if you promise not to die on me, I'll make you breakfast."

"With hash browns, tomatoes, and salsa?"

"Jesus," said Al, "who was your mother last week?"

"You were." Thumps laid his head on his arms. He could smell the coffee. Now if he could find a straw. The bendy kind. It might even be possible to eat without having to change position. He could drag the food off the plate with a fork and catch it with his tongue before it hit the counter.

"Don't you want to know about Archie's new girlfriend?"

"No."

"Asked me to make her a frappé," said Al.

"You don't make frappés."

"Nothing to it," said Al. "Coffee, couple of ice cubes, a little Reddi-wip on top."

"You own a can of Reddi-wip?"

"Fred Gamble liked to use it on his waffles," said Al. "I keep a can in the fridge just for him."

Thumps had to think about that for a moment. "Fred's dead."

"That he is."

"He's been dead, what, three years?"

"More like four," said Al. "Good news is the stuff keeps forever. Figure there's enough left in the can for another dozen frappés."

Thumps tried to imagine Archie with a woman. It wasn't impossible. But where had the man found the time? Archie had barely enough space in his life for himself.

"I made one for Wutty," said Al. "He said it was 'quite cosmopolitan.'"

Thumps looked down the counter. Jimmy was showing Wutty something in the newspaper, and Wutty was shaking his head.

Thumps lowered his voice. "Wutty said 'cosmopolitan'?"

"'Quite cosmopolitan,'" said Al. "His wife says he's been having a good time with the thesaurus function on her computer."

"Hey, Thumps," shouted Wutty. "Your hippie pal is in the papers again."

"Water," said Jimmy. "He wants to save the water."

"Maybe we should start shooting whales," said Wutty, "seeing as how they are prone to defecating in the ocean."

Thumps forced a grin to let both men know that he thought they were funny as hell. Then he turned back to Al.

"You sure she was a girlfriend?"

"Sure as hell wasn't his daughter."

"Where'd Archie find a girlfriend?"

Al shrugged. "How would I know? Maybe he found her on one of those online dating services."

"Archie?"

"Lot of people using those things." Al refilled Thumps's cup and angled her head toward the end of the counter. "Jimmy gave it a try a couple of months back."

"You're kidding."

"World's a big place. Got to be one or two women who go for short, fat guys with hair all over their bodies." Al waved the coffee pot at the two men. "Hey, Jimmy," she said. "Whatever happened with that dating service?"

"Bunch of lesbians." Jimmy scowled.

"Mr. Monroe don't need no dating service," said Wutty. "He is beset with opportunities."

Al shrugged. "I guess it's true what they say about a little knowledge."

Thumps watched the steam rise off the pile of hash browns cooking on the grill. The smell of bacon floated in the air along with onions and warm toast. Thumps wondered if just the smell of food had rejuvenating properties.

"You should consider giving one of those sites a try," said Al, "seeing as Claire has that new boyfriend."

"How about I consider breakfast."

"I could sign you up," said Al. "Successful photographer. Exotic ethnicity. Slightly overweight. Somewhat depressive. Possible health problems. Fixer-upper with potential."

"Fixer-upper?"

"There's lots of women who like fixer-uppers."

"There's a man who would like breakfast," said Thumps. "Please."

"Suit yourself," said Al, "but I wouldn't wait too long. Fixer-uppers don't have near the same shelf life as Reddi-wip."

By THE TIME the food arrived, Thumps discovered that his energy wasn't the only thing missing in action. As he looked at the plate, he realized that his appetite was gone as well.

"That's him."

Thumps looked up to see the sheriff coming in the door with a younger man in tow.

"Right now he's out of sorts," said Hockney, waving a thick finger in his direction. "So you might find him a bit cranky."

The man slid past Duke, which was no mean feat in the narrow confines of the café, especially with the sheriff standing in the way like a landslide.

"Oliver Parrish." The man was in his early forties, blond, with the body of a runner, slim and lithe. Crystal blue eyes and a ready smile that felt as though it was connected to a switch that he could turn on whenever he wanted.

"Ollie here is from Sacramento," said the sheriff. "Flew in this morning from Great Falls."

"It's Oliver," said Parrish, keeping his hands at his sides. "Sheriff tells me that you're heading up the investigation into James Lester's death."

All the visuals said West Coast. Green wire-rim designer glasses, cotton pants, print shirt, casual jacket.

"Sheriff's mistaken." Thumps squirted a glob of ketchup next to the hash browns. "I'm a photographer."

Parrish blinked. "A photographer?"

Duke slapped Parrish on the shoulder and sat down on a stool. "Once you get to know old Thumps here," he said, "you'll appreciate his keen sense of humour."

Al came by with the pot. "You two want coffee?"

"You bet," said the sheriff.

"I'll have an espresso," said Parrish.

Al looked at Thumps and then at Duke to see which one of them was responsible for bringing Parrish into her café.

"He's with the sheriff," said Thumps quickly.

"And a biscotti?"

First impressions suggested that Thumps wasn't going to like Parrish all that much. Everything about the man seemed quick, his eyes, his voice, the way he moved.

Al put a cup on the counter, slowly filled it to the rim with black coffee, and set a packet of saltine crackers next to the saucer. "That look about right?"

"Yes," said Parrish, without the hint of a smile. "That's exactly what I had in mind."

Thumps had to give the man credit. He might look like a weasel with a good haircut, but he was a quick learner.

"Ollie here is the chief of something or other," said Duke.

"Oliver here is the chief operating officer of Orion Technologies," said Parrish. "And it's Parrish with two *r*s."

Thumps's eggs were losing their buttery gloss, and the grease on the potatoes was beginning to cool. Parrish was sharper than Thumps had imagined, and, under different circumstances, he might have found the man amusing.

"Orion Technologies?"

"The very same." The sheriff pushed off the stool. "Ollie and me are going to mosey over to my office and have a little chit-chat. When you're done stuffing your face, why don't you join us."

"Why would I do that?"

Hockney set his hat on his head and cocked the brim to one side. "You going to eat that piece of toast?"

AL WAITED UNTIL the sheriff and Parrish had left before she returned with the coffee pot. "So who the hell wears green glasses with a Hawaiian shirt and a sports coat?"

"California chic." Thumps tested the eggs.

"Well, aren't we the fashion consultant." Al patted her hip. "Any wisdom on the gun?"

Thumps looked up from his food. How had he missed that?

"Right side. Little sucker. I figure he did it."

"Did what?"

"The guy at the Wagon Wheel. The woman out by the test wells." Al pursed her lips together. "Mr. Fancy Specs is your man."

Thumps sighed and rubbed his forehead.

"Chinook's a tight town," said Al. "We take our bodies seriously."

"So Archie knows."

Al nodded. "Wasn't real happy, you forgetting to share."

"Not my job."

The eggs were cold now, the hash browns dry. He had hardly eaten anything, yet he wasn't particularly hungry. Maybe he'd just sit in the café for the rest of the day. Now that he thought about it, there were worse ways to spend his time.

"Archie," Al reminded him. "Room 424. You don't show up, you know what he'll do."

Thumps leaned back on the stool and took a deep breath. "He'll come looking for me."

"And when you get there," said Al, "check out the femme fatale. If Fancy Specs didn't kill 'em, the smart money's on her."

THIRTEEN

In another month, when you could trust the weather, the Tucker would be knee-deep in tourists, camera bags, and guidebooks. Now the lobby was empty and quiet, as though the hotel hadn't yet crawled out of hibernation.

Thumps went straight to the house phones.

"Welcome to the Tucker," said a pleasant voice, "your home in the West. How may I direct your call?"

"Archie Kousoulas's room."

The Tucker was the class hotel in Chinook, what folks in places such as San Francisco, Seattle, Vancouver, and Calgary would call a boutique hotel. It had opened in 1876, the same year that George Armstrong Custer rode into the Little Bighorn Valley and did not ride out.

"Excellent. Could you spell that?"

Thumps did.

"I'm sorry," said the voice, "we have no one of that name registered at the Tucker."

After the First World War, the hotel fell on hard times and the building was turned into a hospital and then a general store. In the 1940s, it was used as a community theatre, a library, a roller-skating rink, and a movie house for art films.

It took Thumps a moment to remember. "Room 424. He's in room 424."

"I'm sorry," said the woman, "but we don't have a Kousoulas in that room."

Archie could certainly afford a room at the Tucker, but there was no good reason why he would spend the money. The man had a perfectly fine house. A hotel, a public building in the middle of town, seemed an odd choice for an assignation.

"Actually, it's Mr. Kousoulas's friend," said Thumps. "The room will be under his friend's name."

"And the friend's name?"

THUMPS RODE THE ELEVATOR with an older couple from southern California who were looking at vacation properties in Glory and Red Tail Lake. The elevator was slow, and for three floors, he listened as they chatted away about the proper ratio of bathrooms to bedrooms and whether a two-car garage was a manageable compromise. By the time they reached the fourth floor, Thumps felt as though he had just lived through an episode of *House Hunters International.*

Room 424 was at the end of the hall. The brass plate on the door said, "Charles Russell Suite." Thumps knocked and tried to imagine what he would say if an "assignation" opened the door.

Assignation.

The word made him smile. He'd have to find other occasions to use it.

"You must be DreadfulWater."

Al was right. The woman standing in the doorway was not Archie's daughter. Archie was short and wiry and beyond middle age. This woman was tall and muscular, early thirties. Whoever she was, she didn't spend her free time in front of a television.

"You want something to eat? There's a fruit plate. Chardonnay, if you're so inclined."

Two empty wineglasses stood next to a tall amber bottle with a gold label.

"Signorello, 2011," said the woman. "A good vintage. Help yourself."

Thumps couldn't see the labels on her clothing, but he was sure that the designers didn't live in North America. A pair of shimmering coffee-coloured slacks and a soft yellow silk blouse. Her hair was dark mahogany and cut shorter than the current fashions.

"Archie here?"

"Somewhere," said the woman, "but we can start without him."

Thumps tried to remember the French word for three people in a house. A phrase with sexual overtones. Something more potent than "assignation." He could feel his mouth begin to dry out.

"Maybe I should come back later."

The woman sat down on the sofa and crossed her legs. The coffee slacks tightened around her thighs. "Archie won't mind."

"What won't Archie mind?"

Archie came out of a room. He was fully clothed.

"Mr. DreadfulWater thinks we're lovers." The woman had a low voice with soft edges. "He thought I was suggesting a . . . ménage à trois."

"That's disgusting." Archie tapped a finger on Thumps's chest. "This is what happens when you listen to gossip."

"You're the one who told Al she was your girlfriend."

"And what if she is my girlfriend?"

"This is my fault," said the woman. "I thought a cover story would be a good idea. Stay under the radar. But I had forgotten about small towns and rumours."

"So, you're not Archie's girlfriend."

"Jayme Redding. Jay, for short."

"But she could be," said Archie.

Thumps had stayed in hotels and motels when he had been a cop, and he had found them all much the same. Bed, bathroom, television. Sometimes there was a small refrigerator, sometimes there wasn't. He had never stayed in a suite, but as he looked around the large, well-lit room, he imagined that this was how a suite might look.

"Is there a separate bedroom?"

Archie frowned. "Why do you want to know about the bedrooms?"

"There's more than one?"

Redding came off the couch. "Why don't you get Mr. DreadfulWater a beer from the kitchen."

"He's on duty," said Archie.

"There's a kitchen?"

"I'm an investigative reporter. *Sacramento Herald.*" Redding set a tablet on the table and turned it so Thumps could see the screen. "This is one of mine."

The banner headline was in bold caps. "Kanji Killer." There was a photograph of one Brian English. Single. White male. Thirty-seven. Clerical job at a large insurance company. He looked ordinary. And happy.

"Kanji Killer?"

Jay grimaced. "English thought it would be cute to mark his victims with a Chinese number. Three dead women before they caught him. One, two, three. You get the idea."

At the bottom of the story was a byline.

Thumps looked up. "So you're . . . Jonathan Green?"

"No," said Redding. "Jonathan Green is my editor's son. Green Senior. Green Junior. Get the picture?"

"Ah."

"Most of the evidence the police had was circumstantial. One woman worked in the same building as English. The other one worked at a Starbucks where English got his coffee."

"The third woman?"

"English lived three blocks away."

"What did English say?"

"First woman, Joan Horton, was killed on a Saturday. English said he was at South Shore, Lake Tahoe. Harrah's club. Said he was there for the entire weekend."

"There would be hotel records. Casino video. Credit card receipts."

Redding shook her head. "English didn't believe in credit cards. Paid cash. Didn't stay at a hotel. Slept in his car. Didn't gamble. Just wanted to walk along the lake in the moonlight."

"Nothing wrong with that," said Archie. "Credit cards are a plague, and walking is good exercise."

"And he was into martial arts in a big way."

Thumps looked at the article again. "Not really a whole lot here."

"Then one of English's co-workers came forward to say that English was aggressive with women. Evidently, social skills are the man's forte."

Thumps waited.

"And he was seen in the same bar as the third victim the same night she was killed."

"And no alibi for that."

"Said he went home and watched television." Redding rolled her eyes. "I was going to go up to South Shore to check English's story, but Green Senior wanted to run with the story."

"Police had already arrested English."

"We argued. I didn't like the loose ends. It was my story, my research, my sources. My reputation."

Thumps tried to look sympathetic. "So they ran the story, and Jonny Junior got the byline."

"Imagine that."

"English claims to be innocent?"

"Death penalty will be in play," said Redding. "What would you say?"

"You're not covering the trial?"

"Jonny's covering the trial," said Redding. "That is, if he can find the courthouse."

"Jay is here for the conference," said Archie, not wanting to be left out of the conversation. "She's going to do a three-part series on water in the West."

"Good news is jury selection doesn't start for another month, so I'll be back in time to hold Jonny's hand." Redding lowered her eyes. "You were involved with a serial killer, weren't you?"

Thumps looked at Archie.

"What was that case called?" Redding waited.

Archie stepped in quickly. "Tell Thumps about Orion Technologies and ClearBlu."

Redding smiled. "I think we're boring Mr. DreadfulWater."

"Thumps is acting sheriff," said Archie. "He's not allowed to be bored."

Redding nodded. "About six years ago, James Lester and Dr. Margo Knight formed a company called Orion Technologies. Lester was the money man. Well connected. Flamboyant. Clever rather than smart. Paranoid as hell. Lester doesn't go anywhere unless he's armed. Makes all his employees carry. It's part of the company dress code."

Thumps shrugged. "Hardly a sin in this part of the world."

"Knight was the scientific muscle. Ph.D. in physics from Stanford. Another in petroleum engineering from the University of Texas, Austin. She came up with a revolutionary way to measure aquifers and oil deposits that involves ions and harmonics. Once she can demonstrate that her technology works, the patent will be worth billions."

Thumps waited.

Redding continued. "Two years ago, Orion took out a ten-year lease on land just north of here."

"The Bear Hump."

"They put in a series of wells to monitor and map the Blackfoot Aquifer."

"To test the technology."

"That's right," said Redding. "They've been gathering data for the last year and a half, and Lester and Knight were going to present the results at the conference."

"And now they're dead," said Archie. "Tell him the rest of it."

Redding helped herself to a strawberry. "There's a company called ClearBlu. Hasn't been around a long time, but it's been a busy little bee, aggressively buying up water rights in the U.S. and Canada."

The grapes looked good. So did the cheese. Thumps wasn't sure why anyone would think of cucumber as a delicacy. He tried to remember the last bottle of wine he had bought. A heavy red for under ten dollars.

"ClearBlu is owned by Southwest Beverage," said Archie. "Southwest is owned by Lone Star International, and Lone Star is owned by Colorado Consolidated."

"These aren't shell companies, if that's what you're thinking," said Jay. "They're real corporate entities. They make profits. They sustain losses."

"And they all have the same master," said Archie.

Thumps knew he should play dumb and let Archie have his moment. But then he remembered how annoying the little Greek could be.

"Austin Resource Capital?"

"What?"

Thumps could see that he had guessed correctly. "Principal shareholder is one Randall Boomper Austin."

"My, my," said Jay, "aren't we the quick study."

Archie had the look of a grenade whose pin had just been pulled. "You *know* who Boomper Austin is?"

Flannery O'Connor was right. There was no pleasure but

meanness. "Tall guy. West Texas. Grey hair. Cowboy hat." Thumps rattled off the details as though he were filling out an accident report. "Blue eyes. Arrogant but friendly. Drives a Cadillac Escalade."

Redding nodded. "Was Cisco Cruz with him?"

"Good-looking guy? Latino. Bit intense? Maybe ex-military?"

The Greek grenade was close to exploding. "How the hell do you know Austin?"

"He stopped by the house." Thumps paused for effect. "He's a photography enthusiast."

"You're just doing this to irritate me."

"Nope," said Thumps. "He wanted to buy some of my prints."

Archie was shouting now. "You actually talked to him!"

"I talk to you."

"Jesus," Archie roared. "He murdered two people!"

Thumps shook his head. "You don't know that."

"Or had them murdered."

"Don't know that either."

"Then what do you know?"

Thumps took in a deep breath. "Talk to the sheriff."

Jay held up a hand. "I thought you said he was the acting sheriff."

"He is," said Archie. "He just hasn't come to terms with his new responsibilities yet."

"Rumours," said Thumps. "You know how they can get out of hand in a small town."

Jay stood and walked to the window. The slacks went with her. "I started work on the story about six months ago when word hit the street that Orion might have developed technology that could change the energy resource industry."

"Because the same technology that could measure an aquifer could also be used to measure oil and gas deposits."

"Exactly."

"And Austin wants the technology."

"That's the rumour."

"And the water conference is where Lester and Knight were going to report on the test results?"

"See," said Archie. "I told you he was quick."

"So," said Thumps, "at this point we don't even know if the technology works."

Archie groaned. "Of course it works. Lester's dead. Knight's dead. What does that tell you?"

Thumps turned to Redding. "Were they lovers?"

"Jesus, Thumps," said Archie. "Is that all you think about?"

"Neither Lester nor Knight were the romantic type," said Redding. "The only love in Lester's life was money. Knight was a loner with a mean streak as long as California. Were they sleeping together? Maybe. Maybe not."

"How much was Lester betting on the new technology?"

"Everything," said Redding. "But it was mostly other people's money."

"Investors?"

"And government grants."

Thumps rolled his shoulders and tried to stretch his neck. That tired feeling was back. He was going to start yawning any minute.

"So, they were business partners and possibly sex buddies. Hardly seems a motive for a murder-suicide."

"That's the way I see it," said Redding.

"But if the technology didn't work, and Lester blamed Knight for destroying the company?"

"Sure," said Redding. "I guess he might shoot her for that."

"And then kill himself?"

"No." Redding shook her head. "Man was too arrogant for that. It would be embarrassing, but he'd just walk away and leave the investors holding the bag."

Thumps couldn't contain the yawn.

Archie's eyes flashed. "Are we boring you?"

"Nope," said Thumps. "I'm having a swell time."

"And if the technology was a success," Redding continued, "there would be no reason to kill Knight and certainly no reason to commit suicide."

"All of which," said Archie, aiming his finger at Thumps's chest once again, "brings us back to Boomper Austin and a double homicide."

Redding held Thumps with her eyes. "But we don't have a motive, do we?"

Her eyes were a soft green with flecks of blue and gold. He'd always liked eyes with colour, eyes that changed and danced in the light.

"No," said Thumps. "We don't."

Archie began pacing the room, cutting figure eights as he prowled the suite. "What are you talking about? Austin wants the technology. Lester and Knight won't sell it. Bam! He has them killed."

"Why?"

"What?"

"Why wouldn't they just sell him the technology? Isn't that what they planned to do with it?"

"Sure," said Archie, "but not to Austin."

"Why not? His money's good."

"That's not the point . . ."

"Just because you don't like the man doesn't mean that Orion wouldn't do business with him. Wouldn't the technology go to the highest bidder?"

Archie picked up the pace. "Maybe Lester was going to release the technology into public domain. The last thing the energy extraction companies want is a method that will accurately measure the reserves. That information could put them out of business. It could be the end of their empires."

"A corporation with a social conscience?" Redding returned to the sofa. "Sure," she said, "that could happen."

Thumps was tempted to ask her where she bought her clothes, ask her if they were as expensive as they looked.

"Okay, so we don't have a *great* motive," said Archie. "But Beth has two bodies in her basement that didn't get dead from natural causes."

Thumps opened the door. "When you figure it out, call Duke."

"Where are you going?" Archie tried standing still for a moment. "Land Titles building? The sheriff's office?"

"Home," said Thumps. "I'm going home."

"You can't go home." Archie paced over to Thumps and stood in the doorway. "You have a murder case to investigate."

"The Obsidian Murders," Redding called out from the sofa. "That was the name the press gave the case, wasn't it? The Obsidian Murders."

THUMPS WAITED in the hallway in front of the elevator. He pressed the button several times, then turned and found the exit sign. The stairwell was empty, and he began the descent quickly, picking up speed until he was almost falling.

The lobby was quiet. The glass doors were standing open. He crossed the threshold of the hotel without pausing or looking back and stepped out into the bright light of a high prairie sky.

FOURTEEN

The sun might have been bright but the air was chilly. It was a game that spring liked to play with people who lived on the high plains. Lots of light. No real warmth.

Thumps stood on the top step of the Tucker and zipped his jacket up all the way. Maybe he'd go shopping. Buy a warm scarf. Invest in a fleece vest.

"*Qué pedo?*" Cisco Cruz was standing at the curb next to the Escalade. Boomper Austin was nowhere in sight. "You have a nice conversation with Jayme and Mr. Kousoulas?"

"What kind of mileage does it get?"

Cruz smiled. "EPA says thirteen city, nineteen highway. Combined sixteen."

"Not so good."

"If you worry about such things."

"And Mr. Austin doesn't."

"No," said Cruz, "he doesn't."

The light might not have been warm, but it was beginning to hurt Thumps's eyes.

"Maybe you want to take it for a test drive?"

"The Escalade?"

"*Claro.*"

"You and me?"

"We could talk, *vato*," said Cruz. "I'll bet we have a lot in common."

THE INSIDE OF the Escalade was warm and extremely comfortable. There were controls that raised and lowered the driver's seat, that tilted it back and adjusted a lumbar support.

"In the summertime," said Cruz, "the front seats can be cooled."

Thumps squeezed the leather-wrapped steering wheel and took in a long, slow breath. So this was the feel of luxury. This was the smell of extravagance.

"Where shall we go?"

"You decide," said Cruz.

"There's a small park down by the river," said Thumps. "We could go there and watch the ducks."

"Perfect," said Cruz. "I love ducks."

* * *

THUMPS TOOK HIS TIME driving to the river. The SUV felt as though it were completely detached from the planet and floating in space by itself. Thumps wasn't sure he liked the sensation.

"Can't really feel the road."

"I prefer standard transmissions and stiffer suspensions," said Cruz, "but the only place you get that shit anymore is in Europe."

THE PARK WAS DESERTED, the trees bare. Except for the ever-greens farther back from the bank, which looked as though they were still asleep. The spring runoff was churning the river into a grey-green boil.

"I thought you said there were ducks."

Thumps walked to the edge of the water and looked upstream and downstream. No ducks. "Ex-military? Law enforcement?"

"Both," said Cruz. "Military police for seven years. San Francisco homicide for ten."

"And now you're a bodyguard for a rich guy."

"And now I'm a bodyguard for a rich guy."

"And the rich guy wants something."

"Yes," said Cruz. "He does."

Thumps was surprised that there were no ducks. He and Claire had come to the park any number of times. There had always been ducks then. Lots of ducks.

"And you're going to tell me what he wants."

"I'll bet you can guess," said Cruz.

Thumps waited to see if Cruz wanted to go first. "A copy of the autopsy reports on Lester and Knight?"

"That would be great," said Cruz.

"Ballistics?"

"Sure."

"Crime scene reports, photographs, fingerprints, cellphone and computer records, any interesting forensics?"

Thumps tried to remember exactly when he and Claire and the ducks had last been here. Later in the summer perhaps. Maybe that was it. Maybe the ducks didn't care for cold springs any more than he did.

"And you're going to tell me why Mr. Austin wants this material."

"No," said Cruz, "I'm not."

"But Mr. Austin is willing to pay me a finder's fee."

"Consultant," said Cruz. "You would be a consultant."

"I imagine that Mr. Austin has a great many consultants."

"From time to time."

Thumps looked at Cruz for a moment. "And you've already told him I'd say no."

"I did," said Cruz.

Thumps waited.

"So you're wondering why we're bothering with this dance?" Cruz walked to an old picnic table and sat down. "We never had anything like this when I was a kid. Just desert. Didn't even rain. You used to live on the coast, that right?"

"Another life."

"Ocean's amazing. First time I saw it was when I was stationed in Okinawa. Couldn't believe all that water." Cruz rocked back on his heels. "You know much about global business?"

"Nothing."

"Mr. Austin has companies all over the world. Australia, Brazil, Mexico, India, China. You ever been to Uruguay?"

"Nope."

"You should see the business deals the man puts together."

"And Austin wanted to deal with Lester and Knight?"

"If you say so," said Cruz.

"And now they're both dead."

Cruz nodded. "If Lester killed Knight and then killed himself, no big deal."

"But if Lester and Knight were murdered?"

Cruz held out his hands. "It could work its way back to Mr. Austin."

"Which is where you come in?"

"Yes." Cruz smiled. "That's where I come in."

"I used to watch *The Cisco Kid*," said Thumps. "Neighbour had a television."

Cruz's face softened. "My mother was crazy about Duncan Renaldo. *Qué oso*. He played Cisco. Leo Carrillo played Pancho."

"Ooooh Cisco," said Thumps, remembering the famous exchange. "Ooooh Pancho."

"My father wanted to name me Emiliano after Emiliano Zapata," said Cruz. "You know that when the series began, Renaldo was forty-six and Carrillo was seventy?"

The sun was warmer now. Thumps could feel it spread out across his shoulders and run up the back of his neck. Behind him there was a sudden flurry and the sound of a body falling and hitting water.

Cruz stood and stretched his legs. "Look at that, *vato*. Ducks. Just like you promised."

FIFTEEN

Cruz drove the Escalade back into town. Thumps would have liked another turn behind the wheel, but sitting in the passenger seat gave him time to acquaint himself with contemporary automobile technology. His Volvo had knobs and switches. The Cadillac had a touch screen. The Volvo had maps stuffed in the side pockets. The Escalade had a GPS system that showed you exactly where you were in the world. At one point, Cruz pressed a button on the steering wheel and told the onboard computer to turn up the heat by two degrees.

And it did.

Thumps talked to his Volvo. Every time he got into the vehicle, he encouraged it to start, and every time he came to a stoplight, he pleaded with it to keep running. He wasn't sure if he could manage a car that actually did what you asked it to do.

Cruz turned a corner and brought the Escalade to a stop in front of the Land Titles building. "You coming to the party at Shadow Ranch?"

"Probably not."

"Free food," said Cruz. "Free booze."

Thumps opened the door and got out. "I suppose this was a coincidence."

"What?"

"Us running into each other," said Thumps. "You dropping me off here."

"This is where you wanted to go, isn't it?" Cruz leaned over and looked through the windshield. "Land Titles building. County coroner. Morgue is in the basement."

"And you would know that because . . ."

"Lucky guess," said Cruz.

Thumps squatted down next to the Escalade. "Because you're bugging Redding's room?"

"That would be illegal." Cruz tapped the wheel. "You remember the names of the horses?"

"Cisco's horse was Diablo," said Thumps. "Pancho's horse was Loco."

"Shadow Ranch." Cruz pulled the SUV into gear. "Who knows what you might learn."

Thumps stood and watched the Escalade disappear down the block. Okay, so Cruz was more than just muscle. The man knew things. Jayme Redding. Lester and Knight and Orion

Technologies. Boomper Austin. And he knew about Beth and her basement.

What else did he know?

The front door was locked. Thumps pressed the button and reminded himself that with two floors above ground, he had a sixty-six percent chance of staying out of the basement.

"Speak."

Beth could be upstairs in the living quarters enjoying a hot cup of tea. Or she could be on the main floor, working on files.

Thumps leaned into the intercom speaker. "It's me. Thumps."

"Basement."

"If we meet upstairs," said Thumps, holding down the button, "we could have tea."

"Basement."

THE LAST TIME he had been in the basement, the stainless steel table had been vacant. Now it wasn't.

"God!"

Margo Knight was on the table. Beth was standing next to her, a very large syringe with a very long needle in one hand.

"Don't be a baby," said Beth. "You've seen lots of dead bodies."

"No, I haven't."

"You here as acting sheriff?"

"Nope."

"Then I can't talk to you."

"Suits me," said Thumps, and he headed for the stairs.

"But you can be the messenger service." Beth waved the syringe at him. "Come here."

"I'm fine where I am."

"You can't see what I want you to see."

Thumps took one step forward.

"Closer."

"What am I looking at?"

"Bullet wounds," said Beth. "One in the chest, one in the head. Either one would have been fatal. You see the stippling patterns?"

"She was shot at close range."

"She was," said Beth. "But look at the wounds themselves."

Thumps leaned over the body. "Okay."

"Symmetrical, right?"

"More or less."

"And the head wound?" Beth took two short dowels from a tray and inserted them into the bullet wounds. "This is not exactly advanced forensics, but what do you see?"

Both dowels stood straight up.

Beth backed away from the table. "Same stippling pattern, same firing angle," she said. "You want to tell me how that is possible?"

Thumps rocked back on his heels.

"First I shoot you in the chest," said Beth. "What would you expect to happen?"

"I'd probably fall down."

"You'd probably fall down. You might fall on your back. You might fall on your face. You might fall on your side. And then I shoot you in the head."

"Pattern changes," said Thumps. "Angle changes."

"What if I shoot you in the head first?"

Thumps shrugged. "Same thing. Pattern changes. Angle changes."

"Unless?"

"Unless Knight was already lying on the ground, on her back, and the killer was standing over her when he shot her."

Beth pulled the dowels out of the wounds. "I didn't find any sign of blunt force trauma. No bruising to indicate a struggle. So, why was she lying on the ground?"

"Drunk? Passed out?"

"Alcohol in the blood barely registered," said Beth. "If she had anything to drink, it wasn't much. Not enough to put her on the ground."

"Drugs."

Beth held up a plastic sack filled with a milky yellow liquid. "Stomach contents may tell us, but your physical gave me an idea."

Thumps hoped he'd be able to get the sack of stomach contents out of his head before he went to sleep that night.

"I'm going to try to test the urine for Rohypnol and GHB."

Thumps looked at the body on the table. Knight wasn't going to pee into a bottle no matter how nicely Beth asked.

Beth held up the syringe. "I'm hoping that there's fluid left in the bladder."

Thumps felt a shudder go through his body.

"If it works," said Beth, "I'll check Lester's urine as well."

"You have a cause of death for him?"

Beth went to her desk and returned with a folder. "Lester had a heart condition. Not a serious one in the pantheon of heart conditions. But he was taking an ACE inhibitor to help dilate the arteries and to lower blood pressure."

"He died of a heart attack?"

"I'll know when I get all the tests back," said Beth, "but yes, I'm betting he died of heart failure."

"Duke is going to love this."

"Good thing you're a photographer and not acting sheriff." Beth laid the syringe to one side and took off her gloves. "I need a break before I get serious with Dr. Knight. You want a cup of tea?"

Thumps looked around the morgue. "Upstairs?" he asked, letting a note of hope creep into his voice.

"Yes," said Beth. "Upstairs."

THUMPS TRIED TO remember the last time he had been to the second floor of the Land Titles building. Before Beth and Ora Mae broke up? Yes, Ora Mae had been painting the place a dark yellow. Now the walls were a seafoam green.

Thumps sat down at the table. "What happened to the yellow?"

"You liked that yellow better?"

Thumps did a quick check to see if Beth had brought the syringe with her.

"No," he said. "I like green."

Beth put the kettle on the stove to boil. "Yellow was Ora Mae."

As Thumps recalled, Ora Mae had painted the place any number of times in all sorts of colour combinations. It had been an annual ritual with her.

"You want regular or herbal?"

Thumps's house had come with off-white walls, and he had never really considered painting them a different colour. But maybe he should. He had read an article that suggested that the colour of walls in the home and workplace could have a marked effect on mood and productivity. Thumps tried to imagine his bedroom in a deep blue.

"Regular is fine."

He could paint his living room a buttercream, maybe spruce the bathroom up with a medium taupe.

"Ora Mae is coming back," said Beth. "To Chinook."

Thumps had never asked why the two women had split up, and he wasn't about to ask now. He'd rather brave dead bodies and creepy morgues.

"She wants to talk." Beth took the kettle off the stove and poured the hot water into the cups. "What do you think I should do?"

Thumps knew instinctively that there was no good answer to that question.

"I won't bite," said Beth.

"Yes, you will."

Beth brought the cups over and banged them down on the table.

"I should get over to the sheriff's office. He's expecting me."

"Drink your damn tea."

"Okay."

"Thought you were a photographer."

"I am."

"Then just sit there and listen," said Beth. "You think you can do that?"

"Sure."

The tea was hot and strong.

"You know why we split up?"

There had been all sorts of rumours at the time. Archie had told him that Ora Mae had found a man somewhere back east. Al swore that it was because Beth wanted a baby, and Ora Mae didn't. Thumps figured that the relationship had fallen apart because that's what relationships tended to do.

"I'm sure you heard all the rumours."

"Don't listen to rumours."

"Everyone listens to rumours," said Beth. "We can't help ourselves."

Thumps put his face in the cup and waited.

"One of us wanted a monogamous relationship," said Beth. "One of us didn't."

"Tea's good."

"End of story."

Thumps waved a hand at the window. "Looks like it's going to warm up."

"What would you do?"

"Me?"

"Never mind," said Beth. "It was a rhetorical question."

Thumps could feel his legs begin to jiggle. They did that when he had sat in one place too long. And when he was anxious.

"Is it okay if I change the subject for a moment?"

Beth nodded.

"If you knew that you were going to go out onto the prairies, how would you dress?"

"You want to know why Knight was dressed for a night out." Beth paused and sipped her tea. "Do you know how hard it is to walk on soft or broken ground in heels?"

"No."

"Another rhetorical question."

"So, she hadn't planned on going out to the test well."

"Be my guess."

Thumps wondered if Knight had seen the bullets coming or if she was already unconscious when she was shot.

"You going to talk to Ora Mae?"

"Sure," said Beth. "No harm in talking. Don't men talk to women?"

"Mostly not," said Thumps.

"They talk to other men?"

"Mostly never." Thumps carried his cup to the sink and rinsed it out. Given the choice of dealing with Hockney or talking about relationships with Beth, he'd pick the sheriff.

"So you don't have any advice as to what I should say to her?"

"Nope."

"You're a good friend, DreadfulWater." Beth pulled the afghan off the back of the sofa and arranged it around her feet. "But I can get more help from the bodies in my basement."

SIXTEEN

E vidently spring was the season to paint things. The last time Thumps had been in the sheriff's office, the walls had been white. There were other changes as well. The ratty leather sofa was gone, replaced with two impersonal metal chairs that reminded Thumps of the chairs in Beth's morgue. Hockney's quarter-sawn oak desk was nowhere to be seen. Instead, the sheriff was now sitting behind a glass slab with chrome legs, in a black metal and mesh chair that looked as though it had escaped from the set of a low-budget space movie.

Not everything had been replaced. The ugly green file cabinets were still stacked against the far wall, and the old percolator that Duke used to smelt his coffee down into black ingots had miraculously survived the renovations.

Oliver Parrish was sitting in one of the morgue chairs.

Thumps stood in the middle of the room and tried to find his bearings. "What happened to the walls?"

"Dusty rose." Hockney made a face. "Mayor felt the place needed brightening."

"Brightening?"

"That's what she said. Brightening."

"It was bright before."

"What do you think of my new desk?"

"Not much," said Thumps.

"Personally," said Parrish, "I like the look. Has a clean, corporate feel."

"A suit." Hockney stretched his neck and turned his head to one side. "She wants me to wear a suit to council meetings."

"Are those curtains?"

Duke cleared his throat. "Ollie here was just about to fill me in on James Lester and Margo Knight. And seeing as it's your case, I figure you'll want to ask some of the questions."

"I don't have a case."

"There's not much to tell," said Parrish. "They were both assholes."

"Were they involved?" Hockney picked up a pencil and began fiddling with it. "As in sex?"

"That was the rumour," said Parrish. "Neither of them was married, so no harm, no foul."

"Ollie here is thinking murder-suicide," said Duke.

"Oliver isn't thinking anything," said Parrish. "That's the job of law enforcement."

Hockney shifted in his new chair. "Sure, but let's say, just for fun, that Lester and Knight were murdered. Who would the smart money be on?"

Parrish frowned. "You think they were both murdered?"

"Oh, I don't think they *were* murdered," said the sheriff. "But on the off chance they were, who do you like for it?"

Parrish ambled over to Duke's percolator and poured himself a cup. The coffee came out in a lump. If the man was still looking for an espresso, he was on the wrong planet.

"Lester was a wheeler-dealer. Liked expensive things. Cars, watches, clothes. He had a condo in Sacramento, another in San Francisco near the Embarcadero, and another at Lake Tahoe."

"Sounds like a swell guy," said Duke.

"Sure, if you like egotistical, misogynous paranoids." Parrish took a sip and instantly recoiled as though he had been struck by a snake.

Hockney closed his eyes and pretended to be bored. "And Knight?"

"She was the brains of the outfit," said Parrish. "But zero social skills. She saw the world as a giant periodic table. Had a mean streak. Liked to pull the wings off her assistants. Spied on everyone."

Hockney swivelled his chair to one side and then he swivelled to the other. "Still, you got along with the two of them."

"I worked for them. There's a difference."

Parrish returned to his chair and sat down. His coffee cup stayed on the file cabinet. Thumps was fairly sure the man wasn't going back for it.

"And if you want to know the truth, there wasn't a week went by where I wasn't ready to strangle the both of them."

"What about your competition?" said Duke. "I hear that business is war."

Parrish looked back at the coffee cup on the file cabinet. "RAM is cutting edge, and Lester kept a tight lid on the technology. We didn't have any competition."

"What about Boomper Austin?" said Thumps.

The sheriff swivelled around. "Boomper?"

Parrish's eyes flashed, as if someone had struck a match. "You know Boomper Austin?"

"He have any reason to kill Lester and Knight?"

"Austin wants to buy RAM," said Parrish. "That's no secret either."

Hockney shifted his weight and tried to find a comfortable position. "You have any idea what Mr. Parrish is trying to tell us?"

Thumps eased himself into the other morgue chair. It was as cold and clammy, as hard and unpleasant as it looked.

"I think he's trying to tell us that if Knight's technology worked, we'd have a precise way to map aquifers and oil and gas deposits throughout the world and that this information could be exceptionally lucrative or exceptionally dangerous, depending on who controlled it."

"That's exactly what Oliver is trying to tell you," said Parrish.

Hockney rocked his new chair back and forth. "Doesn't sound all that dangerous."

Parrish leaned forward and adjusted his glasses. "You ever hear of the Ogallala Aquifer in the Midwest?"

"Sure," said Duke. "Big pot of water that we're draining dry."

"And there's the problem," said Parrish. "The Ogallala Aquifer is part of the High Plains Aquifer. Covers about 174,000 square miles in eight states. Right now we don't know how much water is left in the reserve. In some areas, the aquifer is dry. If we knew exactly how much water was in the Ogallala, a number of industries could be forced to develop expensive conservation protocols they don't want to develop."

Thumps crossed his legs. It didn't help. "Stands to reason that these industries don't want the public to know what's underground."

"Sure," said Parrish. "Worst case scenario is that the big players apply the technology, discover that the deposits are close to collapse, keep that information a secret from the public, and push ahead regardless in order to keep their profits coming in for as long as possible."

"And deal with the shit when it hits the fan?"

"Just business," said Parrish.

Duke rocked forward. "That why you carry a gun?"

Parrish lost a bit of his swagger. "I have a permit."

"Didn't ask you if you had a permit," said Duke. "Asked you why you carry a gun."

"Lester," said Parrish. "He was a gun nut. Insisted that all his executives carry one."

"Calibre?"

"No idea," said Parrish. "You want to see it?"

"Actually," said Duke, "I'd like to hold on to it for a while. That is, if you don't mind."

Parrish slowly opened his jacket. "You can keep it for all I care."

"Slowly," said the sheriff. "We tend to get a little nervous around here when big-city folks show up with guns."

Parrish eased the pistol out of the holster and placed it on Hockney's desk.

"Knight carry a gun?"

"She did," said Parrish. "She liked them as much as Lester did. They used to go shooting together."

Hockney opened the cylinder and dumped the cartridges on the glass top. They made a clicking sound like ball bearings running into each other.

".22 long."

"If you say so," said Parrish. "We all had identical guns. Lester, Knight, me."

"Sort of a dress code?"

"I guess," said Parrish. "He also insisted that we have the same model cellphone and laptop. Man had control issues."

"Lots of that going around."

"Which reminds me," said Parrish. "When can I get their effects?"

Hockney pushed himself out of the chair and went to the percolator.

"Because there may be sensitive material on their phones and the laptops." Parrish's tone had turned serious. "Wouldn't do to have Orion's proprietary material wandering off."

"You staying in town?"

"Is this where you tell me not to leave?"

"Nope," said the sheriff. "That only happens on television. Just want to know where to find you if I have any more questions."

"The Tucker," said Parrish. "I'm staying at the Tucker."

Hockney poured himself a cup. "Not the Wagon Wheel?"

"Lester could be a cheap sonofabitch. I'm not."

"What about it, DreadfulWater," said the sheriff. "You kill someone to keep from staying at the Wagon Wheel?"

"Absolutely," said Thumps.

"Yeah," said the sheriff, putting the cup to his lips and inhaling the warmth. "Me too."

SEVENTEEN

When Parrish left the sheriff's office, he did not take his coffee with him. Hockney rocked back and forth in his new chair and fiddled with several knobs.

"Thing's got a lumbar support. Just haven't found it yet."

"Where's your old chair?"

"In storage," said the sheriff. "Along with my desk."

"Did you know it's National Dark Skies Week?"

Duke stopped playing with the knobs and stared at Thumps.

"No joke," said Thumps. "According to Archie, we're supposed to do what we can to reduce the amount of light we use."

Hockney reached out and turned off his desk lamp. "So tell me about this Boomper guy."

Thumps shrugged his shoulders and tried to breathe out the weariness. "Randall Boomper Austin. Boomper is some kind of family name. He's rich, smart, and has a chauffeur/bodyguard named Cruz. Owns something called Austin Resource Capital."

"And?"

"That's it," said Thumps. "Wants to hire me."

"To do what?"

"Spy on you, I think."

"Pay well?"

"Probably."

"We're in the wrong business," said the sheriff. "You stop by Beth's?"

"I did," said Thumps.

"And?"

"Bits and pieces. Evidently, Knight wasn't shot while she was on her feet. She was shot while she was lying on the ground."

"People wind up on the ground for all sorts of reasons."

"No trauma to the body."

"Blood alcohol?"

"Not enough to be falling-down drunk."

"That still leaves drugs." The sheriff scratched at the side of his thick neck. "Beth say anything about our couple's evening attire?"

Thumps smiled. "She said it's difficult to walk on the prairies in heels."

Duke eased himself out of the chair. "You want a cup?"

"No."

"Don't be a baby. It's fresh."

"Yesterday fresh or last week fresh?"

"When the pot's empty, I refill it." Hockney lumbered back to the chair. "Only time I put on a sports coat is when Macy and me go out to dinner."

"You own a sports coat?"

"Macy generally puts on a dress and heels."

"You think Lester and Knight were going out to dinner?" Duke didn't change his expression.

"And you've already checked the fancy restaurants."

"Hell," said Duke, "I've checked all the restaurants. No reservations anywhere for either Lester or Knight."

"So Lester and Knight get dressed up and go out to the test site. Lester kills Knight and then drives back to the airport, where he shoots himself."

Hockney squeezed his lips together. "Except that before he can pull the trigger, he's already dead."

"Okay, so Lester kills Knight, drives back to the airport, drops dead of a heart attack, is shot by a person or persons unknown, and is then driven back to his room at the Wagon Wheel, where he's staged to look like a suicide."

Hockney turned his head to one side. "And behind door number three?"

Thumps tried not to think about Beth's large syringe. "Lester and Knight are killed by a person or persons unknown."

"That's about it," said the sheriff. "And then the Jeep Lester had rented magically drives itself back to Chivington Motors."

"You think Norm shot Lester?"

"Ah, yes, good old Norm." Duke's face softened. "Can't wait to talk to him."

Thumps glanced at the old percolator. Maybe a cup of the sheriff's coffee wouldn't be such a bad idea. Maybe it would help drive the fatigue away.

"I don't suppose you have any cream or sugar?"

"What?"

"Cream," said Thumps. "Sugar."

"You sure as hell better not be thinking of putting cream and sugar in *my* coffee."

"Just a little."

"Christ," said the sheriff. "Maybe Archie's right. You are sick."

Thumps could feel himself drifting off. Suddenly there was music. Soothing instrumentals that seemed to come out of nowhere. Bach. One of the Brandenburg Concertos.

"Sheriff's office."

Thumps opened his eyes.

"Yeah." Duke had a cellphone to his ear. "Yeah . . . Great . . . On my way."

Thumps took a moment to organize his thoughts. "You have a phone with a ring tone?"

Hockney stuffed the phone back into his pocket. "Nice to see you're awake."

"A Bach ring tone? What happened to good old ring-ring?"

"Brandenburg Concerto no. 3," said the sheriff. "First movement. Part of the mayor's brightening initiative."

"I'm going home."

"Actually," said the sheriff, "going home will have to wait. I need your expertise."

"I'm a photographer."

"Then you'll enjoy this." Hockney fumbled with the knobs at the side of the chair. "Hey, would you look at that."

"What?"

"The lumbar support," said Duke with a big grin. "I found the lumbar support."

EIGHTEEN

A few years back, Thumps had contemplated teaching a photography course at Chinook Community College. He had never taught photography but had thought that it would be an interesting winter activity, an easy way to supplement his income when the weather kept him out of the field.

The woman at the continuing education office had been helpful. "You'll need to submit a course proposal to the curriculum committee." The package she gave him weighed about a pound.

"That's a lot of forms."

"When you fill in the book list, you might want to double-check to make sure all the books you need are in print."

"I don't think I'll be using any books."

"And you should be particularly precise in your course description," the woman had said. "The description is all the students will see when they're making a decision as to which classes to take."

"Okay."

"But the most important thing is the lesson plans."

"Lesson plans?"

"The course is ten weeks," the woman had told him. "The committee will want to see your lesson plan for each of the ten weeks."

Thumps had taken the course proposal package home, spread the forms out on the kitchen table, and began filling in the blanks. When he got to the section on lesson plans, he stopped. He knew the technical process of taking a photograph. And he knew how to print a negative. Digital remained a mystery, but he could probably bull his way through. Still, knowing how to do a thing was not the same as knowing how to teach it.

What are the goal(s) and objective(s) for Week One?

How will progress be measured?

What testing devices and strategies will be used?

Thumps had made himself a cup of coffee. Then he had made a sandwich. Then he had had a nap. Then he had watched television with Freeway on his lap.

Then he had slipped all the forms back into the folder and put everything in the hall closet.

* * *

THE COLLEGE WAS on the eastern edge of town. Hockney drove the ring road around the campus and pulled into a parking lot. Thumps stepped out of the cruiser. From here he could see the land fold and fall into the river. Under the high sun, the water was a curl of polished steel.

"Sterling Noseworthy wanted all of this land for a housing development," said Hockney. "You remember that?"

"Before my time."

"He was not happy when the city gave it to the college." The sheriff took off his hat and wiped the inside of the brim. "Said we shouldn't be using public money to destroy private enterprise."

"Heck of a view for a parking lot."

"That it is." Duke put his hat on. "And to think, it could have been someone's backyard."

"Not mine."

"No," said the sheriff. "You can't even afford a stove."

The campus had grown since Thumps had stopped in to see about teaching the photography course. There were new buildings that looked more like expensive trailers than permanent structures.

"Portables," said the sheriff, making the word sound like phlegm. "They look just like trailers, but they're called 'portables.'"

"What's the difference?"

"Portables cost more."

Duke headed to a portable with a Computer Services sign on the side of the building.

"We got a contract with the college," said Hockney. "They do a lot of our technical stuff."

The temperature outside was pleasantly warm, almost hot. Inside the portable, the temperature plunged.

"Yeah," said the sheriff. "Feels like a meat locker. Evidently, they need it cold to keep the computer stuff from overheating."

The portable was one large open room with a series of free-standing cubicles. Thumps could see the tops of people's heads as they bent over their computers. The scene reminded him in no small measure of Fritz Lang's 1927 dystopia, *Metropolis.*

"There's our boy."

It took Thumps a moment to recognize the young man sitting at the desk.

"I think you two know each other," said the sheriff.

"Hello, Mr. DreadfulWater."

The last time Thumps had seen Stanley Merchant, Claire's only child had been a skinny, long-haired, angry adolescent in dirty jeans and cowboy boots.

"Stick?"

"Stanley, please."

Now Stick's hair was cut short and styled. And he was heavier. Not fat. Just more filled out. Thumps never thought he'd ever see the boy in a dress shirt and slacks.

"Stanley here is on loan to my office," said Hockney. "He helps us with all the newfangled electronics stuff."

"Mom said to say hello."

Not that Stick was a boy any longer. How had that happened?

"Good to see you . . . Stanley."

Stick smiled, all warm and charming. "You should come around more. Mom's always talking about you."

The lawyer from Missoula. That was it. All this friendly chit-chat was simply camouflage. Thumps knew that the old Stick was lurking somewhere in the shadows.

"I hear she's got a new boyfriend."

The smile on Stick's face faded. "Thought you might want to do something about that," he said. "Guess I was wrong."

"Imagine your mother will make up her own mind."

"So why the hell you here?"

"He's with me," said the sheriff. "Thumps is going to be acting sheriff for a week or so."

"No, I'm not."

"That should do wonders for the crime rate," said Stick.

"So," said the sheriff, "what do you have for us?"

The blue plastic container was sitting on a long table. Inside, Thumps could see two laptops and two cellphones all neatly sealed up in evidence bags. Stick arranged the bags on the table in pairs.

"Mr. Lester's cellphone and laptop," he said, touching each bag. "Dr. Knight's cellphone and laptop. Where do you want to start?"

Thumps almost raised a hand. "Weren't the laptops and

phones password protected?" As soon as the words were out of his mouth, Thumps knew he had made a mistake.

"Duh," said Stick. "Of course they're password protected."

"But old Stanley here knows how to get around such inconveniences," said Duke. "Doesn't he?"

Stick screwed his face into a friendly sneer. "Yes, he does."

"And?"

"Lester used his laptop for email in and email out. No Facebook, no Twitter, no social networking whatsoever. Couple of games. Bunch of movies. Porn sites." Stick put the laptop back in the blue container. "Used his cellphone for calling people. Man had no imagination."

"And Knight?"

"Knight, on the other hand," said Stick, "used her laptop for everything. Lot of scientific shit, social networking, games, music, all sorts of apps. Used her phone as a camera. Woman took a photograph of everything she saw."

Hockney laid his large paw on Thumps's shoulder. "You hear that?" said the sheriff. "Photographs. Now there's something you understand."

"I'll make hard copies of all the correspondence and put the photos on a thumb drive," said Stick. "Drop everything off first thing tomorrow."

The sheriff put his hat on and set the brim at an angle. "Anything in the emails that you saw would give us a hint as to why they are dead?"

"Hell," said Stick, grinning like a weasel with a fish in its mouth, "if you believe the emails, they killed each other."

WHEN THEY GOT back to the car, Duke didn't get in right away. He leaned against the roof of the cruiser and considered the land and the sky.

"You know, I never get tired of it."

"What?"

"The land," said the sheriff. "The sky. I know lots of people find it desolate and depressing 'cause it can make them feel small and insignificant, but it's got a grandeur you don't find in places like Los Angeles or Dallas or New York."

"Or Sacramento?"

"Never been to Sacramento."

"You could ask Parrish about the city. Maybe he could give you some geographical insight."

"Ollie and me have already had a nice long talk."

Thumps wasn't going to ask. Asking was just going to encourage the sheriff.

"Don't you want to know what we talked about?"

"Nope."

"Not even a little bit curious?"

"Nope."

"You know," said Duke, "some people might think you don't care."

"I don't."

"But I know better." Hockney shooed a bug away from his face. "Ollie flew in from Sacramento to Great Falls. Afternoon flight. Had to stay overnight in Great Falls. Comfort Inn on Ninth."

"Comfort Inn doesn't sound like our Ollie."

"It does not," said the sheriff. "You know Black Jack Kramer?"

"Chief of police in Great Falls?"

"The very same." Hockney chuckled to himself. "Most people think that Black Jack got his name because he likes to play cards or because he carries a sap."

"But it's not."

"It's the gum," said Duke. "It's the gum he likes to chew."

"So Black Jack checked out Parrish's story?"

"He did," said Hockney. "And so far as Black Jack can tell, Mr. Parrish did indeed spend the night at the motel."

Thumps remembered Black Jack gum from when he was a kid. Each stick was black and tasted like licorice. "It's a little over three hours one way. He could have driven from Great Falls, killed Lester and Knight, and then driven back."

"True," said the sheriff, "but we still don't know if we're dealing with two homicides."

"But you had Black Jack check on the car rental companies."

"I did." Duke sucked his cheeks in. "And nothing appears to have been rented in Ollie's name."

"Orion Technologies?"

"Nope."

"And we know he caught the morning flight from Great Falls."

"We do."

"Al thinks Parrish did it."

"Norm Chivington is my sentimental favourite," said the sheriff.

"What about Knight?" Thumps opened the door and got into the passenger seat. "Find anything in her room?"

"Place was a mess," said the sheriff. "Pizza boxes, soft drink cans, clothes all over the place. Should have seen the bathroom. Woman was a slob."

"You find anything useful?"

"You mean why someone shot her?"

"That would be useful."

"But you know what I didn't find?" Hockney sat in the driver's seat and waited.

"Her gun?"

"Bingo," said the sheriff. "Wasn't in her purse. Wasn't in her room."

"Lester had his gun."

"Indeed, he did," said Duke. "So where is Knight's gun?"

"Maybe she left it in Sacramento."

"Possible, but if carrying a weapon was protocol and seeing as she apparently liked guns, why would she leave hers at home?"

"The killer?"

"Seems reasonable."

"But if Lester killed Knight, then he would have had her gun as well as his own."

"You know, I could sit here all day and listen to your mind work." The sheriff slipped the keys into the ignition. "So, what was all that about?"

"What?"

"Back there," said Duke. "You and Stanley."

Thumps shrugged. "Nothing."

"This about Claire's new boyfriend?"

"You'd have to ask Stick," said Thumps.

"Boy's always been somewhat territorial."

"Yes," said Thumps. "That he has."

The Brandenburg Concerto filled the car. Hockney fished the cellphone out of his pocket. "Speak." Suddenly, the sheriff was a happy man, grinning and bobbing his head. "The hell you say."

Thumps couldn't remember ever seeing Duke this pleased about anything. The man was actually humming to himself.

"On our way," said the sheriff. "Stay right where you are."

Duke dropped the phone on his lap and tore out of the parking lot on the fly. Thumps leaned against the door and watched the landscape fly by.

"Drop me off at my place," said Thumps. "I've had enough fun for today."

"Fun's just beginning," said Duke.

"I take it that was good news."

"That it was."

"They cancel the conference in Costa Rica?"

"Better." Hockney hammered his hand against the steering wheel. "Much, much better."

NINETEEN

It didn't take Thumps long to figure out where the sheriff was headed.

"Chivington Motors?"

"I've had Lance watching the place," said the sheriff. "Just in case."

"And?"

"Just in case just drove up."

The dealership was where they had left it. The late afternoon sun had found the sides of the showroom, setting the glass and aluminum panels on fire, while the slanting light played off the backs of the cars and trucks, giving them the appearance of a herd that had settled down for the evening.

Hockney keyed the mic. "What's he doing?"

There was a moment of static and crackle and then Lance's voice broke through.

"He's putting two suitcases into a maroon late-model Lincoln Navigator. You want me to stop him?"

"No," said Duke. "He's all mine."

Through the windshield, Thumps could see the maroon Navigator come flying down the access road.

"Rodeo time!" Hockney hit a switch on the console and the lights and siren sprang to life. He cranked the wheel hard and slid the cruiser across the road, effectively blocking the Navigator's forward progress.

But the big Lincoln kept coming at speed, and Thumps wasn't sure it was going to stop. He braced himself against the dash just as the Navigator found its brakes and nose-dived into a cloud of dust. Duke didn't wait for the dust to settle. He was out of the cruiser in an instant, his gun clear of its holster, as though he were the star of a crime drama and the director had just yelled, "Action."

"Turn the motor off," the sheriff yelled.

The Lincoln stayed in play, its motor running.

"Turn off the motor! I will not tell you again!"

The Lincoln rolled backwards on its heels, and for a moment, Thumps thought the big car was going to reverse and make a break back up the rise in the hope of losing itself in the acreage of cars and trucks. Not that there was the possibility of escape in that direction, but Thumps knew that panic could trump good sense.

Duke quickly stepped to the driver's side window and fired a round into the belly of the prairies. Even out in the open, where sound was swallowed whole by the land and sky, the crack of the shot was startling. The Navigator's engine immediately went dead.

"Open the door and show me your hands."

Instead, the driver's side window slicked down and there was Norm Chivington, his ferret face bright red and bathed in sweat.

"Duke?" Norm was trying hard to look friendly and aggrieved at the same time. "Is that you, Duke? Jesus, but you scared the daylights out of me. That was some dangerous driving, you know."

"Step out of the car, Norm."

"Dangerous and irresponsible, Duke. You could have got us hurt."

"Out." The sheriff slipped the handcuffs off his belt. "Now."

Norm kept his hands on the steering wheel. "Come on, Duke," he whined. "How about we all drive up to the show-room, sit down, and talk this out like civilized men. Have a cup of coffee. Wait until you see the new machine I got."

WITH CHIVINGTON HANDCUFFED in the back seat, the sheriff took the long scenic route to his office. Norm complained all the way, alternating between appeals and threats.

"Mayor's not going to be happy, you treating a pillar of the community like a criminal."

"You have the right to remain silent."

"Is this about the Buick? Is that what this is about?"

"Anything you say can and will be used against you in a court of law."

"Kidnapping is a federal offence. I hope you realize that."

"You have the right to consult an attorney before speaking to the police."

"You won't think this is so funny when I sue you for everything you have."

"If you cannot afford an attorney, one will be appointed for you before any questioning."

"Damn it, Duke. Think about what you're doing to your career."

"Do you understand your rights as I have explained them to you?"

Norm leaned forward and pressed his face against the wire panel. "For god's sake, Thumps, talk some sense into the man."

Hockney could have pulled the car into the alley and taken Chivington in through the rear door. But he didn't. Instead, Duke parked the car two blocks away and perp-walked Norm back down the street. Hockney took his time, tipping his hat to people as he passed them on the sidewalk, allowing them the thrill of seeing a pillar of the community in handcuffs.

When they got to the office, Thumps stopped.

"I'm going to go home."

"Don't you want to stick around for the questioning?"

"What questioning?" said Norm. "I haven't done anything. This is just police harassment."

"I have better things to do."

"Suit yourself," said the sheriff. "But you're going to miss all the fun."

Norm went pale. "You can't do that, Thumps," he said. "You can't leave me alone with this madman."

THE WALK HOME was pleasant. A high, thin overcast had drifted in and softened the afternoon glare. Thumps stopped in front of Chinook Appliances for a moment and looked in the window. The stove was still there. He considered stepping into the store and having another chat with Danielle, in case she was in a clearance-sale sort of mood.

But he didn't.

He was exhausted. Again. And he was tired of the sheriff and his ideas of temporary employment, tired of dead bodies, tired of Texas billionaires and their hired muscle.

Tired of duplicitous car dealers.

Thumps had a good idea as to Norm's role in Lester's death, and if that were the case, then the sheriff had figured it out as well and was jerking Chivington around on general principles. There was a price to pay for stupidity and arrogance, and, if Thumps was right, Norm had run up quite a bill.

But none of that was his concern. His concerns were what

to eat for dinner and what to watch on television. The sheriff could sort out the victims and the villains on his own. Thumps was going to have a nice, quiet evening by himself.

The porch was deserted. No Pops. No Freeway. But someone had stopped by. An envelope was stuffed between the jamb and the door. Inside was a fancy invitation.

Boomper Austin. The party at Shadow Ranch. That was tonight?

Great.

The house was dark and silent. No grumpy cat complaining that her bowl had not been filled, or that she had been abandoned, or that there had been no one to pet her for an entire day. Thumps wandered the kitchen and the living room. He expected to find Freeway somewhere in the house, but she was nowhere to be seen. Not outside. Not inside. Maybe she had packed her bags and gone to live with Pops. How long would that last?

Maybe longer than Thumps and Claire.

Thumps checked his watch. Three hours before the party at Shadow Ranch. He could stay home, of course, but this Boomper was a curious bird. The Texan was probably richer than anyone Thumps had ever met. That kind of money would make most people nervous, even paranoid. But ostentatious wealth seemed to have had a relaxing effect on the man.

Money appeared to make him cheerful. Money made him friendly.

Not that Austin's general disposition was of any great

concern. What was interesting was that he had come all the way to a hick town in the middle of nowhere to sit around on folding chairs and listen to lectures on water.

Why?

Thumps didn't know all that much about the habits of the rich and famous, but he was sure that the Boompers of the world didn't go just anywhere in the world.

Unless the going was important.

And profitable.

Besides, if he went to Shadow Ranch, he wouldn't have to feed himself. Someone else would do that for him. Always a crowd pleaser.

Three hours.

Time enough for a shower and a shave. Maybe he'd trim his toenails. The invitation hadn't specified a dress code. Probably business casual. Somewhere in his closet was a pair of slacks, a dress shirt, and a jacket, and he was reasonably sure he could find them.

But a free dinner wasn't the only reason he decided to go to the party. Claire would be there. Maybe they could get some time together. Thumps didn't feel particularly proprietary when it came to Claire. She was a grown woman, could make her own choices. Still, it wouldn't hurt to see this mysterious lawyer from Missoula, size up the competition.

And if Lester and Knight had been murdered, maybe Thumps could hang the crime on him.

TWENTY

The drive to Shadow Ranch was a surreal affair. Thumps was barely able to stay awake. He tried slapping himself across the face and chest, pinching the insides of his thighs, and singing 1960s rock and roll songs at the top of his lungs. By the time he rolled into the parking lot, the side of his face was hot and slightly swollen.

And he was hoarse.

SHADOW RANCH WAS the brainchild of Vernon Rockland, a Reagan Republican from Ohio who had made his money in construction. Rockland arrived in Chinook one spring, looked around, bought the old Anderson place for cash, and began "remodelling." A summer retreat, he told everyone, a getaway from the stress of the big city. No one in Chinook thought much about it until several architects arrived, followed closely by a swarm of surveyors, carpenters, electricians, millwrights, and welders, along with a herd of trailers, a pack of earth movers, and a flight of industrial cranes.

And before anyone in town had a chance to react, Rockland had turned a modest ranch into a sprawling, upscale resort and country club cleverly disguised as a western movie set.

The "Bunk House" was a four-star hotel. The "Watering Hole" was a Las Vegas–style nightclub. The "South Forty" was an eighteen-hole golf course. The following year, Rockland quickly added a water slide and pool complex, tennis courts, riding stables, and a skeet-shooting range.

THE RESORT WAS lit up like a Christmas tree. Evidently Rockland hadn't heard of National Dark Skies Week either. Thumps was out of his car and halfway to the main building when he heard the drum. Boomper didn't miss a trick. The Chief Mountain Singers. Thumps recognized the voices and the song, and for the first time all day he began to feel some energy flow back into his body. With any luck, Turley Standing Bull or Wayne Fox would invite him to sit in, and he could lose himself in the community of the drum circle.

It wasn't until he came around the corner of the decorative rock wall that was trying to pretend it was part of a natural formation and he could see the entrance to the resort clearly that Thumps realized he might have been better off staying home.

He had been right about the Chief Mountain Singers.

And he had been right about the drum.

They just weren't part of Boomper's party.

FOR THE FIRST two years of its existence, Shadow Ranch was one of the top destinations in the state, rivalling West Yellowstone, Whitefish, and the rest of the luxury resorts in the Bitterroot Valley.

Then the tribe built Buffalo Mountain.

Buffalo Mountain wasn't as large or as fancy as Shadow Ranch. It didn't have a golf course or a water park. It didn't have a clever theme or a high-end nightclub where you could party till the sun came up.

But it did have the only casino for three hundred miles.

And what it didn't have in terms of glitter and glamour it made up for in location. Part of Buffalo Mountain was set on tribal land, while the other part was set on land the tribe had purchased on the open market. Rather than hotel rooms, Buffalo Mountain offered high-end condos for sale and rent, all with full kitchens and views of the mountains, White Goat Canyon, and the Ironstone River.

All of the condos were on land owned by the tribe but were not on reservation land, a legal distinction that kept condo ownership from running afoul of federal Indian legislation.

The casino, on the other hand, was on tribal land, where it was protected, at least in theory, from state jurisdiction and legislative meddling.

THUMPS MIGHT HAVE mistaken the forty or fifty people standing near the entrance to the resort for partygoers who had stepped outside for a smoke had it not been for the placards that said, "Stop the Theft" and "Our Water Is Not for Sale."

And the television crew.

Most everyone was standing facing the drum, listening to the song, and there was a chance that Thumps could retreat to his car unmarked and head home.

"Thumps!" As if by magic, Archie popped out of the crowd. "Where's your sign?"

Archie's sign said, "Water for People, Not Profits." The printing had been done freehand with a black marker, but it looked professional.

"Nice sign."

"Here," said Archie, "you take it. I have another."

Turley was singing the lead for a Round Dance. Thumps closed his eyes and began to sing along, under his breath.

"But you're not here for the protest, are you?"

Even with his eyes closed, Thumps could feel Archie glowering at him.

"You're here for that asshole's party."

"I was invited."

"That's not an excuse!"

"Archie . . ."

"All right," said Archie, taking Thumps by the arm and leading him around the protesters, "you can be our inside man."

"You want me to spy?"

"Don't be melodramatic. Just keep your eyes open."

"Why don't you go in and spy for yourself?"

"Unlike some people," said Archie, "I wasn't invited."

It was a simple declarative sentence, but Archie was able to make it sound like a federal indictment.

"I didn't ask to be invited."

"Tell your buddy the people won't be defeated."

"He's not my buddy."

"And tell him to turn the damn lights down."

VERNON ROCKLAND WAS not happy about Buffalo Mountain. And he was furious about the casino. Even before construction on the resort began, Rockland sent his lawyers to lobby state and local officials and agencies to shut it down, arguing that the complex and especially the gaming facility represented an unfair advantage for the tribe.

"Level playing field" was the phrase that floated through the air, like smoke from a summer fire.

But because the condo complex was on private land and the casino was on tribal land, there was nothing anyone could do, and for the first time in his life, Rockland, who was used to doing business on a favourable slant, found himself labouring across relatively flat ground.

WHEN THUMPS REACHED the lobby, Cooley Small Elk was waiting for him. Along with a young White guy who was larger than Cooley. If that was possible. Both men had brass badges that said, "Welcome."

"Good evening, sir," said the man.

Thumps guessed that the guy was a football player or a weightlifter. His head and neck were the same size. His shoulders were broad, his chest thick. In a pinch you could have attached hinges to one side of his body, stuck a knob on the other, and hung him in a doorway.

"Do you have an invitation?" The voice sounded pleasant enough, but Thumps was reasonably sure that the man had not been hired solely for his personal relationship skills.

"This is Randy Palmer," said Cooley. "He's from Glory."

The name didn't fit, but that's what you got for naming a baby prematurely. Waiting until a child was old enough to earn a name had always struck Thumps as the intelligent way to do things. Randy looked more like a Bruce or a Jethro or a Billy Bob something.

"Randy's studying photography and graphic arts at the college," said Cooley.

"Your name?"

"Thumps DreadfulWater," said Thumps. "You guys security?"

"Nope," said Cooley. "We're event greeters. Randy is showing me how to welcome people."

"What if Archie and the protesters try to get in?"

"Then we're security," said Cooley.

Randy flipped a couple of pages on the clipboard. "Okay," he said, "it says here we can let you in."

"Archie wants me to spy on the party."

Randy shrugged. "Nothing much to see," said the man, "just a bunch of regular people pretending they're important."

"Wait until you see the food," said Cooley. "If you think about it, you might want to bring us out a plate."

"Sure," said Thumps, "I can do that."

"A large plate," said Randy.

Cooley pointed his lips at Randy. "Better make it two."

"But," said Randy, "you'll have to leave that sign here."

BOOMPER AUSTIN WAS standing in a tight knot of people, holding court. Oliver Parrish had shed his island attire and was dressed in a dark jacket with a Nehru collar. Evidently the man had more than one pair of glasses as well. Thin, black horn-rims with a gold accent at the sides. Beth Mooney was looking lovely in a shiny cocktail dress. Thumps couldn't remember if he had ever seen Beth in high heels and sporting cleavage.

"Mr. DreadfulWater." Boomper reached out from the crowd and dragged Thumps in. "What are you drinking, son?"

The curtains on the side of the room facing the front entrance had been drawn so you couldn't see the protesters, but you could still hear the drum above the crackle of conversation.

"Just water for me."

"Water," said Boomper, cocking his head in the direction of the singers. "That does appear to be the topic of conversation."

Parrish held out a hand. "Tell us," he said, "is that a war dance?"

"Round Dance," said Thumps. "It's a social song."

Parrish nodded. "But not tonight."

"I think they just want to make sure that you know there's an objection to the privatization of water."

"Duly noted," said Boomper. "Course there's always a small minority that objects to everything. That's why the majority rules."

Thumps looked around the room. "So money has nothing to do with it?"

Boomper's smile looked like the sun coming up. "Hell, son, money has everything to do with it. After all, we live in a democracy. And in a democracy, it doesn't matter how much money and power the other guy has. In a democracy, what matters is how much money and power you have."

Thumps wasn't sure if Boomper was joking. "And here I

thought that democracy was about equality and the pursuit of happiness."

"Yeah," said Boomper, "a lot of people think that."

Thumps scanned the room. "Mr. Cruz not here?"

"Oh, he's around," said Boomper. "Here and there. But I'm going to have to ring the bell on this round, seeing as our guest of honour has arrived."

Claire Merchant was standing in the archway. Normally her wardrobe consisted of shirts and jeans with a cotton print dress thrown in, along with a black business suit for when the government came calling. But here she was in a deep-blue evening dress that shimmered even when she was standing still. Her hair was piled on top of her head, and she was wearing dangling earrings. Thumps didn't know she even owned earrings.

"And that's her legal beagle," said Boomper.

Next to Claire was a tall, dark man whose most arresting attribute, besides a muscular body and a handsome face, was a mouthful of perfectly white teeth. So this was the new boyfriend. The lawyer from Missoula. Thumps tried to remember if the beagle had a name.

"That the new boyfriend?" Beth Mooney appeared at his elbow.

"I suppose."

"We need to talk."

"About the boyfriend?"

"No," said Beth, "we need to talk about you."

Thumps glanced at the long table of food and realized that he was hungry. "You want a piece of pie?"

"I don't," said Beth, "and neither do you."

Actually Thumps did want a piece of pie. Perhaps two.

"Here it is," said Beth. "Straight up. You're diabetic."

Thumps thought Beth had said he was diabetic, but he had been trying to decide if he wanted the cherry and the apple or the cherry and the chocolate cream. But only if the cream was real whipped cream and not one of those plastic substitutes.

"What?"

"I have to wait for the blood test to come back to confirm it, but the urine test was good enough for me. You're diabetic."

Thumps had no reason to think that Beth was joking, but he checked her face anyway.

"I'm not joking."

"So, how long do I have?"

Beth put a hand gently on his chest. "At your current blood-sugar levels," she said softly, "you'll be dead in a week. Two tops."

THE LAST THING Thumps remembered was watching the room tilt and wondering why. And then he was lying on the floor. Beth and Claire were both kneeling next to him. This was nice.

"Jesus," said Beth, "you don't do so well with medical humour, do you?"

"Diabetes is funny?"

"I meant the two weeks."

Claire looked even better up close than she had from a distance.

"Thumps has diabetes?"

And she smelled good. In fact, she smelled a little like pie.

"You'll have to ask him," said Beth.

"You're diabetic?"

For some reason, the back of his head hurt. Thumps tried to sit up, but as soon as he lifted his head off the floor, the room began moving again.

"Thumps?" There was concern in Claire's voice. He hoped that Muscles from Missoula could hear it.

"So it would appear." Thumps tried sitting up again. This time the room stayed put.

"Easy," said Beth. "You hit your head when you passed out."

"You didn't catch me?"

"Oh," said Beth, "now you want to joke."

Boomper was waiting for him when he got to his feet. "Damn, son," he said, "you sure know how to spark a party."

"Sorry about that."

"Hell, diabetes is nothing to be sorry about. My uncle was diabetic. Damn fool wouldn't listen to his doctor."

"He died?"

"In a manner of speaking." Boomper took a bite of the slice of banana cream pie he was holding. "They took him apart in pieces. First it was toes. Then a foot. Not long after that, he lost a leg. After he lost the second leg, he dragged himself out to the barn and put a bullet in his head."

The room rolled a little to the right. Thumps leaned against Claire. "Is that real cream?"

"Okay," said Beth, "when was the last time you ate?"

Thumps had to think about that for a moment. "Breakfast."

"Great."

Before Thumps knew it, he was sitting in a chair and Beth was handing him a plate and a fork.

"Pie?"

"Two bites," said Beth. "Just to get the blood sugars up."

"Could I have the cherry instead?"

TWO BITES SEEMED a particularly cruel way to get introduced to a disease. He wasn't that fond of blueberry, and the two mouthfuls only reminded him of how hungry he was. He was set to take a third bite with the claim that he had lost count when Beth took the pie away and came back to the table with a plate of cold vegetables and a small piece of ham.

"You're kidding."

"Get used to it."

The party had re-formed itself. Boomper was talking to Claire, who seemed to have forgotten that Thumps was dying. Mr. Perfect Teeth was standing next to her, his groin hovering dangerously close to Claire's thigh. Parrish was caught in a knot of Chinook's finest, trying to look interested as the mayor talked about her plan for a convention centre.

Beth cut the ham into pieces and handed Thumps the fork. "You drive up here?"

"I'm feeling better now."

"You're not driving home."

"Sure I am."

"You even open the door to your car without my okay and I'll have Motor Vehicles revoke your driver's licence."

Thumps didn't have to look to see if Beth was joking. He could hear the truth in her voice.

"Look, I drove up with Roger Conklin," said Beth. "I'll drive you home."

"Roger Conklin? The city accountant? Mr. Straight Arrow?"

"He's a friend," said Beth. "It may come as a surprise, but lesbians have straight friends."

"I'm your friend."

"Lordy," said Beth, pointing to a piece of carrot on the plate. "It must be an epidemic."

"I have to go to the bathroom."

"Sudden urge to pee?"

"Are doctors allowed to ask questions like that?"

"Only the good ones," said Beth.

* * *

THUMPS HAD TO give the bathroom at Shadow Ranch full marks. The urinals were sparkling white and looked more like little easy chairs, the floor and walls were covered with travertine tiles, and there were newspaper articles in frames above each latrine so you could read while you took care of the business at hand.

Sports, sports, and more sports.

Thumps wondered if the women's bathroom had newspaper articles on the walls of the stalls. He'd have to ask Beth about that, ask her what women like to read. He was reasonably sure that they wouldn't be all that keen on following box scores or batting averages.

When he came out of the bathroom, he made a detour to reception. The woman behind the desk was tall and dark. Hispanic or Native. He didn't think she was from the reserve, but there was something about her that scratched at the back of his mind.

"Hi," he said. "Could you tell me who would take care of reservations for the restaurant?"

"I can do that," said the woman. "When would you like the reservation?"

There it was again. The voice. He knew that voice, and it sent an unexpected jolt of fear through his body.

"Actually, I don't want to make a reservation. I think I made one for the wrong day." Thumps tried to look as foolish and embarrassed as he could. "It was supposed to be for later this week, but I think I made it for two nights ago."

"Was it in your name, Mr. DreadfulWater?"

So they did know each other. Thumps tried his best to place her face.

"Deanna Heavy Runner," said the woman, reading his mind. "Roxanne is my sister."

"Sure," said Thumps, trying to keep the panic out of his voice.

"I know," said Deanna. "Roxanne can be a little intense."

Intense was certainly one way to describe Roxanne Heavy Runner. Terrifying was another. Dangerous. Fearsome. Formidable.

"Best secretary the tribe's ever had."

"That's sweet," said Deanna. "I'll tell her you said that."

There was a story that floated around the reservation about a bear who wandered into the tribal offices without an appointment and wound up as a rug on the floor in front of Roxanne's desk. It was a joke, of course, but every time he heard it, he found himself feeling sorry for the bear.

Deanna smiled and turned to her computer. "So . . . two nights ago?"

"Yes," said Thumps. "It would have been in the name of Austin."

Deanna looked up from the monitor. "You made a reservation for Boomper Austin?"

"Not exactly."

"Are you asking as acting sheriff?"

Thumps looked around quickly. The lobby of the hotel was empty. Everyone was in at the party.

"Roxanne told me that you're going to be the sheriff while Duke is in Costa Rica."

"We're talking about it," said Thumps.

"Is this about those two dead people?"

So much for stealth and cunning. Something like this was easier to do in a large city, where no one knew you and no one cared.

"I'm studying criminology at the college, so if you need any help, let me know." Deanna hit several keys. "Here it is. Reservation for three."

"That's the one."

Deanna lowered her voice. "Is this a clue?"

Behind him, the party seemed to have found new energy. Thumps could hear Boomper's voice rumbling about in the room like a spring storm, and he wondered if the lawyer from Missoula was still perched on Claire's hip or whether she had made a clear space for herself and was waiting for him to return.

"One other thing," said Thumps. "Was the reservation ever cancelled?"

"I remember now." Deanna looked up from the screen. "I was on the desk. Mr. Austin came in and sat at the table by himself for a while and then he left."

"So, the other two didn't show up?"

"Part of the course I'm taking has a practicum requirement." Deanna wrote a number on the back of a business card. "I need to put in twenty hours. Really appreciate it if you could keep me in mind when you're acting sheriff."

THUMPS HAD BEEN wrong about the party finding new energy. It was winding down. Most of the people had already left.

"Took you long enough." Beth had her hands on her hips. "You get lost?"

Claire and her blue dress were nowhere to be seen. Neither was the lawyer.

"Claire leave?"

"How are you feeling?"

"Great."

Thumps followed Beth through the lobby. He didn't want to admit it, but he was still feeling woozy. Maybe it was a good idea that she was driving him home. The diabetes diagnosis hadn't settled in yet. The reality of the disease would come later.

Deanna Heavy Runner was still at the reception desk. Now that he knew she was Roxanne's sister, he could see the resemblance, albeit a younger, friendlier, and less rigid version of the original. As Beth opened the door for him, he glanced back. Deanna came to mock attention and gave him a snappy salute.

He'd have to remember to mention her practicum to the sheriff.

TWENTY-ONE

The night was black and solid. If there had been any part of a moon in the sky, it was long gone. Thumps was halfway to the car when he realized that the protesters had disappeared.

"Archie and the gang go home?"

"Vernon had security help them off the property." Beth slid the seat belt across his chest. "Said the drum was disturbing the guests."

"Before or after the television crew left?"

"After."

THUMPS DIDN'T REMEMBER going to sleep, but when Beth shook him awake, they were on the outskirts of Chinook.

"Wake up. You're not supposed to go to sleep."

"You have to stay awake if you're diabetic?"

"No," said Beth. "But I'm concerned you may have a concussion."

Thumps felt the back of his head. There was a large lump. "You just missed my street."

"I'm not taking you home." Beth put in the clutch and tried to coax the Volvo into third gear. "You know, this car isn't in much better shape than you."

"It's just temperamental."

"You can buy a new car, but you can't buy a new body."

Thumps had not seen the old Land Titles building at night. It had always looked slightly ominous during the day. Night didn't improve that impression one little bit.

"Where we going?"

"First floor."

"You talk to Ora Mae yet?"

Beth scowled. "You're not well enough to ask that question."

"I'm here if you want to talk."

"You're here because you're sick."

The basement was just as dark and creepy as Thumps remembered. Deep shadows. Nasty smells. Dead bodies trapped in metal lockers.

"I thought you said we were going to the main floor."

"Sit down." Beth went to the white metal cabinet and unlocked it.

On the main floor, there were cushy chairs. Here in the

basement, there was nothing but the steel stools and the metal table where Beth did her work. Thumps picked the stool that looked to be the warmer of the two.

"This is a blood testing kit." The thing in Beth's hand looked like a black cloth wallet with a zipper. Inside was a meter of some sort, a longish plastic tube, and a small canister. None of it looked particularly dangerous.

"Did you know that they have newspaper articles in frames over the urinals in the men's room at Shadow Ranch?"

Beth opened the canister. "These are the test strips."

"Mostly sports," said Thumps. "You can read them while you pee."

"You put them in the meter like this."

"What do they have in the women's washrooms?"

"Toilet paper," said Beth. "Then you load the plunger like this."

"Is this going to hurt?"

"Then you put the plunger against a finger like this . . ."

Thumps tried to ease his finger out of Beth's grip. "Because if it's going to hurt, you should tell me . . ."

The pain was instant and dramatic.

"Oh, don't be a baby." Beth squeezed his finger so that a blood drop formed on the skin.

"That hurt!"

"Then you gently push the tip of the test strip into the blood drop."

"I'm bleeding."

"125. That's pretty good."

"Are you angry with me?"

"I want you to do this before each meal," said Beth. "And keep track of the results."

"You're kidding." The tip of his finger was still stinging. "I don't have that many fingers."

"Tell that to a kid with Type 1 diabetes."

"Do I have to . . ."

"Inject yourself with insulin?" said Beth. "No. Not if you're good. You might be able to control it with diet and medication."

"Medication." Thumps sucked on his finger. The bleeding had stopped. "Like in pills?"

"And you need to lose ten pounds. Fifteen would be better."

"Okay," said Thumps, holding up his hands. "I won't mention Ora Mae again."

"Don't be an ass." Beth went to her desk and took out a pad. "This is a referral to the diabetes clinic at the hospital and a prescription for the testing kit and the medications you'll need. You have any health coverage?"

"Are you kidding?"

"Now if you were Canadian, the diabetes kit and the drugs would be covered."

"I'm not Canadian."

"So, you're going to have to buy a kit." Beth handed him several slips. "Chinook Pharmacy. First thing tomorrow."

"And all this stuff is going to cure me?"

"No cure for diabetes," said Beth. "Only good news is we can control it."

Thumps's stomach began to rumble and he felt light-headed. Maybe 125, whatever it meant, was too low. Maybe he was going to have to eat something.

"I want you to fast for the rest of the night," said Beth.

"What if I get hungry?"

"And I want you here first thing in the morning for a blood test. Before you eat anything. That's important. Nothing to eat before you see me."

"You know that there are laws against assault."

Beth rolled her eyes. "Anything else I can tell you?"

"James Lester and Margo Knight?"

"I'd concentrate on your health first," said Beth. "At this point, there's not much medical science can do for either of them."

TWENTY-TWO

Beth let him drive home alone on the promise that he wouldn't make any stops along the way. It was after two, and Thumps couldn't think of anywhere to stop even if he wanted to stop. Al's was closed, the two restaurants at the Tucker were closed. Even the convenience store out at the truck stop would be dark at this hour.

Freeway was curled up on the kitchen table. Thumps wasn't sure why he bothered making rules when the cat ignored them.

"Tonight's an exception," he told Freeway. "I'm diabetic."

Freeway lowered her eyes and pretended not to care.

"You think ice cream is on the list?" Thumps opened the brochure Beth had given him. Sure enough, ice cream was on the list.

Under food he couldn't eat.

Along with bananas, potato chips, watermelon, fruit juices, white bread, pasta, pizza, and cheeses with high fat content.

He opened the refrigerator. If he threw out all the offending items, the only things he'd be left with were green beans and broccoli. Along with a package of frozen fish that Cooley had missed.

According to the brochure, a half-cup serving of Häagen-Dazs vanilla ice cream had twenty-one grams of sugar and eighteen grams of fat. One ounce of Kellogg's Raisin Bran, which Thumps had always considered a healthy cereal, had twenty-one grams of carbohydrates and one gram of fat. One-quarter of a Sara Lee pound cake contained nineteen grams of sugar and thirteen grams of fat, which didn't seem unreasonable until he remembered that he would normally eat half a cake at a sitting. Even a cup of spaghetti—before you factored in the sauce and the Parmigiano Reggiano—had thirty-nine grams of carbohydrates.

One waffle had twenty-seven grams of carbohydrates. One slice of watermelon had thirty-five grams of carbohydrates. Eight ounces of low-fat yogurt with fruit had forty-three grams of carbohydrates. One pat of salted butter had four grams of fat, but no carbohydrates.

Thank God for small mercies.

By the time the phone rang, Thumps had calculated the sugar, fat, and carbohydrate levels of everything in his kitchen and was working on the nutritional values of individual meals that he had eaten for the past month.

Thumps glanced at his watch. Only one person would call him at this hour.

"Archie, do you know what time it is?"

"Hi." Claire didn't sound happy, and she didn't sound angry.

"Hi."

"You busy?"

It was a strange question for Claire to ask at three in the morning, but it had been a strange day all around.

"No."

"Can I come in?"

"Where are you?"

"On the porch."

Cellphones, Thumps had to admit, had certainly changed patterns of social interaction.

"Why didn't you just knock?"

"If you were busy, I didn't want to disturb you."

"Busy? With what?"

"Busy," said Claire with that fragile detachment that had marked much of their relationship. "You know."

When Thumps opened the door, he still had the phone in his hand, and he still didn't know what it was he might have been doing. Claire was on the porch in the moonlight, the blue dress sparkling like a starry night.

"We should probably hang up now."

Actually, it was the porch light and not the moon, but the effect was the same.

"So, how bad is it?" Claire slipped through the door, set her handbag on the table, and sat down.

"The diabetes?"

"You have other medical problems I don't know about?"

"I think getting it is the bad part."

"His name is Quincy."

"Quincy?"

"Quincy Comes at Night. He's a lawyer from Missoula. We're not sleeping together."

"Okay."

"So, we're clear on that?"

"Sure." Thumps went to the sink. "You want coffee?"

LAST YEAR, he had gone to Planet Earth, a new free-trade coffee store that had just opened across from old city hall. Thumps had spent over an hour picking out a Bodum French press and then another hour sniffing his way through the different varieties of coffee beans. In the end, he bought a Colombian, an Ethiopian Limu, and an expensive Nicaragua FT.

However, the Nicaragua FT was nowhere as expensive as something called kopi luwak, a coffee from Sumatra. According to the guy at the store, these particular coffee beans had been eaten by a small marsupial, passed through its digestive tract, and excreted. The beans were then gathered, cleaned up, roasted, and turned into the world's most expensive coffee.

He didn't carry kopi luwak, the man told Thumps, but the

beans could be ordered online. If you had the money and were so inclined.

"Is this the list of foods you can and can't eat?" Claire held up the pamphlet that Beth had given him.

"Yeah."

"Have you looked at the lists yet?"

"Just a glance." Thumps poured the boiling water into the Bodum.

"What's on the good food list?"

"Things I don't like."

"What's on the bad food list?"

Thumps was pretty sure the guy at the store was having him on about fecal coffee beans, but the man swore the story was true, told him that there were places on the internet where you could buy a gift box of Arabica kopi luwak for about $220 or Robusta kopi luwak for $160, though Thumps had no idea what the difference might be.

And, if you wanted the full boutique coffee experience, you could pass on the gift box, order a pound of unprocessed kopi luwak for little more than a hundred dollars, and roast it yourself.

* * *

"WHAT DO YOU know about water?"

Thumps held the cup close to his mouth and let the steam wash over his face. "Not a lot."

"What about the Blackfoot Aquifer?"

"Even less."

"A large part of the aquifer runs under the reservation," said Claire. "But most of the water is in a sandstone formation under the Bear Hump."

"Orion Technologies."

"Two years ago, Orion negotiated a ten-year lease with the state to drill monitoring wells on the Bear Hump to measure the water in the aquifer. When we discovered what had happened, we tried to get an injunction."

"The 1836 Treaty."

"In the original treaty, the Bear Hump was part of the reservation, but before it could be ratified, the terms were unilaterally changed by the U.S. Senate."

It was a familiar story, one Thumps had heard before. "And Bear Hump was removed from the reservation boundaries."

Claire nodded. "Evidently Congress didn't think we needed all that land."

"An early version of government assistance."

"There would have been a written record of the negotiations, but we've never been able to find it." Claire wrapped her hands around the cup. "There's a strong oral record of exactly what was agreed to, but every time we go to court, oral testimony has been ruled unreliable."

1836. THUMPS KNEW the decade well. In 1830, Andrew Jackson signed the 1830 Removal Act, which allowed the government to strip the tribes along the eastern seaboard of their land. But it was his successor, Martin Van Buren, less a friend to Native people than Jackson, who in 1838 issued the order for the U.S. army to invade Cherokee territory, force more than thirteen thousand people into concentration camps, and then march them west in a series of removes to Indian Territory.

Nu na da ul tsun yi.

"The Place Where They Cried." More than four thousand Cherokee died on the two-thousand-mile trek. Two deaths for every mile.

"BUT ALL THAT has changed." Claire was suddenly animated. "Eight months ago, Benjamin Thomas, a history professor at the University of Saskatchewan in Saskatoon, was doing research at the Glenbow Museum in Calgary and came across the diary of a Canadian named William Holland, who was present at the treaty negotiations. Holland was there as an interpreter, and the man kept detailed notes."

"Bear Hump."

"In black and white. We have a court date in October." Claire looked away, her eyes glistening. "We're going to get the land back."

"That's great."

"Yes, it is. But even if we win the case, we won't get control of the land right away."

Thumps slowly saw where Claire was heading. "The lease."

"Exactly," said Claire. "It doesn't expire for eight more years, and there are few restrictions. While Orion can't cut any timber, they could, if they wanted, pump water out of the aquifer."

"Archie know about this?"

Claire chuckled. "I'm not looking for trouble."

"I think he's beginning to mellow."

"We're not worried about Orion. They don't have the wherewithal or the interest to put that kind of a venture together. Everything they have is tied up in their Resource Analysis Mapping technology."

Thumps waited for the other shoe.

"But," said Claire, "Orion could sell the lease to another company."

There it was. A piece to the puzzle that hadn't been available until now. "Boomper Austin."

"Boomper Austin." Claire shifted in her chair and her dress came to life. "He called this morning. Asked to meet with me."

"About what?"

"Didn't say. He just asked to meet."

"You and Oscar?"

"Quincy," said Claire without any hint of annoyance. "Maybe. He's a water rights lawyer."

"So, he's not really a . . . boyfriend?"

If it hadn't been so late and if he hadn't just discovered he was diabetic and if he hadn't been feeling sorry for himself, Thumps might have come up with a better way to phrase that question.

"Do you want him to be?"

Thumps wondered if there was something genetic or instinctual that allowed women to answer questions with questions.

"You want to stay the night?"

"Not much of it left." Claire stood and put her cup in the sink. "Is this the dress talking?"

"It's a great dress."

"Yes," said Claire, "it is."

Thumps moved in behind her and gently put his hands on her shoulders. "Stick is worried that you might be serious about Oscar."

"Are you doing that to piss me off?"

"Yeah." Thumps nuzzled Claire's hair. "I am."

"And what about you?" Claire turned so she could see Thumps's face. But it was already too late. He had hesitated that fraction of a second, and now the opportunity was gone.

"I don't know."

"Me neither," said Claire. "And until we do, things such as sex will have to wait."

"Okay."

"Besides, I have to get up early tomorrow and fly to Great Falls."

"Business?"

"More or less." The kiss was soft, almost apologetic.

Thumps followed her to the door. "I didn't mean I don't know."

Claire watched Thumps's face. "Does it work with other women?"

"What?"

"The confusion. The helplessness."

"There aren't any other women." It had been a dumb thing to say and it sounded stupid, maybe even desperate.

Claire opened the door and let the night flow in around the dress. "Call me when you get it figured out."

TWENTY-THREE

Thumps hardly slept at all, and by six in the morning, he was wide awake. Three hours of sleep. Not even that. He had tried to work out his relationship with Claire, what he might want, what she might want, what they might want together.

But in spite of his best efforts, his mind kept flying off to the prairies and circling around James Lester and Margo Knight. Like the vultures out on the coulees. The birds had seen something they couldn't explain and had stayed away. Thumps should have learned from their good example.

But he hadn't.

James Lester and Margo Knight. Boomper Austin and Cisco Cruz. Jayme Redding and Oliver Parrish. Thumps was beginning to feel as though he were stuck in the middle of a Russian novel.

Lester and Knight had come to Chinook to present their report on the mapping of the Blackfoot Aquifer and to showcase their new technology. Boomper's motives for being in town were equally transparent. The only reason for a rich Texan to race off to the middle of nowhere was money. The dinner for three at Shadow Ranch had to have been a negotiation for Orion's mapping system. Or a celebration to mark the completion of a deal.

Or both.

Cruz was here because Austin was here, and Redding had come to town in hot pursuit of the Orion story.

Oliver Parrish was the wild card. Why had he come? Maybe corporate teams travelled in packs of three. But with the deaths of the company's principals, Thumps would have expected Parrish to have run back to Sacramento to do whatever it was that chief operating officers did to keep the corporate ship afloat.

Yet he had stayed in town.

In the end, Thumps didn't trust any of them. Duke was going to squeeze Chivington until he found out how an already dead James Lester had got himself from the airport back to the motel. Norm hadn't looked as though it would take all that much squeezing. From there the sheriff might be able to walk his way back to Knight. Perhaps Hockney had already solved the puzzle and Thumps was wasting his time looking for the missing pieces.

* * *

THUMPS WAS DRESSED and standing in front of the refrigerator when he remembered two things. One, there was nothing in the refrigerator to eat. And two, he was diabetic. What the hell did diabetics eat for breakfast?

Maybe Al would know.

Of course, there was no reason to bother Al. Thumps could always read the brochure that Beth had given him. Recommended foods. Foods to be avoided. Thumps was reasonably sure that eggs were on the side of the angels and that hash browns were not. He didn't need a brochure to tell him that. But maybe if you ate one good food and one bad food, you wound up with a balance.

Balance. Wasn't that the basis of a healthy life?

THE LAND HAD warmed up overnight. The sun was bright. The wind had disappeared. As Thumps stepped outside, he could actually smell things growing, and for the moment, winter was nothing more than a vague memory.

"Mr. Awfulwater." His new next-door neighbour was standing on his porch. Pops was draped over a wicker chair. Freeway was perched on the dog's enormous head, her tail dangling in his face. It was a disturbing tableau. "Have you got a minute?"

Thumps wanted to say no. He hadn't had a good night's sleep, and he was hungry.

"Sure."

Dixie came off the porch with the agility of a stork. Jerky. All wings and legs.

"Don't think it's a problem," said Dixie, "but last night when I let Pops out to do his business, there was someone parked in front of your house."

Thumps wondered just how much business a dog that size could do. Enough to turn a yard into a minefield.

"All the houses on the block have parking off the alley," said Dixie. "So nobody much uses the street. You probably already know that."

Thumps looked down the street. "What kind of car?"

"Not a car guy," said Dixie. "Software, computers, programs. That's my game. So the car was sitting all by itself, and when I stepped off the porch to get a better look, they drove off."

"They?"

"Couldn't really tell that either. It was dark." Dixie paused as though he were trying to remember something he had forgotten. "I tend to be a little security conscious. Hope you don't mind."

"No. Security's good."

"That's why I have Pops."

As soon as the dog heard his name, he struggled to his feet, spilling Freeway off his head.

The cat took the disturbance in stride. She rolled onto one side and leisurely licked her groin.

Lovely. The queen at her toilette.

"My plan is to remodel the kitchen," said Dixie. "I'll try to keep the noise down."

"No problem."

"New counters. New cupboards. The works."

"Sounds great."

"You like espresso?"

"Sure."

"Just got my machine set up," said Dixie. "As soon as the kitchen is done, I'm going to bake a bunch of pies. Everyone says I make great pie."

CHINTAK RAWAT WAS where Thumps had left him. Standing behind the counter of Chinook Pharmacy in his white jacket.

"Ah, Mr. DreadfulWater," said Rawat, "will you be wanting a standard or an ultra-mini?"

Thumps heard every word Rawat had said, but he had no idea what the man was talking about.

"Your glucose meter." Rawat set two boxes on the counter. "For the diabetes."

The prescription Beth had given him was still in his pocket. Thumps could feel it right next to his keys. "How did you know I was diabetic?"

"Dr. Mooney," said Rawat. "She called in the prescription. She was concerned you might neglect her instructions."

Thumps had hoped to keep his health information under wraps, but as he stood in the store he realized that it was hopeless. Beth knew, but she was his doctor. Claire knew. And now Rawat knew. Along with anyone who was at Shadow Ranch the night before.

Even his cat knew.

Rawat stretched out a wrist and tapped his watch. "She was most firm. If you did not arrive by nine-thirty, I was to call you at your house."

"You're kidding."

"Dr. Mooney was quite insistent," said Rawat. "Many doctors do not possess this level of dedication."

Thumps had no quarrel with Beth's level of dedication. But she was also pushy. And meddlesome. Isn't that how Henry II had described Thomas Becket? Or had the king used the word "troublesome"? Maybe priests and doctors had more in common than met the eye.

"Has Dr. Mooney performed your fasting blood test yet?"

Thumps closed his eyes. Damn. He had forgotten about the blood test.

"It is a most important test."

"Absolutely." Thumps made a casual gesture with his hand. "All done."

"Excellent," said Rawat. "Shall we begin?"

"Sure."

"This one," said Rawat, holding up the first box, "is perfectly fine, but it is larger than the mini."

"Okay."

"Whereas this one is smaller." Rawat held up the second box. "Some of my customers prefer the reduced size as they can slip it into a pocket."

"Is there a difference in price?"

"Of course."

"Which one is cheaper?"

Rawat smiled. "That depends."

For the next fifteen minutes, Rawat gave Thumps a consumer tour of glucose meters.

"So you see, the cost of the meter is not the important issue. It is also the cost of the strips and the lancets and how easy these are to obtain."

"Pick one for me."

"You have no preference?" Rawat sounded somewhat astonished. "This is a most important decision."

"Something cheap and simple."

Rawat went to the shelves and came back with two more boxes. "These are both convenient and affordable," he said. "This one comes with a book where you are to write down all the things you eat each day."

"And this one?"

"Does not have the book."

Thumps looked at both boxes. "The one without the writing book."

"A good choice," said Rawat. "Writing in the book is quite depressing. Did Dr. Mooney speak to you about losing weight?"

"She might have mentioned it."

"Then I shall say no more about it," said Rawat. "And did she talk to you about the medical regime she has prescribed?"

"She said I could control it with diet."

Rawat smiled. It was a broad smile, almost a chuckle. "Yes, this is possible for a period of time, but evidently you have exceeded that period already."

"I was just diagnosed."

"This drug has been rigorously tested." Rawat held up a plastic bottle. "And the side effects are generally mild."

"Such as?"

"A slight metallic taste in the mouth. Diarrhea. Upset stomach. Impotence."

"Impotence?"

"Did Dr. Mooney talk to you about insulin and the insulin pump?"

"Pump?" Thumps could feel the sweat beginning to rise out of his body. "No, she didn't."

"Then," said Rawat, "I shall say no more about it."

* * *

By the time Rawat had finished compiling all the lancets and test strips and alcohol swabs along with the meter and the pills, a bottle of multivitamins, and several brochures on diabetes, Thumps had a sizable sack to lug around.

"Do you have a drug plan, Mr. DreadfulWater?"

"No drug plan."

"Ah," said Rawat, handing him the bill. "A misfortune to be sure."

Thumps knew the medication wasn't going to be cheap, but the figure on the slip stopped him dead. "You're kidding."

"I'm afraid not."

"You could die from the cost of the disease."

"Yes," said Rawat. "Many people do. It's unfortunate you do not live in Canada. In Canada, many of these costs are covered."

Thumps took out his wallet. "At least they're working on a cure."

"Oh, the drug companies don't want to find a cure," said Rawat. "All the profit is in controlling the disease."

Thumps slowly laid each bill out on the counter. The stove was going to have to wait a little longer.

"Diabetes, cancer, heart disease," said Rawat, "all most profitable."

The conversation with Rawat had been mildly depressing. But as Thumps walked down the street with his bag, the main emotion he felt was embarrassment, as though he were fifteen again and his mother had caught him with a box of contraceptives.

Not that diabetes was embarrassing.

Thumps paused for a moment in front of Budd's Clothing and tried to find the right word. Inconvenient. Diabetes was inconvenient. And somewhat scary. Thumps had always thought that he would die suddenly. A heart attack. A car crash. When he was a cop, there had always been the chance that he would be killed on the job. Disease had not been on the radar then, and now, suddenly, here it was.

It took him a minute to realize that he was staring at himself in the store window. So that's what diabetes looked like. Somewhat middle-aged, somewhat out of shape, somewhat sad.

And very much alone.

TWENTY-FOUR

When Thumps got to Al's, Wutty Youngbeaver and Jimmy Monroe were sitting where they always sat, near the front door across from the grill.

"The key is a positive attitude," Jimmy called out to him, as Thumps made his way to the far end of the counter. "They're curing all sorts of cancers these days."

"Diabetes," said Wutty, shaking his head. "Still not an auspicious prognosis."

"Russell Plunkett had cancer," said Jimmy, "and he beat it."

"Russell had gallstones," said Wutty.

Al was waiting for him with the coffee pot. "Looks like your little buddy was right all along."

"Is there someone in town who doesn't know?"

"I'm willing to swap the hash browns for some nice sliced tomatoes," said Al. "How does that sound?"

"Eggs, scrambled. No milk, no cream, just butter. Multi-grain toast. Hash browns with salsa. Coffee. Black."

"That sounds like the usual."

"It is the usual."

"Okay," said Al. "I'm not your mother."

Thumps looked around the café.

"That guy from Sacramento been in?"

"Mr. Fancy Specs?" Al shook her head. "Haven't seen Archie's girlfriend either, now that I think about it."

"She's not Archie's girlfriend."

"But I've been working on my frappés," said Al. "Just in case she shows up again."

Thumps set the pharmacy bag on the floor next to the stool where no one could see it. He didn't want to take the medication and the testing kit out until he was somewhere private. Opening the bag in the café would just bring Wutty and Jimmy to his end of the counter with sympathy and advice. In terms of his overall health, the sooner people forgot that he was diabetic, the better he'd feel.

"Hear the sheriff arrested Norm Chivington."

"He did."

"You were there?"

"I was."

Al grinned as though she had just told herself a good joke. "That must have put a spring in Duke's step."

"It did."

"Hear Norm's threatening to sue."

"You know what would put a spring in *my* step?"

"Breakfast?"

"Breakfast."

"Did you get the mini or the standard?"

"Al . . ."

Al glanced back at Wutty and Jimmy. "If you're going to stick your finger, the guys said that they'd like to watch."

"I'm not going to stick my finger."

"Suit yourself." Al strolled back to the grill. "But you're going to have to get into the bag sometime. Archie says you're supposed to take the pills with food."

"My aunt had diabetes," Wutty called out from the front of the café. "They had to appropriate her toes."

"Guy I bowl with," said Jimmy, "couldn't control his blood sugars and wound up with a heart problem."

Thumps closed his eyes and tried to shut out the Greek chorus. He didn't hear the front door open and close until it was too late.

"Damn it, DreadfulWater."

Beth slid onto the stool next to him.

"Last night. What was the last thing I said last night?"

"Something about a blood test?"

"Before you ate breakfast."

"I haven't had breakfast."

"Good." Beth put her bag on the counter and opened it.

"You're joking."

"Roll up your sleeve and relax."

THE REST OF breakfast was a tortured affair. Beth drained his body of blood, and his arm ached so badly he had to eat with his left hand. Al cut back on his hash browns and gave him two slices of fresh tomato, so he could see how delicious healthy eating could be, and when Thumps complained about the shortage, Wutty and Jimmy raced to her defence.

"They didn't confiscate Auntie's toes all at once," Wutty explained. "They eradicated them one at a time."

"Wasn't all bad news," said Jimmy. "Frank had to give up bowling, but he was able to get one of those handicap parking stickers."

Thumps tried to sneak into the bag while the two men were debating whether they'd rather have a wonky heart or no toes, but he wasn't completely successful. Each time he reached in, the plastic packaging made a crackling sound, and he could feel Wutty and Jimmy rise off their stools like a pair of hunting dogs looking for a rabbit.

In the end, he left the bag on the floor next to the stool and stayed hunched over his coffee, holding his arm and feeling sorry for himself.

TWENTY-FIVE

The sheriff was sitting behind his desk, bent over a folder. The old percolator was making strange wheezing noises, as though it were gasping for air.

"That doesn't sound good."

"Ran out of coffee," said Duke without looking up. "Had to make a new batch."

Thumps couldn't remember the last time he had caught Duke brewing a fresh pot of coffee. Not in the last six months. Maybe not in the last year. Mostly he just added water to the resident sludge.

"Fresh coffee is always hard on the pot."

"Maybe I'll take a photograph," said Thumps. "Call the newspaper."

Hockney raised his head. "You keep making jokes about

my coffee and I'm not going to tell you about my exciting day in law enforcement."

Thumps listened for a moment. Except for the percolator, the building was quiet.

"You let Norm go?"

Duke shut the folder. "Mr. Chivington is enjoying the amenities of the west wing."

"The cell with the foul stench?"

"Lance found a dead rat in the floor drain," said Hockney. "It doesn't smell that bad anymore."

Thumps tried to settle onto one of the new chairs. "So, Norm shot Lester?"

The sheriff made a sour face. "Norm couldn't shoot himself in the foot."

Thumps tried resting on his right hip. Then he tried resting on his left. He didn't know who had designed the chairs. Someone who didn't have a butt.

"So, Norm didn't shoot Lester."

"According to Norm," said Duke, "he was at home with the wife when he got a call from Orem at the airport to alert him to a possible problem with one of the rentals. And being an honest businessman . . ."

"Honest businessman?"

"His words, not mine." Duke wasn't smiling, but he was thinking about it. "Anyway, Norm goes to the airport and finds James Lester passed out in one of the rentals."

"Passed out?"

"Passed out," said the sheriff. "Norm swears he didn't notice the gun or the hole in Lester's head until he got to the motel."

"Amazing."

"That's exactly what I said," said the sheriff. "And this is the part I like the best. Norm, upon finding said gun and said hole, determined that Lester had committed suicide, and he further determined that a suicide in a Chivington Motors' rental and a suicide in a Wagon Wheel motel room were, in fact, the same suicide."

"The argument being that it didn't matter where the suicide was found."

"Indeed," said Hockney. "And what should Norm have done?"

"Call the sheriff's office."

"Exactly," said Duke. "But as Norm explained to me, while he is an honest businessman, he was also fearful . . ."

"Fearful?"

"That's the word he used," said the sheriff. "Fearful that if he reported a dead body, I would impound the Jeep as part of my investigation."

"Which you would have done."

"Which I would have done had I had the chance." Hockney got up and went to the percolator. "So, Norm . . . fearful that I would do exactly that, decided to make some minor adjustments to the crime scene. He told Orem that Lester was just drunk, drove the body back to the motel, left it in the room, and drove away in the Jeep."

The coffee that came from the spout of the percolator looked almost normal. It was dark brown, not blue-black, and had a viscosity that was closer to water than it was to warm tar. Thumps considered trying a cup.

"You believe him?"

The sheriff took a sip, made a face, and poured the coffee back into the pot.

"Unfortunately," said Hockney, "Norm's story fits most of the facts."

"Yet he's still in jail."

"Yes, he is."

Thumps held up one hand and began ticking off the offences on his fingers. "Disturbing a crime scene, impeding an ongoing investigation, removing evidence . . ."

"Pissing me off."

"He tried to avoid arrest."

"I'd forgotten that one," said Duke. "Anyway, I'm going to let the city's attorney and Norm's lawyer sort things out."

"He'll make bail."

"I imagine he will," said the sheriff. "Just not today."

"I guess that wraps it all up."

The sheriff banged the percolator on the table and swirled the liquid around. "A little agitation helps to sweeten the brew."

"Except for the gunshot wound." Thumps waited to see if Duke wanted to step in.

"Yes," said the sheriff, banging the percolator, harder this time. "Everything except for the gunshot wound. You got any ideas?"

Thumps tried sitting up straight in the chair. He could feel the chrome bars digging into his back and thighs. "I think Lester and Knight had dinner reservations at Shadow Ranch the night they were killed."

Hockney shook his head. "I checked all the restaurants personally including Shadow Ranch. No reservations."

"Wasn't in either of their names," said Thumps. "Boomper Austin made the reservation. He showed up, but the other two didn't."

"Austin? Again?"

"Talked to the front desk." Thumps pulled Deanna's card out of his pocket and slid it across the desk. "Reservation was for three."

The sheriff looked at the card. "Deanna Heavy Runner? She related to Roxanne?"

"Sister."

"She as fierce as Roxanne?"

"Major in criminology at the college. She's working on a practicum."

The sheriff didn't bite. "Reservation could have been for anyone."

"True enough," said Thumps.

"But it's a shitload of coincidences." The sheriff cocked his head and gave Thumps a squinty look. "Lester and Knight get all dressed up for an evening out. Austin makes a reservation for three the same night they're killed. He shows up for the dinner, but the other two, whoever they are, don't. Is that about it?"

"That's about it."

"And Mr. Austin didn't bother to mention this?"

"No reason he should."

"I guess I'll have to have a little talk with our Texas billionaire."

"Maybe you could talk to Deanna while you're at it."

"Damn it, DreadfulWater," said Duke, "I'm not an employment agency."

"You've been trying to hire me."

From somewhere deep in the back of the sheriff's office, Thumps could hear what might have been muffled shouts followed by the vague sounds of someone banging on metal.

"That's Norm," said Duke. "He must have heard your voice and thinks you've come to rescue him."

"So Norm didn't shoot Lester."

"Swears on his mother's grave," said Duke. "And other clichés."

"Hard to discount a cliché."

"And truth be told, I believe him." Hockney reached down and twiddled with one of the knobs at the side of the chair and the back reclined. "Why put a bullet in a dead body? A corpse in one of his cars was trouble enough."

Thumps took a moment to consider the percolator. "Maybe I'll try a cup of coffee."

"Help yourself." Duke twiddled with the knobs again and the back of the chair came up. "It's sort of like a recliner," he said. "But without the comfort."

"So you think Lester and Knight were murdered."

"I'll wait until I hear from Beth." Duke opened the drawer of his desk and took out a large manila envelope. "In the meantime, why don't you take a look at this."

"That the stuff Stick got off the cellphones and laptops?"

"He dropped it off this morning."

The envelope wasn't all that thick. The college's logo was in one corner in gold and blue lettering. "Computer Services" was printed below it in basic black. Someone had written, "Eyes Only," across the face of the envelope with a bold marker.

Thumps held the envelope up. "You couldn't find your 'Top Secret' stamp?"

Hockney ignored him. "How about you take a gander. See what you can find."

Thumps could see that Duke wasn't going to take no for an answer. "Okay," he said, "I'll do it if you stop bugging me about being acting sheriff."

"How about doing it because you're a concerned citizen?"

"And I'm concerned about what again?"

"Not getting on my bad side."

"Some folks would argue that you don't have a good side."

"That's because they don't know me." The sheriff spun the chair in a slow circle. "I'm a generous and forgiving man."

"What about Norm?" Thumps weighed the envelope. "Maybe you should let Norm go."

"Now why would I do that?"

"Because you're a generous and forgiving man?"

"Yes, I am," said the sheriff, bringing the chair to a stop. "Yes, I am."

THE LOBBY OF the Tucker was in the same condition as he had left it. Thumps went directly to the house phones.

"Welcome to the Tucker, your home in the West."

"Could you tell me if Oliver Parrish is still a guest?"

"I'm afraid I can't give out that information."

Thumps tried again. "Could you connect me with Oliver Parrish's room?"

"Certainly."

The phone rang six times and then went to voice mail. Thumps hung up and then dialed zero. The woman was just as cheery.

"Could you connect me with Jayme Redding's room?"

"Absolutely."

Six rings. Voice mail. Okay, so neither Parrish nor Redding was in their room. Thumps stood in front of the massive ornate mirror that took up much of the far wall and tried to imagine where he might go.

Food.

Food was the answer to most questions in life.

The Tucker had two restaurants. The Mother Lode over-looked the river and the mountains and offered patrons an elegant dining experience of dark wood and brass, where the Texas striploin was trucked down from Alberta and the New England lobster was flown in from Halifax. Dinner for two could be had for just under a hundred dollars provided you went without wine and shared a dessert.

The Quick Claim served breakfast and lunch. It was a bright room tucked away in a corner on the main floor, done up to look like a Hollywood version of a western saloon. The prices, however, were all East Coast. The breakfast buffet including orange juice and coffee was around twenty-seven dollars, or you could order off the menu and pay more for less.

The restaurant was all but empty. There were four business types in suits and ties in a booth and an older couple hunkered down over books, hardly looking at their food or at each other. Thumps wondered what could be so engrossing. A novel? Non-fiction? There were better places to read, Thumps told himself, than over a meal.

Neither Parrish nor Redding was to be seen. Disappointing, but no great surprise.

"Pancho!"

Cisco Cruz was sitting by himself in a corner.

"Join me." Cruz waved him over and signalled the server, who glided to the table with a carafe of orange juice. Cruz reached across the table and tapped the menu. "Order whatever you like."

"We're known for our waffles," said the server.

"Not a great idea," said Cruz. "My friend here has just discovered that he's diabetic."

"Coffee's fine."

The server was all smiles. "We have a very nice vanilla-flavoured Viennese roast."

"Black."

As soon as the server was out of hearing, Cruz held his hands up in apology. "Sorry about the diabetes. I don't suppose you want the world knowing your business."

"Small town," said Thumps. "Sooner or later, everyone knows your business."

"So how's the acting-sheriff job going?"

There was an extra menu and place setting on the table.

"Thought you were staying out at Shadow Ranch."

"I am," said Cruz, "but I heard the food's good here."

Thumps played along. "And?"

"Cook can't tell a steak from a *zapato*."

"Then again, you didn't really come for the food."

The pendant Cruz had around his neck was silver with a stylized face. Thumps recalled seeing the same sort of figure on a small totem pole when he was in a Native art store in Victoria, British Columbia.

"If you're a single," said Thumps, "they generally clear the second place setting away."

"And?"

"Whoever you're waiting for didn't show."

Cruz shifted in his seat. "You play poker?"

"Not much."

"But you know the basic idea of the game."

"Sure," said Thumps. "I try to take your money. You try to take mine."

"Mr. Austin doesn't play poker," said Cruz. "Does that surprise you?"

"He doesn't like to lose."

"He doesn't like to leave winning and losing to luck."

"Thought poker was a game of skill."

"Lot of people make that mistake," said Cruz. "They think the game begins *after* the deal. Hell, even a *pendejo* can bet four aces."

"And Mr. Austin likes to have all the aces in hand before he bets."

Cruz pushed his plate to one side. "Man likes to have the whole deck."

Thumps gestured to the second place setting. "Redding?"

"You asking as acting sheriff, or is this just innate curiosity?"

"Little of both."

Cruz pushed back his chair. "You take care of yourself, *vato*," he said, dropping his napkin on the table. "Diabetes is nothing to mess with."

* * *

THE COFFEE WASN'T BAD, and it wasn't good. It was black and it was hot. Thumps sat back and checked the room again. The suits were gone, off to do battle with supply and demand. The old couple hadn't moved. Library books. He could see the stickers on the spines. Thumps found himself feeling sorry for them. Maybe they couldn't afford to buy books. Maybe they were living on a pension, and this meal was a monthly treat.

The man looked up and said something to the woman. Then he reached out and put his hand on hers. It was a gentle gesture that took Thumps by surprise. Whatever else they had, they had each other.

Here he was sitting in the same restaurant by himself with only the menu to read.

TWENTY-SIX

The Aegean was quiet and even darker than before. Several customers were wandering through the stacks, and there was a young man sitting on a sofa, thumbing through a large book on Rembrandt, turning the volume to try to catch whatever stray light might be available. Archie was nowhere to be seen. With any luck, he was at lunch, and Thumps would be able to get in and out of the store before the little Greek even knew he had been here.

"Thumps!"

So much for luck.

Archie hurried out of the back area, waving a sandwich in one hand. "You should have told me you were coming."

"Just needed to borrow your computer."

"You still don't have one?"

Thumps did have a computer. It just didn't work. And he

was in no rush to get it fixed. When it was working, he had had to wade through a daily blizzard of obnoxious emails. Free trips to Paris, pleas from Nubian princesses to help them with their fortunes, easy and inexpensive ways to enlarge your penis.

"I won't be long."

"Sure, sure," said Archie. He set the sandwich down on the desk and moved the mouse. "You want the internet?"

Thumps opened the envelope and took out the flash drive. "Just need to take a look at a couple of things."

Archie raised his eyebrows. "Evidence?"

"Archie . . ."

"This the files from their cellphones and laptops?"

"Archie . . ."

"What? You don't trust me?"

"It's an ongoing investigation."

"So, what's wrong with a little ongoing help?" Archie moved into a blocking position, putting himself between Thumps and the computer. "Besides, you don't even know where to put that drive."

Thumps reached around and plugged the drive into a USB port.

"Lucky guess," said Archie. "Now let's see you open the file."

Thumps hoped that a window was going to pop up with a prompt and he would be able to look at the files Stick had loaded onto the drive without having to involve Archie.

No window.

Thumps dragged the mouse around and clicked on an icon he didn't recognize.

"That's Windows Media Player."

Thumps clicked on a second icon.

"And that's Dropbox." Archie was smiling.

Thumps took the flash drive out and then eased it in again. Still no icon. This was why he didn't care if his computer was working. Functioning computers were just as frustrating as non-functioning ones.

"You know they offer computer courses at the college." Archie forced Thumps out of the chair and worked the mouse. "Okay, there are two files. 'Lester JPEGs' and 'Knight JPEGs.' Which do you want to see first?"

"Lester."

Archie ran the mouse to the bottom of the page, clicked on an icon. Thumps tried to watch what the little Greek was doing, but it was like following a sleight-of-hand artist with three cups and a pea.

"Nothing much," said Archie. "Four photos."

The first photo was of a car.

"BMW," said Archie. "Looks like a 7 Series."

The second and third photos were taken on a golf course overlooking the ocean. Thumps recognized the hole immediately.

"Pebble Beach."

The fourth photograph was of a young woman sitting at an outdoor café with a busy cityscape in the background.

"Girlfriend?"

The woman was young, not yet thirty, with auburn hair that she wore to her shoulders. Professionally dressed. If Thumps were guessing, he'd imagine that she worked for an insurance company or a brokerage firm. Maybe government.

"Not Chinook," said Thumps. "Bigger city."

"Sacramento?"

The woman wasn't looking at the camera. She was looking away as though lost in thought.

"Probably." Thumps leaned back in the chair. "What about Knight?"

Archie clicked the mouse and suddenly the screen came alive with thumbnails.

"Someone likes to take pictures." Archie began scrolling through the images. "Woman didn't understand the concept of 'delete.'"

"Can you arrange them by date," said Thumps, "from the last picture taken to the first?"

Archie clicked the mouse again and the thumbnails magically rearranged themselves. There were some general landscapes of the Ironstone River Valley. By the look of them, they were taken from a moving car. Others were of downtown Chinook.

Thumps watched the images move across the screen. "Is that the Flying J truck stop?"

"And the main street of Chinook." Archie shook his head.

"But not one picture of the Aegean. You believe that? Woman had no sense of history."

The next twenty photographs were of the interior of an office complex: cubicles, file cabinets, people standing in doorways, a conference room with Lester sitting at the head of the table, looking presidential. On the wall above his head was the Orion Technologies logo.

"Someone should have taken her phone away." Archie pushed back in the chair. "Or turned off the camera function."

Knight might have been a scientific genius, but she was a terrible photographer. Most of the photographs were badly composed, and many were out of focus.

"That it?"

"That's it," said Archie. "Did we find anything?"

"Nope." Thumps pulled the flash drive out of the computer.

"Hey," shouted Archie. "You can't just pull it out. You have to log out of the program. You could destroy the data on the drive."

"Sorry."

Archie cocked his head to one side and glared at Thumps. "You know something."

"Just picking up pieces."

"And you're not going to tell me?"

"Nothing to tell."

"You figured it out, didn't you?" Archie stabbed a finger at Thumps's chest. "They were murdered. That's it, isn't it?"

"Ongoing investigation."

"That's what the Nazis said."

"That's not what they said."

"It could have been."

"Okay, you want to help?"

Archie wasn't convinced. "Is this where you tell me that I can help by minding my own business?"

"No," said Thumps, "this is where I ask you to do some research."

"Quid pro quo. Were Lester and Knight murdered?" Archie crossed his arms and waited.

"Probably."

"Okay," said Archie, "I'll do the research. What do you need?"

Thumps slipped the flash drive back into the envelope. "I need you to find out everything you can on Boomper Austin, Cisco Cruz, Jayme Redding, and Oliver Parrish."

Archie frowned. "Redding is one of the good guys, and Cruz and Parrish are just hired guns."

"Everything you can find."

Archie followed Thumps to the front of the store. "And while I'm researching, what are you going to be doing?"

"Shopping," said Thumps, as he pushed through the doors. "I'm going shopping."

THE CHINOOK Cash and Carry was the inexpensive grocery in town, and it was where Thumps shopped when his bank account was low. He preferred the Albertsons on the west side because it generally had the better produce.

Today, the tomatoes at the Cash and Carry looked reasonably good. For hothouse tomatoes. Thumps had had vine-grown tomatoes when he was a kid, so he knew the sweet taste of a real tomato. Maybe next year he'd clear part of the backyard and put in tomatoes and bush beans, a little lettuce.

He didn't see Eleanor Lake until it was too late.

"Well, if it isn't the photographer." Eleanor didn't look any happier than she had at the motel.

"Hello, Eleanor."

"Hear you're acting sheriff."

"You heard wrong."

"How about you open up my rooms so I can rent them."

"Can't do that."

"Honeymooners came by this morning. Wanted to rent Number 11 real bad. Offered me triple what I normally charge." Eleanor picked up an apple, turned it over in her hand, and then put it back in the bin. "Said it was their lucky number."

"I'm sure the sheriff is working as fast as he can."

"Triple," said Eleanor, looking at another apple. "And can I rent Number 11?"

Thumps put a head of lettuce in his cart.

"I cannot." Eleanor tossed the apple back in the bin. "Because Number 11 is all tied up in yellow police tape and making me poor instead of making me money. And because I'm not making money, I get to waste my time shopping and getting my hair cut."

Thumps reached for a sack of onions.

"And if that isn't bad enough," said Eleanor, "here I am standing in produce, talking to a photographer who doesn't know the first thing about running a motel."

"I'll talk to the sheriff," said Thumps. "I run a small business. I know how tough it is to make ends meet."

"That lump of a sheriff sure as hell don't," said Eleanor. "Man's been glued to the public tit so long, it would take a crowbar and half a dozen strong men to pry him loose."

"Must have been hard saying no to that couple."

"Don't get me started." Eleanor snorted as though she were a small whale coming up for air.

"You happen to remember what kind of car they were driving?"

"Of course I remember. Fancy black thing, so you know they had money."

"Black Cadillac Escalade?"

"Triple," said Eleanor, picking out another apple and holding it up to the light. "They were going to pay me triple."

THUMPS LEFT ELEANOR to her apples and pushed the cart around the store at race pace—eggs, potatoes, ice cream, tomatoes, cheese, chicken—replacing the damage that Cooley had done to his refrigerator, and was through the checkout, into the Volvo, and out of the parking lot in record time.

In the bright sunshine, the Wagon Wheel looked as though it had been abandoned somewhere back in the twentieth century, and perhaps that's how all motels looked in the middle of a day. There was only one other car in attendance. A blue Toyota was parked in front of the ice dispenser, a hatchback shot through with rust and listing to one side as though it were in need of a hip replacement.

Thumps parked the Volvo under a tree at the far end of the motel lot. From there he had a clear view of the office and the long line of rooms. When he had left the Cash and Carry, Eleanor was still pushing her cart up and down the aisles, and allowing time for the shopping and her haircut, Thumps reckoned that he had at least an hour before she returned.

The envelope was on the passenger seat. Thumps picked it up, gave it a quick shake, and tossed it in the back on top of his jacket with more force than was necessary.

Enough was enough.

The sheriff could do his own investigative work. What the hell was Thumps thinking? Here he was sitting in his car in the middle of a day watching a motel room. He wasn't a cop. Not anymore. Maybe Eleanor's couple in their fancy car and the peculiar interest in Number 11 had been Redding and Cruz, or maybe the man and woman had been exactly what they said they were, honeymooners whose favourite number was the next prime after seven.

Seven-eleven.

Craps or a convenience store.

But if it was Redding and Cruz, what was a bodyguard for a billionaire doing with a newspaper reporter? The sheriff had already searched both rooms, and Thumps couldn't believe that Duke would have missed anything. Why would Redding and Cruz take a chance on getting caught breaking into a crime scene?

Of course, one way to find out would be to break in himself. Hockney might not take kindly to finding Redding or Cruz in either of the rooms, but Thumps had the dubious protection of Costa Rica and the sheriff's wife.

As he sat in his car, he tried to remember the various techniques for breaking into a room. If the lock was as old as the motel, he might be able to get in with a credit card, though that always worked better in the movies than it did in real life. There was a trick with a car jack where you spread the frame until the door swung open. He could give that a try. If he had a jack.

But he didn't.

Or he could just yell, "Acting sheriff," kick the door down, and rush into the room with guns blazing.

And what would he do once he got inside? Tear up the carpet? Pull down the ceiling tiles? Slice open the mattress? Unscrew the vents and search the furnace ducts? Stick a hand down the toilet and feel around for a plastic bag filled with evidence of some sort or another?

God.

No. Best to forget all this cloak and dagger stuff, drive home, and put the groceries away. He could make a pot of coffee, eat toast with a little jam, sit on the sofa, and read a book.

Have a nap.

Thumps snapped his seat belt in place and was reaching for the ignition when the door to Number 11 opened.

TWENTY-SEVEN

Jayme Redding slipped out of Number 11, closed the door behind her, and took out her cellphone, all in one fluid motion. She was in the middle of dialing a number when she spotted the Volvo. Thumps gave a little wave, started the engine, slipped the clutch, and let the car idle its way to where she was standing.

Redding was smiling and didn't look at all like a felon who had just been busted.

"Mr. DreadfulWater," she said. "You are certainly full of surprises."

"Why is it," said Thumps, "that you can never find a reporter when you need one?"

"Are you asking as acting sheriff?"

"Not yet."

"I could use a coffee." Redding opened the passenger door

246

and tossed her purse onto the back seat. "And a doughnut. My treat. Any place in this town make good doughnuts?"

THERE WERE ANY number of spots in Chinook that could come up with a decent cup of coffee, but there was only one establishment that made doughnuts that were worth eating.

Dumbo's.

Dumbo's was a dog-shit brown, one-storey clapboard at the end of Main Street. The building sat in the middle of a parking lot and resembled a double-wide that had been renovated to look like an abandoned service station.

Thumps was at the door when he realized that Redding was still standing by the car, frozen in place.

"You're kidding."

"You wanted good doughnuts."

"Sure," she said, "but is it safe to eat in there?"

"That depends on how much you like doughnuts."

"I better bring my purse." Redding opened the rear door of the car and leaned in. "Just in case I have to shoot my way out of the place."

The interior of Dumbo's was the same as any number of beat-to-shit western cafés. Tables with plastic cloths and mismatched chairs. Wood floors. Bathrooms marked "Stags" and "Does."

Thumps could feel Redding's body tense as she stepped

inside and was hit with the smell of coffee, grease, and the dank odour of wet clothes left too long in a plastic bag.

Redding wrinkled her nose. "You bring a lot of women here?"

Morris Dumbo was sitting where he always sat, behind the counter in his brown Naugahyde recliner, watching a baseball game on a small black-and-white set. On the wall just under the big Budweiser clock, Morris had used a black marker to write, "I Don't Serve Those I Don't Like," in large block letters.

"Hey, chief. Long time, no see."

Morris was a skinny man with a thin, grizzled face and bright blue eyes. He had a thin, razor mouth and short brown hair that sat atop his bony head like a scrub brush that had been nailed to a brick.

Morris eased himself out of the recliner. "Who's the doll?"

Thumps felt Redding draw in a deep breath and hold it.

"Couple cups of coffee, Morris." Thumps herded Redding to a table near the back wall. "And two doughnuts."

Morris threw a dirty towel over his shoulder and strolled to the gun-metal-grey coffee urn near the register. "Cake or raised?"

"The old-fashioneds are good," said Thumps.

Redding nodded, her eyes never leaving Morris.

"Two old-fashioneds," said Thumps. "Please."

Morris took his time getting to the table with the plates and cups. He quickly ran the towel around the Formica and set a knife and fork in front of Redding.

"I made your old-fashioned plain, chief, on account of the diabetes," said Morris, "though if you ask me it's nothing but a hoax."

"Diabetes?"

"Damn straight," said Morris. "Who do you think profits if the sugar industry goes under?"

Redding was a fast learner. Thumps could see she wasn't even tempted to ask.

"What about you, sweet pants?" said Morris. "You like a little sugar in your life?"

"I think the nice man is talking to you, darling," said Redding.

Morris's face darkened. "You calling me a fag?"

Thumps closed his eyes. "Just a joke, Morris."

"You don't joke about shit like that." Morris stared at Redding as though he hoped his eyes could slice through her. "You might want to put a muzzle on your bitch." Then he slapped the towel over his shoulder and marched back to his recliner and the game.

Redding breathed out and took a bite of the doughnut. "You didn't warn me that this place was trapped in nineteenth-century Alabama."

"Morris is Morris."

"Morris is an asshole," said Redding, keeping her voice low. "But you're right."

"About?"

"He makes good doughnuts."

Thumps would have preferred his old-fashioned doughnut with glaze, but eating it plain made the enterprise seem somewhat virtuous and almost healthy.

"Okay," said Redding. "Ask away."

Thumps took a bite of his doughnut and let the flavour fill his mouth. Since it wasn't glazed, maybe he'd have a second.

"I imagine you want to know what I was doing at the motel."

"Nope."

"No?" Redding frowned. "Why not?"

"Because you'll just lie."

"You certainly know how to hurt a girl's feelings."

"And," said Thumps, "it's not my problem, so I don't care."

"I wanted to get photos of the crime scene." Redding pushed the doughnut around her plate with a fork. "You're not going to tell the sheriff about my being in the room?"

"Did you find anything?"

"No."

"Did you take anything?"

"No."

A second doughnut was probably out of the question. Thumps was sure that doughnuts were on the "do not eat" list, with or without glaze. Still, it hadn't been a particularly large doughnut.

Redding stood and brushed the crumbs off her lap. "Is it safe to go to the bathroom?"

"Think of it as an adventure."

Redding kept her back to Morris. "When I get to the hotel, I may have to burn my clothes."

As soon as Redding had disappeared into the back, Morris slid out of his chair and came over with the coffee pot.

"She belong to you, chief, or are you just renting her?"

"She's a reporter. For a paper in Sacramento."

"The hell you say."

"She's doing a series on doughnuts."

Thumps had never heard Morris laugh, and he wasn't sure that the noise coming out of the man's mouth qualified as that. It sounded more like a dull band-saw blade cutting through plywood. Morris filled both cups and wiped his eyes with the towel.

"You got some white in you, chief." Morris's teeth were large and yellow, like old ivory. "No doubt about that. A series on doughnuts? You're a regular Abbott and Costello."

Thumps smiled back.

"Reporter like that don't come all this way for doughnuts." Morris leaned in. "This is about those bodies, isn't it?"

"You'll have to ask her that yourself."

Morris wiped his hands on the towel. "Woman like that got no time for Morris Dumbo. She's too good for an old cracker like me, and I ain't got the inclination to waste any time with the likes of her. You finish up your doughnut and get her out of here 'cause she's not welcome."

"She said your doughnut was the best she's tasted."

"You see that sign." Morris retreated to his chair. "It means what it says."

THUMPS HADN'T NOTICED that Redding hadn't returned until Morris came by with the pot again.

"Two refills," he said. "After that you start paying again."

"I'm fine." Thumps put his hand over his cup and turned toward the restrooms.

"Maybe she's having her period," said Morris. "She damn well better not make a mess in there."

"Just the bill."

"Maybe she's dumped you for some guy with a better car." Morris carried the coffee pot back to the counter. "That's the way women are. No pleasing them. You think you're going to get into her pants with a doughnut and a cup of coffee?"

The thought had come out of nowhere, and Thumps was not happy to have it arrive. "Is there another door?"

"Sure," said Morris, waving his hand toward the back. "Jesus, you think she's already run off on you?"

The women's room was down a long hall past the men's room. Between the two was a door that led to the back parking lot. Thumps knocked softly on the door to the women's room. Nothing. He knocked harder.

"Jay, you all right?"

The bathroom was empty.

Morris was waiting for him. He was smiling, his big yellow teeth looking as though they wanted to bite someone. "You order a Cadillac?"

Thumps groaned a little groan. "A black Escalade?"

"Saw one pull into the parking lot," said Morris. "And I saw it pull out."

"Great."

"Shit, Geronimo, no wonder we kicked your ass." Morris started cackling and choking all at the same time. "You can't even keep your women in line."

There was a Mason jar near the register with a handwritten sign that said, "Tips Expected."

Thumps paid the bill but put the change in his pocket.

The afternoon sky had settled on robin-egg blue. It wasn't hot yet. That would come later. But it was warmer than it had been in the morning. The Volvo was basking happily in the sun. And maybe that's what he should do. Go home, break out the chaise longue, and lie in the backyard until the day ran into evening and the air turned cold.

Thumps was halfway to the car when he realized what had happened.

"Shit!"

He opened the back door and checked the rear seat, but it was as he had suspected. His jacket was still there, crumpled into a ball, but the manila envelope was gone.

TWENTY-EIGHT

Thumps pulled in behind a dark-blue car that was parked in front of his house and was halfway up the walk with his groceries before he saw Ora Mae Foreman sitting on his front porch. Pops and Freeway were sprawled at her feet.

"You get a dog?"

"Not mine."

"Good," said Ora Mae, "'cause this hound has got a serious digestive problem."

Thumps hadn't seen Ora Mae in over a year, not since she and Beth had broken up and Ora Mae had moved to Chicago or New York or California or wherever it was that injured relationships went to die.

"Your neighbour brought over a piece of apple pie. Trixie?"

"Dixie."

"Whatever," said Ora Mae. "Cooley said it was pretty good."

"Cooley?"

"He came to leave you a message. When you didn't show, he ate the pie."

Ora Mae held up a plate. A couple of crumbs were the only indication that there had ever been anything on it.

"Cooley ate my pie?"

"He said you wouldn't mind, seeing as how you're diabetic." Ora Mae paused for a moment. "When did that happen?"

"I have to put the food away."

"You do that," said Ora Mae. "Then we need to talk."

Thumps had forgotten about the ice cream. It had begun to soften. He could feel it moving in the carton. He set it upright in the freezer. Not a problem. A few hours and all would be well. Thumps lined up the perishables on the counter, making decisions about their positions in the refrigerator. But now that Cooley had effectively emptied it, he was tempted to take the time and clean the shelves. He had done that last month, but with Ora Mae wanting to talk, he could see doing it again.

"I made a pot of coffee," said Ora Mae. "Didn't think you'd mind."

"Coffee's good."

"But you don't want to talk."

"Not much to talk about."

"You're not curious?" said Ora Mae. "About where I've been or what I've been doing or what happened with Beth and me?"

Thumps got two cups from the dish drainer. "Not really."

Ora Mae watched Thumps fill her cup. "This is why men die alone."

She looked older now. There were signs of grey at her temples, and her skin was lighter than he remembered. It had been a soft maroon, deep and radiant. Now her face was more chestnut, as though the darker tones had been worn away.

Not that he was going to mention any of this.

"Went to Salt Lake to spend some time with my sister and her kids," said Ora Mae. "Taya's thirteen and Derron is eleven. They were cuter as babies."

Thumps put a little sugar in his coffee and swirled it slowly with his spoon.

"That lasted two weeks." There was sadness in her voice, as though she had lost something precious. "Then I drove up to Seattle. Always wanted to give the coast a try."

When he was a cop in Northern California, Thumps had gone to Seattle several times as part of law enforcement get-togethers. It wasn't exactly on the coast. The city was inland on the Sound. If you wanted the coast, you had to jump across to La Push on the Olympic Peninsula. Or drive down to Olympia and head west.

"Strange place," said Ora Mae. "Highway cuts the city in half. They got a Space Needle that looks better on a postcard and a market where they toss fish back and forth for the tourists. Seattle's not so much a city as it's a bag of neighbourhoods. Never gets too hot, and the only time the drizzle stops is when it rains."

Eureka, on California's North Coast, had been like that. Overcast days with rain and wind, occasional bursts of sunlight, followed by more grey. Thumps remembered the long months of coastal weather when the days were dark and your shoes never dried. Either you liked the dreary and the damp—or you moved.

"Rain can get to you."

"Wasn't the rain," said Ora Mae. "Place was claustrophobic. Couldn't see the sky. Couldn't see the horizon."

Ora Mae had worked for Sterling Noseworthy and Wild Rose Realty, had been the lead agent at Buffalo Mountain when the complex first opened.

Thumps sipped at his coffee. "So you came home."

"I guess," said Ora Mae. "I guess that's what I did."

Thumps considered cleaning the stove. With any luck, Ora Mae would get bored watching him, give up, and leave, and he would be able to avoid the conversation he could feel looming in front of him. If Ora Mae wanted to talk to Beth, she should talk to Beth. If Beth wanted to talk to Ora Mae, she should talk to Ora Mae. The two women might need someone to mediate, but Thumps had no intention of applying for the position.

"You know that Beth and I own the Land Titles building." Ora Mae tapped her spoon on the rim of the cup. It made a hard, brittle sound. "We own it together."

Okay, so it was worse than he thought. Thumps had assumed that Ora Mae had come back to Chinook so that she and Beth could give their relationship another try.

But that wasn't it.

"Ever since Sterling moved to Denver and bought some big, old, ugly house up in the mountains, he's been hurting for money." Ora Mae rubbed the back of her neck. "Wild Rose is dead weight. He's willing to sell it cheap."

Beth hadn't mentioned anything about selling the Land Titles building, and Thumps was guessing that she wouldn't be all that keen on the idea.

"I don't want to force the issue. We were friends." Ora Mae's face softened. "We were lovers."

So that was it. Ora Mae wanted Thumps to talk to Beth about selling, wanted Thumps to explain to her that Ora Mae needed the money in order to buy Wild Rose Realty, wanted Thumps to be the messenger who got shot.

Ora Mae looked around the kitchen. "You paint the place?"

"No."

"You should," she said. "Maybe a warm tone, so it doesn't feel so sad."

Thumps tried steering the conversation out of harm's way. "You said something about Cooley coming by."

"That's right," said Ora Mae. "He said you're to go to the airport tonight to pick up Claire when she flies in from Great Falls. According to Cooley, you're to take flowers and a box of candy."

"Cooley said all that?"

"Actually, it was Roxanne Heavy Runner. Cooley wanted to

make it clear that he had no hand in any of this. Boy actually looked frightened."

"Roxanne will do that to you."

"Then he got hungry and ate the pie." Ora Mae pushed away from the table and walked to the door. "Cooley said that you're supposed to buy red roses and that expensive dark chocolate in the gold foil and not the milk chocolate junk you get at the mall."

Thumps followed her out to the car. "You discuss the Land Titles building with Beth?"

"Not yet," she said.

"Don't think she wants to sell."

"Probably not." Ora Mae tried to smile. "But Sterling isn't going to wait forever."

"Not much I can do." Thumps considered Ora Mae's car for a moment. "Did you come by the other night?"

Ora Mae nodded. "I did but you weren't here. I suppose Trixie told you that."

"Dixie's a little security conscious."

"Uh-huh. Man gives me the creeps. Looked like a scarecrow escaped from a cornfield, him standing on his porch and staring at me like that. When he started lurking over, I took off."

"I'll tell him you're okay."

"You could mention it. Beth respects you." Ora Mae looked back to the porch. "But whatever you do, try to stay upwind from that dog."

TWENTY-NINE

Left to his own devices, Thumps could have come up with any number of ideas as to how he might spend his evening. None of them involved flowers and candy. He didn't mind picking Claire up at the airport, would have welcomed the chance to spend time with her again. He just didn't like the idea of being ordered to do it. Roxanne wasn't his mother. His mother had loved him.

And flowers and candy? Roxanne was watching too many soaps. Adults didn't do that sort of thing anymore, did they?

He wasn't even sure that there was a florist in Chinook until he looked in the Yellow Pages and found one at the end of Main Street. The woman was just closing for the day and didn't have any roses in stock.

"You have to order those special," said the woman. "And ahead of time."

"What do you have?"

"What's the occasion?"

"Occasion?"

"Romance, celebration?" The woman paused and looked him up and down. "Contrition?"

Thumps settled for a bouquet of yellow flowers that reminded him of daisies, along with a fringe of something called baby's breath and some green stuff to hold it all together.

Baby's breath. Who thought up these names?

The bill came to over thirty dollars.

"Were the roses cheaper?"

The woman was still laughing as she pushed Thumps out the door and locked the shop.

The chocolate was harder. Thumps would have thought that this would be the easy part, but the first two stores he stopped at only had milk chocolate. A clerk at the Albertsons told him that dark chocolate wasn't as popular as the milk.

"If it doesn't sell," the man told Thumps, "we don't carry it."

"Any place in town that might carry dark chocolate?"

"Only place I can think of," said the clerk, "is Chinook Pharmacy."

HE HAD SEEN enough of Chintak Rawat, but when Thumps walked into the pharmacy, there Rawat was, standing behind the counter as though he had been waiting for Thumps to return.

"Ah, Mr. DreadfulWater," said Rawat. "You have just missed your good friend Mr. Archie."

Thumps could feel sweat forming in his underarms. "Was he looking for me?"

"Unhappily, no," said Rawat. "He came to explain to me the obligations and goals of National Dark Skies Week."

"The lights in the store?"

"Yes," said Rawat. "Sadly, it is an old store and there is only one switch for the lights. If I turn that off, I cannot read the prescriptions nor find the medicines on the shelves."

"Archie will understand."

"He was not as understanding as one would hope," said Rawat.

Thumps should have been sympathetic, but he found himself enjoying the anxiety that Archie had left in his wake. What did that say about him?

"And you, Mr. DreadfulWater," said Rawat. "I hope you are feeling better."

"I am," said Thumps, because saying anything else would have plunged him into a medical discussion he would prefer to avoid. "I'm looking for dark chocolate."

"That is not a good idea," said Rawat. "While dark chocolate has less sugar than milk chocolate, it is still a sugar product and should be avoided, especially in the early stages of establishing a healthy diet."

"It's not for me."

"Denial," cautioned Rawat, "is not an effective strategy. There are a great many studies which confirm this."

"No," said Thumps, "the chocolate really is for someone else."

"Ah," said Rawat, his eyes brightening. "Romance. May I inquire whether this is a dalliance or something more enthusiastic?"

Thumps couldn't see where that would make any difference.

"Most assuredly it makes a difference," said Rawat. "One should not rush to the most excellent and expensive chocolate to service a liaison. To do so would limit your ability to provide future tokens of ascending value."

"I think I'd like a box of the good stuff."

"You are a sly dog, Mr. DreadfulWater," said Rawat. "And will you be needing flowers?"

"You sell flowers?"

"Of course not," said Rawat. "This is a pharmacy. You would need to go to a florist to find flowers."

"I'm okay for flowers," said Thumps.

"There are also a great many libations that one might consider," said Rawat, "though I would be remiss if I did not alert you to the possible perils of such an adventure."

Thumps didn't want to ask.

"Romantic undertakings that are supplemented with flowers and candy and alcohol have an excellent possibility of culminating in sexual activity."

"The chocolates?" said Thumps quickly.

"And, if one is not alert, sexual activity can lead to procreation." Rawat reached under the counter and came up with a box of condoms. "Very thin with only the slightest reduction in sensitivity."

Thumps looked over his shoulder to see who else might be in the store.

"And with what we now know about drinking and birth defects," said Rawat, "we must be quite vigilant to separate fermented spirits from conception and pregnancy at any stage."

Thumps held his wrist up and rotated the watch so Rawat could see the time. "I have to get to the airport."

"Has anyone discussed fetal alcohol spectrum disorder with you?"

Thumps put the credit card back in his wallet and took out cash. "I really have to run."

Rawat smiled and folded the top of the bag in a neat crease. "Then," he said, "I shall say no more about it."

BY THE TIME he pulled into the airport parking lot, there were already a number of cars resting in the spaces closest to the terminal. Several Jeeps were huddled in a bunch under one of the security lamps. They were probably part of Chivington's rental fleet, and for just an instant, Thumps considered checking them for additional dead bodies.

And then the instant passed.

Outside, the sky was beginning to darken, and he paused for a moment to enjoy the heavens as they turned soft and velvet. Inside, the terminal was bright and ghastly, the light hard and cold, as though some genius had decided to capture the ambience of a meat locker.

Orem was standing at the rental desk, looking spiffy in his red blazer with the gold name tag. And bored. Thumps wasn't sure Orem would recognize him, but the young man spotted him immediately.

"Mr. DreadfulWater."

Thumps smiled and wandered over, the flowers in one hand, the box of chocolate in the other.

"I'm guessing you're not here to rent a car."

"Meeting a friend."

"My girlfriend likes me to bring flowers," said Orem. "She's not so keen on chocolate. She likes ice cream better."

"Plane from Great Falls on time?"

"It is," said Orem. "I've got three rentals coming in on that flight. And then I'm done."

"No more flights tonight?"

"There's one from Fargo at ten with two rentals," said Orem. "But Sandy is going to handle that."

"Andy?"

"Right, Andy," said Orem, his voice flattening a bit. "It's a little embarrassing."

"Embarrassing?"

"I've been fired," said Orem. "Mr. Chivington said I shouldn't have talked to the sheriff. Says I got him into trouble."

Thumps shook his head. "You didn't get Norm into trouble. He did that himself."

"That's what Deanna said."

It took Thumps a few seconds to make the connection. "Deanna? Deanna Heavy Runner?"

"My girlfriend. She works up at Shadow Ranch." Orem was suddenly beaming, beaming the way only people in love can beam. "We're thinking about getting married after we graduate from college."

Thumps tried to remember if he had ever been that happy. Maybe once upon a time. Not now. But maybe once.

Orem continued to beam. "Anyway, it's for the best."

"Marriage?"

"No," said Orem, "losing my job. Deanna says there's going to be an opening in the pro shop at Shadow Ranch. I carry a two handicap, and this job has given me some experience in sales and service, so I've got a shot at it."

"That sounds great."

"Pays a lot better, too," said Orem. "Course I don't know if Mr. Chivington is going to give me a recommendation."

Thumps had played a couple of rounds at Shadow Ranch's South Forty. It was a good course. He didn't know what his handicap was, but it wasn't a two.

"Maybe I can talk to Norm."

"Wow," said Orem. "That would be great."

Thumps checked his watch. He could see the runway through the windows at the far end of the terminal. No plane.

"They always list it as on time," said Orem, reading Thumps's mind. "Even when it's late. Mr. Chivington always likes it when the planes are late."

Thumps couldn't see where Chivington would care one way or the other.

"He makes more money off the parking lot when people have to park and then wait for the plane to arrive."

Thumps put the flowers and the chocolate on the rental counter. "The night that Lester died, the plane was late, wasn't it?"

"That's right," said Orem. "It was."

"Andy Hooper came by to check the cars in the lot that night. You remember what time that was?"

Orem wasn't beaming anymore. His face was somewhere between guilty and embarrassed.

"Am I in trouble?"

Thumps frowned. "Why would you be in trouble?"

Orem looked around the terminal and lowered his voice. "I think I might have misled you and the sheriff. Andy normally checks the cars in the lot, but sometimes he calls in and asks me to do it."

"He called in that night."

"He did," said Orem. "Said he wasn't feeling well and asked me to check on the cars. I'm not supposed to leave the desk, but there's time between the flights. It's really not a problem."

"So Andy didn't check the cars the evening that Lester was found dead."

"No," said Orem, "I did the count that night."

Thumps was working on the next question when the runway lights came on.

"There she is."

The terminal came to life. The PA system crackled, and a young woman's voice announced the arrival of Flight 20 from Great Falls. Orem stepped to the computer and began punching in numbers.

"Have to get the rental forms ready," he said. "If you can talk to Mr. Chivington, I'd really appreciate it."

Thumps felt somewhat foolish standing in the arrivals lounge with flowers and candy. Who did that anymore? He didn't even know if Claire liked flowers. He had never bought her any. Nor candy for that matter.

And he hadn't considered who else might be getting off the plane, or that he would have to stand there on public display as the passengers filed by him.

Raymond Tullie, the high school football coach. "Someone getting lucky?"

Ginger Williams, the loan officer at Cattleman's Bank and Trust. "Nice flowers."

Sarah Brandt, who ran the feed store north of town. Just a quick smile.

Rebecca Turner, accountant at Chinook Tax Services. "Maybe you could give my husband lessons."

Thumps smiled and nodded as everyone had a quick shot at him. He imagined that this was the contemporary version of the medieval practice of dragging a person out to the village square and putting them in stocks, and he was beginning to wonder if Claire had made the plane at all or if this public dismembering was for naught.

Claire was not among the first fifteen passengers. And she wasn't in the next ten.

And then there she was. Looking tired. As though she had travelled a very long way and still had a distance to go.

Thumps didn't know whether to wave or call out or just stand there until she found him. In his immediate fantasy, Claire would see him with the flowers and chocolate, drop her bags, and rush into his arms. She might be smiling. She might be crying. Either way, she was happy, telling him he shouldn't have, or that she missed him, or that being with him made her feel complete.

Instead, Claire stopped and let her shoulders slump, as though she had just been told that she had to get back on the plane and return to Great Falls. Then she marched over to where he was standing.

"This is Roxanne's idea," she said. "Isn't it?"

It wasn't so much a question as it was an accusation.

"Thought you might like flowers."

"And I suppose there's dark chocolate in the bag."

"There is."

"And you're here to take me home?"

Thumps wasn't sure that getting the right answer to the questions was doing him any good.

"Okay," said Claire with another heavy sigh. And she headed for the doors of the terminal, leaving Thumps in her wake. "Let's get on with it."

THIRTY

For the first part of the drive, Claire slumped against the passenger door with her eyes closed. Thumps knew he wasn't to say anything, and he took the interlude to go back over what he might have done wrong.

Flowers. Chocolate. He had showered and shaved, even put on some cologne that he had found on a shelf in the bathroom. He had answered all her questions truthfully and hadn't made any obvious mistakes. He wanted to break the silence and open up the conversation in the hopes that something such as warmth or affection might fall out. But he didn't know where to begin.

Women had a way of walling themselves off from the world, and Claire was particularly good at it. As he drove through the night, Thumps felt as though he was transporting a marble statue that might at any moment roll over and crush him.

Maybe he'd start with something simple and innocuous.

"So, how was Great Falls?"

At which point, the statue rolled over.

"Damn it." Claire's voice was a gunshot in the confines of the Volvo. "I'm going to strangle that woman."

Roxanne seemed the obvious answer to the unspoken question.

"Roxanne told you, didn't she?"

Thumps wasn't sure what it was that Roxanne might have told him, and he wasn't about to ask.

"Cooley came by. Asked me if I would pick you up."

Thumps could feel the car picking up speed. The speedometer read seventy-six. He eased up on the accelerator and touched the brakes.

"And the flowers and chocolate?" said Claire. "You came up with all that on your own?"

No ONE ON the reservation owned land outright, but different families had occupied particular pieces for so long that no one questioned their right to be there. The high, hard ridge at the foot of the mountains and the circle of bottomland that had been created as the Ironstone looped its way south had always been Merchant land.

Claire's house sat on high ground overlooking the river. It was a prefab house, a remnant of one of the many economic ventures that the tribe had been encouraged to try.

The majority of these had been the bright ideas of some eager bureaucrats in Washington, ideas that were generally ill-conceived, always underfunded, and never supported any longer than the next election.

The house was a long rectangle wrapped in sky-blue and white aluminum siding. It was not a pretty house, nothing like the ones featured in the magazines, and Claire's only attempt at landscaping had been to form a pad in front of the porch out of four large concrete slabs. The rest of the yard was dirt and short grass. Thumps had always thought that houses on the prairies looked tentative, as though they didn't quite belong, as though they had paused on the land to rest a while before moving on.

The last time Thumps had been to Claire's house, there hadn't been a tree standing right in the middle of the driveway.

"You planted a tree?"

It was a spindly thing, ghostly grey, as though it was on the verge of dying and would never recover. In the headlights of the Volvo, the branches glowed with biblical intensity.

"Russian olive," said Claire, as though that was an answer. "The house needed some shade."

"They're not exactly a shade tree." Thumps steered around the tree and parked the car at the side of the house. "They're mostly ornamental."

Thumps had seen Claire exhausted and he had seen her sad and disheartened, but the Claire who sat in his car and watched the night sky through the windshield was none of these. This Claire was diminished.

"What was Roxanne supposed to tell me?"

"She wasn't supposed to tell you anything."

"Okay," said Thumps, "what wasn't she supposed to tell me?"

Claire sat quietly for a moment, and then she opened the door and stepped out. "Bring the flowers and chocolate," she said. "I'll make coffee."

No one who knew Claire would accuse her of being a tidy person. All things considered, she was something of a slob. There were dirty dishes floating in the sink. Thumps didn't want to know how long they had been there. A couple of days? A week? One side of the counter next to the toaster was covered with crumbs, and the stove looked as though spaghetti had been on the menu in the not-so-distant past. The last time he had been here, Thumps had taken the time to clean the place. Organize the boxes in her cupboards. Arrange the dishes and the glasses according to pattern and size. Yet look where he might, there was no sign of his handiwork. It was as though the jungle had returned and swallowed all signs of civilization.

Thumps held the flowers out. "Vase?"

Claire shook her head. "Put them in a stew pot."

Thumps didn't want to open the refrigerator, but curiosity got the better of him. It was a mistake.

"You looking for milk?"

"Sure."

"I think it's still good."

Thumps shook the carton. He could hear the clots rattling against each other. There was no need to open the carton. It could go straight into the toilet.

"I've also got some of that powdered creamer somewhere."

The sour milk wasn't the only thing in the refrigerator that had lived a long and full life. There was a weepy, brown lump that might have been an apple, a plastic sack of green mush that had probably been a cucumber, and a plate with what looked to be a sandwich of some sort that had grown fur.

Along with a carton of eggs, half a loaf of bread that still looked to be alive, and a jar of peanut butter that had been in residence during his last visit and that appeared none the worse for wear.

Claire stood in the middle of the room, looking defiant. "You want something to eat?"

"No."

"Are you going to give me another kitchen lecture?"

"Nope."

"Good," said Claire, "because I'm not in the mood for it."

Thumps set the bag on the table. He wondered where his blood sugars were and if eating a chocolate might be a danger or a necessity. Which is when he realized that his testing kit was back at his house.

Brilliant.

So he'd have to guess, and since he was guessing, he decided that one chocolate wasn't going to be the end of the world.

He turned back to share this piece of wisdom with Claire. "Are you crying?"

Which was a truly dumb thing to ask, since Thumps could clearly see that she was indeed crying.

Claire wiped her eyes. "You didn't do anything."

"Do you want me to hold you?"

"I don't want you to ask." Claire poured a cup of coffee, stalked over to the table, and helped herself to a chocolate. "We should talk."

"Absolutely."

Thumps took his coffee to the table and waited.

"Sit down."

Thumps sat.

Claire took a sip of her coffee and then pushed the cup away. "What do you know about breast cancer?"

Thumps stopped breathing and waited.

"Now's your chance," said Claire.

He could feel her eyes searching his face. He tried a supportive smile that wasn't particularly successful.

"Stay or go."

"Stay."

"That's the easy answer," said Claire. "I need you to think about it."

"Stay."

Claire's face softened. "Okay," she said. "You'll change your mind later."

"No, I won't."

"Then maybe I will."

Thumps found himself hoping that a *deus ex machina* would suddenly appear and push the conversation off to one side. Stick arriving home. A phone call from the sheriff. A sudden snowstorm.

"So, Roxanne didn't tell you."

"Roxanne never tells me anything."

"And the flowers and the chocolate weren't because you were feeling sorry for me."

"No."

Claire stood. "I'd like to be held now."

Thumps came out of his chair and gathered Claire in his arms. And as he stood there with Claire pressed against his body, movie clichés began to play in his head. Hero saves fair damsel. Sensitive man comforts dying heroine. Knight slays dragon.

Claire pushed away. "I'm still going to kill Roxanne."

"Can I help?"

Thumps would have preferred to continue holding Claire. Holding someone who was upset was like standing in the eye of a storm. So long as you were able to stay in that calm place, you were safe.

Claire went to the sofa. She was composed now. Not happy. Not dejected. Thumps stayed standing and at a distance.

"About four months ago, I had a mammogram. They called

the next day and had me come back in for a second test. There was a suspicious area. The second test wasn't conclusive and they gave me two options. We could wait and see and monitor the area, or I could get a biopsy."

"You went for the biopsy."

"No," said Claire. "Not right away. I decided to wait. Watchful waiting is what they call it. There was a third mammogram. The area had gotten larger."

"That's why you were in Great Falls."

Claire nodded. "That's why I was in Great Falls."

Thumps knew there was a question, probably several, that he could ask that would keep Claire talking and that would keep him from making a mess of the situation. But he couldn't think of any.

"Which breast?"

Thumps thought he saw a smile flash on Claire's face. "Why?" she said. "You have a favourite?"

Okay, so it hadn't been a smile.

"Sorry."

"Not your fault." Claire wrapped her arms around her. "I get the results back in about a week."

"So it might not be cancer."

"Why are you standing?" Claire put a hand on the cushion next to her. "Could you sit with me?"

Thumps liked standing where he was, but now that was no longer possible.

"I'm going to have some decisions to make." Claire stretched out and put her feet on Thumps's lap. "How would you feel if I lost a breast?"

"Me?" Again, a wrong answer.

"I know how I'd feel." Thumps could hear the snap in her voice. "I want to know how you would feel."

"I wouldn't like it."

"Duh," said Claire. "I don't know many men who go looking for a woman with one breast."

Claire's feet were in his lap. They were warm and that should have been mildly erotic. But it wasn't. In fact, the proximity of her heels to his testicles was slightly alarming.

"That's not what I meant."

Claire's eyes flashed. "Then what did you mean?"

"It wouldn't make a difference."

"Bullshit!"

Thumps remembered that Claire liked having her feet rubbed. He quickly eased both hands under her heels and began softly kneading her instep. Safety first.

"Okay," he said. "I don't know how I'd feel."

"Better," said Claire.

"I don't think you know how you'd feel."

"No," said Claire. "I can't imagine how I'd feel with one breast. How eager I'd be to have sex. How keen I'd be to spend money on fancy lingerie."

So far as Thumps could remember, Claire's taste in underwear consisted of white and cotton. White cotton bras. White cotton panties.

"You want to see?" Claire began unbuttoning her blouse. "After the biopsy, I went shopping."

The bra was not white cotton. In fact, so far as Thumps could tell from his end of the sofa, it wasn't cotton at all.

"It's silk muslin," said Claire, opening her blouse completely so Thumps could have a proper look. "And lace."

The bra was purple. Not a flat, dull purple. A rich, shimmering purple like ripe plums or wet grapes. He tried to find a word to describe the colour, but all he could come up with was "engorged."

"It's a set," said Claire. "The panties match."

And she got up and walked to the bedroom.

THIRTY-ONE

When Thumps woke the next morning, he found Claire's purple silk bra stuck to the side of his face. The night had been a lovely mix of gentle touching and passionate coupling. All conducted in complete silence. No mention of mammograms. No talk of dead bodies. No allusions to rich Texans and muscular lawyers.

Everything pushed aside. The world forgotten.

Claire hadn't said and Thumps hadn't asked, but there was a flesh-coloured bandage on the side of her left breast. It didn't look dangerous. Yet each time his lips stumbled against the dressing, he could feel Claire tense.

So he concentrated on holding her.

Thumps set the bra next to the pillow. Claire's panties were somewhere in the bed as well. He remembered sliding them down her thighs. He just couldn't remember where he had put them. Tangled up in the covers, no doubt.

It might be fun to rummage through the bedding to see who could find them first.

Thumps stretched but kept his eyes closed. No sense rushing the day. Here he was safe in Claire's bed, safe in Claire's house. Safe with Claire. The perfect morning after a perfect night. He had nowhere to go, nothing to do. There was no Archie calling him. No surly cat wanting to be fed. No sheriff with job opportunities. No Beth and her medieval basement.

Thumps rolled over and went sorting through the blankets and the pillows, looking for Claire's warm body. He could still feel the gentle aftershocks of the evening, and he hoped that Claire might be interested in taking up where they had left off.

But first he had to find her.

No Claire.

Thumps opened his eyes and propped himself up on an elbow. The bed was empty. Claire could have slipped out to the bathroom to freshen up. She could be on her way back. But now that he was sitting up, he could smell the faint aroma of coffee. And fried onions. And bacon.

Okay, no morning encore.

Worse, now he had to face one of Claire's breakfasts. It wasn't that she couldn't cook, it was just that he would prefer she didn't try. She had a trick for microwaving eggs in a cup, and a fire-hazard technique for cooking a basket weave of bacon in a toaster oven. She didn't make much use of the stove, and when she did, she liked to set the burner on high because she believed food cooked faster at higher temperatures.

Which was true so far as it went.

Still the coffee and the onions and the bacon smelled remarkably like coffee, onions, and bacon. Maybe if he was fast, Thumps could get to the kitchen before the meal began to blacken and smoke.

But what to say? Last night had been easy enough. He had had sex to hide behind. Now Claire would be waiting for him, expecting that he'd say something profound without being clichéd, something sympathetic without being maudlin, something inspirational without being trite.

And all that came to mind was Monty Python and that silly song about always looking on the bright side of life.

Thumps went back to sorting through the covers. Forget Claire's panties. Where were his?

THUMPS HAD CONSIDERED wandering into the kitchen with just a towel wrapped around his waist and reprising that commercial for men's cologne. "Anything is possible," he would have said, tightening his stomach and lowering his voice an octave, "when your man smells like Old Spice."

But he didn't.

And just as well. Moses was at the stove, scrambling eggs

and frying bacon. In a separate pan were about a dozen sausages. Cooley was sitting at the table, waiting expectantly for food to arrive.

"Ho," said Moses, "you're just in time. Cooley was concerned he was going to have to eat everything by himself."

Claire was nowhere to be seen.

"Claire had to go to Buffalo Mountain," said Cooley. "To get ready for the water conference."

"You want bacon and sausage with your eggs?" asked Moses. "There's orange juice too."

"Sounds good."

"Claire said to tell you that she's staying two nights at Buffalo Mountain," said Cooley. "In one of those fancy condos."

"We bought some pastries from that new bakery," said Moses, "but Cooley was worried that you would be tempted, so he ate them on the way here."

"I think she was hinting that you could stay with her," said Cooley. "But I can't be sure."

There was coffee in the pot, food cooking on the stove, bread in the toaster. Even fruit in a bowl. Thumps had to remind himself that he was standing in Claire's kitchen.

"Claire doesn't believe in food," said Cooley, "so we brought our own."

Moses carried the meat and eggs over on two large plates. "Yes," he said, "Claire needs a good man to shop for her. She needs a good man to cook for her."

Cooley nodded as he took half of everything. "A healthy diet is the key to a healthy life."

Moses returned with the coffee pot. He settled in his chair, sat back, and sighed. "The women have been talking."

Cooley nodded. "And you know what that means."

Thumps didn't know what that meant, but a feeling of panic rippled through his body.

"And when the women are talking," said Moses, "people need to listen."

"That's why we're here," said Cooley, and he reached across and helped himself to one of Thumps's sausages. "To help you listen."

Thumps pulled his plate out of harm's way.

"The Magpies," said Moses.

"The women's society?"

"They want you to look after Claire."

"Sure," said Thumps. "I can do that."

Moses pursed his lips. "Yes, I told Roxanne that you would do that."

The panic ripple was back. "Is Roxanne still head of the Magpies?"

"But," said Cooley, "Auntie wasn't sure that you would know what to do."

Moses reached into his jacket pocket and put an envelope on the table. "Instructions," he said. "Roxanne's real good at organizing these kinds of things."

"It's true," said Cooley. "Auntie has things on the list I would never have thought of."

Thumps lifted the edge of the envelope with a finger. It was heavier than it looked. "A list?"

"Yes," said Moses. "Of things that will make Claire happy and help her through the difficult times ahead."

"How long is the list?"

Moses shook his head. "I didn't have the courage to look."

Cooley fished the last piece of bacon off Thumps's plate and swallowed it whole. "Auntie has her doubts that you're up to the job, so I'm supposed to report back on how you're doing."

"You're supposed to spy on me?"

"Observe," said Cooley. "The word Auntie used was 'observe.'"

"But in the meantime," said Moses, "we need your help on that second thing."

It took Thumps a moment to remember the promise he had made Moses when he was at the old man's place.

"Remember," said Cooley. "You said you would help us with two things."

"I'll do what I can."

Moses stood and waited for his body to straighten itself. "We have to go for a drive. The thing we need help with is not here."

Thumps took the plates to the sink, cleaned them, and set them in the drainer. He was still hungry, and he wondered if this was a side effect of diabetes. Being hungry and not being able to eat. He was sorry the pastries from the new bakery hadn't made it to the house. He wouldn't have eaten one, of course, but a small taste wouldn't have hurt.

Cooley put on his coat and checked the refrigerator in case there was something he had overlooked on one of the shelves.

The three men had started for the door when Moses stopped suddenly and went back to the table.

"Holy," he said, holding up the envelope. "You almost forgot your list."

THIRTY-TWO

The day was surprisingly cool and there were no signs of clouds to help break the high glare. Cooley drove north through the heart of the reservation. Thumps didn't ask, but he was sure that they were headed to Bear Hump.

"When Orion Technologies got their lease, they put in twenty wells," said Cooley, as he negotiated the dirt track with its ruts and washboards. "When we get the land back, we'll probably sell the wellheads for scrap."

This part of the reservation was rolling hills, heavy greens and burnished golds, with dark mountains in the distance and a steel sky set along the horizon like the edge of a knife. From the cab of Cooley's truck, the land seemed untouched and forgotten by the clamour and destruction of modern existence.

"These days," said Cooley, "you can get pretty good money for scrap."

"Lots of the people have been coming up with good ideas about the monitoring wells," said Moses. "Raymond Horse Capture wants to paint them so they look like politicians with their heads buried in the earth."

Cooley concentrated on skirting the larger potholes. "How we going to know they're politicians?"

"No idea," said Moses.

"'Cause with their heads buried like that, they could just as well be voters."

"Yes," said Moses. "Someone should mention that to Raymond."

Thumps hadn't been looking forward to a morning conversation with Claire, but now that there was no conversation, he felt as though he had let her down, and he hoped that Roxanne and the rest of the women in the Magpie Society didn't hear of his poor beginning.

Still, it hadn't been his fault. Claire had left before he was awake. And the conversation they should have had had just been delayed, put off for the time being. He was still going to have to figure out what he would say to Claire and how he would say it.

Moses put a hand out the window to catch the wind. "But first we have to help Claire."

"We?"

"Yes," said Moses. "The women are hoping that three men will be enough."

"Auntie says it normally takes at least four men to do the job of one woman," said Cooley, "but she's willing to count Moses as two."

"You got to feel good about that," said Moses.

"I don't need any help."

"Everybody needs help," said Moses. "We just forget to ask."

THE TOUR OF the monitoring stations was more boring than Thumps would have imagined. At each one, they got out of the truck and walked around the wellhead and the fence. Then Moses and Cooley would wander off into the prairie grass and explore the surrounding area. As though they were trying to find something they had lost.

And then they got back in the truck and headed for the next station.

"When I was a child," said Moses, "the grass was over my head. My brother and sisters and I would hide in it and try to scare each other."

"Being scared," said Cooley, "can be fun."

"When I got older, the grass wasn't as high," said Moses, "and it was harder to hide. That's how they caught me."

Thumps turned in his seat.

"Residential school," said Cooley. "I never had to go, but I hear it was scary."

"It was," said Moses. "But it wasn't much fun."

The road rose steeply as the land opened up onto a broad swell. In the distance, Thumps could see another monitoring station.

"There's the last one," said Cooley.

The last monitoring station looked exactly like all the rest. Wellhead. Cyclone fence. Moses got out of the truck slowly and sat down on the running boards.

"In the old days, much of the grass around here was thick and tall," said Moses. "The tall grass was my favourite. But there was other grass that was shorter and there was some that was in the middle."

"Not much of the tall stuff left," said Cooley.

"My mother knew all the grasses," said Moses. "She paid attention to the land."

"Auntie knows the grasses," said Cooley. "It's one of the things that women do."

Moses stood and walked to the fence. "If my mother was still alive, I could ask her about this."

At first, Thumps didn't see it. And then he did. About a hundred yards from the wellhead, there were six perfectly straight mounded swatches of new-growth short grass, thick lines drawn on the prairies, each line about fifty yards long and about twenty yards wide.

"This grass doesn't belong here," said Cooley.

"No." Moses reached down and touched the earth. "This grass is White man grass."

Thumps walked one of the trench lines. It was perfectly straight with squared corners. "This was made by a machine."

"Yes," said Moses. "The White man's machines are everywhere."

"My truck is a White man's machine," said Cooley.

"I prefer a horse," said Moses, "but a truck can certainly be handy."

Thumps tested the surface of each trench. The earth was soft. The trenches or furrows or whatever they were had been dug deep, and the earth hadn't settled.

"Tire tracks over here," said Cooley. "Fresh."

The tracks were faint, slight depressions on the grass and dirt.

"Big tire," said Cooley. "Truck or an SUV."

Moses turned to Thumps. "So maybe you can help us."

"Help you with what?"

"You've lived with the White man for much of your life," said Moses, pointing his lips at the trenches. "Maybe you know what these are."

"No idea," said Thumps. "But someone went to some trouble to cover them up."

"We thought it might have something to do with the testing," said Moses, "but this is the only station with these marks."

"Moses said we should ask you," said Cooley, "before we considered the question of aliens."

"I don't think aliens made these."

"No," said Moses, "aliens would have used better grass."

Thumps tried to find a discernable pattern to the trenches, but nothing came to mind. The tire tracks were interesting. Someone had come out here in the last few days.

"It could be a burial site for the mob," said Cooley. "But it's a four-day drive from New Jersey to here."

"We could ask Mr. Lester or Dr. Knight," said Moses, "but they're dead."

"Oliver Parrish might know," said Thumps.

"See," said Moses. "I told you your uncle wouldn't let us down."

COOLEY AND MOSES dropped him off at Claire's place. Thumps checked the house on the off chance she had returned. He hadn't expected that she would. She'd be busy with the conference at Buffalo Mountain all day and into the night. And it was just as well. He had no idea what to say.

The Volvo was sleeping next to the barn and didn't look to be in any hurry to wake up. Thumps set the envelope on the passenger seat beside him. He didn't plan to look at Roxanne's list any time soon.

Maybe never.

Like most of the important things in life, he knew he was going to have to figure this one out on his own.

THIRTY-THREE

Thumps pulled up in front of the sheriff's office and parked in the only spot on the street that didn't have any shade. He wasn't sure how he was going to tell Duke that he had lost the envelope with the emails and the photos. In his defence, he would point out that it wasn't his fault, that he had been robbed, but that confession would make him look more incompetent than victim.

When he caught up with Jayme Redding, the two of them were going to have a meaningful conversation.

The sheriff had changed out of his tan uniform into slacks and a short-sleeve shirt. He had a tie knotted around his neck that looked as comfortable as a hangman's noose.

"We're still waiting for the stomach-content results," said Duke, "but Beth did some fancy test with urine and she's pretty sure that both Lester and Knight were drugged."

"Rohypnol?"

"That's her guess."

"So Lester didn't kill Knight."

"Lester died of a coronary," said Hockney. "Man has a history of heart problems. The drug probably triggered a massive seizure."

"Which is why he was dead before he was shot."

"Exactly," said Duke. "You get a chance to look at those emails and at the stuff on the thumb drive?"

"Sort of."

The sheriff's head came up. "Sort of?"

"I looked at the photographs on the thumb drives, and I was going to look at the hard copies, but I lost the envelope."

"Lost the envelope?"

"Actually," said Thumps, "it was stolen."

Duke waited.

"By Redding."

Duke waited some more.

"I caught her coming out of Knight's room at the Wagon Wheel."

"Our crime scene."

"That's right," said Thumps. "So, we went to Dumbo's for doughnuts and coffee, and when I wasn't looking, she took the envelope from my car."

"Okay," said the sheriff, "let's recap. You saw Ms. Redding come out of a police crime scene and instead of arresting her, you took her out for doughnuts and coffee, and then, in a gesture of good will and generosity, you let her help herself to police property. Is that accurate?"

"I like the tie," said Thumps. "Goes nicely with the shirt."

"Don't change the subject," said Duke. "You actually ate at Dumbo's?"

"Just a doughnut and coffee," said Thumps.

"And while you were enjoying your caffeine and sugar fix, Redding took the envelope?"

"She pretended to go to the bathroom and slipped out the back," said Thumps. "I think Cruz picked her up."

"So now it's Cruz and Redding?"

"Somehow they're connected."

"God, but I love conspiracy theories." Hockney sighed. "Deanna Heavy Runner called. Left a message for you."

"For me?"

"Something about a practicum?" Duke didn't bother to try to hide his annoyance. "Said that Mr. Parrish and Mr. Austin are having lunch at Buffalo Mountain, in case we wanted to talk to them?"

"You go."

Hockney stood and grabbed a sports jacket from the back of the chair. "Can't," he said. "Have to go to a council meeting. Besides, it's good practice for you."

"I'm going home."

"Someone's going to have to sign off on Heavy Runner's

practicum," said Duke. "You want to be the one to tell Roxanne that you wouldn't help her sister?"

Thumps felt a cold front pass over his body.

"I hear Roxanne doesn't have a well-developed sense of humour." Duke struggled into his jacket. "Not real forgiving either."

"That's low."

"It's the job talking." Hockney opened the door and let the spring light stream in. "It's not me."

"Sure sounds like you."

"You say that," said the sheriff, "because you don't understand the complexities of personal interaction and the dynamics of group motivation."

THUMPS LEANED BACK and considered the new curtains on the window. Here wasn't where he wanted to be, but all in all, the sheriff's office wasn't bad. It was cool and quiet. He might even find a cozy cell and lock the door behind him.

Outside he could hear the vague sounds of the human herd going about its business. Work. Play. Raising children. Trying to make sense of life. And he wondered how many were dreaming of some new beginning, of sailing away, of striking out for the territories, telling themselves all the while that nothing would go wrong this time.

THIRTY-FOUR

The inside of the Volvo was hot and sweaty. Thumps opened the doors and retreated to the shade of one of the trees that the council had planted to help beautify the city. While he waited for the car to exhale.

Ginkgos and red maples.

Neither tree was native to the area, but then neither were most of the people who lived in the state. According to the last census, over half of the population had moved in from places such as Colorado and Wyoming and Utah and eastern Washington.

Predominately White, with Indians a distant second.

As if that told you anything about people. Or trees for that matter.

* * *

IT WAS AFTER TWO by the time Thumps turned off the highway and onto the winding road that led to Buffalo Mountain Resort. The complex had been designed by Douglas Cardinal and had won numerous awards for the innovative ways in which the architect had settled the casino, along with the conference centre and condominium complexes, into the natural contours of the land while maintaining views of the mountains and the Ironstone River as it raced down White Goat Canyon and leaped over the edge of the Bozeman Fault.

The main parking lot was full, and Thumps had to leave the Volvo in the overflow area behind the administration offices. The car baulked as he squeezed it in between an overweight dump truck and a shifty panel van whose wheel wells had rusted away.

"They won't bite," he told the car. "And I won't be long."

But the Volvo wasn't having any of it. It puttered and sputtered, the engine continuing to turn over slowly, as though it were gasping for breath or gearing up for a minor coronary. He was halfway to the conference centre before the car gave up the post-ignition dramatics and reluctantly settled into a sullen heap.

DEANNA HEAVY RUNNER caught him as he crossed the atrium.

"You're late," she said.

Thumps had to take a moment to remember where he was. "I thought you worked at Shadow Ranch."

"Sure," said Deanna, "but I don't get enough hours there, so I work the special events here."

"Big conference?"

"Big enough," said Deanna. "But you missed Austin."

Thumps felt a little air go out of his body. He didn't know what it was he had hoped to accomplish, but now that Boomper wasn't here, there seemed no reason to have made the trip.

"But Mr. Parrish is still in the restaurant." Deanna's eyes were sparkling with excitement. "He's having dessert."

"Dessert?"

"Crème brûlée," said Deanna. "Did he kill those two people?"

Thumps turned toward the dining room. And then he turned back. "Do you know how long their lunch was?"

Deanna reached into a pocket and came up with a notebook, the kind that Thumps had carried when he had been a cop in Northern California.

"Mr. Parrish was shown to his table at 11:47," said Deanna. "Mr. Austin joined him at 12:13."

Thumps couldn't help the smile.

"Mr. Austin left at 1:52. Lola said that both men were friendly and that Mr. Parrish seemed especially happy."

"Lola?"

"One of the servers," said Deanna. "She's a criminology major as well."

"So, you asked Lola to spy on Austin and Parrish?"

"Observe," said Deanna. "As of right now, I figure I've put in five and a half hours on the practicum. Does that sound right to you?"

"Absolutely," said Thumps.

"Are you going to interrogate Mr. Parrish?"

"Probably just talk."

Deanna moved closer and lowered her voice. "Can I watch?"

OLIVER PARRISH WAS by the window. He had his cellphone out and was staring at it as though it contained the formula for eternal life. He didn't look up until Thumps reached the table.

"Mr. DreadfulWater." Parrish slipped his cell into his pocket and gestured to the chair. "Please, sit down."

Parrish looked like a mannequin in the window of an upscale men's store. A black knit T-shirt, a lightweight seersucker jacket, and a pair of charcoal slacks. All expensive. All complementary. He had exchanged his fancy wire-rim glasses for fancy red plastic ones.

"No espresso," said Parrish, "but the pie is decent."

"Good to know."

Thumps glanced at Parrish's watch. It was a complicated-looking thing with gears and wheels showing, all encased in rose gold, and a black leather strap. He guessed it cost more than his house.

"I'm told that Lester and Knight were murdered."

"Where did you hear that?"

Parrish poked at the brûlée with his spoon. "Is that why you're here?"

Thumps turned to see if one of the servers was nearby with a coffee pot. "You recall how many monitoring wells Orion has on Bear Hump?"

Parrish shook his head. "Not my area," he said. "Margo took care of all the science."

"So you've never been out to see the wells?"

"Why would I want to do that?"

"Curiosity?"

Parrish laced his fingers together and closed his eyes. "I manage the office. I tell the clerical staff what to do. I arrange meetings and make sure that everything runs smoothly. I don't hike through the wilderness because I'm curious."

"Okay."

"Have you ever seen a monitoring well?" Parrish's blue eyes flashed behind the red frames. "How exciting can they be?"

Thumps raised his cup and a young woman hurried over with a coffee pot and a menu. "Would you like something to eat?" she asked.

"Just coffee," said Thumps.

"I'll take my bill," said Parrish. "Put his coffee on it."

Thumps waited until the server left. "One last question. Do you know who built the monitoring wells?"

Parrish frowned.

"I mean, Orion isn't in the business of digging wells and

putting in monitoring stations, so it stands to reason that they would hire another company to do that. That would be your area, wouldn't it?"

"Hardly," said Parrish. "Again, Knight took care of stuff like that. Or it might have been Lester. I'm just a glorified office boy."

Thumps tried the coffee. It was unremarkable.

"I take it I'm a suspect," said Parrish.

"What?"

"If Lester and Knight were murdered," said Parrish. "I assume I'm a suspect."

"You'd have to ask the sheriff about that," said Thumps.

Parrish chuckled. For the mess that Orion Technologies found itself in, the man seemed inappropriately jolly and pleased with himself.

"It's rather exciting." Parrish straightened his jacket. "Being a suspect. Tell me, what do suspects do?"

"Sometimes they confess," said Thumps. "Other times they make mistakes."

"Are Boomper Austin and his man Cruz also suspects?"

"You'd have to ask the sheriff about that as well."

"And Jayme Redding?" Parrish was on his feet. "She seems . . . dangerous."

"You'd have to . . ."

"Yes, ask the sheriff about that." Parrish put his napkin on the table. "We should talk more often."

* * *

THE VOLVO DIDN'T seem happy to see him. The dump truck and the panel van were still there, and there was no indication that the three of them had even tried to find common ground. Thumps climbed in behind the wheel and turned the key in the ignition. Nothing. He tried it again. Nothing.

"I didn't desert you."

Another turn. Another nothing.

"I bet that Jeep at Chivington's would start first time."

Thumps worked the key once again, and the engine reluctantly turned over.

"Thank you."

The engine sputtered and coughed, but it didn't die. Thumps sat and waited for the car to sort itself out. Deanna was right. Parrish did seem inordinately happy. And the only thing that Thumps could think of that made people like Parrish happy was money.

THIRTY-FIVE

The Volvo complained all the way back to Chinook. Thumps tried to ignore the car and concentrate on the puzzle that was James Lester and Margo Knight.

Several years ago, Orion Technologies had leased land on the Bear Hump and put in monitoring wells to test their Resource Analysis Mapping technology. Lester and Knight had come to Chinook to report their findings, and Thumps found it hard to believe that they had come all this way if their system had proven to be a failure.

So the technology worked.

The water conference was to be a victory lap, a chance to show it off. Certainly the findings themselves would generate interest, but what Orion was hoping for was that the scientific data would start a bidding war. Instead someone had drugged and murdered the two principals and tried to make it look like a murder-suicide. Indeed, if Lester hadn't had a wonky heart and died before he was shot, that's probably what a coroner's inquest would have concluded. A lover's quarrel. A business disagreement. Corporate espionage. Greed.

Take your pick. Case closed.

Neither Lester nor Knight had been local, so it stood to reason that they had brought their destruction with them. Boomper Austin. Cisco Cruz. Oliver Parrish. Jayme Redding. Not that any of them had a logical motive for killing the two partners. At least, not one that was readily apparent.

Of course, it could have been someone from the reservation, someone who was angry with the construction of the monitoring wells, but Thumps dismissed the idea. There had been no serious protests when the stations were first built and there were no protests now. Moreover, with the discovery of the Holland journal, the tribe was on the verge of winning the land claim and getting the Hump back. There was little to be gained, Thumps reasoned, with killing off a businessman and a scientist.

Austin and/or Cruz were the most likely suspects. Austin had a strong interest in Orion's technology. Cruz worked for Boomper. Would he kill for his boss? Thumps didn't think so. Cruz seemed smarter than that. And why would Austin have Lester and Knight killed when he could just buy the technology or the company? Or both.

Jayme Redding didn't seem to figure into any of the scenarios that Thumps created. She was a reporter. If she was doing research on Orion, then she would know Lester and Knight, might have even interviewed them. Still, no matter which way Thumps turned it, he couldn't see where Redding would have found a reason to kill two people she barely knew.

Oliver Parrish was the wild card. But Parrish hadn't arrived in Chinook until after the murders. The sheriff had checked the man's story once, and now that the case was officially a double homicide, he would check it again. Carefully this time and in detail. And Hockney would find out if Parrish had anything to gain from the deaths of Lester and Knight. This line of reasoning appeared to have the most potential. Parrish had a direct link with the victims. He worked for them. He was aware of the value of the technology. All that was missing was motive and opportunity.

Maybe Archie would find something in the research Thumps had asked him to do.

By the time Thumps got back to town, he had gone through every variation of the case that he could imagine, and he had come up with nothing. Absolutely nothing. And he was tired. He should check his blood sugar. He should eat something. He should go to bed.

Instead he found a space in front of Chinook Appliances. Maybe a little retail therapy would help chase away the exhaustion. Maybe Danielle Fischlin had finally put the stove on sale and he could afford to think about a purchase.

"See," Thumps said to the Volvo, "you're in the shade."

The car began making its post-ignition pinging noises.

"I want you to remember that."

The stove was no longer in the window. A large fire-engine-red, bottom-freezer refrigerator had taken its place. Thumps took this to be a good sign. The stove hadn't sold, so Danielle had moved it back onto the floor. What would be a reasonable reduction? Twenty-five percent? Thirty? Thumps had seen ads on the internet where high-end appliances were reduced by as much as fifty percent.

Danielle was talking with a customer. Thumps wandered the store, touching the stoves and refrigerators. He stopped at a display that had an oven, a microwave, and a warming drawer all stacked neatly and recessed into a wall. All stainless. It reminded him of the kitchens in the high-end condos at Buffalo Mountain.

"Mr. DreadfulWater," said Danielle. "So good to see you again."

"Still thinking about that stove."

"The six-burner gas?"

Thumps smiled. Just the thought of the stove made him happy. And feel energized. Maybe today was the day.

"Is it on sale?"

"Actually," said Danielle, "it sold."

Thumps thought Danielle had said that his stove was sold.

"Nice young man came in and bought it yesterday."

She had said it was sold.

"But I can always order you one."

What the hell? How could Danielle sell his stove? He was going to buy it. He just needed some time. Surely she had understood that.

"Unfortunately, the price for the new models has gone up," said Danielle.

The exhaustion was back. Thumps could feel his shoulders sag.

"Delivery time is around four months," said Danielle. "So if you want one before winter, you should order it now."

WHEN THUMPS GOT back to his car, he found Cisco Cruz sitting on the hood.

"This yours, Pancho?"

"All mine."

Cruz walked the length of the Volvo. "1982 two-door GLT 240. MacPherson strut front suspension."

"If you say so."

"2.3 litre?"

"No idea."

"Not a car guy?"

"Nope."

"Hence the Volvo," said Cruz.

The sale of his stove had put Thumps in a foul mood, and Cruz wasn't helping.

"So, what does Boomper Austin want now?"

"*Nada*," said Cruz. "But I heard that your murder-suicide is now a double homicide."

"Word travels fast."

"Small town," said Cruz. "You know how that is."

Thumps wondered if the sale was final. The stove was expensive. There was always the chance that the buyer would come to his senses and regret an impulse purchase. He might not have even picked it up yet. It could be sitting at Fischlin's warehouse, waiting for Thumps to step in and save the day.

"Mr. Austin is up at Buffalo Ranch for the conference, so I have some free time. Thought I'd see if I could be of any help."

"Help?"

"With your investigation," said Cruz. "*Mira*. I used to be a cop."

"So you didn't come to confess."

"I'd make a lousy suspect."

"'Cause you've got a really good alibi."

Cruz grinned. "You watch much television, *vato*?"

"Nope."

"Neither do I," said Cruz. "Television's too neat. Life is a lot messier. You want to find out who killed Lester and Knight, you're probably going to have to figure out why."

"So you don't think this is about the mapping technology?"

"Neither do you." Cruz pushed off the hood. "Mr. Austin was hoping you might come to Buffalo Mountain tomorrow.

Bring along some of your photographic prints. Do lunch if you have the time."

"Mr. Austin have any thoughts on why Lester and Knight were murdered?"

"That's not something Mr. Austin thinks about."

Thumps glanced at his watch. It was after four. "What about you?"

Cruz patted the Volvo as though it were a friend. "If it were me, I'd take better care of it. They don't make them like this anymore."

WHEN HE GOT HOME, the answering machine was blinking. Thumps didn't know why he had ever bought the thing. An answering machine, Thumps had discovered, brings with it the obligation of returning calls, whether you want to return them or not.

The first call was from Claire.

"Hi. I'm at Buffalo Mountain. Where are you?"

Hell. He had forgotten. Claire had taken one of the condos for the conference, had invited him to stay there with her. She didn't sound angry or disappointed. Her voice was flat and calm. Resigned perhaps. Or indifferent.

The second call was a hang up. So was the third. And the fourth. Thumps knew there was a way to find the number of every call that came in, but in the six months that he had

had the machine, he hadn't been able to figure out how.

It wasn't Archie. Archie would have left a message. Ora Mae perhaps, wondering if he had had a chance to speak with Beth.

Thumps set the phone back on its cradle, opened the refrigerator door, and stood there hoping that something would slide off one of the shelves, cooked and ready to eat. Coq au vin perhaps or a ratatouille or a wild mushroom risotto.

The phone saved him from the reality of a toasted cheese sandwich.

"We need to talk."

Redding didn't sound all that happy.

"Lester and Knight," said Redding. "Their cellphones. Do you have a copy of those files?"

"You took my copy."

"That was a misunderstanding." Redding sounded upset, angry. "I need to look at those files."

"What happened to the copy you stole?"

"I didn't steal it."

Thumps waited and listened to Redding breathe.

"Buffalo Mountain. Tomorrow at ten."

"You want to tell me what this is about?"

"Bring a copy of those files," said Redding. "It's important."

THUMPS SETTLED ON quinoa for dinner. Two cups of water. One cup of the Andean grain. Bring it to a boil and then simmer with a lid for eighteen minutes. A little butter. A little Parmesan. Cottage cheese on top. A meal in twenty minutes. Nutty. High in protein and, best of all, on the list of approved foods for diabetics.

Redding's call was a puzzle. She had taken the files. Of that, Thumps had no doubt. But now she didn't have them. And if she didn't, then who did? Thumps couldn't imagine that she had lost the envelope. Redding didn't strike him as someone who lost much of anything.

And having seen the files once, why did she need to see them again?

Thumps carried his bowl outside. "Freeway!"

There were no lights on at Dixie's house, and no Pops piled up in a mound on the porch.

"Treat!"

The quinoa was tasty. Maybe eating healthy wasn't going to be as bad as he had supposed. He had never been a big fan of spinach or broccoli, but perhaps it was time to give these neglected vegetables a second try.

Eggplant, for example.

"Freeway!"

Thumps sat on the porch and watched the afternoon turn to evening. He might even read Roxanne's list, just in case it contained something of value. Or he could play it safe and go back into the house and watch some television while he waited for the cat to come home.

THIRTY-SIX

Thumps was not looking forward to locking horns with Stanley Merchant for a second time, and as he drove to Chinook Community College the next morning, he tried to imagine how best to negotiate his way through a conversation with Claire's surly son.

He had thought about calling ahead and asking Stick to make a second copy of the files. That way Thumps could swing by and pick it up. In and out. A quick exchange. No questions asked. But calling ahead would have given Stick time to wonder about the request, would have given him time to come up with questions that Thumps didn't want asked. Better to take him by surprise.

The computer lab was just as depressing as it had been the day before. Fluorescent lights. Grey institutional furniture. Air chilled to the point where you could see your own breath. The place was brighter than Beth's morgue and it was larger, but that was where the differences ended.

Stanley was standing by the coffee machine at the far end of the room. When he saw Thumps, he straightened up and held out a cup. He wasn't smiling. But he was trying.

Something wasn't right. The Stick Thumps knew was churlish and rude.

"Sheriff called. Said you'd be stopping in this morning." Stick held up a manila envelope. "Said the state crime lab needed a set."

Thumps took the envelope. "Everything in triplicate."

"Yeah," said Stick, "just like the college."

Worry. That's what Thumps was hearing and why he hadn't recognized it. He had seen Stick grumpy and disagreeable. He had never seen him worried.

"Roxanne said you picked Mom up at the airport the other night."

Thumps nodded.

"She say anything to you?"

"Not much."

"You stayed with her." Stick's eyes were damp and slightly swollen. "I appreciate you doing that."

"She'll be okay." It sounded hollow, more lie than truth, and Thumps didn't know why he said it, but he said it nonetheless.

Stick rolled his shoulders forward. "I know about the biopsy."

Something was wrong. Thumps hadn't thought about it until now. Claire was a private person. Why would she have told

Stick about the biopsy? She would have waited until she had the results. And if she had shut Stick out, where did that leave him?

"She doesn't want me to worry." Stick's voice was no more than a whisper now. "But she's all I've got."

Thumps couldn't think of anything else to say.

"You understand?"

Thumps took the scenic route back to the car, a deer trail that ran along the front of the campus. He could see the river bottom from here and the long run of cottonwoods that hugged the banks. He'd have to come back with his camera sometime, maybe catch a foggy day when the heavy mist rose off the river like smoke from a cauldron.

So, the sheriff wasn't as dozy as he looked. Duke had second-guessed him, had correctly assumed that since he had lost the original file, he'd sneak back to the college to pick up a replacement. Hockney must have called Stick first thing that morning to make the bogus "state lab" request for the files formal, so Thumps wouldn't have to suffer the indignity of explaining to Claire's son just how he had come to lose the first set.

I put the envelope on the back seat.

I took this reporter out for doughnuts.

She stole the file when I wasn't looking.

No, she's not my girlfriend.

No, I'm not sleeping with her.

Yes, it was a dumb thing to do.

Okay, he owed Hockney one. But what next? It was after ten. By now, all the principals would be at Buffalo Mountain for the conference. All the pieces to the puzzle. If there was still a puzzle left to be solved.

Most of all, Thumps needed to hear Claire tell him that he was mistaken, that she hadn't already gotten the results of the biopsy, that he was someone with whom she could share the bad times as well as the good.

Thumps turned right out of the parking lot and pointed the car toward the mountains. If there were any answers, that's where they would be. But right now, he wasn't thinking about the murders. He was thinking about the small bandage on Claire's breast, and he was remembering Stick's face, how it came alive as he talked about his mother, and how, for one bright moment, Thumps had seen the sweet and vulnerable child that Claire saw every time she looked at her son.

THIRTY-SEVEN

Thumps made a quick stop at the house to grab a toothbrush and a clean pair of underwear. Just in case Claire hadn't changed her mind. Freeway was still among the missing. The food in her bowl was untouched. The cat didn't miss meals, which meant someone else was feeding her. Probably the next-door neighbour and his lump of a dog.

Thumps thought about leaving a note on Dixie's door.

Where is my cat? Have you seen my cat? Do you have my cat?

Thumps realized that the operative word here was "my." It was an inadvertent error. He was fairly certain that Freeway had little appreciation for possessive pronouns. But she did appreciate treats. He shook out a handful of fish-shaped Kitty Num-Nums and left them on the floor in front of the refrigerator. A cat trap. If Freeway was still on the planet, she would find them, and Thumps would know that she was alive and well.

Photographs. Cruz had asked him to bring some of his photographs. Thumps wasn't sure he wanted to sell any of his photographs to Austin. A sale might make him feel obligated to the man, which was probably how Boomper did business. Still, Austin seemed to have a genuine interest in photography, and, Thumps reminded himself, the stove he wanted had just gotten more expensive.

DEANNA HEAVY RUNNER was at the reception desk. Thumps wondered when the woman slept or if she ever went home.

"Welcome to Buffalo Mountain," said Deanna. "Do you have a reservation?"

"A reservation?"

Deanna lowered her voice. "I don't want to blow your cover."

Thumps smiled. "I'm not undercover."

"Okay," said Deanna, "so what's up? How's our case going?"

"Good," said Thumps. "I'm trying to find Jayme Redding."

"Hasn't checked in," said Deanna. "And she doesn't have a reservation."

"No reservation?"

"And you're not the first person to ask." Deanna gestured with her lips. "He's been bugging me for the last hour."

"Thumps!"

Thumps didn't have to turn to know who was coming up behind him.

"Where have you been? The conference has already started."

Deanna leaned forward on the front desk. "She still hasn't showed up."

"She was supposed to meet me here for breakfast," said Archie. "And now she's disappeared."

"Redding?"

"Of course, Redding." Archie grabbed Thumps's arm and dragged him across the lobby. "There's a conference buffet. We can eat and talk."

Thumps had a list of things to avoid that he carried around in his head. Buffets were about in the middle, well below guns and smoking but above crowds and politicians. When he was at university, he had seen a French film called *La Grande Bouffe*, where a group of rich guys rented a villa and proceeded to eat themselves to death. Thumps recalled that there were prostitutes involved and more than a little sex, but it was the food that he remembered most clearly. Great mounds that the characters shovelled into themselves.

"You hungry?" Archie picked up a large plate. "I'm starved."

Even before he saw that film, Thumps had understood that buffets are not about food. They are about quantity, and Buffalo Mountain's buffet was no exception. Hot trays lined up in a row, platters of vegetables, cheese boards, stations with slabs of roast beef and pork and turkey. Farther along and out of sight were the desserts, slices of pie, squares of cake, custard, ice cream, maybe some fruit.

"Don't take too much salad stuff," warned Archie. "You need to leave room on your plate for the protein."

"I'm not hungry."

"Small meals," said the little Greek. "That's the trick with diabetes. Small meals."

ARCHIE FOUND A TABLE that overlooked the Ironstone. On any other day, Thumps would have been content to sit and enjoy the view.

"No coffee?"

"Not hungry."

"Coffee's not food," said Archie. "It's a necessary part of a civilized day."

"So, what did you find out?"

"Did you know the Greeks invented coffee?"

"The research I asked you to do?"

Archie buttered a dinner roll. "Okay. First thing, Redding doesn't work for the *Sacramento Herald* anymore."

Thumps looked at his plate. There wasn't much there to inspire an appetite. Eggplant-okra stir-fry. A chunk of very dry pork loin smothered in tan gravy. Cottage cheese. The desserts had been disappointing. Blueberry pie, pecan-caramel cake, coconut custard, and something that looked like green Jell-O but wasn't. Thumps had taken a gluten-free cookie, but now that he saw it up close, he doubted he would eat it.

"Fired or quit?"

"Don't know," said Archie.

Thumps stabbed at the meat. The meat stabbed back. He tried the eggplant-okra stir-fry. It had the consistency of soft snot.

"But guess where she worked before she got the job at the newspaper?"

Maybe Archie was right. Maybe he should get coffee. It wouldn't be as good as Al's, but a cup of something dark and hot might make the cookie tolerable.

"Colorado Consolidated," said Archie. "Austin's holding company. She worked there for three years."

"And she didn't happen to mention that."

"No," said Archie, "she didn't."

Thumps had missed it. With Redding in the hotel room. With Cruz at the river. And later at Dumbo's. It had been right there in front of him, and he had missed it. "They know each other. Redding and Cruz know each other."

Archie looked up from his macaroni and cheese. "Again with the sex?"

Thumps tried the cottage cheese. It was room temperature and starting to melt. "What else did you find?"

"Didn't find much new on Austin. Billionaire. Oil, gas, water, minerals. He started off as a geologist. Made his first million in Colombia and Brazil."

"Gemstones?"

Archie cocked his head. "How'd you know that?"

"Lucky guess."

Archie's face hardened. "The sonofabitch is after the water in the Blackfoot Aquifer."

"I thought you said he was after Orion's mapping technology."

"That too."

Thumps's stomach was rumbling. He was going to have to get something else to eat. "How's the macaroni and cheese?"

"Cruz and Parrish are pretty much what they seem," said Archie.

The noodles would be pure carbohydrate, which according to a brochure Rawat had given him was the same thing as sugar. But the cheese was protein. It also contained a large amount of fat, but food wasn't a perfect world.

"Hired help," said Archie. "The both of them."

A small bowl probably wouldn't hurt. Thumps leaned back and looked out the window. The sun had gone in behind a bank of clouds, and the mountains and the forest had darkened to a soft purple.

"I saw Claire," said Archie. "She was looking for you."

"What'd she say?"

"Asked if I had seen you."

The new information about Redding wasn't much help. Maybe she was covering the conference as a freelancer. Maybe she was embarrassed about being fired from the paper and didn't want people to know. Colorado Consolidated was probably a large company. Maybe she had never met Cisco Cruz or Boomper Austin.

Archie checked his watch. "There was supposed to be a presentation on Orion Technologies' Resource Analysis Mapping technology, but it was cancelled."

"Cancelled?"

"No Margo Knight. No James Lester. No presentation."

"What about Oliver Parrish?"

"Said he didn't know the science well enough to make the presentation," said Archie. "So instead, we're showing Irena Salina's documentary *Flow: For Love of Water*. You should come."

"I should find Claire."

"Sure." Archie pointed his fork at Thumps's plate. "You going to finish your stir-fry?"

THIRTY-EIGHT

Thumps went straight to reception. "I need room numbers."

Deanna's face lit up. "Are you asking as acting sheriff?"

"Yes."

"Shoot."

"Boomper Austin and Oliver Parrish."

Deanna wrote the numbers down on a yellow sticky. "You want phone records?"

Thumps thought about it for a moment. "Sure."

Deanna began working her keyboard. "No outgoing phone calls for Parrish, but that's not unusual. Everyone uses cellphones these days. And at a dollar a call from your room phone, I don't blame them."

"Austin?"

"A dozen calls," said Deanna. "All to two numbers. Area codes 713 and 66."

"Sixty-six is an area code?"

"Bangkok," said Deanna.

"Thailand?"

"And 713 is downtown Houston. How am I doing?"

"Claire Merchant," said Thumps. "Which condo is hers?"

"Is she a suspect?"

"No."

"Good," said Deanna. "I like her."

"Me too," said Thumps.

"So, you think I'll be able to get the sheriff's signature on my practicum?"

BOOMPER AUSTIN WAS staying in one of the Cascades, a three-bedroom, two-bath, cathedral-ceilinged affair with a greenhouse master bath, where you could lie in a whirlpool tub and watch the clouds float across the sky. Thumps had toured the models when Buffalo Mountain first opened, and the Cascade had been the high-end unit, the one for folks who had what economists liked to call "disposable incomes," bags of money that they could afford to toss out with the trash. Did the place have a six-burner gas stove? Yes, he believed it did.

"Mr. DreadfulWater." Austin was dressed in a dark silk shirt and a pair of soft cream pants. Behind him was a balcony with a panoramic view of the Ironstone and the mountains. "What a nice surprise."

Claire Merchant was standing on the balcony.

"You want a beer?" Austin retreated to the kitchen. "I've got wine and a shitload of the hard stuff as well."

Against the bright mountain light, Claire looked small and cold. "Hello, Thumps."

"You're in time for the celebration," said Austin. "Ms. Merchant and I have just hammered out an agreement."

Claire stepped in off the balcony. "What are you doing here?"

Boomper came back with two beers and handed one to Thumps. "I believe Mr. DreadfulWater sees me as a person of interest in the unfortunate demise of James Lester and Margo Knight. Isn't that right?"

Claire looked tired. Thumps wondered if she had gotten much sleep.

"Course, he doesn't believe that I did the deed or caused it to be done," said Boomper, "but he's stumped for the moment and has decided to beat the bushes to see what flies out." Austin helped himself to a large easy chair. "I imagine you have one or two questions, so let me see if I can answer them."

Thumps waited.

"You're wondering if I was able to secure the rights to Orion Technologies' Resource Analysis Mapping system."

Thumps waited some more.

"And the answer is, yes, I have." Boomper pointed the beer bottle at Thumps. "Actually, I had worked out a preliminary agreement with Mr. Lester and Dr. Knight before we all got to

Chinook. All hush-hush, you understand. We were supposed to have a celebratory dinner up at Shadow Ranch the night they were killed. But I suspect you know that already."

"Must have been awkward." Thumps tried not to look at Claire. "Their deaths."

"Indeed it was," said Austin. "Just about had to start the whole negotiation thing all over again."

"But Mr. Parrish was helpful?"

"Saved the day, actually," said Boomper. "But then that's what the Parrishes of the world do."

"So you own RAM."

"Enough of it to call the shots," said Boomper. "Hell of a deal."

"Which means you own the Bear Hump as well?"

"The lease on the land did come with the mapping system."

"The lease was originally for ten years," said Claire. "There are eight years left."

"And that's what Ms. Merchant and I were discussing," said Austin. "Because of my interests in bottled water, you might be supposing that I'm going to spend those eight years draining the aquifer."

"Stands to reason."

"Yes," said Austin, "there's good money in water. I won't deny it. But if I tried to do that, Ms. Merchant here would slap me with an injunction, and we'd be spending all our time in court, knee-deep in lawyers and bleeding money."

"It's our land," said Claire, her voice thin and sharp.

"Yes, it is," said Boomper. "And I've no quarrel with that."

"So, you're not going to touch the aquifer?" Thumps watched Austin's face to see if he could spot the lie.

Claire leaned forward on the sofa. "Mr. Austin is going to sign an agreement stating that he will not take any of the water from Bear Hump."

"Even going one step further," said Boomper. "I'll keep the monitoring stations in play for now so I can recheck Orion's findings, but I'm going to begin to take them out, one by one, and return the land to its natural state."

Thumps took a sip of the beer. With all this corporate generosity in the air, he might need something stronger.

"Where's the profit?"

"Good will," said Boomper. "Never underestimate the profit in good will."

Claire stood up. "I have to go chair a panel."

"My lawyers will send a PDF of the agreement to your office first thing Monday morning," said Boomper. "Have your legal team check it out and get back to me."

Claire walked past both men without a word and was out the door before Thumps knew what had happened.

Boomper walked to the balcony and looked down at the river. "Hell of a view," he shouted back to Thumps. "Hell of a view."

"We still need to talk," said Thumps.

"Better hurry." Austin waved a hand at the open door. "In my experience, you only get so many chances."

THUMPS CAUGHT UP with Claire at the elevators, and they rode down together, standing apart in opposite corners. He hadn't noticed it before, but the car felt like a miniature boxing ring, a square so small that every punch thrown would hit something.

"I'm sorry I wasn't here last night."

"It's okay," said Claire. "It was a long day. Conference dinner. After midnight before I got to bed."

"How you doing?"

"Good."

It was a slow elevator, and now Thumps was sorry he hadn't looked at Roxanne's list. There might have been a good tip on how to start a difficult conversation.

"You want to talk about Great Falls?"

"Nothing to talk about."

"I saw Stanley."

Silence.

"He's worried about you."

More silence.

Roxanne's list was in the car. On the back seat. Where it wasn't going to do anyone any good. The elevator was only about three feet square, but Thumps could feel Claire pulling further and further away. If this kept up, he'd be alone in the car when it got to the lobby. People liked to say that honesty was the best policy. It didn't seem to apply to politics, and Thumps wasn't sure it applied to tenuous relationships either.

"Look, it's none of my business . . ."

"No, it's not."

"Still . . ."

"There is no still."

The elevator stopped and the doors opened. Claire didn't move. Thumps reached out and pressed the button for the top floor. The doors shut and the car began its slow climb.

"You didn't go to Great Falls for a biopsy." Thumps watched Claire to see if he was right. "The bandage was new, but it had been replaced a couple of times. There was a bit of the old adhesive just at the edges."

Claire crossed her arms tightly around her body.

"The trip to Great Falls was for the results."

"It's not your business."

"I should have figured it out. You would never have told anyone that you were going to Great Falls for a biopsy. Not Roxanne. Not Stick. Not me. If the test came back negative, then there would be no reason for anyone to know. If the test came back positive . . ."

Claire let out a long, slow breath. "What did you say to Stanley?"

"Nothing," said Thumps. "How serious is it?"

"You want a scale of one to ten?"

"No," said Thumps. "I don't want numbers."

"It's cancer," said Claire. "They're going to try to remove it."

"Great Falls?"

"They're sending me to the University of Washington Medical Center in Seattle."

"I'll go with you."

"No, you won't."

"Why not? I can handle it."

"I don't want you to *handle* it."

"Roxanne gave me a list of things I'm supposed to do," said Thumps. "First thing on the list is 'Don't listen to Claire.'"

"There's no list."

"It's in my car. I'll bring it tonight and show you."

The elevator slowed, and the doors slicked open. Claire pressed the lobby button and stepped off the car.

"I'll walk down," she said, as the doors started to shut. "I can use the exercise."

THIRTY-NINE

The ride down gave Thumps time to think, and by the time he reached the lobby he had something in mind that resembled a plan. It wasn't a good plan, but he figured he could adjust it on the fly.

Archie was at the front desk, talking to Deanna Heavy Runner. *Okay*, Thumps told himself, *time to adjust*.

"Thumps." Archie's tone reminded Thumps of the way he talked to Freeway. "You missed the film."

Thumps held out his hand. "I need your cellphone."

Archie took a step back. "What's wrong with yours?"

"I don't have one."

"Borrowing someone else's cellphone is like using another person's toothbrush."

"No, it's not."

"Actually," said Deanna, "it is."

"See this?" Archie held up his cellphone, which was the size of a small tablet.

"That's a cellphone?"

"This phone has addresses, phone numbers, emails, photos, apps, and can connect to the internet almost anywhere you are." Archie ran his finger across the screen and brightly coloured icons jumped about. "If you know how to look, you can find a person's entire life, all on a chip."

"I'd lend you mine," said Deanna, "but there's personal stuff from my boyfriend."

"I need a phone."

Archie shook his head. "Not happening. There's information on this phone that's top secret."

"Archie . . ."

"I could lend you one of the phones that the security guys use," said Deanna, "seeing as you're acting sheriff and all."

"That'll do."

"They're kind of old."

"Will it call long distance?"

Archie and Deanna looked at Thumps as though he had just arrived from the eighteenth century without any luggage.

Deanna opened a drawer and came up with a lump of black plastic. "No games, no WiFi capability," she said apologetically, "but you can call long distance."

"We still haven't found Redding," said Archie, "but Deanna saw Cruz heading toward the casino."

Deanna consulted her notebook. "Sixteen minutes ago."

Thumps turned to Archie. "I need your room."

"First my phone and now my room?"

"I need a quiet place to make some calls."

"What about the bathroom in the restaurant?" said Archie. "You could sit in one of the stalls. Bathrooms are quiet."

"Archie . . ."

"All right," said the little Greek. "But don't sit on the beds. They were just made."

"You have two beds?"

"And don't take anything from the mini-bar." Archie reluctantly took the key card out of his pocket. "You know how much they want for a candy bar?"

ARCHIE'S ROOM WAS spacious, with two beds and a small sitting area near the window. There wasn't much of a view. The parking lot. The casino and its geodesic dome. The road as it came out of the trees.

Thumps settled on the sofa and opened the cellphone. Cooley answered on the second ring.

"Small Elk Enterprises."

"Hey, Cooley . . ."

"Mr. Small Elk is currently in a meeting. May I take a message?"

"Cooley, it's me. Thumps."

"Oh, hi, Thumps."

"What's with the 'Mr. Small Elk is in a meeting'?"

"Roxanne said that every successful business has to have an office secretary who screens calls."

"Makes sense."

"But I can't afford a secretary."

"And you don't have an office."

"Yes," said Cooley. "There's that."

"I need a favour."

"Does it have anything to do with law and order?"

"Maybe."

"Can I be a deputy?"

Thumps's first impulse was to say no, but if Cooley and Moses were temporary deputies and they found anything, the chain of evidence would remain intact.

"Okay."

"Moses is here with me," said Cooley. "He'd like to be a deputy too."

Thumps wasn't sure deputizing the two men over the phone was legal. The question had never come up when he was a cop in Northern California.

"Okay," said Thumps, dropping his voice down a bit for effect. "Raise your right hand and repeat after me . . ."

It didn't take Thumps long to explain to Cooley what he wanted him to do. And it wasn't complicated. But he went through the plan a second time to make sure he hadn't missed anything.

"You think Randy is available?"

"I can check," said Cooley, "but I may need more help with the heavy stuff."

"Not sure I can deputize anyone else."

"It's okay," said Cooley. "Just so long as you pay for the pizza and soft drinks."

THE SECOND CALL was to the *Sacramento Herald*. The phone was answered by an electronic voice that gave him a list of options. He picked the option "For the front desk, press one," and got another electronic voice and another set of options. After five electronic voices and options that included "If you wish to renew your subscription, press three," and "If you wish to report a news story, press two," and "If your newspaper wasn't delivered, press five," Thumps hung up and called again. This time he pressed zero right off the bat and got an electronic voice that said he had reached the newspaper's voice mail box but that the box was full, and thank you for your call.

The option he wanted was "To talk to a living person, press four," but that didn't seem to be a choice.

Thumps hung up and tried again. This time, he pressed the option for the staff directory and used the keypad to spell "Green."

"Jonathan Green."

For a moment, Thumps wasn't sure if this was a live person or another recording with options. "Mr. Green?"

"Yeah. What?"

"I'm calling about Jayme Redding," said Thumps. "I understand she works for the paper."

"She did," said Green.

"We're trying to locate her."

"Can't help you."

"This is a police matter."

"What's she done?"

"She was working on a serial-killer story."

Green had all the charm of a telemarketer and was just about as forthcoming. The conversation with the man left Thumps tired and grumpy.

"She screwed up."

There was a long silence on the phone. Thumps could hear the man breathing. "When you see Jay, tell her to stop calling me."

Thumps was trying to pump more authority into his voice when he realized that the line was dead. Okay, so Redding hadn't been exaggerating. Jonny Junior was an ass. Thumps could call back, pretend to be the sheriff or an FBI agent out of the Denver office, hint at the need to bring the man in for questioning, but he suspected that people such as Green didn't bully that easily.

There was an iPad on the desk next to the phone. Thumps raised the cover and the thing came to life. But instead of a browser icon he recognized, the screen had ten circles with numbers and a small message that asked him for a password. Thumps had no idea how many numbers were in Archie's password. Three? Four? Five? And even if he knew, the possible combinations were probably endless.

"My iPad?"

Archie was in the doorway, a horrified look on his face, as though he had walked in on Thumps in bed with his wife.

"You're trying to break into my iPad?"

"I can't break in." Thumps tried a few numbers. "The thing is password protected."

"Of course it's password protected." Archie rushed to the desk and grabbed the tablet. "That's so people like you can't break in."

"I need to get on the internet."

"First my phone and now my iPad."

"You wouldn't let me use your phone."

"And I won't let you use my iPad."

Thumps closed his eyes and took several deep breaths. "Don't make me arrest you."

"Acting sheriffs don't arrest people." Archie sat on the edge of one of the beds, opened the iPad, and poked at the screen. "What do you need?"

Thumps took another deep breath. "*Sacramento Herald.* Start with yesterday."

"What are we looking for?"

"Redding called Jonathan Green several times. I need to know why."

"That makes it easy." Archie ran his finger across the screen. "Okay . . . 'Governor to Run for Re-election'?"

"No."

"'State Legislature Sets New Corporate Tax Rates'?"

"No."

"'Suspect Released'?"

"Next."

"'Body Found on Levee'?"

"Wait." Thumps went to the bed and sat down next to Archie. "That last story."

Archie tapped the screen and the full article appeared. "Brian English," said Archie. "Hey, isn't this the guy that Redding did the story on?"

"The Kanji Killer."

"He's been released. Says English is no longer a person of interest in the case."

"Why?"

"Doesn't say."

"Go to the story on the body."

The decomposed body of a young woman had been found on the banks of the Sacramento River under the Tower Bridge. According to the article, the body had been hidden under a piece of plywood.

"No name?"

"Nope," said Archie. "Is that it?"

"I need another favour."

"Again with the favours."

"I need you to find out how much Austin paid for Orion's RAM technology."

Archie made a face. "He's not going to tell me that."

"Millions?" asked Thumps. "Tens of millions?"

"Easy."

"That's the kind of money that doesn't stay quiet. That's the kind of money that gets in the wind fast."

"And you want me to find out which way the wind is blowing."

Thumps stood and walked to the door. "Let's call it a weather report."

Archie pushed his glasses up his nose. "And here I thought you were a fine-art photographer."

"Not today." Thumps paused at the doorway. "Today I'm acting sheriff."

FORTY

The casino at Buffalo Mountain was housed in a giant copper-coloured geodesic dome set on stone risers. In the bright sun, the casino glowed like a mound of gold. Thumps wasn't much of a gambler, had better things to spend his money on than twinkling lights, spinning fruit, and dinging bells.

Still, the inside of the building was impressive. There were no walls in the place, just an enormous open space with a ceiling that rose high above the floor in an arch like the prairie sky.

A cave.

That's what the casino was supposed to resemble. A cave filled with money. As Thumps stepped through the first set of doors, he silently whispered the magic words from *Ali Baba and the Forty Thieves*.

Cisco Cruz was sitting at one end of a blackjack table with a small stack of chips in front of him.

"Pancho! *Qué pedo*?" Cruz moved a bit to make room for Thumps. "I thought I might be seeing you again."

"Winning or losing?"

"Not sure." Cruz was showing seventeen. The dealer's top card was a ten. "What do you think?"

"What?"

"Stay or hit."

"Thought you didn't like gambling."

"That's Mr. Austin." Cruz motioned with his hand for another card. A four came out. The dealer's hole card was a ten. "I'm just killing time."

Thumps did a quick visual tour of the floor. There were people wandering the rows of slots or sitting in front of the machines. Others were hovering over the gaming tables in the half-light of the casino.

Cruz pushed a stack of chips into the betting circle. "You know why there aren't any windows or clocks in a casino?"

The dealer dealt the cards. Cruz got a face card and then he caught an ace.

"Blackjack." Cruz leaned back. "My lucky day."

"How long has Redding been working for Boomper Austin?"

"Why don't we walk and talk." Cruz picked up his chips and slid off the chair. "Maybe we can find some more ducks."

* * *

THE SUN WAS exactly where Thumps had left it, but after the gloom of the casino, it seemed twice as bright. Even with his eyes closed, the mountain light was dazzling.

"You know what I wanted to be when I was a kid?" Cruz headed up the path to the condos. "I wanted to be a jazz musician."

Thumps tried to remember what he wanted to be.

"Chet Baker," said Cruz. "I wanted to be Chet Baker."

Professional golfer. At one point in his life, Thumps thought he might be a professional golfer.

"But the army didn't have much use for a horn player."

"More about guns than horns."

"Wars aren't won with music," said Cruz.

"Maybe that's the problem with war."

There were three condo complexes at Buffalo Mountain. One complex was used for seasonal rentals: skiing in the winter, hiking in the summer. A second complex was a time-share, an inexpensive way to enjoy mountain life a week at a time. The third complex contained the high-end condos, condos with the largest square footage, the best finishes, the more spectacular views.

"You play an instrument, *vato*?"

Thumps shook his head.

"About ten years ago, I saw a cornet for sale, a used Besson Sovereign. Came with a case and a Bob Reeves mouthpiece. Before the trumpet took over in the 50s, all the great jazz horn players played cornet." Cruz stopped and looked back at the casino. "So, I bought it."

"Where are we going with this?"

"Don't you want to hear about my cornet?"

"Not particularly."

"Just as well," said Cruz. "I can't play for shit."

"How long have you and Redding been lovers?"

"That a question or a guess?"

"Little of both."

"Any reason why I should tell you?"

"I think you just did." Thumps smiled. "Redding wasn't here for the *Sacramento Herald*. She was fired from the paper. Only reason for her coming to Chinook was if the two of you were lovers or if she was working for Austin."

"Mr. Austin's business is confidential."

"Or both." Thumps walked to where the path swung out to the edge of the canyon. "You ever play 'Hypothetical'?"

Cruz was grinning. "As in, 'Hypothetically speaking, was Redding working for Austin Inc.?'"

"That's the one."

"Okay," said Cruz. "Let's say she was. Hypothetically."

"Was?"

"Let's say that she is no longer working for Austin Inc."

"Because?"

"Let's say that she finished the job she had been hired to do."

Thumps thought about the possibilities for a moment. "The only thing Austin was interested in was Orion Technologies and their RAM system."

"Let's say that when Jayme got fired from the paper, we hired her to do research on Orion."

"You mean spy on the company."

"Research, *pendejo*," repeated Cruz. "Hypothetically."

"And Lester and Knight?"

"Part of the company," said Cruz. "Part of the job."

Thumps fit the new pieces into the puzzle. He still couldn't see the full picture, but it felt as though he had the edges of the thing. "But then Austin purchased Orion's technology. And after that you didn't need Redding."

"Business," said Cruz. "It's not kind, and it's not caring. It's just business."

Thumps could almost see what had happened next. "But that wasn't the end of it."

Cruz said nothing.

"Redding had something to sell."

Cruz turned to the view. "I'll bet it's cold as hell in winter."

"An envelope." Thumps was talking to himself now. "Lester and Knight. Their cellphones and laptops. Emails, phone records, photographs. But when she called me last night, she didn't have the envelope."

Cruz waited.

"She asked me to get another copy of the files and to meet her here today."

"She was supposed to meet me here this morning," said Cruz. "But she never showed."

"Who else might want that envelope?"

Cruz thought about it for a moment. "Oliver Parrish?"

"Why?"

"Company secrets that Orion might not want getting out."

"So why is Redding missing, and what happened to the envelope?"

"Maybe she went back to Sacramento."

"Would she have left without telling you?"

"No." Cruz turned away from the view. "You know what happened to Baker?"

"The musician?"

"He fell out of a second-storey window at the Hotel Prins Hendrik in Amsterdam. May 13, 1988."

"A Friday?"

"Yes," said Cruz, "as a matter of fact, it was."

Thumps couldn't see Cruz's face clearly. The man was backlit against the light, more a silhouette.

Cruz shook his head. "This doesn't feel right."

"We'll find her."

"They found Baker too." Cruz's voice was soft and melancholic. "But by the time they did, he was dead."

FORTY-ONE

Cruz went as far as the lobby. "Remember when I said that Jay wouldn't have gone back to Sacramento without saying goodbye?"

"You think she might be chasing a lead?"

"Lester and Knight," said Cruz. "Double murder makes for great press."

"You think there was something in those files?"

"You're the acting sheriff," said Cruz. "I'm just hired muscle."

"You know I'm going to need to talk to Austin again."

Cruz considered the idea for a moment. "Did you bring any of your photographs?"

"I did."

"Okay." Cruz took his cellphone from his pocket. "Let's go see Mr. Austin."

* * *

RANDALL BOOMPER AUSTIN was lounging on the balcony, enjoying the dying light. He didn't get up when Cruz and Thumps came into the room.

"Come and see this," he shouted to them from his perch.

The sun was already down, but the light was still ringing the tops of the mountains.

"Don't see that in Texas."

Thumps put the portfolio case on the coffee table. Boomper rose slowly and stepped back into the condo.

"I'm going to buy this beauty," said Boomper. "I can't resist. I'll probably regret it in a month or two. May never get back up here again. But that view is worth the impulse."

"Mr. DreadfulWater has a few questions."

"Didn't we just have a conversation?"

"We did," said Thumps.

"You know," said Boomper, "for a photographer, you are one hell of a detective. I would not like to have you on my tail."

"I'm harmless."

Boomper threw his head back and laughed long and hard. "Son," he said, "you are the most dangerous man I know. You're after the truth, even though you know there's no such thing."

"I'll settle for getting close."

"Then fire away." Boomper held out his arms. "Not sure I can help, but it could be fun trying."

Boomper opened a bottle of red wine. Thumps settled for water. Cruz waited by the door, his arms loose and ready in case Archie or an army of zombies tried to storm the room.

"Tell me what you know."

Thumps took a moment to figure out where he wanted to start.

"I know that Jayme used to work for you at Colorado Consolidated. I know that she didn't come to Chinook to cover the water conference. I know she had been fired from the *Herald* about three weeks before. I believe that she's been working for you, again, collecting information on Orion Technologies. I'm not sure why she was in Chinook."

"Couple of murders makes for some tasty headlines."

"Redding didn't know about the murders until after she got here."

"Touché." Boomper glanced at Cruz. "You're correct. She was working for me."

Thumps stared at the floor. "But she had already finished that work."

Boomper closed his eyes for a moment. "A vacation perhaps. See the West. Maybe she saw a good story in Orion's mapping technology."

"Don't think so," said Thumps. "Seeing as the technology doesn't work."

Thumps felt Cruz stiffen behind him.

"Are you saying that I've gone and bought a pig in a poke?"

"Let's try this." Thumps checked to see that Cruz was still standing by the door. "Redding found evidence that RAM wasn't what it claimed to be. She passed that information on to you."

Boomper went to the bar and poured himself another drink.

"But instead of revealing the fraud, you bought it. How much did you pay?"

"Afraid that's corporate business."

Thumps pushed ahead. "Three million? Five million? Couldn't have been more than that. Just enough to make it look like a sale. Not enough to cause you any inconvenience."

"Four million and change," said Boomper.

"Nowhere near what the technology would be worth if it worked as advertised." Thumps waited for Boomper to get settled on the sofa. "The point is that no one else knows that RAM doesn't work. Lester and Knight are dead. Parrish may or may not know, but if he does know, he's not going to talk. The only other person who knows is Redding, and she's missing. You see where this is leading?"

"Lot of smoke," said Boomper. "Lot of smoke."

"You know what they say about smoke."

"Got to be fire close by," said Boomper. "All right. RAM works. Just not as well as Mr. Lester and Dr. Knight advertised. But, as you say, I knew that before I got in bed with Orion. Figure I can take what they started and improve upon it. And even if I can't, I can dangle RAM in front of my competitors."

"Threaten to make the technology public domain."

"Nothing quite that drastic," said Boomper. "But yes, that's the idea. Might even be able to get folks to buy shares in keeping the technology out of the industry."

"The electric car."

"Business, Mr. DreadfulWater." Boomper raised his glass. "Business."

"So your defence is that you had no reason to harm Lester or Knight. Or Redding for that matter?"

"None whatsoever." Boomper's voice lost its friendly edge. "I don't know what happened to Lester and Knight, and I can't see how Redding might be in harm's way. Can you?"

Thumps ran through what he knew one more time. "No."

Cruz cleared his throat. "She may have returned to Sacramento."

"Then we should check on that," said Boomper. "Make sure the good Ms. Redding is safe."

The interview was over. Thumps could feel Austin begin to withdraw into himself.

"As a token of my good will," said Boomper, "Mr. Cruz will make himself available to you until we find Ms. Redding." Boomper got up and strolled to the table where Thumps's portfolio lay. "I'd like to look at these in good light. Do you mind leaving them with me?"

CRUZ STOOD WITH Thumps as they waited for the elevator.

"What's your next move?"

"I'm going to get dinner," said Thumps. "You?"

"Go back into town," said Cruz. "See what I can find."

"You believe Austin?"

"I work for the man," said Cruz. "He pays me to believe."

"Any limits to that faith?"

"Nothing to do with faith," said Cruz. "He's rich. He's arrogant. He's smart. He's hard. He changes staff like you and I change socks. I suspect I won't be working for him much longer."

The elevator dinged and the doors opened. Thumps hit the lobby button.

"Seeing as you're about to be unemployed, is there anything you want to add to that conversation we just had?"

Cruz rolled his neck in a circle. "Just odd."

"What?"

"I can see buying Orion's technology for the corporate-leverage angle," said Cruz, "but why come all the way to Buffalo Chip by the Lake?"

"Buffalo Chip by the Lake?"

"No offence," said Cruz. "It's just that he could have made the same deal from the comfort of his office tower in Houston."

"Office tower?"

"Big sucker. Glass and granite. Looks like a dildo."

"Does he have an office tower in Bangkok?"

"Thailand?" Cruz looked genuinely surprised.

"Or a business deal on the go in that part of the world?"

"Not that I know of."

"It would be a mistake."

"What?"

"Firing you," said Thumps.

"It's okay," said Cruz. "You'd be amazed at the number of guys like him who need a guy like me."

THE LOBBY WAS QUIET. Deanna wasn't at reception. Thumps wandered into the dining room, with its banks of floor-to-ceiling windows that looked out onto the land. The evening had turned to night, and the trees and the mountains were silhouettes against a dark sky.

"Thumps!"

Archie was sitting with seven other people. Thumps stopped in his tracks and began to think of an excuse as to why he couldn't stay, when he saw Claire at the far end of the table.

"Join us." Archie grabbed a chair and began wedging it in next to Claire. "We got food coming."

An evening out with one other person was ideal. Four was okay. Anything more than that was problematic. Eight was impossible. And exhausting.

For the next hour, Thumps sat next to Claire, while plates of food came and went, and Archie held court on every subject from bottled water to the national debt. Every so often Claire would smile or nod or both. Thumps wanted to tell her that he wasn't going anywhere, that he'd be there for her, but the voices at the table drowned out any hope of intimacy.

The party began to crack apart around ten. A couple whom Thumps did not know excused themselves and then two guys from the state environmental agency drifted away. By ten-thirty, it was just Archie and Claire.

"Nothing on the Orion deal so far." Archie helped himself to a spoonful of chocolate mousse.

"Don't need it," said Thumps.

Archie stopped the spoon in mid-air. "Because?"

"Austin bought RAM for a little over four million."

Archie put the spoon down. "That's crazy. That technology is worth a hundred times that much."

Claire stood and straightened her dress. "I'm going to bed. Big day tomorrow."

"Sure, sure," said Archie. "Me and Thumps have to talk."

Thumps stood and shook his head. "No, we don't."

"You need to fill me in. Tell me what's happening."

"No, I don't."

Thumps could see Archie's eyes flit from him to Claire and then back again. "Oh," he said. "Right. I get it. Sure, we can talk later."

Claire waited until Archie was in the lobby on his way to the elevators. "That wasn't subtle."

"Subtle doesn't work with Archie."

"So, is this where you try to charm your way into my chamber?"

"I'm hoping for an invitation."

"You need a second?"

* * *

CLAIRE'S CONDO WASN'T as fancy as the one that Austin had, but the balcony had just as good a view. The night air was cool but not uncomfortable. Each day from now on, it would warm until it got August hot. And then fall would come to the High Plains, and the earth would begin to go quiet again.

"I have to do this myself."

"Why?"

"Because I do."

"That doesn't sound like a reason," said Thumps. "That sounds like depression."

"What do you know about depression?"

"How about I come to Seattle with you? Drive you around. Feed you. Be your Cisco Kid."

"My what?"

"Television show," said Thumps. "I could be your chauffeur, your chef, your massage therapist, your bodyguard."

"Someone who would hold me?"

"Definitely."

"I don't like depending on anyone."

"I know."

Claire leaned in, and Thumps took her in his arms. Just like in the movies. Moonlight, stars, a river running through a canyon, a night breeze, a bedroom.

A phone.

At first, Thumps tried to imagine that it wasn't a phone ringing. But it was. He was going to suggest that Claire not answer
it. Phone calls at this time of night were never good news.

"Hello . . . Yes . . . Hi, sheriff . . ."

Thumps began making frantic throat-cutting motions for
Claire to hang up.

"He is," she said, a small smile forming on her lips. "Do you
want to speak to him?"

The sheriff was brief and to the point.

Claire waited for Thumps to hang up the phone. "Is it as bad
as you look?"

"It is."

"And you have to go back into town."

"I do."

"If this were a movie," said Claire, "this would be the scene
where I get upset, the scene where you tell me you love me,
the scene where I cry and say that if you really loved me, you
wouldn't leave."

Thumps sighed, more a groan. "I never did like that scene."

"Me neither," said Claire. "Be careful. Come back when
you can."

Thumps touched Claire's cheek. "You know the Spartan
women used to tell their men to either come back victorious or
come back on their shields."

"God." Claire kissed him gently on the lips. "You guys are
such drama queens."

FORTY-TWO

When Thumps got to the Tucker, the place looked like a movie set for a cop show. All of Chinook's finest were on duty. The entrance to the hotel was cordoned off, and Lance Packard was directing traffic. The news media had been herded off to one side, and Thumps could see that no one was going to get in or out of the hotel unless they had an invite and knew the special handshake.

Thumps stood against the yellow crime-scene tape and waited for Lance to notice him.

"Hey, Thumps."

Lance was about thirty-two, tall with a head of thick brown hair that reminded Thumps of fudge.

"Busy night."

Lance smiled. "You don't know the half of it. Duke's not a happy camper. I can tell you that."

"Can I get through?"

Lance checked an imaginary guest list. "You're among the anointed."

The deputy made it sound as though the distinction was first prize in a raffle.

"Fourth floor," said Lance. "You can't miss it."

"At least the weather's good."

Lance nodded. "Temperature's supposed to drop. When you see the sheriff, could you ask him if we could get some coffee sent out?"

DUKE WAS STANDING in the middle of room 424 with Beth Mooney at his side. Cisco Cruz was sitting on the far sofa, flanked by two more deputies. The air was heavy from too many bodies in too small a space, and everyone was talking in half tones, as though there was someone sleeping in the next room whom they did not want to disturb.

Thumps didn't have to ask.

Hockney looked up from his conversation with Beth. "About time."

"How?"

"Well," said Duke, "on the surface, it appears to be an accident."

Thumps glanced around the room. Hockney and his deputies. Beth. A couple of paramedics from the hospital.

"Doesn't look like the accident investigation squad."

"Cruz found the body," said Duke. "Claims he got to the hotel around eight, knocked on the door, got no answer, so he let himself in."

"Let himself in?"

"Seems he had a key card."

"Body's in the bathroom," said Beth. "In the tub."

Cruz was not looking good. His eyes were swollen and there was a tired tilt to his body.

"Cisco here says he was with you at Buffalo Mountain."

Thumps looked at Beth and then back at Duke. "Time of death?"

"No idea," said Beth.

The bathroom was larger than Thumps expected. There was a double sink and a free-standing shower stall, along with a new toilet that looked like an old toilet. And a bidet. The bathtub was a porcelain trough, expensive with thick sides, a sloping back, and a chrome basket for soap and shampoo. There were clothes—slacks, blouse, panties, bra—strewn in clumps on the floor. In front of the tub was a thick bath mat, and next to the mat was a long-stem glass of what looked to be white wine.

The tub was full. Jayme Redding was floating in water the colour of blood. She had a small ring on her left hand. Aside from that she was naked.

"If we are to believe the initial impression," said Beth, "we might conclude that Ms. Redding drew herself a bath, disrobed, stepped into the tub, slipped, hit her head, and drowned."

Thumps stood and waited. Death was a funny business. Naked live bodies and naked dead bodies had little in common.

"But there are two problems," said the sheriff.

"Cruz having a key for the room?"

"Three," said Duke.

"Cruz and Redding were on-again, off-again lovers."

"Yes," said the sheriff. "Mr. Cruz has already offered up that piece of information."

Beth waved a hand over the pile of clothes. "Valli slacks, Phillip Lim blouse, Fleur of England undergarments. Those aren't brands you just dump on the floor."

"That's problem number one," said Duke.

"She'd been drinking?"

"Maybe," said Beth.

"What's number two?"

Hockney rubbed the back of his head. "Why don't you take a run at number two."

Thumps stepped back into the doorway so he could see the room whole and at once. Then he slowly walked to the bath mat, reached down, and pressed his hand into the thick pile.

"How long has she been in the tub?"

"That will be a bad guess at best," said Beth. "The water in the tub is room temperature. I'm guessing that it was hotter to begin with."

"Because no woman would fill a tub with lukewarm water."

"Sexist," said Beth, "but true."

"And the temperature of the water is going to screw up the time of death."

"The best we can hope for is to run it back to the last time anyone saw her alive and run it forward to when she was found."

"And," said Duke, "it appears the first person to find her dead was also the last person to see her alive."

"Don't think Cruz did it."

"Didn't say it was murder," said Beth.

Thumps shook his head. "High-end clothes in a pile can be explained. But I don't see how you can get around the water."

"How do you take a bath?" asked Beth.

"I take showers."

"Okay," said Beth, "if you took a bath, how would you do it?"

"Macy takes baths," said Duke. "She fills the tub, tosses in some of that oil stuff, lights a couple of candles."

Beth nodded. "And then she gets into the tub."

"And then she gets into the tub."

Thumps reached down and felt the mat again. "And if she stepped into a tub full of water and slipped, there would be water all over the place."

"That's problem number two," said Beth.

"No water on the floor," said Thumps. "The bath mat is dead dry."

"Cruz says he saw Redding at seven last night," said the

sheriff. "Says he was here for about twenty minutes and when he left, Redding was alive."

"And if we believe him," said Beth, "that gives us a time frame of about fifteen hours."

"Plenty of time for the floor to dry," said Duke.

"Sure." Thumps rubbed his eyes. "But not the bath mat."

"Marble," said Beth. "Any water that dried on this floor would have left marks. I figure Redding was put into an empty tub." Beth took off her gloves. "Her head was bashed against the porcelain, the tub was filled, and someone held her under until she drowned."

"The wineglass?"

"Stagecraft," said Duke. "Act one, scene one."

Thumps turned back toward the living room. "You talk to Cruz yet?"

"We have," said the sheriff. "But maybe you should have a chat with your friend."

"He's not my friend."

"Have a chat with him anyway."

Cruz was still sitting on the sofa. The two deputies were still standing on either side. Cruz looked relaxed. The deputies looked as though they needed to sit down. On the coffee table was an envelope. Thumps recognized the college logo.

"I found Jayme."

Thumps nodded. "So I heard."

"Didn't kill her."

"Don't think the sheriff is going to take your word for that."

"Hell," said Cruz, "I wouldn't take my word either."

Thumps sat on the chair across from Cruz and opened the envelope. The files were all there. So was the thumb drive.

"Okay, so you left Buffalo Mountain, came here to find Redding."

"I called on the way in," said Cruz. "No answer. I knocked when I got here. Again, no answer. So I let myself in. Found her in the tub."

"And you called the sheriff."

"I called the sheriff."

"Right away?"

Cruz shifted on the sofa. "No."

"Because?"

"It's not going to make a lot of sense."

"Try me," said Thumps.

Cruz leaned back. "Finding her like that was . . ."

"A shock?"

"Yeah," said Cruz, "it was."

"But?"

"A phone call," said Cruz. "I had just found Jayme's body when the phone rang. I let it go to voice mail. It was that *fresa* Oliver Parrish. Said he was running late but that he'd be there shortly."

"So you waited."

"Sure," said Cruz. "Sometimes waiting is the best strategy."

"And?"

Cruz glanced at Duke. "About twenty minutes later, there was a knock at the door."

"Parrish?"

"*No se*," said Cruz. "I didn't answer it."

"You wanted to see if Parrish had a key card as well?"

Cruz shrugged.

"And then you phoned the sheriff?"

Duke snorted louder than necessary.

"No," said Cruz. "I ran the crime scene first."

"As in cleaning up evidence?" The sheriff had his "not amused" face on.

"Didn't touch anything," said Cruz. "I just looked."

"Well," said Duke, "we certainly appreciate your assistance in this matter."

"She was murdered." Cruz touched his finger. "The ring. Black opal set in gold. Jayme got it when she was in Australia. Expensive. Opal doesn't do well in soapy water. She'd never take a bath with that ring."

Hockney rubbed his forehead. "Well, this is jolly. We all seem to be in agreement that what we have here is a homicide. Maybe we can put our heads together and figure out who killed Ms. Redding."

"I'm good with that," said Cruz.

"I wasn't talking to you." Duke took his handcuffs off his belt. "You're under arrest."

Cruz turned around and put his hands behind his back.

"Don't think I'm not sympathetic," said Duke. "Which is why I'm going to let Thumps read you your rights."

"Didn't do it, *vato*."

"I know," said the sheriff. "But you can ask Thumps. I just like arresting people."

FORTY-THREE

It was almost midnight by the time Thumps and Duke and a handcuffed Cisco Cruz arrived at the sheriff's office. Hockney turned on the lights and plugged in the old percolator. Which Thumps saw as an ominous sign.

"Just how long you figure we're going to be here?"

Duke rearranged the handcuffs and fastened Cruz to the arm of one of the morgue chairs.

Cruz tried to look hurt. "Is this really necessary?"

Duke put two evidence bags on his desk. Redding's cellphone was in one. Her laptop was in the other.

"Either of you know anything about phone logs and browsing history?"

Cruz raised his free hand.

"Don't look at me," said Thumps. "I have trouble with my answering machine."

"But you'll have to take the handcuffs off," said Cruz.

Duke sat in his chair and tried to look like a stone wall. "I'll bet you can check things out with one hand."

"I can," said Cruz. "But I won't."

Hockney tossed the keys to Cruz. "You take the cellphone. I'll try the computer."

Thumps yawned. "They're probably both password protected."

Cruz was already tapping his finger on the phone. "Try NellieBly2."

"The journalist?"

"Did you know Bly faked insanity in order to get committed to the asylum on Blackwell's Island?" Cruz looked up from the phone. "*Qué mujer*. Spent ten days in appalling conditions just to be able to write a first-hand exposé on the brutality of the place. She was one tough cookie."

"Hence the password."

"Everyone has heroes."

Duke squinted at the computer. "Redding appears to have emailed a Detective Walter Chang of the Sacramento Police Department. Any idea why?"

Cruz shook his head. "Jayme had sources. Or maybe he was a friend."

Duke picked up the phone and began dialing. "There's coffee if you want."

Cruz started to stand. Thumps held out a hand and mouthed a silent no.

"Looking for Detective Walter Chang," said the sheriff. "Sheriff Duke Hockney, Chinook, Montana."

Thumps debated whether he should call Claire. It was late and he didn't want to wake her. But he didn't want her to think that he'd forgotten either. It wasn't that he didn't want to be with her. She'd understand that. If he explained it correctly.

"The phone message," said Thumps. "Parrish said he was running late?"

"He's not at the Tucker anymore," said Cruz. "He moved to Buffalo Mountain for the conference."

"So he would have had to drive down just to see Redding."

"You think this is about the envelope?" said Cruz.

Thumps lined the pieces up as best he could. Redding takes the envelope from his car. What does she do next? She looks through the emails and the photos. That much is a given. She makes a copy? A copy would be the smart thing to do. Maybe she's looking to use the information for a story. Maybe she's looking to sell the file to Austin or Parrish. Or both.

"Yes," said the sheriff, the phone wedged between his cheek and shoulder. "I understand."

But then she calls Thumps and asks to look at the files as though she no longer has the envelope. Yet when her body is found in the hotel room, the files that she took from the Volvo are there on the coffee table.

"I very much appreciate that," said Duke, and he put the phone back on its cradle.

Cruz shifted in the chair. "*Qué pedo?*"

"That was the duty sergeant at the Sacramento Police Department. Detective Walter Chang is currently off duty but will be available first thing in the morning."

"You're not going to make me spend the night in a cell."

"That depends."

"On what?" said Cruz.

"Why would Redding want to talk to Detective Chang?"

Conferences, as Thumps remembered, tended to run into the early hours of the morning. If he drove a little over the speed limit, he might be able to get to Buffalo Mountain before Claire called it a night.

"The serial-killer case." Thumps tried to make the explanation as concise as possible. "I talked to Jonathan Green at the *Sacramento Herald*. The guy the police had arrested came up with an alibi, and they had to release him. And then they found another body. I think Green blames Redding for getting the story wrong."

"You think Redding was calling Chang about the case."

"If I know Jayme," said Cruz, "she probably asked him for a copy of the crime scene report."

"Which he would not send her," said Duke. "Because contrary to television wisdom, police departments are not information centres for reporters and private eyes."

"But we won't know exactly what she wanted, until we talk to Detective Chang in the morning."

Cruz looked at Thumps and then at the sheriff. "So I can go home and get a good night's sleep?"

"That depends."

"You know," said Cruz, "'depends' isn't the only active verb in the world."

Thumps could feel his eyes beginning to droop. It might be a good idea to check his blood sugars. "How about you release him into my custody?"

"Wouldn't be prudent to release a possible felon into the custody of a photographer," said Duke.

"How about an acting sheriff?"

"That," said the sheriff, "would be an entirely different matter."

CRUZ LET THUMPS drive the Escalade back to Buffalo Mountain.

"You want to talk about it?"

"About what?"

"Redding," said Thumps. "Finding her like that."

"I was in Kandahar province in 2007. Saw my share of bodies."

Even after all these years, Thumps could still remember that night on Clam Beach on the Northern California coast. He could remember the walk across the sand to where the bodies lay under dark tarps. Anna Tripp, thirty-nine. Callie Tripp, ten. He could remember looking at the still faces of his lover and her child. The Obsidian Murders. Nothing had faded. Everything was still in sharp relief.

"Not the same."

"No, *vato*," said Cruz. "It's not."

Thumps let the SUV float. The heavy vehicle felt like a boat on a quiet lake, gently rolling as it followed the current up to the resort.

"So what are you going to do with your new-found freedom?"

Cruz stared out the window. "Get some sleep. Find who killed Redding."

"And then?"

"What would you do?"

That was the question Thumps had asked himself any number of times. What if he was able to find the person who killed Anna and Callie? What would he do? What would the cop do? What would the man do?

"I don't know."

"An honest answer," said Cruz. "Most guys go all macho and start waving their dicks around, but talk is different than action."

"So action makes it better?"

"Shit, no," said Cruz. "Nothing makes it better. Nothing makes it go away."

"But you do something anyway?"

"You asking me about Redding, or you doing research?"

Thumps ran his hands across the leather steering wheel. The thing was actually heated. "Little of both, I guess."

"Nothing helps," said Cruz. "But I'm guessing you know that already."

Thumps drove the Cadillac to the front entrance of Buffalo Mountain and got out.

Cruz slid behind the wheel. "You going to find Parrish?"

Thumps looked at his watch. "Got something else to do first."

"Smart," said Cruz. "Take care of the important stuff."

"Breakfast?"

"I'm an early riser."

"What about Parrish?"

Cruz dropped the Escalade into gear. "Maybe he's an early riser too."

FORTY-FOUR

Claire wasn't in the dining room or in the bar. Thumps went up to her condo, stood outside the door, and listened for any sound that might suggest someone was still awake. Nothing.

He ran through his available choices. He could stand in the hall and try to reach Claire mentally. He had read that people who have a strong, long-term relationship can sometimes sense what the other person is thinking.

So, that wasn't going to work.

He could always knock. What's the worst that could happen? Claire could open the door and tell him that she had been asleep, that she thought he had forgotten, that she didn't want to talk, that it was past midnight.

Or she might open the door and take him in her arms, tell him that she hadn't been asleep, that she hadn't thought he had forgotten, that she needed to talk, that he shouldn't worry about the hour.

The simple answer was to phone. He could go down to the front desk and call Claire from there. That way there would be some distance between success and failure. He could explain the crime scene delay and the late hour. He could give her the opportunity to invite him up or the occasion to turn him away. They could talk without having to face each other.

Standing in the hallway like a stump in a field wasn't an option. Knock or call. In the end, those were the only choices.

His first attempt at knocking was a failure. He could barely hear the sound his knuckles made on the wood. The second attempt rang out like a volley of gunfire. Thumps waited and watched the security peephole for the change in light that would indicate that someone was looking out from the other side.

Nothing.

He was about to knock for a third time when the door opened. Thumps was prepared to see Claire fully clothed, and he was prepared to see her in a bathrobe. What he was not prepared for was Stick Merchant in his underpants.

"Hey, Thumps."

"Stick?"

"Did you know this place has premium cable and the sports package?"

Thumps looked over Stick's shoulder to see if Claire was somewhere in the room.

"Come on in," said Stick. "Just watching a show about a bunch of kings and knights and witches and dragons."

The sofa in front of the television was piled with blankets and pillows. There were dirty plates on the coffee table, along with several empty beer bottles. The television was on, but there was no sound.

"They spend all their time sword fighting and taking off their clothes." Stick flopped on the sofa. "Power, violence, and nudity. What's not to like?"

"Your mother here?"

"Asleep."

Thumps glanced at the bedroom door. He wondered if Claire was lying in bed awake and could hear the conversation. A part of him wanted the door to open. A part of him wanted Claire to appear and send her son home.

Stick waved the remote at the television. "You don't even have to have the sound on to know what's happening."

Another part of him wanted to leave well enough alone.

"She's going to be okay," said Stick. "She's going to get better."

"That's what everyone's hoping."

"Fuck hope," said Stick. "She's going to get better." Stick looked at Thumps, his eyes darkening. "'Cause I'm here now, and I'm going to look after her. I mean, I appreciate all you did, but I'm her son."

As hints go, it wasn't subtle. "When she wakes up," said Thumps, "could you tell her I stopped by?"

"We're taking it one day at a time." Stick began working his way back under the blankets and pillows. "Mom and me."

THUMPS CONSIDERED DRIVING home, turning off the phone, and staying out of sight for the next week, out of harm's way. And he considered throwing his camera gear into the car and heading up into Canada and Waterton Park. There were several hikes he had been meaning to do. Crypt Lake. Wall Lake. The Carthew-Alderson Trail. Lineham Ridge. Each choice had its appeal and photo opportunities. Instead, he took the elevator down to the third floor.

ARCHIE DID NOT appear happy to see him.

"Thumps?"

"I need a place to stay."

Archie stood rooted in the doorway, not looking as though he wanted to move. "It's one in the morning."

"And you have two beds."

"And you have a home."

"Jayme Redding has been murdered."

Thumps knew he should have eased into Redding's death, should have managed the news with more tact and sensitivity, but he was diabetic and his stove had been sold to someone else and Claire's obnoxious and annoying son had gone all Oedipal on him.

"What?"

Then again, Archie was equally obnoxious and annoying.

"Redding's dead."

Archie's room was as Thumps had left it. The bed nearest the window was rumpled. It was the bed he would have chosen if he had had first choice.

"Sit," said Archie. "Tell me everything."

"Not much to tell."

Archie scowled. "That's what you always say."

"She was found in her room at the Tucker, in the bathtub. Someone tried to make it look like an accident."

"Austin."

"We don't know that."

"Or his man Cruz."

"Doubt it."

"Or Oliver Parrish," said Archie, ticking names off his fingers. "Or a hired assassin who is already on a plane to Morocco."

"Morocco?"

"We don't have an extradition treaty with Morocco," said Archie, "and there's a really nice beach at Al Hoceima."

Thumps spent the next half-hour walking Archie through the crime scene—Redding's body in the tub, Cruz in the living room, the stolen envelope on the coffee table, Parrish calling and coming by the room.

"Why are you telling me all this?" Archie waited for a moment. "What happened to 'Talk to the sheriff'?"

Thumps shrugged.

"Be pretty dumb for Cruz to get caught with the body."

"Cruz called it in."

"If it were television," said Archie, "Parrish would be the killer because he doesn't seem to have a motive."

"But it isn't television."

Archie pushed off the bed and went to the window. "The only thing that makes any sense is that all three murders are connected."

"Okay."

"So what connects them?"

Thumps kicked off his shoes and stretched out on the bed. The mattress was comfortable and the white duvet was soft and deep. Even the pillows felt luxurious.

"You're not going to sleep."

"Yes, I am."

"We have a murder to solve."

"Three murders," said Thumps, "and now I'm going to go to sleep."

"Duke won't be impressed."

"I'm closing my eyes."

With his eyes closed, Thumps could no longer see Archie, but he could hear the man as he paced the room and tapped at his tablet. And then the lights went out, and he heard Archie get into bed. Now that the room was quiet, Thumps hoped sleep would come quickly, but it didn't. He lay awake, trying to force square pieces into a round hole.

And just as he could feel his mind and body relax, just as he began to drift off on a sea of white foam and polished cotton, Archie began to snore.

FORTY-FIVE

Thumps didn't open his eyes right away. He could feel the light on his face, knew it was morning, understood that he should get up, but couldn't think of a good reason to leave a comfortable bed. He had no place to go and nothing to do. Claire would be tied up with the conference or with her suddenly overly protective son. Or both. The sheriff would be chasing down leads. Beth would be processing yet another body. Austin and Parrish would be having breakfast.

That left Cruz and Archie. Thumps had no idea what Cruz was doing, and he didn't want to know what was keeping the little Greek busy.

"Morning, Pancho."

Cisco Cruz was sitting in one of the club chairs. There were two cups on the table in front of him, along with a white square box.

"Where's Archie?"

"No idea," said Cruz. "He was gone when I arrived."

It took Thumps a moment to connect the dots. "Then how did you get in?"

Cruz smiled. "I brought coffee. And doughnuts."

"Doughnuts?"

"I forgot about the diabetes."

Thumps sat up. He was still fully dressed. Wrinkled, but fully dressed.

"You're going to need to do something with your hair, *vato*." Cruz opened the box and fished out a doughnut. "You look like a rooster."

The coffee wasn't particularly good, but it was hot. Thumps broke one of the doughnuts in half, seeing this as a compromise with temptation, and when he finished the first half, he ate the second.

"You know the trick for getting wrinkles out of clothes?"

"Why are you here?"

"*Mira.* You turn the shower on really hot until the bathroom fills with steam." Cruz took another bite of doughnut. "And then you stand in it."

Thumps padded into the bathroom and stood in front of the mirror. Cruz was right. He did look like a rooster. A badly rumpled rooster. Thumps turned on the tap and let the water run hot. He quickly washed his face and wet his hair. Not much of an improvement, but an improvement nonetheless.

Cruz was brushing doughnut crumbs off his pants. "You still acting sheriff?"

Thumps looked into the doughnut box. It was empty.

Cruz crushed the box and placed it on top of the trash can. "My good deed for today."

"Bringing doughnuts?"

"Eating the last one," said Cruz, "and saving you from yourself."

"Generous."

"That's me, *vato*," said Cruz. "You ready to go to work?"

IF THUMPS REMEMBERED correctly, the unit Oliver Parrish currently occupied was called the Canyon, a two-bedroom, two-bath model with a fireplace. Parrish answered the door in grey slacks, a soft, green shirt, and a black-on-black sports jacket with silver thread. The man still reminded Thumps of a weasel, but he knew how to dress.

"Mr. DreadfulWater. Mr. Cruz. Come on in," said Parrish. "You just missed Sheriff Hockney."

Thumps glanced at Cruz.

"There's fruit if you like," said Parrish. "And cheese."

"So you know about Jayme Redding."

"I do," said Parrish. "A tragedy. Didn't know her well. She was doing a story on Orion. She interviewed Lester and Knight. We spoke a couple of times. Seemed nice."

"She was," said Cruz.

"You want coffee? There's a fresh pot."

Thumps helped himself to some cheese. There was the chance it might counteract the effects of the doughnut.

"But you didn't come here for the food," said Parrish. "You want to know about my relationship with Ms. Redding."

"Mr. Austin has a vested interest," said Cruz. "I look after Mr. Austin's vested interests."

"Yes," said Parrish. "Mr. Austin mentioned that you were quite good at vested interests."

The two men were smiling at one another, but Thumps could feel the warmth begin to flee the room. "You called Redding last night."

"I did," said Parrish. "We were supposed to meet at the Tucker. I called to tell her I was running late and when I got to her room, there was no answer."

"What was the meeting about?"

Parrish arranged himself in one of the easy chairs. "Not sure. Redding said she had something that I would want to see. I think she was hoping to make a sale."

Thumps took several grapes. "She didn't say what she had for sale?"

"We never got together," said Parrish. "The sheriff has my full statement."

Thumps nodded. "The sheriff probably asked you where you were when Redding was killed."

"He did."

"And?"

"Here," said Parrish. "Buffalo Mountain. Ms. Redding called me here around five yesterday afternoon. We arranged to meet around nine that night. I was late."

"And from five until you drove to Chinook?"

"This is all in the statement I gave the sheriff."

Cruz tapped the edge of the table. "Humour him, *pendejo*. He used to be a cop."

"Early dinner," said Parrish. "In the resort dining room. I had the risotto. Surprisingly good. After that, the casino. Didn't do so well there."

Thumps stood and motioned to Cruz. "Thank you for your time."

"My pleasure," said Parrish.

Thumps was at the door before he stopped and turned. "You were in Great Falls when Lester and Knight were killed."

"That's right."

"At a motel."

"Comfort Inn," said Parrish. "Wouldn't recommend it."

"And then you flew into Chinook the next day."

Parrish waited.

"Did you know it's a little under three hours to drive from Great Falls?"

Parrish's face brightened. "Are you asking me if I drove over from Great Falls, killed James and Margo, drove back, and jumped on the plane the next morning?"

"Sure sounded like that was the question," said Cruz.

"You think I killed them?" Parrish was smiling now. "Lester, Knight? What, and Redding?"

"But you didn't have opportunity or motive, did you?"

"No," said Parrish, the smile slipping into something harder and colder. "I didn't. But while you're at it, maybe you should ask Boomper Austin the same question."

Thumps frowned. "Now why didn't I think of that?"

Parrish checked his fancy watch. "I have to get to a panel on aquifer measurement technology or something like that. Help yourself to the food and coffee. Make sure the place is locked when you leave."

Thumps stayed seated. Cruz wandered the room, looking at the furnishings.

"How much you figure one of these places costs?"

"To rent?"

"No, *vato*, to buy." Cruz reached into his jacket, took out his cellphone, and looked at the screen.

"Problem?"

"Mr. Austin wants to see me."

Thumps helped himself to a handful of grapes. "Why would Parrish stay at a Comfort Inn?"

"Great Falls has better hotels?"

Thumps rubbed his eyes. "There's a Hilton, a Holiday, and a Hampton. If you like boutique, there's the Arvon on First Avenue."

"Probably close to the airport."

Thumps shook his head. "There are two Comfort Inns. One is right at the airport. The second one is on Ninth. It's as far away from the airport as you can get."

"And Parrish stayed at the Comfort Inn on Ninth?"

"He did."

"Curious." Cruz wandered into the kitchen. "What are your plans for the day?"

"Get some breakfast."

"I brought you breakfast." Cruz opened and shut the refrigerator door. "Jayme told me about Eureka."

Thumps stiffened. "Long time ago."

"Sure," said Cruz. "And it's none of my business."

"What are you going to do?"

"See *el jefe*." Cruz ran a hand across the granite countertop. "Rattle the bushes. See what flies out."

Cruz left. Thumps stayed in the chair. He thought about checking his blood sugars to see how much damage the one doughnut had done. Instead he waited for the memories of that night on the North Coast to crawl back into the shadows.

And for his heart to stop pounding.

FORTY-SIX

The dining room was a beehive. There were people everywhere with name cards clipped to lanyards hanging around their necks. As Thumps made his way through the pack, he couldn't help but think of dog collars and leashes.

The breakfast buffet was extensive, and he took his time wandering around the hot trays and platters, looking at the choices and trying to decide what he could eat. The meat selections would probably be fine, except for the sausage, which had a high fat content, and the bacon, which had no nutritional value to speak of. The scrambled eggs would be okay, though the ones in the tray looked somewhat tired and worn out. There was cottage cheese and fruit and pastries of all sorts, as well as three different kinds of bread along with French toast, waffle squares, and hash-brown patties.

"Thumps." Archie and the sheriff were sitting at a small table piled with dirty dishes. "We've gone national." Archie held up his tablet so Thumps could see the screen. The banner line read, "Water Conference Turns Deadly."

Thumps read the first paragraph. It was about the murders. "Don't imagine this is the kind of publicity you wanted."

"Publicity is publicity," said Archie. "Sure, they'll show up for the blood, but some of them will stay for the water."

Duke was toying with a sausage. He didn't look particularly happy. Not that he ever looked happy. Even when he was.

"I've got to chair a panel," said Archie. "But if you find anything, I want to be the first to know."

Thumps watched the little Greek work his way through the room, stopping almost every step to shake hands and say a few words of encouragement—the conference version of speed dating.

"You get a good night's sleep?" asked Duke. The bags under the sheriff's eyes were a little fuller and there was a noticeable droop to his jowls.

"You were up all night?"

"Dead bodies will do that to a person," said Duke.

Thumps's stomach began to growl. He could hear the buffet calling.

"I talked to Detective Walter Chang this morning." Duke worked the keyboard of his laptop. "Sent me the crime-scene report."

"And?"

Duke turned the laptop around. "Amanda Douglas. Thirty-one. Worked for the state. Chang is sure it's the work of the Kanji Killer."

"Great."

"Don't know why they do it."

"I'm not sure anyone knows what makes serial killers tick."

"Not the perp," said Hockney. "The media. Why those idiots give this idiot a fancy nickname. 'Kanji Killer' my ass. Sounds like something out of one of those stupid zombie movies."

"You watch zombie movies?"

"Macy," said the sheriff. "She loves the damn things."

Thumps scrolled down the crime-scene report. "They don't have much."

"There's a photo," said Duke.

The image on the screen was of a young woman in a black robe and mortarboard hat. A university graduation picture. Amanda Douglas smiling out at the world, imagining what lay ahead, never suspecting what she would find.

The report didn't say if she was married or if she had children, and Thumps didn't want to know. Reports such as this were always cold and impersonal. Sad. A life reduced to a series of notations on a sheet of paper.

"A child." Duke's voice was almost a whisper. "Just a child."

It was difficult looking at Douglas's face. Auburn hair. Blue eyes. A crooked smile. She didn't remind Thumps of Anna or of Callie. And then again, she did.

"I'm guessing Redding was going to pick up where she had left off."

"Work the serial-killer story?"

"Didn't strike me as someone who liked to let sleeping dogs lie," said Duke.

The smile. It hit Thumps like a punch. He had seen that smile before. Another place. Another time.

"You had breakfast?" Hockney waved a hand at the buffet. "It's okay if you like steam-table food."

Thumps pushed the laptop across the table. "You got the files from Lester's cellphone on this thing?"

"Sure."

"I need to see his photos."

Duke shrugged and started working the keys. Then he stopped. "Shit."

"Yeah," said Thumps. "I think it's her."

The photograph of the young woman on Lester's cellphone was taken from a distance.

Duke squinted at the screen. "What do you think?"

"Can you make it bigger?"

"Probably," said the sheriff. "If I knew how."

"It's the same woman," said Thumps. "It's Amanda Douglas."

"So what the hell is her photo doing on Lester's cellphone?"

Thumps tried to think of the combinations that made sense. "Someone he knew?"

"Or a friend of a friend," said Hockney. "She was a state

employee. Maybe she worked for an agency that had dealings with Orion."

Thumps shook his head. "No," he said. "You see the way she's looking off at something to the side?"

"This some sort of photography quiz?"

"She doesn't know her picture is being taken."

Hockney tried to sound impressed. "And how would you know that?"

"Women are sensitive about pictures." Thumps moved his finger across the touchpad. "Look at the way she's slouching. Look at the way her hair is partly in her face. If she knew she was being photographed, she would have sat up and fixed her hair. She would have looked at the camera."

"You think Lester was the Kanji Killer?"

"You know how cellphone cameras work?"

"Nope."

"Neither do I," said Thumps. "But as luck would have it, we know someone who does."

FORTY-SEVEN

Stick answered the door. Claire was in the kitchen. As soon as she saw Thumps and the sheriff, she mouthed a silent plea, "Help me." Stick stood in the doorway like the three hundred Spartans at Thermopylae.

"She doesn't want to see anyone."

"Stick." Claire looked ready to butcher her son on the spot. "Let them in."

"You don't need this bullshit, Mom."

"I've just made coffee."

"Actually," said Duke, "we're here to see Stanley."

"Thank God," said Claire.

Claire looked tired. If she had gotten any sleep last night, it didn't show. Thumps had a twinge of admiration for Stick's protective instincts, but he couldn't imagine that Claire was all that crazy about her son bunking with her and pulling round-the-clock guard duty, keeping everyone away, friend and foe alike.

Hockney tried his congenial face. "You remember the cellphones and laptops you processed?"

"The two stiffs?"

Claire closed her eyes. "James Lester and Margo Knight," she said. "Not 'two stiffs.'"

"Whatever."

"As it turns out," said Duke, "we need you to look at those files again."

"Stanley will be happy to help," said Claire.

"Sure," said Stick, "but I'm not leaving you."

Hockney nodded. "There's a photo on Lester's phone. We need to know who took it."

"Lester's phone," said Stick. "Lester's photo."

"That's why we need you to look at the file," said Duke. "We're thinking someone sent it to him."

Stick looked at his mother. "I can't do that here. I'd have to go to the lab."

It wasn't a smile on Claire's face, but it was close enough. "Then go. If it will help with the investigation, then we need to help."

"But . . ."

"Thumps will look after me," said Claire. "Won't you, Thumps?"

"Absolutely."

"This is official police business," said Duke.

"Okay." Stick was grinding his teeth. "But as soon as we're done, I'll be back."

Duke draped his large arm around Stick's shoulders. "I'll drive you back myself."

Claire waited until she was sure her son was gone before she let out a long breath. "Thank you."

"No problem."

"If I had had to put up with his empathy and help for another minute . . ."

"He's your son," said Thumps. "He loves you."

Claire held Thumps's eyes with hers. "And you think that would have saved him?"

There was a word for mothers who ate their young, but Thumps couldn't remember what it was. Savaging? Filial infanticide? Something like that.

"He's got his own place now. He wants me to move in with him."

Thumps didn't mean to laugh.

"It's not funny." Claire poured herself a cup of coffee. "My son goes from petulant brat to dog soldier."

"He's worried about you. You won't talk to him." Thumps put his arms around Claire and drew her in. "You won't talk to me."

"Yes, I will," said Claire. "When I have to."

Thumps could smell the shampoo in Claire's hair. A floral scent. Soft, white flowers. Delicate petals that bruised easily.

"Maybe you can come with me to Seattle." Claire didn't sound particularly happy about the prospect. "I'll probably need someone to drive me around."

Claire's body was warm and alive. He could feel her breathing against his neck, feel the beat of her heart against his chest. Somewhere in the distance, he could hear bells ringing.

Claire pushed away and went to the door. "You expecting someone?"

Thumps wasn't expecting anyone. He certainly wasn't expecting Cooley and Moses, but there they were, standing in the doorway. Cooley had a pizza box in one hand. Moses was carrying a paper bag.

"We had some pizza left over," said Moses. "Cooley didn't want to eat it until he checked to see if you wanted it."

"It's pepperoni and onions," said Cooley, "with extra cheese."

Thumps shook his head. Claire grabbed the box and took out a large slice that bent under the weight of the toppings.

"Stanley wants me to eat vegetables and yogurt."

"Vegetables are good food for rabbits," said Moses.

"I've tried yogurt," said Cooley, "but I prefer ice cream."

Claire finished the pizza slice in five bites. "God, that was good."

"There's one slice left," said Cooley.

Claire didn't have to be asked twice. "Don't you dare tell Stanley."

Thumps zipped his lips. Cooley and Moses stood still as stones.

"Why are you guys here?" Claire licked at her fingers.

"Thumps deputized Cooley and me," said Moses. "Deputy Blood. You got to like the sound of that."

"And Deputy Small Elk," said Cooley. "Makes you feel important."

Thumps looked to see if there was a third slice of pizza.

"It was an expensive job." Cooley took a piece of paper out of his pocket and handed it to Thumps. "There was the pizza, the soft drinks, the gas for Randy's truck, and the rental."

Thumps looked at the total. More than he had hoped.

"The pizza and the soft drinks were on sale," said Cooley. "The gas and the rental were regular price."

"Randy's still at the site?"

"He is." Cooley held up his cellphone. "As soon as he gets those photos, he'll send them to us."

Moses set the bag on the counter. "I don't know if this is what you wanted," he said, "but it's what we found."

Thumps opened the bag. "You guys did well."

Claire stopped licking her fingers. "What is it?"

"Not sure," said Thumps. "But I'll let you know as soon as I am."

"And now you're going to run off," said Claire.

"I have to go meet Stanley and Duke at the college."

Claire pursed her lips. "Then you'll miss lunch."

"Lunch?" said Cooley.

"Cooley's pretty hungry," said Moses. "He was thinking about those pizza slices all the way over."

Claire took a card from her purse and slipped it to Thumps. "I'll take care of Stanley. When you get back, let yourself in. I don't care what time it is."

"Yes," said Cooley. "It was difficult sitting in my truck with the smell of fresh pizza in the air."

Claire turned to the two men. "Come on," she said. "Lunch is on me."

"See." Moses patted Cooley on the shoulder. "Being a deputy is full of unanticipated benefits."

He wasn't sure how he was going to start the conversation. Maybe when Boomper opened the door, Thumps would just show him the bag and see where things went. But Boomper didn't open the door.

"Pancho." Cruz stepped back and waved him in. "If you're looking for me, you're in luck."

"Actually, I'm looking for Austin."

"Not so lucky then," said Cruz. "He took off. Be back this afternoon."

"Not at the conference?"

"Never came for the conference," said Cruz. "He came for the deal."

Thumps let the bag swing against his thigh. "Deal's done. Why is he still here?"

"Good question." Cruz waited to see if Thumps had an answer. "What's in the bag?"

"Don't know."

"You haven't looked?"

"I've looked."

Cruz pointed at the bag with his chin. "Can I look?"

Thumps put the bag on the counter. Cruz opened the top.

"Yeah," he said. "I see your problem."

"I'm going into town, to the college. May have something new."

"On Redding?" said Cruz.

"On everything," said Thumps.

"Okay," said Cruz. "But can we take your car?"

"What happened to the Cadillac?"

"Mr. Austin took it," said Cruz. "And besides, I've been fired."

CRUZ DROVE THE Volvo down the winding laneway to the main road with practised efficiency. Slow into the turns, power out. Thumps couldn't be sure, but the car seemed to be enjoying this new approach to driving.

"Brakes pull to the left."

"Why were you fired?"

"And you should have your front end checked out."

"So, what are you going to do?"

"Enjoy the drive."

Sheriff Duke Hockney and Stanley Merchant were waiting for them when Thumps and Cruz got to campus and the computer lab.

"You're just in time," said the sheriff. "We've already done all the hard work."

"I've already done all the hard work," said Stick.

"Which is why," said Duke, "I'll let Mr. Merchant explain what he has discovered."

Stick swivelled in the chair. "I checked Lester's phone. He didn't take the photo."

"Who did?"

"Someone sent it to him as an email attachment."

"Same question," said Thumps.

"Margo Knight," said Stick.

"Margo Knight took a photo of Amanda Douglas?" Thumps tried to connect the dots. "Knight took a photo of a murder victim?"

"This is where things get a little muddy," said the sheriff.

Stick held up a cellphone. "This is Knight's phone. I'm sure the photo was sent from this phone. But there's no such photo on her phone."

"Which means it was erased," said Cruz.

"That's what Stanley figures," said Duke.

"Whoever erased the file knew what they were doing," said Stick.

"But you can retrieve the file?"

"Maybe."

"So, Knight takes a picture of a woman who is murdered by a serial killer and sends it to Lester. The image is erased from Knight's phone but not from Lester's. Does any of this make sense?"

"How long will it take you to restore the missing file?" said Cruz.

"Anything from a couple of hours to never," said Stick.

"Lots of ways this could go," said Duke.

Cruz shifted his weight. "Am I still a suspect?"

Hockney slapped Cruz on the shoulder. "Hell, no," he said. "You're just the closest thing I've got to one."

"I'm going home," said Thumps. "Don't call me. You guys can take it from here."

"Going to miss all the fun."

"Diabetics," said Thumps. "We can only handle so much fun."

FORTY-EIGHT

Thumps left Cruz to fend for himself. He was sure the sheriff would take good care of Austin's bodyguard. Stick was trying to explain cellphones and how computer memory and SIM cards worked. The last thing he saw as he slipped out the door were three grown men staring at a computer screen, the electronic version of watching paint dry.

The weather had turned, and Thumps could feel his body open up to take in the unexpected warmth. Summer was around the corner. Too bad Claire had to go to Seattle. Even in the summer, the city could be damp and cold. Summer never saved the Northwest Coast the way it did the High Plains. Then again, winter didn't bury it either.

The two of them would manage. Maybe the time together, even on the back of a crisis, would pull the relationship out of the rut into which it had fallen. Best of all, they wouldn't have Stick in their face or in their bedroom.

DIXIE WAS SITTING on the front porch, enjoying the day. Pops was lying next to him and Freeway was on his lap. "Traitor" was the first word that came to mind. The second word that popped into his head was not nearly as nice.

"Hi, Mr. Awfulwater."

"Dixie."

"Remodelling started yesterday. New cupboards, countertops, appliances. Going to take about a month, but it will be worth it."

"Great."

"Friend of yours stopped by," said Dixie. "Wanted to talk to you. When he saw you weren't here, he talked to me."

Thumps gave Freeway the hardest look he could muster. The cat didn't flinch. "About?"

"Cars," said Dixie. "He seemed quite concerned that you might buy a car privately."

"Andy."

"That's right," said Dixie. "Andy. Said you were looking to get a Jeep."

"Not anymore."

"He wanted to sell me a car, but I already have a late-model Honda."

"Good car."

"It is," said Dixie. "Bought it off the internet. When I knew I was coming to Chinook, I jumped on a couple of websites, found the car I wanted, and bought it. Easy as it could be. Was waiting for me when I got to town."

"You tell Andy that?"

Dixie shook his head. "No," he said. "Didn't seem friendly. Him being a salesman and all."

"Wouldn't mind seeing your kitchen when it's done."

Dixie sprang out of the chair. Freeway landed on the floor with all the grace of an Olympic gymnast. "Come on. Show you what we've done so far."

Dixie's kitchen was a mess. The old cupboards had been torn out, and plastic was hanging from all the doorways to keep the dust out of the rest of the house. Against one wall was a brand new stainless steel refrigerator.

"Freezer's on the bottom," said Dixie. "It's better that way."

"Big fridge."

"It's just me for now," said Dixie. "But you never know what might happen."

Sitting close to the new refrigerator was a large lump draped in a heavy drop cloth.

"I always wanted a six-burner gas." Dixie raised a corner of the cloth. "And the store had one left."

Thumps stood and stared.

"Got lucky." Dixie ran a hand across one of the dull-black

cast-iron grills. "The woman at the store said there was another guy looking at the stove but that he hadn't been able to make up his mind."

Thumps left Dixie to double-check the measurements for the cabinets. The stove was going to look good in his neighbour's new kitchen, better than it would have looked in Thumps's. Maybe that was the universe reminding him of necessary balances. New stoves needed new kitchens. You couldn't put them into worn-out spaces and expect them to be happy.

Pops and Freeway had disappeared. Run off again, so it seemed. Just as well. Thumps wasn't in the mood for society. The cat had made her choice. The only bright spot in his day was Claire, and she could change her mind in a moment. In fact, as Thumps thought about it, he imagined that she already had.

He didn't see the car at the curb until he was almost on his porch. A black sedan. Thumps stood and waited for the door to open. He was pretty sure he knew who it was, but there was still the chance he might be surprised.

"I hope you don't mind."

Thumps spun around to find the voice. Oliver Parrish was standing in the doorway of Thumps's house, resplendent in a polished grey sports jacket and charcoal slacks. The red plastic glasses were gone. In their place was a designer model with yellow lenses that made Parrish look like a blond Elvis Presley. Freeway was rubbing herself against the Orion executive's leg.

"The door was open," said Parrish, "and your cat didn't seem to object."

"She's a fierce watchdog."

"I thought we might talk."

"Sure," said Thumps. "You want coffee?"

"You make your coffee like the sheriff makes his?"

"No."

"Then I'd love a cup," said Parrish.

Thumps filled the kettle and set it on the boil. He was struck by how shabby his kitchen looked compared to the imagined kitchen that Dixie was building. Even under plastic, with only the refrigerator and stove in place, Dixie's looked better. Thumps's cabinets and countertop were outdated. His appliances were prehistoric. The linoleum floor was scuffed and beginning to curl up at the edges. Overall, the place looked sad, as though someone had left it alone in the dark too long.

"Great kitchen," said Parrish. "Is that a 1959 Frigidaire Imperial?"

"The stove?"

"Have never seen one in this condition," said Parrish. "Does it work?"

Thumps wasn't sure whether Parrish was having him on.

"Really smart."

"What?"

"Not getting rid of it," said Parrish. "A lot of people with houses of this vintage remodel their kitchen and put in all new appliances. Ruins the ambience. If you had this bungalow in Sacramento in the right area, you could get half a million just as it stands. But remodel the kitchen, and the price drops by seventy grand."

"You're kidding."

"You could get an easy twelve hundred for the stove on eBay," said Parrish. "It's a beauty. And you have the matching refrigerator."

Thumps poured the water into the Bodum and let the coffee steep. Maybe his kitchen wasn't so bad. Maybe it was authentic. Nothing wrong with that. Cuffs and collars that matched.

"I wanted to talk to you before I talked to the sheriff."

Thumps carried the Bodum and two cups to the table. "You want milk or sugar?"

Parrish pulled out a chair and sat down. "Black."

"This about Redding?"

Parrish waited while Thumps poured the coffee. "I lied."

Thumps wondered if Frigidaire had made a gas stove in 1959. Maybe a collectible was the way to go. Maybe Parrish was right about the importance of tradition and ambience. Thumps glanced around the kitchen. It didn't look that bad after all.

"When Redding called me, she told me about the files," said Parrish. "Lester and Knight. Their cellphones and laptops."

"She wanted to sell the files."

"She did," said Parrish. "Ten thousand dollars."

"And you said no."

Parrish shrugged. "I said five thousand dollars."

"Negotiation."

"Everything's a negotiation."

"When was this?"

"Late yesterday afternoon," said Parrish. "If she made the call on her cellphone, you can check the time."

Thumps tried to remember the timeline, but he couldn't. "So, why lie?"

"Looks bad," said Parrish. "Redding asking for money, and then she's dead."

"But you never saw the files."

"No," said Parrish. "I'm guessing that by the time I got to the Tucker, Redding was already dead."

Thumps sipped the coffee. He could always replace the floor, clean up the cabinets, put on a fresh coat of paint. A six-burner stove was probably too large for the space anyway. It would dominate the kitchen.

"Evidently there was RAM data in the emails. Redding claimed that the data showed that Orion's RAM technology didn't work as well as Knight had claimed."

"Austin already knew that."

"Sure," said Parrish, "but the publicity could have been bad for the company. Corporations are already seen as shifty at best. Something like that could hurt the share price."

"So, you were going to pay?"

"Probably. We were supposed to meet around nine that night and she was going to show me a sample of the altered data."

"Maybe a motive for murder?"

"Now you sound like the sheriff."

Thumps took a moment to look at the sequence. Redding calls Parrish in the late afternoon and offers to sell him the files for ten thousand dollars. Parrish agrees to meet Redding at nine that night. By the time he gets to the Tucker, Redding is already dead. Cruz is in the room with Redding's body when Parrish calls in to say he'll be late, and Cruz is in the room when Parrish knocks on the door.

"You could have come much earlier and killed her then."

"Why?"

"For the files."

Parrish shook his head. "The files were still in the room. On the coffee table. If I had killed Redding, I would have taken the files."

"So, what do you want me to do?"

"Talk to the sheriff," said Parrish. "I don't have time to spend in jail. I'm sorry I lied. Redding's death just threw me."

Freeway had parked herself under the table and was chewing on one of Thumps's shoelaces. Thumps moved his foot. Amnesty wasn't won that easily.

"Which do you prefer," said Thumps, "electric or gas?"

"What?"

"To cook on."

Parrish smiled and drank the last of his coffee. "Who the hell cooks anymore?"

FORTY-NINE

The last place Thumps wanted to be was the old Land Titles building, but here he was, yet again, standing outside the front door with his finger on the intercom button.

"Yes?"

"Thumps."

"Basement."

The buzzer sounded, the door snapped open, and Thumps took a deep breath and stepped inside. There was an elevator somewhere on the main floor that took you to Beth's basement, but in all these years, Thumps had always used the stairs.

Beth's Basement. It sounded like the name of an upscale nightclub. Someplace you could dance the night away. With dead bodies.

Beth was sitting at her desk, making notes in a book. "Not

going to start the autopsy on Redding until morning," she said. "I need a night off."

"Three murders in a week has to be a record."

"That's not the half of it."

Thumps took a moment to replay the last few days. "Ora Mae?"

Beth nodded. "We talked."

Thumps waited.

"You're supposed to ask about what," said Beth.

"I know about what," said Thumps.

"Then you're supposed to ask what happened."

"I don't want to know what happened."

Beth took her glasses off and laid them on the table. "Then why are you here?"

"You said that, because of the temperature of the bathwater, you couldn't give an accurate time of death."

"That's right," said Beth. "Don't you want to know what Ora Mae and I decided?"

Thumps sighed. "Is there any chance I can get out of here without knowing what you two decided?"

"Probably not."

Thumps sat down on one of the stainless steel chairs. "So tell me."

Beth put her glasses back on and tucked her hair behind her ear. "This building is paid for. Current value is somewhere north of half a million."

"For this?"

"The land," said Beth. "If we sell the building, some developer will tear it down and use the land for a hotel or a condo or a new commercial building."

"It's a heritage building."

"That's what everyone thinks," said Beth, "but it was never designated heritage."

"Don't tell Archie."

"We're not going to sell," said Beth. "We're going to take out a mortgage for $350,000. That way Ora Mae can buy Wild Rose Realty."

"Half of that money is yours," said Thumps.

"An investment," said Beth. "My share will be an investment in Ora Mae's business."

"So, you two are back together?" Thumps was sorry as soon as the question was out of his mouth.

"So, why did you want to know about time of death?"

Thumps held up a finger. "One, Redding is killed and placed in a tub of hot water. Two, Cruz finds her around nine o'clock and calls it in at nine-thirty. By the time you and the sheriff get there, the water is tepid, close to room temperature. Oliver Parrish says Redding called him in the late afternoon and arranged for him to come to the Tucker around nine that night. Cruz hears the phone call Parrish makes to say he's late, and later hears the knock on the door and assumes it's Parrish. That about right?"

"We still don't know when she was killed," said Beth. "There's a formula for the time it takes water to cool, which works off the ambient air temperature, but it's not much help because we don't know how hot the water was in the first place."

"Then she could have been killed any time during the day or even the night before and left in the tub until Cruz found her." Thumps pushed off the chair. "That's a nice thing you're doing for Ora Mae."

Beth leaned back. "Not doing it for her."

"It's still a nice thing."

Beth pushed an autopsy form across her desk to Thumps. "There's one other thing you need to know, and you're not going to like it."

Thumps stared at the lines that had been filled in and the blank boxes that had been checked. "You're sure?"

"Yes."

"Does Duke know?"

"Not yet," said Beth. "I'll tell him in the morning. Sometimes it helps to spread bad news out."

EVENING HAD SNUCK IN when Thumps wasn't looking. As he came out of the old Land Titles building, the last sliver of day had slipped below the horizon. There were lights on in the sheriff's office, and, through the window, Thumps could see Duke sitting behind his space-age desk.

The sheriff didn't seem all that happy to see him. "It better damn well be important."

"You took Parrish's statement?"

"I did." Duke rolled his shoulders. "And yes, I checked his alibi. Buffalo Mountain has video of him eating dinner at five-thirty. Afterwards he went to the casino, and we have video of him there until just before nine."

"Then he drove to the Tucker for his meeting with Redding."

"And, yes, I checked Redding's cellphone," said Duke. "She called Parrish at five."

"So, that's our timeline?" said Thumps. "Five to nine?"

"Just like the movie."

"The movie was called *Nine to Five*," said Thumps. "Dolly Parton, Jane Fonda, Lily Tomlin."

"Same idea." Hockney looked at Thumps over his glasses. "What the hell do you want?"

"Figured I'd solve the case."

"Good," said Duke, "because the whole thing is going to hell in a handbasket."

There was a new folder on Duke's desk.

"Is that the crime-scene report?"

"Such as it is."

"When you talked to Parrish, did you share the specifics with him?"

"You mean like where we found Redding, the dry bath mat, the brand of wine?"

"Like that."

"Of course not." Hockney shifted forward. The chair came with him. "Are you screwing with me?"

"What about crime-scene photos," said Thumps. "Did he see any of them?"

"Is this where you shout eureka and solve the case?"

"Eureka."

"Shit," said Duke. "Go home. I've got real police work to do."

"Stick come up with anything?"

Duke let out a long, irritated breath. "Dead end. All we know is that Knight sent the photo, and that the photo isn't on her phone."

"So it was erased," said Thumps. "And she didn't take it."

"How the hell you know that?"

"Look at the remaining photos on Knight's phone. All badly framed, some out of focus, every one taken by someone who hasn't a clue about photography."

"Everybody's a critic," said Duke.

"Ms. Point and Shoot," said Thumps. "That was our Dr. Knight."

Duke closed his eyes and put his fingers to his temples.

"Then look at the photograph of Amanda Douglas," said Thumps. "Well framed, in focus, well lit. Taken by someone who knows something about taking a good picture."

"You think you know who killed Redding?"

"Along with Lester and Knight," said Thumps. "One killer, three victims."

"And you can prove any of this?" said Duke.

Thumps pinched his nose. "I think I know why."

Duke heaved himself out of the chair and poured a cup of coffee. It came out of the pot like soft tar. "When your thinking gets to proving, you let me know."

"What's wrong with educated guesses?"

"They're still guesses," said the sheriff. "Have some coffee. You'll feel better."

"No, I won't."

Duke banged the percolator on the table. "Have some anyway."

FIFTY

Thumps had left the Volvo parked in front of the old Land Titles building. There had been no sense in moving it the two and a half blocks to the sheriff's office. A light mist was hovering around the street lights, a rare thing in this part of the country, and for a moment, Thumps found himself back on the North Coast on that lonely stretch of beach where Anna and Callie had been found. There had been a mist that night as well, heavier, denser. He had always thought of coastal fog as gentle and comforting, a soft, peaceful grey.

Not anymore.

Not after that night. Not after all the nights that had followed.

"Pancho." Cisco Cruz was sitting on the hood of the Volvo. "I took you for an early-to-bed, early-to-rise kind of hombre."

Thumps stood there, wanting to say something soothing, something with healing powers. But he knew there was nothing language could offer.

"So you know." Cruz looked off into the night. "She told me when I picked her up at that doughnut shop."

"How far along?"

"About two months. She found out a couple of weeks back." Cruz pushed off the hood. "It wasn't the clothes, and it wasn't the ring. It wasn't even the dry bath mat," said Cruz. "It was the wineglass. The minute I saw that, I knew she had been murdered."

"The wineglass?"

"A year ago, she did a three-part story on alcohol and birth defects and fetal alcohol spectrum disorder." Cruz wiped at his eyes. "No way was she drinking."

"She didn't come for the conference. She came to be with you."

Cruz smiled. "And then Lester and Knight were killed."

"And Redding smelled a story."

"No stopping that woman when she was chasing a story."

"So, she wasn't working for Austin."

"Partly true," said Cruz. "She did do some background work on Orion and on Lester and Knight. Particularly the imaging technology. Mr. Austin doesn't like to go into a deal blind."

"You know why she took the envelope?"

"She felt bad about that," said Cruz.

"It was a fishing expedition, wasn't it?" Thumps took a

moment to look at the matter from different angles. "Offer to sell the information and see which fish took the bait."

"Except there was nothing there that would have got her killed," said Cruz. "She showed me the files. The emails, the data from the monitoring wells, the photographs. We spent most of a day reading that crap. Knight whining. Lester huffing and puffing. Did Jayme tell you Knight was one paranoid and secretive lady?"

"Said Lester was pretty paranoid himself."

"Knight loved to spy on everyone," said Cruz. "Personal emails, phone logs. Orion had video cameras all over the place, and Knight's idea of an evening out was to watch the security footage. A real piece of work. Knight appears to have had the hots for someone, but nothing to suggest that it was Lester."

"So what are you going to do now?"

"First, I'm going to find who killed Jayme and our baby," said Cruz. "You going back to Buffalo Mountain?"

"I am."

"Your lady friend?"

"Yes."

"Can I catch a ride? Most of my stuff is still there."

"Sure."

Cruz looked at the Volvo. "Can I drive?"

The road from Chinook up to Buffalo Mountain was dark and empty. If there was a moon, it was buried in cloud cover.

Thumps couldn't think of anything else to say, so he kept his mouth shut.

"Where I come from," said Cruz, "you could always see the stars. Bright heavens. Cold sky."

"Southwest?"

"Pie Town, New Mexico," said Cruz. "West-central New Mexico. Population, nothing. Get a lot of cyclists through during the fall, and there are a couple of Indian ruins. Anasazi stuff. Pottery shards, axe heads."

"They make pies in Pie Town?"

"They do," said Cruz. "*Mira.* CBS News did a story on the place in 2015."

"Sounds peaceful."

"It is." Cruz leaned on the wheel. "I'll probably go to San Francisco. Rich people always need *brazos* like me."

"What about Los Angeles? Place is lousy with movie stars."

"Don't like L.A.," said Cruz. "Place is bullshit and silicone. Seattle would be okay. Rainy, cold. Jayme liked Seattle."

"Austin fire you because of Redding?"

"Didn't need a reason," said Cruz. "Man does what he wants."

"Your parents still alive?"

"No."

"Brothers or sisters?"

"No."

"Just a mercenary travelling the world."

"Have gun, will travel," said Cruz. "You always this nosy, *vato?*"

* * *

THE PARKING LOT was deserted, and Cruz was able to park the car near the front door to the resort.

"Look after your lady friend."

"I will," said Thumps. "How do I reach you?"

"I'll find you," said Cruz. "I'm good at finding people."

Thumps was already at the elevators when he remembered the bag. It was in the car. He thought about retrieving it, but that could wait. It was Claire who needed his attention. He stepped into the elevator and pressed the button. Of course, there was always the chance that Claire had been unsuccessful at removing Stick and the boy was still encamped. Stanley could be tenacious when it came to comfort and attention. Thumps had heard of yearling male bear cubs who would follow their mothers around long after the sows had sent their sons packing.

Then again, Claire wasn't a mother bear. She was much tougher than that.

Thumps fished the key card out of his pocket, slid it into the slot in the door, and watched the light turn green. If Stick was still in the condo, Thumps might have to take him aside for a stern lecture on adults and relationships.

The place was dark, but Thumps could see Claire sitting on the sofa in the shadows. He had anticipated the depression that would come with the cancer. He just didn't know what to do about it.

"Hey, Claire."

There was no response, and as he moved closer, he could see that her eyes were closed, as though she had fallen asleep in a sitting position.

"Don't worry. She's not dead."

Thumps spun around to the sound.

"Easy. Very easy."

Oliver Parrish was sitting in a chair in the far corner in the shadows. He had a small gun resting on his lap.

"Sit down, Mr. DreadfulWater," he said, gesturing with the pistol. "There, where I can see you."

"What's going on?"

"Oh, I'm sure you know what's going on." Parrish had gone back to the austere wire-rim glasses. They made his eyes seem small and sharp. "I slipped up, didn't I?"

Thumps tried to see if Claire was breathing. "I don't know what you're talking about."

"When I mentioned that the Orion file was on the coffee table." Parrish took a breath and let it out. "Stupid. How would I know it was on the coffee table unless I had put it there?"

"You're the Kanji Killer."

"Very good," said Parrish.

"Redding figured it out."

"No," said Parrish. "Actually, she hadn't. She would have, but she hadn't made the connection yet."

"And Lester and Knight?"

"Why don't you tell me."

"I'd only be guessing."

Parrish smiled. "I love guessing."

Thumps could feel all the pieces falling into place, like a well-shuffled deck of cards.

"The photograph of Amanda Douglas," said Thumps. "You took it."

"Bravo," said Parrish. "A needless bit of egotism."

"Knight found the photo somehow."

"A mistake on my part. Stupid, really. Left my phone on the nightstand, and she found the photo. She thought Ms. Douglas was a love interest."

"You and Knight?"

"Another mistake," said Parrish. "You know what they say about office romances. There was some yelling and some hurt feelings. Woman could be jealous and quite possessive."

"Why send the photo to Lester?"

"Margo was determined to find out who the woman was. I think she was hoping that Lester might know."

Thumps looked back at Claire. "You drugged her."

"I need to know what the police know," said Parrish.

"The sheriff will figure it out."

"I don't think so," said Parrish. "After I discovered that Knight had seen the photo, I changed the memory card on my phone. No one will ever be able to find a trace of Amanda Douglas or any of the others in my electronic footprint."

"How many?"

"Do you really care?"

Thumps knew it was a matter of buying time. The more time he could buy, the more chance he had of figuring a way out of this mess.

"So, how did I do it?" said Parrish. "I wasn't even in town when they died. Impress me with your deductive powers."

"You were in town, all right," said Thumps. "I'm guessing you bought a car. Off the internet? Something cheap? Picked it up when you flew into Great Falls. Comfort Inn isn't your style, but it's on the highway out of town, and inexpensive motels don't pay that much attention to their guests, and they don't have the same surveillance as the more expensive places."

Parrish tilted his head. "I am impressed."

"But I don't know how you got Lester and Knight out to the monitoring well."

"Ah, yes," said Parrish. "Well, let's say I called Lester and told him that I was coming in on an evening flight and that he and Knight should pick me up at the airport."

"You had good news for them," said Thumps. "The Austin deal?"

"A counter offer," said Parrish. "Ten million over what Austin had put on the table."

"A celebration."

"Champagne under the stars. Profits on the prairies."

"But the champagne was drugged." Thumps stiffened. "And you shot Knight where she lay, put Lester into his Jeep, drove him back to the airport, shot him in the head, and tried to make it look like it was suicide."

"Just bad luck the idiot had a heart condition and died before I shot him."

"And then you got into the car you bought and drove back to Great Falls."

"Do you know how easy it is to buy a car on the internet?"

Thumps looked at the gun in Parrish's hand. "And that's Knight's gun."

"Well," said Parrish, "the sheriff did take mine."

"So, now what?"

"No, no," said Parrish. "We're not done guessing."

"Redding?"

"Exactly."

Suddenly, Thumps could see what had happened. "You bought the file."

Parrish was smiling, pleased with himself. "Yes, I did. The same day she took it from you, I suspect."

"That's why she didn't have it when she called me." Thumps waited. "But then she found out about the new victim and called Jonathan Green at the *Herald*. When she saw the photograph, she recognized the woman."

"She called me, said she suspected that Lester was the Kanji Killer, said she wanted to see the file she had sold me." Parrish waved the gun in a circle. "I told her I had already sent it to main office and didn't have it anymore."

"So she called me."

"Evidently."

"She didn't know that the photo had come from your phone."

"I will allow that luck did turn in my favour."

"How did you get into her room?"

"That was easy," said Parrish. "Redding was a reporter, so I told her there were some things she might want to know about Lester."

"And you drugged the wine."

"Fruit juice," said Parrish. "I was ready to drug the wine, but Ms. Redding wanted fruit juice." Parrish turned toward Claire on the sofa. "Much like your Ms. Merchant."

"She was pregnant."

"Redding?" Parrish seemed surprised. "Now that is unfortunate."

Claire began to stir, trying to climb her way back to consciousness.

"Excellent," said Parrish. "It's time for me to make my exit. Would you help Ms. Merchant to her feet?"

"If I don't?"

"I can shoot you here," said Parrish. "The gun is not quiet by any means, but you'd be amazed how quickly the sound of a gunshot vanishes and how little attention it generates."

"Where are we going?"

"The parking lot," said Parrish. "Let's start there."

FIFTY-ONE

The drug was beginning to wear off, but Claire was still groggy and barely able to walk. Thumps supported her as best he could as Parrish forced them down the stairs. At each landing, Thumps had to stop and reposition his arm around Claire's waist. When they got to the ground floor, Parrish motioned for Thumps to stop.

"We'll take your car, Mr. DreadfulWater," he said.

Thumps half turned. Parrish had the gun pointed at his chest. "What's wrong with your car?"

"Late-model rental," said Parrish. "You drive a beat-to-shit Volvo. My car has GPS and an anti-theft tracking system. Yours does not."

The exit door on the ground floor had a crash bar. Thumps looked for wires or a junction box.

Parrish read Thumps's mind. "The door's not alarmed."

"Why should I help you?" said Thumps. "You're just going to kill us."

"Killing you isn't the smart play," said Parrish. "Even if the sheriff hasn't put all the pieces together, he doesn't strike me as a stupid man. Your bodies would only confirm what he might already suspect. Better to keep him chasing his tail for as long as possible."

Thumps had expected a well-lit parking lot of sodium-vapour lights that would make it difficult for Parrish to get to the car without being seen. But the lot was dark and cold, all the lights turned off.

Archie. National Dark Skies Week. One of these days, the little Greek was going to get him killed. Thumps leaned against the side of the building with Claire in his arms. She was moving in and out of consciousness.

"Where's your car?" said Parrish.

"By the front entrance."

Parrish made a face. "Not exactly private."

"I didn't know you were going to kidnap us."

"Irony," said Parrish. "It's overrated."

The Volvo was about fifty yards away. There was a large van between it and the entrance to the resort, blocking the sightline of anyone who happened to step outside for a breath of mountain air or a smoke. And on the other side of the parking lot, a shelter of dark trees. Close enough to see. Too far to reach.

"Here's what's going to happen." Parrish nudged Thumps with the barrel of the pistol. "We're going to walk to the car, no silly moves, no calling out for help. You're going to put Ms. Merchant in the back seat. Then I'm going to get in the passenger side and you're going to drive."

"Doesn't sound like a good idea," said Thumps.

"You have a better one?"

"There's probably nothing to link you to the murders in Sacramento," said Thumps. "Not much to link you to Lester and Knight. Or to Redding for that matter. Without the photograph of Amanda Douglas and a way of demonstrating that you took it, everything else is vaguely circumstantial."

"Yes," said Parrish, "but you know the truth."

"Doesn't matter," said Thumps. "My word against yours. Disgruntled, washed-up cop. Couldn't solve his own serial-killer case. Looking for a scapegoat."

"And Ms. Merchant?"

"Rohypnol?" Thumps waited to see if he was right. "She won't remember a thing."

"Bravo," said Parrish. "Now let's get in the car."

The interior of the car was dark and cold. Thumps slid behind the wheel and slipped the key into the ignition.

"Walking away is the smart move," said Thumps. "I'll even give you a head start."

"And then you'll release the hounds?"

"Even if they catch you, you'll walk," said Thumps. "In the end, you'll walk."

"Start the car."

Out of the corner of his eye, Thumps saw something hanging from the rear-view mirror. A round silver pendant on a piece of rawhide that hadn't been there when he had parked the car.

Cruz.

"Don't make me shoot the girl."

Thumps leaned forward and turned the key. Nothing. He tried again. More nothing. The Volvo wouldn't start. Generally, the starter motor would make an effort, but now he couldn't coax a spark of life out of the car.

Parrish leaned over and tapped the barrel of the gun against Thumps's head. "Do we need some encouragement?"

"It won't start."

"Bullshit!"

Thumps turned the key again. "It won't start."

"Fix it." Parrish sighed deeply. "Quickly."

There had been problems in the past. A dead battery. Worn spark plugs. A timing belt. Annoying problems. Expensive problems. Tonight was more serious.

"Maybe it's the cables," said Thumps. "Battery's new, so I should be getting a spark."

Parrish opened his door and stepped out. "Easy," he said. "Very slowly."

Thumps walked to the front of the car and opened the hood. There was just enough light spill from the resort windows to see the engine. The battery looked fine. Except for the positive cable. It had been pulled off the post, and that didn't happen by chance. Cable terminals were clamped onto the posts with a wrench. They didn't pop off like buttons on a shirt.

Thumps hoped that Oliver Parrish was the new breed of car owner who had never peered under a hood, who didn't know a head cover from a dipstick.

Parrish stared at the battery for a moment, and then he stepped in behind Thumps and pulled him in tight. "Where is he?"

"Who?"

"Mr. Cisco Fucking Cruz." Parrish ground the gun into Thumps's back. "Where is the sonofabitch?"

"Here." Cruz stepped out of the trees. "I'm right here."

Parrish spun around, taking Thumps with him as a shield. "Stay where you are!"

Cruz lazily raised his pistol. "How you doing, *vato*?"

"Been better," said Thumps.

Cruz rotated his neck. "I think I can shoot him from here."

"Think?"

"Put your gun down." Parrish brought the gun up to Thumps's head. "Or I shoot your friend."

Cruz smiled. In the dark, his teeth looked like stars. "He's not my friend."

"Yes, I am."

"You can shoot him," said Cruz, "but then he falls down, and then I shoot you."

Thumps could see the copper top of the casino through the trees. The odds weren't all that good in there, but they were worse out here.

"Here's the thing," said Cruz. "We're about thirty-five yards away from each other. You have a .22 calibre pistol with a short barrel. Effective range is around twenty-five feet. I have a SIG Sauer P210, 9mm, loaded with Parabellums. My gun has more kick, and so it tends to be less accurate. I could miss. Unfortunately for you, I'm a damn good marksman, so I won't. Your gun is probably a bit more accurate because there's no recoil, but I'm willing to bet that you're not a particularly good shot."

"I can kill Mr. DreadfulWater," said Parrish.

"Or you can give yourself up," said Thumps. "What about it, Cruz? You think we could get a conviction?"

Thumps could see Cruz lining up the sights.

"Not a chance in hell," said Cruz. "So I'm really hoping El Guapo shoots you."

"Don't mind him," Thumps told Parrish. "That's just the testosterone talking."

"Tell you what," said Cruz, "you take a shot at me. Maybe you hit me, maybe you don't. Then I'll take a shot at you. I'm thinking I can probably miss Thumps and put a bullet in your head."

"Probably?"

"The light's not all that good," said Cruz.

"Fuck you," shouted Parrish, pulling the trigger.

The shot was quick and hard, and Cruz didn't move. "Missed," he shouted. "My turn."

Thumps felt Parrish hesitate, and then the man slowly raised his hands. "Okay," he shouted. "Okay, I'm putting down my gun."

"You sure?"

"Yes."

"Hand it to Thumps."

Parrish let the pistol swing down by the trigger guard. Thumps took it and stepped to one side.

"I'm unarmed." Parrish put his hands above his head.

"That you are." Cruz looked at Thumps and gestured toward the Volvo. "Better check on Ms. Merchant."

Thumps had taken three steps toward the car when the first shot hit Parrish.

"That was for Redding." Cruz's voice was low and fierce.

Thumps turned. Parrish was still upright, unable to come to terms with what had just happened. His face was twisted in pain, his mouth was open, as though he were going to complain. But there was no sound.

And then, with a quickness that Thumps had never seen before, Cruz's arm came up, the gun cracked three more times, and Parrish was driven backwards onto the asphalt.

"And that was for *mi hijo*."

Parrish lay on his back, his arms and legs splayed out at unnatural angles, his eyes wide open, a surprised look on his face, and four neat holes in his chest. Cruz held his shooting stance for a moment, and then he straightened up and slipped the gun back into its holster.

Thumps realized that he had stopped breathing. "You shot him."

"I did."

"He was unarmed."

"He was."

Cruz walked to the car, reached in, and slipped the pendant off the mirror. Thumps watched him tie the small disc around his neck.

"Redding gave you that."

"She did," said Cruz. "*Mira*. Face of the moon. Said I needed some light because I spent so much of my time in the dark." There was no emotion in Cruz's eyes, nothing but determined concentration. "Woman could be sentimental at times."

It was only when Cruz turned that Thumps saw the tear in the man's jacket. Blood had begun to soak the material.

"You're hit."

"He got lucky." Cruz shrugged. "Caught a piece of the deltoid."

"Jesus."

"Ruined a good jacket," said Cruz. "And it'll probably leave a scar."

"You could have been killed."

"Scars are cool."

"Would you really have let him shoot me?" Thumps didn't know why he had even asked the question. He knew the answer.

"Your fault, Pancho," said Cruz.

"My fault?"

"You were right." Cruz touched the silver pendant. "No chance of a conviction. He would have walked."

FIFTY-TWO

The scene in the Buffalo Mountain parking lot was somewhat surreal, like a black-and-white movie that had once
been in colour. Lance Packard had gone to talk to the
resort manager about getting the sodium-vapours back on, while
two of Duke's other deputies were setting up remote lighting
units and stringing yellow crime-scene tape around the area.

Thumps helped Beth Mooney get a tarp from her station
wagon to throw over the body.

"You ever think about taking suspects alive?"

Thumps held up his hands. "I didn't kill him."

Sheriff Duke Hockney was not happy. He had Cruz up
against a police cruiser. "You know you're under arrest," Duke
told him.

"Again?"

"You shot a man."

"He killed Lester and Knight," said Cruz. "He killed Redding."

"Parrish shot first," said Thumps. "He wounded Cruz."

"I was in fear of my life," said Cruz.

Hockney made a grumbling sound in his throat that sounded like a diesel truck on a steep incline.

Thumps ignored the noise. "And he's also the Kanji Killer."

"Parrish?" Duke tried to keep the surprise out of his voice. "The serial killer in Sacramento?"

"The photo on Lester's phone," said Thumps. "Amanda Douglas? Knight sent it to Lester, but I think she found it on Parrish's phone."

"Jesus," said the sheriff, "you two are a real Cheech and Chong."

"*A la verga*," said Cruz. "I must be Cheech."

"Shut up," said Duke. "You're still under arrest."

"He drugged Claire," said Thumps. "He held me at gunpoint. He was going to shoot me. Cruz shot him."

"Sure," said Duke. "It's the space between 'He was going to shoot me' and 'Cruz shot him' that I want to explore. And don't tell me it happened fast, and that it was dark."

Thumps looked at Cruz. "It happened fast. It was dark."

"Damn it, DreadfulWater," said the sheriff. "You remind me of a cat Macy had. Animal would go out and kill squirrels and bring me their bodies. I was not fond of that beast."

"How's Claire?"

"Deanna Heavy Runner's looking after her. Beth said she'll be okay." Duke looked down at the tarp that was covering Parrish's body. "I'll talk to her later, but I'm guessing she didn't see anything."

"Parrish bought a car in Great Falls," said Thumps. "Probably the internet. Cash sale. Drove over. Killed Lester and Knight. Drove back. Caught the morning flight the next day. I'm guessing you'll find it in long-term parking at the airport."

Duke scratched his cheek. "So, Parrish is our local killer as well as a serial killer?"

"You were kidding about arresting me," said Cruz. "Right?"

"Wrong," said the sheriff.

Thumps tried to keep the tone calm and reasonable. "The sheriff just wants to know why you had to shoot Parrish four times."

"I could have shot him five times," said Cruz.

"Here's my problem," said Duke. "Why would someone like Oliver Parrish, armed with a .22 calibre snub nose that isn't worth shit after twenty yards, throw down on a professional bodyguard with military training and holding a SIG Sauer 9mm pistol? Can you explain that to me?"

"Arrogance?"

"And why, having fired once, didn't he fire again?"

Thumps and Cruz waited for the sheriff to make his point.

"The only way I see Oliver Parrish with four bullets in his chest," said Duke, "is if he had already given up his gun and was trying to surrender."

"It happened fast," said Thumps. "It was dark."

Hockney tried to come at the shooting from several angles and each time he hit a dead end, until he finally gave up and put Cruz in the back of his cruiser. Thumps wandered over to see if Beth needed a hand.

"You can't be here." Beth didn't even look up from her work. "You're a suspect in a shooting."

"I'm not a suspect," said Thumps. "Cruz is a suspect. I'm one of the victims."

"Man's one hell of a shot." Beth pulled the tarp back so Thumps could see the torso. "Thirty-five, forty yards in bad light. Killer with a gun and a hostage. Yet our hero is able to put four shots in our perp, centre mass, eight-inch spread."

"You and Ora Mae do any more talking?"

Beth pointed her pencil at Thumps's chest. "What it feels like," she said, "is target practice."

"It happened fast. It was dark."

THUMPS STILL HAD the key card. He wasn't superstitious, but the last time he had let himself in, a killer with a gun had been waiting for him.

Deanna answered on the first knock. "She's okay. Just groggy."

Claire was on the sofa, wrapped up in a blanket, holding a cup of something steaming. Thumps sat down beside her and waited.

"I have to get back to the desk," said Deanna. "If you need anything from the mini-bar, help yourself."

"Thanks."

"It's on the house."

Thumps didn't know if he should talk or wait. Claire's hair was dishevelled, and he was tempted to try to fix it, to push it out of her face and pull it into place. Instead, he put his hand on her neck and gently rubbed her shoulders.

Claire took a sip of her drink. "That's nice."

"Is that tea?"

"Hot water and honey," said Claire. "He called. Said he needed to talk to me about Austin and the agreement."

"It was a set-up."

Claire took another sip. "So, I met him in the bar. We talked. And then I wasn't feeling well."

"Parrish needed leverage over me," said Thumps. "I'm sorry."

"The last thing I remember was him helping me back to my room. Is that when you arrived?"

"More or less."

Claire put her cup down and snuggled up against Thumps. "My hero."

Claire's body was warm and soft. Being a hero wasn't so bad. Except he wasn't. Granted, Claire hadn't been awake to see how little of a hero he had been, and maybe it was better to leave it alone.

And then again, maybe it wasn't.

"Look," he began, "I didn't have anything to do with stopping Parrish. It was Cisco Cruz. He saved us."

Claire pushed away and held up an envelope. It looked vaguely familiar.

"This was on the back seat," said Claire. "It's the list Roxanne made up."

Thumps felt the blood drain away.

"Have you read it?" Claire's face was shimmering with delight. "Number three is great."

"Claire . . ."

"And number four . . ." Claire started laughing, low at first, and then collapsing into a full-blown cackle. "You have to look at number four."

It took the better part of an hour to get Claire calmed down and back in his arms again. She slowly moulded herself against his chest and began to snore. Softly. More a flutter. So this was how a happy ending looked. The heroine in the arms of the hero. Okay, he could get used to this.

Thumps reached across and borrowed a corner of the blanket. He eased his shoes off and put his legs up on the coffee table. It wasn't a comfortable position, but he'd manage. The French doors were open, and he watched a starless night sky until his breathing slowed and he closed his eyes.

In the morning, he'd take the list and burn it.

FIFTY-THREE

The next morning when Thumps and Claire came down for breakfast, the crime scene was still cordoned off and Sheriff Duke Hockney's cruiser was parked where it had been the night before.

Deanna Heavy Runner was at the reception desk, looking fresh and efficient.

"Sheriff Hockney is having breakfast with Mr. Austin. He said if I saw you to tell you that you should join him."

"Ask us or tell us?" said Thumps.

"Tell you," said Deanna. "He's a little grumpy."

Claire pressed Thumps's arm. "I think breakfast with the sheriff is just the thing."

"Sure," said Thumps, "sounds great."

"He signed my practicum," said Deanna. "And he offered me a summer internship."

"Congratulations. You earned it."

"You're the best, Mr. DreadfulWater," said Deanna.

"Maybe you could mention that to your sister."

Claire gently punched Thumps's shoulder. "Don't push your luck."

Duke and Boomper were sitting at a table in the far corner where the floor-to-ceiling glass windows gave an unobstructed view of the Ironstone. They looked like a couple of old friends on vacation, which confirmed what people liked to say about appearances.

Thumps was working on how he was going to keep Duke at bay when he remembered the bag.

"Think you can handle those two on your own?" Thumps tried to look charming. "I have to get something."

"I believe I have a chair and a whip somewhere in my purse." Claire squeezed Thumps's arm. "Have you seen Roxanne's list?"

Thumps shrugged.

"I had it last night," said Claire, "but now I can't find it."

"It'll show up."

"You know," said Claire, "those aren't the kinds of things that I want. They're what Roxanne wants."

"Are you kidding?"

"Don't be like that," said Claire. "Everyone has different needs."

By the time Thumps got back to the table with the bag, Duke and Boomper were relaxing in their seats, smiling like idiots.

"Grab a chair." Austin laughed and whacked the edge of the

table, shaking the glass and the coffee cups. "Ms. Merchant was just telling us about a canoe trip the two of you took."

"Seems you overestimated your traditional skills," said Duke.

Thumps settled himself in the chair and put the bag on the table. "The river was higher than usual that year."

"Would have paid to see you shoot those rapids," said Duke.

"Did you ever find the canoe?" asked Boomper.

Thumps ignored the Texan. "Did you really arrest Cruz?"

Duke sucked at his teeth. "It was high on my to-do list, but I'm going to have enough paperwork, what with four bodies. There's no more room in Beth's basement. We get another corpse and we'll have to FedEx it to Great Falls."

"Cruz is a good man." Thumps turned to Austin. "Was a mistake to fire him."

Austin looked startled. "Fire? Hell, I didn't fire the boy. He resigned. Tried to get him to change his mind, but he was adamant."

"What?"

"Best damn associate I've ever had. Going to be hard to replace," said Boomper. "I can tell you that."

Duke gestured at the bag. "I hope that's not someone's head."

"Nope," said Thumps. "Not a head."

"Then I'm off," said the sheriff. "Got a desk full of messages and a truckload of questions that are wanting answers. Mayor has requested a personal briefing, so I got to wear that damn tie and jacket."

"Are acting sheriffs required to be sympathetic?" asked Thumps.

Duke stood and shook his head. "Your lucky day," he said. "I don't need you anymore."

"I don't have to be acting sheriff?"

"Nope," said Hockney. "Black Jack Kramer is going to take some vacation time and look after the office."

"Black Jack is going to take vacation time to come to Chinook? To work?"

"Fishing's better around here," said Duke, "and there's nothing that Black Jack loves more than fishing."

"Great."

"So you're off the hook," said Hockney, "in a manner of speaking. And I don't owe you a fancy stove."

"Fair enough," said Thumps. "But I need a favour. You remember the kid at the airport rental desk?"

"Sure," said the sheriff, after Thumps had explained the situation. "Nothing I'd like better than to pull old Norm's chain again."

"It was a pleasure meeting you, sheriff." Boomper took a card out of his pocket. "If you're ever in Houston, you give me a call."

Duke walked across the dining room with the same slow, bowlegged gait that movie star cowboys favoured just before they got to the gunfight scene.

"So if it's not someone's head," said Boomper, pointing to the bag, "what is it?"

"A present for Claire," said Thumps.

Claire snorted. "You bought me a present?"

"Well, don't keep us in suspense," said Austin.

Thumps untied the bag and emptied the contents on the table. Claire's smile faded.

"Rocks?" she said.

Boomper leaned back in the chair, his face flat and impassive.

"You bought me rocks?"

"You should ask Mr. Austin," said Thumps. "He's quite the authority on rocks."

Claire picked up one of the rocks and held it up to the light. It was a dark and dirty-looking piece of stone with red flashes at the edges.

"Had some friends do a little digging," said Thumps. "And then there were the phone calls to your gem broker in Thailand."

"Damn, son," said Boomper. "You sure know how to land on someone's cake."

"Friend of mine sent you a photo," said Thumps. "You might want to take a look."

Boomper fished his phone out of a pocket and tapped the screen.

"Randy Palmer took it," said Thumps. "He's studying photography at the college. That's you and the Escalade and the monitoring station. Yesterday afternoon."

Claire turned the rock around in her hand. "I take it this is valuable?"

"Red beryl," said Boomper. "Finest quality I've ever seen."

Claire put the rock down and picked up a second piece. "And you found this on . . . Bear Hump?"

"One of Mr. Austin's companies did the drilling for the monitoring stations," said Thumps. "He wanted to keep track of the progress Orion was making with their technology."

"Gemstones are a hobby of mine," said Austin. "Man who was in charge of the drilling has worked for me for years. Knows his minerals. He recognized the beryl as soon as he saw it."

Claire put on her pleasant face, the one she saved for government bureaucrats and annoying children. "That's tribal land."

"Yes," sighed Boomper. "It is."

"And you were going to tell me about this . . . when?"

Thumps gestured at Boomper's ring. "That didn't come from the mine in Utah either, did it? It came from Bear Hump."

"Guilty." Boomper rubbed the stone with his finger. "A beauty, isn't it?"

Claire pushed the rocks on the table into a tight pattern. "Well," she said, "this is certainly a different present than a girl normally gets."

"I know this doesn't look good," said Boomper, "but I'm hoping we can hammer out an agreement that is mutually beneficial."

Claire nodded. "You mean where we allow you to mine the beryl and you pay us for the privilege."

"That sounds about right."

Claire stretched and signalled the server. "Then I suppose we're going to need more coffee."

Thumps left Claire and Boomper to work out the details. He had had more than enough fun for a while. He had film to develop, negatives to print, and a surly cat to cajole. Full-time work if there ever was.

And there was Claire. Right now, she was willing to let him go with her to Seattle, but Thumps knew her well enough to know that that could change. Once the intense emotions of almost getting killed wore off, the old, independent Claire might resurface, and then Thumps would have to begin the process of being included in her life all over again.

Cisco Cruz was sitting on the hood of the Volvo. Again. Thumps wondered if the man did this just to annoy him.

"Pancho."

"You're on the hood of my car again."

"Good steel," said Cruz. "If I sat on the hood of one of the new Fords, I'd crush it."

"So the sheriff didn't arrest you."

"I appreciate what you did," said Cruz, "but I was willing to go to jail."

"I know," said Thumps.

"I couldn't let that pass," said Cruz. "*Tú entiendes?*"

Thumps wanted to ask if killing Parrish had made any difference. But he didn't. "How did you know?"

"About Parrish?"

"You were waiting for us."

Cruz slid off the hood. "The girl at reception. She's sharp."

"That she is."

"She saw Parrish and your lady in the bar together," said Cruz. "Saw them come out. Noticed that Merchant wasn't feeling all that well."

"And she told you?"

"Like I said," said Cruz, "she's sharp. So, I went up to Merchant's room, listened at the door, heard a little bit of Parrish's plan."

"What if we had taken his car?"

Cruz shook his head. "Wasn't going to happen."

"You didn't know that."

"His car had a problem," said Cruz. "Flat tire."

Thumps grunted. "Imagine that."

Cruz jammed his hands in his pockets. "I was hoping you might drop me off at the airport."

"Sure."

"Figure I'll go home, remind myself why I left Pie Town in the first place." Cruz shaded his eyes from the bright sun. "That should take about a week."

Thumps smiled. "So just how much Spanish do you really speak?"

Cruz grinned back. "Enough to frighten the tourists."

"And Austin didn't fire you."

"No," said Cruz, "he didn't."

"You blame yourself," said Thumps.

"Wouldn't you?" Cruz climbed into the passenger seat. "Why don't you drive this time."

"You want to talk?"

"No offence, *vato*," said Cruz, "but all things considered, I'd rather listen to music and just watch the sky."

FIFTY-FOUR

Thumps took Cruz to the airport and waited with him until the plane boarded. Thumps didn't think Cruz saw him as a friend, and he wasn't sure how he felt about the man from Pie Town, New Mexico. There was hard tragedy in both their lives, and perhaps that was what they shared.

Perhaps that was all they shared.

He spent that night with Claire at her house. She had had a spirited discussion with Boomper Austin about the price of red beryl and the cost of deceit, and was in a playful mood, which translated into a game of bedroom hide-and-seek, complete with shrieks and soft moaning. They didn't talk about the cancer or about Seattle, didn't make any promises, didn't try to tell each other that everything was going to be okay.

And in the morning, they went their separate ways, Claire to her office at the tribal centre and Thumps back to his house with its basement darkroom and its grumpy cat. He didn't stop in at Al's for breakfast, and he didn't call Archie. He considered checking in with the sheriff but decided to leave that dog lie.

Beth and Ora Mae could work out their relationship on their own.

Instead, he packed his photo gear into the trunk of the car and began driving toward the Canadian border and the Rockies. He'd lose himself in the mountains for a few days and then drive to Lethbridge to see old friends on the Blood reserve.

And when he ran out of money and excuses, he'd come home.

It was a good plan and he got as far as Sunburst and the Early Bird Coffee Shop before he turned around and drove the five hours back to Chinook without stopping, the memories of that night in the Buffalo Mountain Resort parking lot still vivid and alive.

Claire drugged and in the back seat. Oliver Parrish standing with his arms over his head, a smile on his face, knowing that his chances of walking away from the murders were excellent. Cruz lining up the front sight of his pistol on Parrish's chest and squeezing the trigger four times.

Thumps hadn't asked him how it felt to kill the man who had killed his lover, the man who had killed his child. There was a great deal written about revenge and how it wasn't as satisfying as a person might expect, but Thumps had seen the look in Cruz's eyes. There had been no confusion, no regret, and no hesitation. He had found Jayme's killer and he had shot him in cold blood.

Thumps tried to imagine what he would do in a similar circumstance, what he would do if he found the man responsible for the Obsidian Murders, for the deaths of Anna and Callie.

It was after midnight when he crossed the Ironstone, and by the time he could finally see the lights of Chinook in the distance, he knew there was only one way to find out.